THE GOLDEN DOLPHIN

(AND OTHER PIRATE TALES FROM THE PULPS)

THE GOLDEN DOLPHIN

(AND OTHER PIRATE TALES FROM THE PULPS)

J. ALLAN DUNN

WILDSIDE PRESS

THE GOLDEN DOLPHIN
AND OTHER PIRATE TALES FROM THE PULPS

The Golden Dolphin originally appeared in *Short Stories*, Dec. 10, 1921.
"The Marooner" originally appeared in *Adventure*. August 3, 1918.
"Forced Luck" originally appeared in *Adventure*, February 10, 1922.

CONTENTS

THE GOLDEN
DOLPHIN

I

Opportunity Knocks

Jim Lyman, wandering aimlessly down North Street, Foxfield, had it borne in upon him that jobs were hard to catch. The paper mills and the woolen mills and the big electric supplies factory that, taking advantage of cheap water power, had transformed Foxfield the village into Foxfield the city of fifty thousand, were either shut down or running half time with a greatly reduced number of employees. It seemed to Jim that the rest of these unemployed were standing on the curbings and lounging on the Common, parked wherever there were vacant spaces, their savings gone, their faces more or less disconsolate. Yet Jim Lyman had turned down a job no later than that morning.

It is true that he had regarded it almost as an insult, that he had found difficulty in gracing his refusal. Yet he was beginning to regret his rashness. He had a few dollars in his pocket but they were very few, and the high cost of living had not reduced on the same scale as the lowering average of wages. Most of the chaps standing about would have jumped at Jim's offer, he reflected, provided they could have qualified.

The job was out at Winnesota Lake where the summer season for holiday makers from the big cities was in full swing. A man was wanted to help in the hiring and care of boats — a launch, rowboats and canoes — to help people get into them without upsetting or stepping through the bottoms, to shove out and haul in, to swab, to generally stand by and hang around a wharf in a bathing suit — for fifteen dollars a month and found; the findings meaning fair meals and an indifferent bunk at the mock-bungalow of the owner of the boathouse, and boating privileges. A soft snap to almost anyone out of a job, a vacation in itself, a chance for a good time with the city girls who were not averse to flirting with men of the "handsome brave life-saver" variety, but —

Jim Lyman was a sailor, a man who had served as second and first mate, who was qualified as a master mariner, who loved the sea and regarded a freshwater pond like Winnesota Lake much as a salmon would regard a bathtub. That comparison is not vigorous enough. To Jim the idea of the job on the placid lake, handling toy boats when his heart longed for a stiff breeze, big seas and a heeling vessel working into the wind's eye, was a good deal like the offering to a lion tamer a position taking care of guinea pigs.

Beggars may not be choosers, but Jim would never be a beggar, and he had a strong belief in his own star or in the general fairness of Providence. All of which was a testimony to his good nature, his vitality and his good digestion, since he had just come through a severe pummeling at the hands of Fate: wrecked in the South Pacific; hungry, thirsty, blazing days in an open boat; despair; rescue; return to Panama aboard a smelly, inefficient ship inadequately run by Portuguese whose ideas of food were as limited as their larder; a chance to work his way back north and east as a handler on a fruit freighter, a brief visit at the New England home of the wrecked ship's purser-steward, companion of his misfortunes, and then the long hunt and the ultimate conviction that a sailor man was out-of-date, obsolete, and not much to be desired; a job as a rigger in an emergency contract, two or three jobs painting flagpoles and straightening vanes, wandering inland the while, the supposed opportunity to get on as rigger again with a contractor in Foxfield, only to find the man with barely work enough to keep his oldest hands together on half time.

There was adventure for you — or misadventure — which Jim had suffered and taken as part of the day's job, the risk that sharpened the edge of things. It was the tabasco sauce on life's oyster to Jim, just an appetizer. One could get too much of it, but now — now life was as flat and stale as ditchwater or the placid green and blue reflecting wavelets of Lake Winnesota.

The ancient adages — and you will generally find them well based — depict Opportunity as Knocking at the Door and Adventure Waiting Around the Corner. Jim was fairly confident of the truth of the latter saying, he was beginning to doubt the verity of the former. Or else he was always out or asleep when the knock came. Even adventure seemed infinitely remote, despite his comparatively recent experience.

There are few of us — older than Jim, who was midway between twenty and thirty — who have much of life to look back to and remember, who have not had times when, swathed in the bonds of the commonplace, either complacent resentful or despondent, seemingly as fixed as an oyster to its rock-bed, the swift change of circumstance has not swept down upon us like a whirlwind from a clear sky and transported us to scenes and happenings we never dreamed of encountering. Opportunity and Adventure are sisters of the fates. Often the first, coming down the street hand in hand with the one who has opened the door to her knock, will turn the corner where Adventure lurks and the trio go on together, while Fortune smiles at another successful combination. So with Jim when he first saw clearly the gleaming emblem of the golden dolphin shining in the afternoon sun and felt that subtle quickening of spirit that we call presentment.

He turned from North Street, with its loafing tribute to slack times, and was strolling down a side avenue where elms met overhead in their June tracery of crisp green against the blue and gold of the sky. On either side he began to find the commercial district changing to the residential. He crossed the Winnetac River on its broad white-railed bridge and walked past old-time Colonial houses, not indicative of great wealth, but of vast comfort. There were lawns and lilacs, glimpses of more flowers at the back, robins listening-in for worms, grackles, and catbirds calling from the maples. It was a homey street and the sights and sounds and scents had their due effect upon Jim Lyman. Even as North Street had raised the ruff of his spirit in protest against the times, now it smoothed down like the ruff of a collie under the touch of a known and friendly hand.

Then he caught sight of the dolphin, ablaze in a direct shaft of sunlight, a heraldic dolphin, skillfully wrought in metal and nobly covered with burnished gold-leaf, not merely bronzed with baser metal.

It swung in a wrought iron frame — ungilded — that projected from a doorway with a Colonial Dutch hood. On either side the glazed-in porches showed old furniture, chairs, rockers, spinning wheels, rag rugs, warming pans, knockers, andirons —all of which confirmed the legend of the sign:

THE GOLDEN DOLPHIN
ANTIQUES
K. Whiting, Prop.

Jim did not notice the lettering at first, he was too busy looking at the dolphin. In a way it was his totem, it was the symbol of the sea that he loved. Jim knew dolphins, the porpoises of the Pacific and their sharper-snouted cousins of the Atlantic, the acrobats of the ocean. He knew too the true dolphin, the *dorado*, with its protuberant forehead and long dorsal fin, the fish that really changes into exquisite degrees and blends of color as it dies upon the deck. The conventional form shown in the sign he knew also. He had seen it in ships' decorations, on ancient charts that he had studied; once, at least, as the figurehead of a ship. It was as a figurehead he had last seen it.

He shifted his gaze from sign to porch-window. His pupils dilated, his lids narrowed. He pushed open the picket-gate and walked in a daze up the path toward the left-hand porch, walked as a hypnotic subject will, with gaze fixed on the object that has enchained the senses.

In the window was a background of old furnishings, enlivened here and there with bits of Oriental embroidery, lacquered trays, batiks, gleaming seashells. All these were subordinated — in the eyes of Jim — to the beautiful model of a ship, set on a low stand. The vessel was of exquisite design and its fashioning of rare artistry. The veriest landsman might see speed and buoyancy in the swelling streamlines of the hull, sweet as the contours of a *bonito*; the ambitious sheer of the stem, the curving counter, the rake of the four masts — the fore square-rigged, the others fore and aft. The model was complete with rigging and canvas, with boats slung in davits, skylights and awnings, minia-ture wheel, and binnacle; the tiniest details made a part of the loving, skilful craftsmanship.

On the bow and on the stern, there showed in golden lettering the name:

Golden Dolphin
BOSTON

And the figurehead was a replica of the sign that swung above the door of the shop, a supple, twisting body armored with golden scales, set with outspread golden fins that clung like fingers to the stem of the ship, a flowing tail and the goblin-like head with its rounded forehead and protruding lips that kissed the foam, as the windful sails drove on the gallant vessel. Any ship-lover and sea-lover could readily replace the stand with curling waves, creaming at the stem and along the run to fan-like wake; ignore the background of antiques and visualize instead the flowing sea and bright horizon where cloud argosies sailed before the wind. But that was not what Jim Lyman, standing entranced with contracting pupils, with parted lips, beheld back of the graceful hull and tapering masts. To him the actuality of the model had suddenly blended with a vision, as pictures blend upon the film-screen, reality of the present with recollection of the past.

He saw a tropic tangle, rather — so completely did the fantasy enthrall him — he was *in* a tropic tangle, peering through the rank growth of brush; palms and broad-leaved trees shot up high crowns that interlocked to bar out the sunshine and rendered daylight into a green twilight shot with golden beams hardly thicker than a cord and blobs of amber mottling the verdant floor. All about a riot of green growth wattled together with vines and ground shrubbery. Orchids were a-swing, giving out waves of intoxicant perfume. Two great butterflies, scarlet and black, hovered about like protesting guardian spirits of the place to which he had unwittingly forced his way. In his ears were the faint swish of the breeze in the treetops, the hiss of surf on the nearby beach and its heavier drumming on the barrier reef.

Verdure had flung itself, writhing, tentacled, embracing the hull of a vessel as if the jungle claimed a prize and was striving to hide it from prior ownership or the envy of discoverers; a ship whose stem — battered a little but unbroken — bore the shape of a golden dolphin as figurehead. The dolphin was tarnished and half hidden by creepers, but sunlight spotted it with flecks of flame.

The masts, four of them, had gone by the board. One of them slanted from ground to smashed rail, cordage twining it like snakes, a handy ladder for a handy man.

Now at this point Jim took on double embodiment — scarcely triple, for he was quite unconscious of being in front of the porch-window. Still *in* the jungle, he saw, *from* the jungle, one Jim Lyman forcing his way through resistant boughs to a closer view of the jungle stranded ship. On the bows the name had been applied in metal letters. Some of them were missing. On the starboard bow he read:

G LDE   D LP N

On the counter, in sunken carving, was the full legend:

Golden Dolphin
BOSTON

He saw himself climbing that angling mast, reaching the deck, disappearing. The sudden shutting off of all sunlight, the deepening of the green twilight to gloom, the switch of palmtops in strengthening wind, the signal of a recall gun, voices calling his name — all dimmed. Even the ship — now a model again — faded. Something else absorbed him, something made contact with his inner self, brought it back to the present with a strange sensation — the identical quickening of the spirit that had accompanied his first sight of the sign, yet deeper, more intimate.

At the back of the display someone was opening a French window from the inner room. Brocades had parted to the touch of a white hand, a girl's face appearing, pale in the dusk, with luminous eyes, looking at Jim. The expression, emphasized by piquant eyebrows, registered surprise at what the owner read in Jim's bemused gaze. A slightly amused smile came to the red lips, but there was no ridicule in it, only friendliness; a sort of intimacy, as if she, too, liked that ship's model, and knowing he did, acknowledged the link between them.

She leaned forward. A slender arm, bare to the elbow, rounded, soft and white of skin, reached out and slim fingers took up a blue and white pitcher. Jug and girl disappeared through the brocades.

The spell was broken. Jim, self-convicted of staring, imagined he must have looked like a moonstruck fool. While every lass may love a sailor, it is not every sailor that loves every lass, despite the ballads. The sweetheart in every port is a calumny born of jealousy. Your blue water salt is perforce a hermit for long periods. If he has brains he becomes a bit of a philosopher. He learns to think while on watch; and the rolling sea, the roving clouds, the chanting winds, the sun, the moon and the stars rolling in their appointed courses, are all good teachers. Jim was a bit of a poet at heart. So is every true sailor. He had had his own dreams of the measure of a girl, but he had had few opportunities for metrical diversion. Also he was a bit flustered in their presence. He did not understand them, they were like fine lace to a carpet weaver, admirable but strange to his craft. The girl, so far, was but incidental to the main point. His jaw lines tensed as he went up the steps beneath the Dutch hood and through the door with the tinkling of an automatic bell. He half expected to see a customer inside in connection with the blue and white pitcher. And there would be the K. Whiting, proprietor. But the girl came forward to meet him out of shadows empty of other humanity though close set with furniture, tip-tables, chairs, sofas, standard lamps, and century-old belongings.

Jim's eyes were good, dark or light. He saw that she had on a dress of deep blue, ocean blue, flicked with small dots of lighter blue. Her eyebrows again arched quizzically as Jim stood, hat in hand, lost for opening words.

"Mr. Whiting in?" he asked. Somehow the girl took his breath a bit. Cool and dainty, self reliant, but utterly feminine. A face so good to look at that he did not know whether she was pretty or not. Womanhood, that was what she represented to Jim, though she was young yet, young and sweet. She was disturbing. He had come in to see about the ship and she made his desire vacillating. His will struck for the original motive, therefore he asked to talk with a man.

"There is no Mr. Whiting — here," she answered, a slight hesitancy before the last word, a fleeting shadow over her face. "I am the proprietor. You were looking at the ship? You are a sailor, aren't you?"

This is what the girl saw:

A man who had boyhood in his eyes and about his mouth, though the first were steady, the second firm enough; a face tanned deep; eyes of gray with little traceries of sun and wind about them; aquiline nose; good forehead; brown hair that was a little sunburned here and there, plenty of it and the barest suggestion of a wave; tall — about six feet — a hundred and seventy pounds of solidity, chest like a barrel and a lean waist; clothes, blue serge, fairly new, well kept; hands, well kept, but hands that were used to work and showed it, hands held slightly curved inward as if ready to grasp a rope. Being a woman, she took this all in at a glance, while to Jim's equal opportunity she was more or less a vague pleasantness. It was the combination of blue serge, the half open hands and the look in his eyes as he viewed the ship that had set him down as a sailor to the girl. She knew something of sailors. Also she knew that she liked Jim. Instinctively she felt that she could trust him. Women and dogs can do that at first sight — scent also, with the dogs. Man's intuitions are less blunted. It is not so necessary for him to be attracted or warned through his senses; he has developed other ways of obtaining information, other ways of protection which often prove far less infallible.

"Yes, I am a sailor," he said. "Was, at least. Hope to be so again. Is the ship for sale? I mean does it belong to somebody here or did you buy it outright to sell again?"

Something of his excitement had spread to the girl; the atmosphere in the shop, transformed from original parlors, dusky save for the lighter space by the door where they stood, was becoming charged with magnetism.

"Why do you ask?" she said.

"I'm not a purchaser — though I'd like to be if I could afford it and had a place to put it." Subconsciously he was stalling, delaying the information that momentarily he more and more felt was going to start something. There was a knocking at the door of his inner self. Then he blurted it out.

"I've seen that ship before. Not the model but the ship itself, ashore in the bush on an island in the South Pacific."

The girl blanched, all color draining from her face and even her lips. Jim put out a hand to steady her as she swayed, but she caught at the high back of a chair and stood with the corner of her underlip caught between small teeth, her eyes masked for a moment. Then they widened, rounded, searched him.

"That was my father's ship," she said. "We have believed him lost at sea. Tell me about it, please." Jim hesitated, reluctant. He felt that he had unveiled a tragedy, that he had struck a deadly blow at this girl who met disaster so bravely. She even smiled at him, wanly but bravely.

"Please," she repeated and Jim knew then that her voice had power to compel him to do its bidding, now and for always; knew instantly that here was the last girl on earth he would have wounded.

"I know," she said. "You think he must be dead. But he is not. I have always been sure of that, quite sure." And despite Jim's contrary belief her tone carried conviction to him. "I knew he was lost somewhere, but he is not dead. You have brought me the best of news. And you will tell me all about it? It is closing time anyway, and time for lights."

She closed the door and set the latch, drew down a blind and turned a switch. Two old standing lamps with Chinese shades illuminated the place. She led the way toward the back of the room and motioned to a seat on a settle that formed a screen from the rest of the shop. There was a little table there and a businesslike looking desk.

"I shall be back in a moment," she said and vanished toward the back of the house. "Smoke, if you want to."

Jim did not want to smoke. With her departure the momentary belief he had shared with her that her father was not dead oozed out through his pores. The searchlight of his will was summoning details of his discovery in the jungle and now he could see, gleaming white among the ground vines distinctly as if it lay on the floor in front of him, a skeleton, the bones picked clean by ants, the cage of the ribs bound to backbone and pelvis by a network of tendrils — and a skull, with a gold bridge gleaming in its fallen jaw. It was not that of a victim of the sea. The dome had been rudely cleft by a blunt weapon. Surely the skull of a white man.

❚❚

Adventure

The girl came back accompanied by a bony person with a bony face that suggested a horse, a thin, tall austere person who looked as if most of the blood had been drained out of her, and with it all of the milk of human kindness that her veins might have contained. She smiled at Jim, displaying big teeth liberally inset with gold. She was dressed in rusty black material that hung on her like stuff flung hastily over a clothes-rack. Her pale hair had brassy streaks in it. Her eyes were almost colorless, lacking eyebrows. The whole was redeemed, almost nullified, by a voice of wonderful contralto richness, suggesting in its beauty everything that the rest of her did not.

She bore a tray with plates and cups and saucers upon it, napkins of fine old linen, a dish of cake and cookies. The girl brought a pewter trencher bearing a teapot, cream ewer and sugar bowl of old Sheffield plate; the teapot under a quilted cozy shaped like a helmet. These they set down upon the table. To think of tea at a moment tense with the first news after months of suspense — years perhaps, for it was hard to guess how long the ship had lain in its canting jungle bed! The hospitality of gentlewomen. Jim recognized the quality though he was not used to sharing its niceties.

"I am Katherine Whiting," said the girl. "I should like to introduce you to my cousin, Lynda Warner, Mr. —?"

"Lyman, Jim Lyman." Jim stood up, heard the marvelous richness of that voice — though it did not seem as sweet to him as the clear, high note of the girl's — sat down, sipped some tea, broke a cookie and began his yarn. North Street and its unemployed seemed a thousand miles away. The whirligig of time was bringing about its own revenges.

"It's not much of a yarn — my end of it. It happened on my last voyage. I've sailed on both oceans, Atlantic and Pacific, but I like the Pacific best. I was on this side, as it happened, the trip before last, and after we'd landed cargo at Porto Bello, we laid up for repairs. I took a notion to cross to the Pacific side. The skipper was agreeable. The owners were always willing to cut expenses and the ports these days are full of sailormen looking for a berth.

"Things were slack at Panama, but after a bit I shipped on the four-masted schooner *Whitewing*, bound for Tahiti, a forty-five hundred mile run. We never got there. East of the Paumotus we ran into a wicked storm, a hurricane. They call the group the Dangerous Islands and they've named 'em right. The danger is all around 'em. First our mizzen mast smashed off as if some giant had hit it with an axe. All we had set to that gale was a storm staysail and a bit of the spanker, but that was yards too much. That storm fair wrenched us apart. Before we could hack the mizzen clear it had smashed the rudder.

"There we bucked, five foot of water in the hold, and rising, seams opening, three men out of eleven hurt, to say nothing of the skipper himself with his head split by the spanker-boom. We got the steam-pump assembled finally and the water out of her, but not till after we'd been blown way out of our course, far south of Pitcairn, south of Rapa. Twice the jury rudder we had rigged gave way on us, and we were in a sad mess the morning we picked up that bit of land, a mountain top lifting up from the sea in a wrack of vapor clouds, like a finger stuck through a veil — and beckoning. Some of us fancied we saw loom of high land way to the west, but you couldn't be sure, the weather 'ud open up a bit and shut down again with all the horizon banked up with clouds that looked like dark gray wool.

"It was a lee shore at that, the wind still blowing northeast, and blowing hard. The barometer was jumpy and it looked as if it might boil up and over again into another hurricane any minute. Ordinary times we'd have kept clear of that place, but we had to have water, we needed fresh meat, and we wanted to get a chance to strengthen our rudder a bit. As we got closer we caught glimpses of patches of green. By the looks of the island we hoped to find pigs, doves, fish, and fruit: coconuts, papus, guavas, wild oranges, and bananas. If there were natives they'd do the provisioning, and if not we'd forage for ourselves.

"You must understand, miss, that we'd all, from the skipper down, had a tough time of it; cold victuals for days at a time, no chance to light the galley fire, soaked through, up day and night with just snatches of sleep. Sick and well, we were nigh tuckered out. Thought of getting ashore for the fruit and meat, most of all for some fresh water, got us close to crazy to make it. We discounted the risks. But we might not have, at that, if the sun hadn't suddenly rent through the sky like it was rotten cloth. For a minute it hung over the jagged peak and turned the green of the trees to emerald before it faded. That settled it. The first mate and myself — I was second — took four men apiece with water barrels, while the old man, with his head tied up, handled the schooner, off and on, outside the barrier reef. We didn't dare try to get into the lagoon unless it moderated, though we wanted to 'count of fixing the rudder. But we made sure of the water, anyhow.

"We were careful in landing for we didn't have any guns but a pistol apiece for the first and myself and the skipper's shotgun that I took along to try to get some fresh meat. My boat hung back a bit like a covering boat. It's the usual way in the islands, and we figured the natives would argue we were well armed. I show my shotgun barrel plainly enough. There was one freshwater creek opposite the gap in the outer reef, its flow having made the gate in the coral. It looked like another one flowed into the lagoon at the far end of the curving bay. Anyway there were cocoa palms there and we planned for the first mate to tackle the first creek and me the one by the palms. If there was no fresh water we'd get nuts.

"It was a narrow reef, as barrier reefs go, little more than a hundred yards wide but with a mean, jaggy entrance and the waves spouting over the slabs of coral that looked like stone sponge layers. We didn't see a sign of natives. We worked fast in case of a hurry signal from the ship for, while the sun was blinking in and out, the sea was running high and every now and then the wind would blow in gusts that came like the explosions of big guns.

"There was no creek after all, where my boat went, so we went after the nuts. A native could have climbed the trees and thrown them down but none of us were monkeys enough for that — and we were all battered and bruised up anyhow — so we cut down the palms. I hate to cut down palms like that, they are so mighty useful, but we had no time to lose.

"I heard doves cooing and I thought I heard the grunting of a pig, so I worked into the stiff jungle that came bristling down to the beach, best way I could. Looking for pigs in there, unless you found a runway and had luck, was next to impossible. Most places the bush was woven together like high hurdles with the creepers and vines twisted about the trees. But I came across a lot of deadfall — trees uprooted in some big blow that hadn't happened so very long ago, to judge by the looks of them and the new growth. I had got half a dozen ringdoves, a jumper-full of vi-apples, oranges, bananas, and mangoes when the sun worked through again and suddenly I saw something shine in the trees. First I thought it was some sort of idol — I was new to these South Seas and didn't know but what they had 'em of metal — and I went mighty careful, watching for savages. I was there after food, not to furnish it.

"Presently I saw what it was — the figurehead of a ship lying there prow on to the mountain, the decks aslant a bit but all cradled up in vines, half a mile inland from the lagoon and, so far as I had time to determine, undamaged. It was just as if it had been picked up from the sea like Gulliver did with the fleet at Lilliput; picked up by a kid giant for a toy and dropped in the forest like a toy yacht might fall on the grass."

Jim paused, sipping his tea, nearly cold now, declaring he liked it, making it an excuse to gather his thoughts. He wanted to eliminate certain details, to color others optimistically, but was not sure if that would be the right thing.

The girl and her cousin, the bony spinster, hung on his words with growing excitement, their eyes urging him on to the finish. Moreover, it was fairly evident that not only was his tale magic to them by reason of their personal interest, but that he had made it vivid to their imaginations. Under the glow of the lamp the girl leaned forward as eagerly as Desdemona must have done, her eyes luminous, her lips, soft and red as rose petals, slightly apart, her breath short. The glamour of the thing was upon the older woman. Finishing his cup of tea, Jim Lyman decided to submit the more gruesome details to her privately, and took up the thread of his yarn.

"It was a good ship. If the sea could have been brought to her I believe she would have floated. Strained a bit, of course, but sound. The masts were gone by the board. One lay over the port rail like a companion ladder. The others might have been alongside hidden in the heavy growth. I've got an idea they snapped off like carrots when she landed.

"You see, I figure she must have been flung ashore in some combination of great wind and tidal wave. Great rollers sometimes come up out of the ocean and sweep the islands. The skipper said afterward that they had them at Tahiti every so often. That would account for the ship riding unbroken over barrier and fringing reef, to be left high and dry inland. I have heard of such ships before.

"I went up by the mast. The deck was a mess, and the glass of the skylights broken. The slide of the main companionway was jammed, so I swung down through the skylight. Vines had worked their way in and the rains had mouldered things, but there was no sign of looting, no disorder outside of that natural to the jolt of such a landing. Now that, Miss, was proof positive to me there were no natives on the island. They would have dismantled the ship, gutted it, and probably burned it. I'd seen some lettering on the bows, raised letters with some of 'em dropped off, and I'd seen the full name on the stern. They tied up with the figurehead and name of that model in the window; they were the same as that sign you've got hanging up outside:

THE GOLDEN DOLPHIN
BOSTON

That was the name of her.

"The cabin was much the same as other cabins — a mast running through, transom cushions between the doors leading off to the staterooms, fixed table and chairs in the middle, swinging lamp with the chimney busted, but oil in the container. She was well fitted up. It was getting dark outside and I could hear the wind rising, tossing about the treetops. I had to hurry. There was an empty birdcage, I remember, and books on shelves behind doors with the glass broken. The books were mouldy and had mostly come apart with the damp. I took along one of them that was small enough to get into my pocket. *Gulliver's Travels.* That's how I happened to read it."

"Oh!" The girl gave the exclamation with shining eyes. "Father thinks that Swift is the most wonderful of satirists. He always had Gulliver with him. I gave him that copy that was in the little library. And the canary. Poor Dick! Go on."

"Well, Miss, that's about all, so far as the island goes. I told you it was getting dark. There was a recall from the ship, three shots from the saluting gun. My men were shouting for me and there was the schooner with a flag streaming from the main spreader. It was about mid-afternoon, but by the time we got aboard it was black as midnight. It was as if that big hurricane had been blowing in a circle and we had come from one edge of it through comparative calm only to go smack into it again.

We clawed off that island by some miracle and away we went again, south and east. Our rudder went for the third and last time, we were blown along the top of the waste with no more control than a chip in a millrace.

"There are leagues of open water down where we were, to look at the chart, but there are deeps in the South Pacific, troughs, they call 'em, where the depth is five thousand fathoms — thirty thousand feet — and more, and right close to those troughs you'll find great reefs built up. I suppose they are built to sea level by the coral insects working on top of big peaks. They make big patches of shallows where, if it is calm, you see the sea breaking for miles at low tide. We saw nothing. There was as much water in the air as the ocean, it seemed. The spume blew level and stung like hail from the force of the wind back of it. There was no sky, no horizon, only a white welter, and the ship leaking, staggering along till she went smashing and dragging over coral that ripped her almost to splinters. There was no bottom left to the old hooker.

"And, then, just as if it had done what it set out to do, though you can't imagine such a hullabaloo to sink one schooner, or a dozen, for that matter, the wind vanished, blew out, the snarling sea worried over us for a bit and went down, though where it was deep the waves ran high enough, as we soon found out. The sky had cleared by sunset. It was the most gorgeous sight I've ever seen. The stars were out and the moon up before midnight, shining down on our two boats running before a sweet southeaster.

"We parted company that night. The skipper and the first mate were in the other boat. Far as I know they've never been heard of. Insurance has been collected on the *Whitewing*, I know that. We'd broken up on the Maria Theresa Reef, I imagine, or maybe the Legouve Reef. The last reckoning taken and set down was the one made by the skipper when the sun broke through at noon off the island; Dolphin Island, I've always called it, for want of a better name. There's nothing down on the charts.

"That's as far as you're interested, Miss, and farther. We had a pretty mean time. Ran out of grub and water, the usual open boat luck. Two poor devils died and another went mad with drinking salt water, but we were picked up at last and brought back to Panama. There was a chap who was half purser, half steward along with me, and I came up north with him looking for a job. There was nothing doing on the coast so I worked inland after I'd stayed with his folks till I was ashamed of myself.

"That's all."

He had dodged the skeleton successfully and the fallen jaw with the golden bridge. He could ask the spinster if Captain Whiting had bridge work in his teeth. It might establish his death and, if so, a relative could better break it to the girl. It seemed convincing that there were no survivors. For one thing — he had avoided mention of it — the ship's boats were gone. They might have been carried away in the storm that had flung her on the island; they might have been launched during that storm; they might have been launched from the island after the final catastrophe. If the crew had not been swept overboard, if they had not escaped in boats, they would surely have stayed with the ship and used it as headquarters, if not for a permanent habitation. Supposing the ship had been there a year even — in the hurry of departure Lyman had not thought to look for ship's papers — that meant that the boats had been lost, like the skipper of the *Whitewing*, long ago.

The island was uninhabited. Natives or white survivors of the *Golden Dolphin* would always have been looking for a ship. They would have seen the *Whitewing*, come down to the beach or signaled. Yet proof that one, at least, of the *Golden Dolphin*'s crew had come ashore, lay in the skeleton of the man who had been murdered. Such dentistry would hardly be that of a common sailor. It was an enigma probably insoluble this side of the grave. But Jim Lyman had not begun to gauge the intricacies of the riddle.

The girl turned questioner and her inquisition showed that her knowledge of sea-craft was not merely inherent, but acquired, and that she knew how to apply it.

"You said that the captain of the *Whitewing* took an observation that would give the position of the island?"

"Yes, Miss."

"And set it down in the ship's log?" Jim nodded. He saw what she was driving at.

"I suppose he had the ship's papers with him when you took to the boats?"

"Yes. I saw the entry in the log and copied it. I have a master's certificate and I have always kept a log of my own, as a matter of habit, whether acting as first or second. Just a pocket diary that trip. I told the skipper about the ship in the jungle and he noted it. He didn't seem to attach much importance to it. We had troubles of our own. And all of us in my boat were in pretty bad shape when we were picked up. The Portugee that rescued us wasn't over well found, though we were grateful enough to them. But they didn't have much of a medicine chest and Spigotty grub needs lifelong training. We had boat sores and scurvy on top of being famished, and we just about crawled ashore at Panama. I didn't know then but what our skipper might have been picked up or made a landing. It was his duty to report such a find and he would have turned in his log. But there's no question but what he's perished at sea, I'm afraid. I was in hospital on the Isthmus for awhile with Stallings, the steward — the rest, too, for that matter. I got a quick chance with Stallings to work north on a fruit freighter when I got out, and — though it may seem strange to you, being personally interested — I forgot about the *Golden Dolphin* until I saw your sign. It all came back in a flash when I saw the model in the window."

"Naturally. But you've got the position?"

"Yes. The diary is with my things in my room here."

"Ah!" The girl stood up with shining eyes. "Mr. Lyman, I am going to make you an offer for those figures."

"Why, they're yours Miss, of course, without the asking." She checked him.

"Wait. I am positive my father is alive. We were closer than most fathers and daughters. I have sailed with him and been his constant companion up to the trip of the *Golden Dolphin*. There were special reasons why he would not take me on that voyage. But if he had died I should have known it. I am sure of it — here."

She put her hand over her heart, speaking with a ring to her voice that carried the assurance of an ancient sybil. Jim supposed many people had felt that way about their loved ones, desire fanning the flame of hope. Again he felt the force of her conviction against his own force of logic.

"And now you have come here, a special messenger, coming as you thought by chance or coincidence. I do not believe in such things. It was not by chance you forced your way through that jungle; God brought you to me. I am a sailor's daughter. I am going to that island and I know that there I shall find the clew that will help me find my father, *alive*."

Jim sat dumbfounded. He looked appeal at the spinster cousin and managed to convey a meaning in his glance that he had something to tell her in private. That the girl did not realize the magnitude, the expense, the forlorn chances of the quest she so proudly announced, he was certain.

"I shall find my father," she said again. "You are a sailor; you have been a mate; you have a master's certificate and you have been looking in vain for a berth. I offer it to you in exchange for the position of the island. More than that, I offer you a share in a fortune that is hidden safely aboard the *Golden Dolphin.*" She paused for a moment with her forehead wrinkled. "I am not alone in the matter," she went on, "but I have a third interest in the affair, my father another third. I offer you a sixteenth of all that we recover, in addition, of course, to your pay as master. Your share should be in the neighborhood of sixty thousand dollars."

Jim wondered if the girl was insane; if grief for her father had unsettled her mind. But the eminently practical face of Miss Warner showed no such apprehension.

"It would cost a lot of money," he said. "And the chances of finding your father are —"

"I shall find him. I can find the money for outfitting. I have had good offers for this business. This old furniture is valuable. I have collected it personally and sold much at a good profit already."

"But I do not want pay for giving you your clue. I should despise myself if I did. Common humanity —"

"It is common justice that you should share if you bring the means of restoration. The money means nothing to me compared to the finding of dad. You are the only person in the world who could have furnished me with this clue. You have been brought halfway across the world to me. I cannot tell you how grateful I am to you. You found the ship; I ask you to go back to it with me. I cannot take your information unless you agree to my terms. You would not rob me of my chance to find my father?"

This was placing him in the small end of the horn with a vengeance, Jim reflected. Common justice, she called it. He supposed it was the working of the New England conscience. But it was a fool's errand.

"You'll have to tell me more about it," he temporized.

"I will. But that should come with a full consultation. The *Golden*

Dolphin was outfitted for a special purpose. There are others, two others, who have a third share between them. My uncle — the husband of my aunt, and his son. I can get in touch with them by telephone. We will hold a meeting tonight. I think it can be arranged. I'll see."

She went toward the front of the shop where the telephone stood upon a wall table. If she was insane, there was method in her madness, Jim told himself. He could imagine her capable in business. But this wild undertaking? He seized his opportunity and leaned toward the spinster, whispering:

"Did Captain Whiting have a gold bridge in his lower jaw?"

Lynda Warner's own jaw sagged momentarily, but she rallied to the occasion. Here was a keen-witted woman. Jim realized. And she did not answer one question with another.

"No. Every tooth in his head sound," she answered in the same tone. "Why?"

Katherine Whiting had got her connection and was talking over the wire.

"Found a skeleton beside the ship," said Jim. "Skull had gold teeth. I was afraid it was her father. Afraid to tell her."

"You needn't have been," retorted the spinster. "Though I appreciate your idea. Any signs of foul play?"

Jim nodded. The girl had hung up and was coming back. But how did Lynda Warner come to suspect that there should have been murder committed?

"They'll be over by eight o'clock," the girl announced, excitement glowing in her face. "You'll stay for supper, Mr. Lyman. We — we can't lose sight of you."

"But —" Jim wanted to spruce up a little. Here was an atmosphere of refinement, of elegance to which he was not accustomed. He felt suddenly self-conscious, unkempt. "I should get that diary," he suggested.

"That will keep for a little while. I have a thousand questions to ask you, lots to tell you. Will you wait for a few minutes here, alone? Lynda, will you come with me?" She vanished.

Her cousin, lingering at the door, said softly, "I will tell her."

Meaning the skeleton, Jim told himself. His head buzzed a bit. Here were adventure and opportunity hand in hand, bowing to him, like a pair of friendly djinns. Things had happened too swiftly for him to properly adjust them. He was like a player given a hand by a swift dealer. He had picked up the cards, glanced at them, but he had yet to arrange them in sequence, separate them into suits, appraise their true value. At first glance he saw he had some heart cards, but he was doubtful about them. Jim had not considered himself the type to fall headlong into love. On the other hand, he had never met a girl like this before. Jim was well enough born and bred. But he had a fair education and had taken postgraduate work in the greatest of all universities — the world at large. Long ago, in the little village of Maine, he had seen and known such things as surrounded Katherine — the diminutive of that would be Kitty, he supposed, if a chap ever got familiar enough with her to use it — and her cousin. There had been antiques and old silver and fine linen with all the niceties that go with them in his mother's house. But of late years those things had gone by the board. He had roughened and toughened. He had lost his finer manners, perhaps his sensibilities.

He looked at his suit of serge. It had been cheap, because he could not afford any more than he paid. Cheap clothes in this day and time are shoddy and it had worn quickly and badly. It looked like a suit from the slop chest. The same way with his shoes, his tie, his hat, everything. A chap like he was would constantly offend the girl's ideas of life, he imagined. Then took himself to task for a fool for thinking about such things.

The chance to go away in a ship of his own — she had hinted he would be master — down to the South Seas, with her! She crept in again to the foreground of his dreams, tugged at him with a hundred warps of interest. To find a missing man and a missing treasure, here was romance, or folly, and Jim was not old or world-worn enough to entertain the suggestion that the two are twins.

It was Lynda Warner who reappeared and escorted him up a white, thin-spindled, mahogany-railed stairway, curving to the next floor. He found himself in a guest room with furnishings of white, and hangings of gay chintz, rag rugs on the floor, a door half open to a tiled bathroom. It was as different from the room he had at the National House, uptown, as the forecastle of a ship is to the cabins aft. Jim was used to the latter, but this increased his ill ease till he caught sight of himself in the glass and laughed at his reflection for that of an egregious ass.

"It isn't the clothes, you chump," he told himself; "it's the man. You're straight enough and decent enough under your artificial hide.

You can always buy duds. You can always mend your manners. As for the girl, you've got to do your best to persuade her, or her cousin, that she'll be throwing her money away. Without butting in too personally, of course. If you can't, or if you get in too deep, it's up to you to drift off and fade away. She's a yacht built for speed in summer waters and summer winds; you're a trading schooner and out of her class. You belong moored to a copra wharf, not off a yacht club float."

The heart-to-heart talk did him good, and after he had washed up and brushed his hair and clothes, be went downstairs cheerfully with recovered poise. He appreciated the courtesy that left all talk of the vital question out of the meal, covering it so successfully that it appeared dismissed. And he appreciated the meal: crisp waffles with honey, fresh asparagus with poached eggs and a sublime sauce over all, a huckleberry pie that melted, crust and all, in one's mouth, and coffee such as he had not tasted for ten years. Lynda Warner exhibited a rare fund of anecdote and a sense of humor that the girl reflected and Jim enjoyed. The supper was savored with the best of condiments — laughter.

Only the porches and the two front rooms of the house had been given over to business, it seemed, though there were some goods stored in the barn back of the little garden. The rest of the house was private and the property of the girl's father — or the girl herself, Jim feared. The dining room held portraits of Avery Churchill Whiting, the missing skipper, a ruddy-faced mariner with gray hair and a blend of kindliness and determination in his strong features; and of James Avery Whiting, father of the aforesaid, also a captain, but in naval uniform. His sword hung below the frame.

There was a serving maid, angular almost as Lynda Warner, privileged by custom and her own indomitable determination to know all about everything that was going on. The elimination of all reference to the *Golden Dolphin* might partly have been staged for her benefit, Jim surmised. She was patently devoured with anxiety to know who he was, and how he came to be invited. She surveyed him between service with a puzzled face, her head cocked to one side like an undetermined hen.

They remained in the dining room, which appeared to be also used as a general living room, and the maid dawdled over clearing away. But she was gone at last and both women insisted upon Lyman smoking, producing cigars that were both good and properly moist. Gratefully enjoying it, he listened in his turn.

Avery Churchill Whiting had, it seemed, retired from the sea, inland to Foxfield where relatives had settled for land commerce. He had married late and was forty when Katherine Whiting was born — the only child. Her mother died soon after and the two became chums, the girl going on voyages until Captain Avery decided he was fairly well fixed, that the merchant marine was rapidly going to the dogs, and that he hated steam worse than ever. Therefore he settled to enjoy his three delights; his daughter, trotting horses, and flowers.

His wife's brother, Stephen Foster, native of Foxfield, was the uncle who was coming at eight o'clock, with his son, Newton. He was a manufacturer of blankets and woolen goods and Jim gathered that he had made almost a million during the war. Gathered also from a hint of Lynda Warner that he was not averse at anytime to making more; that, born on a farm, gaining footing in the office of a mill after factory experience, he had finally made good as producer in a small way until the war gave him his great opportunity. Now, having tasted power, he was obsessed with the desire of great wealth and what it might do to make him a ruler of men.

The son, it seemed, was a more negligible quantity, confining most of his activities to various amusements, a Yale graduate. Lynda Warner, with an inimitable trick of suggestion, drew these sketches, which Jim felt were excellent portraits, in a few words. It appeared that she was not over friendly to the Fosters, father and son, and Jim noticed that the girl entered no especial protest, save to disregard her caustic interjections.

The important factor was that the Fosters owned a third share in the *Golden Dolphin* and its hidden treasure. Lyman was glad that a man — and a successful business one — with a real interest in the affair, was to take part in the council. The talk of hidden treasure was attractive enough, but if it was of bulk small enough to be concealed on the ship it did not seem likely that it would have been left there. There was that skeleton! He wondered whether Lynda Warner had already told the girl about it. It would have to be mentioned at the conference.

"My father," said the girl, "once got to be very friendly with a chief named Mafulu, ruler of an island somewhere near the Bismarck Archipelago. That is, he had been ruler until the Germans took his island away from him and made plantation slaves out of all his people. After that he hated all white men. He even mistrusted father for a long while after dad had saved his life. But they got to be blood brothers and called each other by the other's name. Mafulu was Vaitini — the nearest his tongue could come to Whiting — and father was Mafulu. They had not seen each other for years and father had quitted the sea.

"Mafulu, and some of his islanders, were employed as pilot and crew by a man, an eccentric millionaire who had taken up anthropology, with the tracing of the drift of the Malayo-Polynesian races as his especial hobby. As father understood it, Mafulu had graduated from pilot and come to be his right hand man. At all events, he accompanied this millionaire through the archipelagoes, to Tahiti, to Hawaii and at last to San Francisco. He was still on the ship, or yacht, when the owner dropped dead of heart disease. There was some squabble among the heirs, and Mafulu was dismissed. He had been too proud to accept actual wages, so he was practically penniless, unable to speak much of the language, bewildered by the bustle of a city, robbed, and cheated. Finally the fogs of San Francisco proved too much for him. He was a magnificent specimen of manhood, father said, and probably would have lived to be almost a hundred in his native haunts. As it was, he was found in a dying condition in a miserable sailors' lodging house where he had been the drudge — that fearless chief and warrior — for enough to eat and a hole to crawl to at night. It was consumption of the most rapid sort. Some reporter got part of his yarn and pieced together more, enough to make a feature story. It was copied by the Associated Press, more briefly.

"Father left for San Francisco within six hours after he had read the item in the local paper. That was like dad. Mafulu was a man, he said, and there were few men nowadays. He respected the obligations of his blood brotherhood. And Mafulu literally died in father's arms, died still hating all white men — was it any wonder? — save one, the one he called by his own name and who called him Vaitini.

"Father had the body cremated, much in the custom of Mafulu's tribe, and he promised Mafulu to take back his ashes and have them properly buried on his own island. And Mafulu told father of the existence of a double atoll rich with virgin oyster shell, drawn on by Mafulu's ancestors for the pearls they used for trading. Its whereabouts were known only to the ruling chief and his son. Mafulu had no son. After the Germans annexed his land his people went no more to the atoll. He gave father the chart he had always carried and explained it to him. The hospital people had thought it was a charm and nobody had ever thought it worth while to steal it. Mafulu had kept it on a sinnet string about his neck. Father translated its directions into more modern shape and he gave the chart to me when he sailed. Here it is. Mafulu swore — and father knew him to be absolutely truthful under his oath of blood — that there were pearls there of such value that dad calculated there must be a dozen fortunes in the two lagoons."

Lyman took the chart and surveyed it with enthralled interest. It did not look much like a map. It consisted of slender reed sections bound flat, mat fashion, with strands of fiber woven into them in crosswise curves and lines. Here and there a small shell was attached. The whole thing barely covered the palm of his hand. No one would have guessed it to be the key to fortune.

"The fibers," said the girl, "represent currents and sailing courses; the shells are islands. The trip has to be taken at a certain time of the year when certain winds prevail and certain constellations are above the horizon.

"On the strength of it my father persuaded my uncle, Mr. Foster, who was just beginning to make money then, to go shares in the expedition. They needed a ship and ships were scarce at that time, three years ago, when the war used every available bottom. They wouldn't take father for the war because of his age but he was in wonderful health and strength, really in his prime. They got a small shipbuilder father knew in Maine to build the *Golden Dolphin*, Mr. Foster thought a ship a good investment aside from the treasure hunt, and he believed in that. His son was at Camp Devens."

"Until the armistice," put in Lynda Warner.

"So the ship was built and launched. I christened it. I saw it built from the laying of the keel. Father almost lived at the yard. All his love of the sea returned. I begged for him to take me but he said the trip was too hazardous, especially with the added risks of German raiders. Only he and I knew the secret place where he intended to keep the pearls after he had got them. They were to visit Mafulu's island first, and if possible, recruit native divers, though they carried modern apparatus.

"It was hard work to get a crew at all. There was the draft and high wages for those who stayed ashore. Father was not satisfied with those he got. He said they were a rascally lot of longshore riffraff, but that he would make sailors out of them before they came back. At that, he was forced to sail short-handed, expecting to fill the complement with natives. So — they sailed."

The girl ceased talking and sat with her hands idle in her lap, lost in recollection. A tall clock ticked woodenly, wheezed and struck seven, arousing her.

"Lynda told me about you finding that skeleton," she said. "It was not my father. I do not know who it could have been. But it was thoughtful of you to ask my cousin to break it to me. I know this, that father delivered Mafulu's ashes and that they held ritualistic ceremonies over them. In gratitude many islanders shipped with him. I know that he found the island and the pearls. He wrote from Viti Levu in the Fijis. He was on his way home, and he was having trouble with his men. He did not think that it was serious or he would not have written me about it, and he has handled many a rough crowd before. I'll read you a part of that letter."

She got it from a lacquered box inlaid with mother of pearl, several sheets covered in distinctive writing. The date she read was twenty-seven months old.

"I can trust my Bioto boys absolutely (Mafulu's men) but I shall be glad to get rid of some of the others. Tomlinson has been slack in discipline throughout and, if he were not a good navigating officer and hard to replace these days, I would have got rid of him. He is too friendly with the crew; I mean not only the whites but the other natives. It is much the same with Harvey, a first-class steward when he is sober, but drunk whenever he can get the chance and an inveterate smuggler aboard of liquor. Bird is a weakling. I have made fairly good sailors out of those longshoremen, but it has not been willing service. You can't make a silk purse out of a sow's ear, but you can use it as a receptacle in a pinch. One would think they would all be happy as clams at high tide on this return voyage with the pearls aboard, looking forward to the bonuses promised them. But they are a surly lot. I should like to discharge them at Tahiti if there is any chance. You know Tahiti is the great pearl market, and I shall get ours appraised there, and possibly dispose of some of them. But I should soon glut the market. We had wonderful luck. I could go back and get as many more and then again, but it would take long weeks and I am anxious to get home. And we are rich. We must have almost a million dollars worth of fine gems aboard — safely stowed where only you and I know. So I shall soon see you again and then for a trip to Europe as soon as the war ends.

"The Germans have all been driven out of the Pacific, thanks largely to the British cruisers. Our boys are nearer home or in the Atlantic waters, I understand. I am writing your uncle by this mail. The Bioto boys are to be sent home from here. Good, faithful lads and I hate to part with them."

"The rest," concluded the girl, folding up the sheets and putting them away, "is personal and various remembrances. Tomlinson was a man who shipped as first mate. He applied for the job when father was almost despairing of filling it. He recommended Harvey and Harvey brought two or three men that he rounded up. Bird was second mate. They got him at Colon. He was an older man.

"So you see they started for home. I have imagined all sorts of happenings — storm, a German raider, fire at sea, even mutiny, but I have always been positive that father would come through. If you knew him you would think so too, Mr. Lyman."

"I am sure I hope so. But he was not with the ship. Would he have left the pearls behind him? If I found no trace of him —"

"You were on the island only a short time and then in the jungle. The weather was cloudy. They might have been on the other side. They might have been ill, away on a trip to that highland you spoke of seeing. A hundred things might have happened; there might be a thousand traces if one searched. And I will scour the island for him. Suppose he is there, waiting for succor? I cannot be dissuaded."

She spoke imperiously, passionately. It hardly needed the covert sign Lynda Wagner made him for Jim to keep silent. Yet he could not help but feel that a man of Captain Whiting's character and experience would have left the lonely isle, if not in his own ship's boats then in some craft he would build from the forest timbers. Only, it would have been the easiest thing to reconstruct a smaller vessel from the ship itself. The mystery deepened, the more one tried to solve it. And he could understand the love of the girl for her father refusing to pass over the one tangible clue.

In the back of his mind the thought of mutiny grew, the revolt of men who knew they carried a treasure aboard in which they held but slight shares compared with the possibility of even distribution. Piracy was not dead. He admired her pluck and beauty; he was amazed when he saw reaction suddenly set in. Her lip quivered; her eyes filled with tears that she made vain effort to stem; then her slim, lithe body was wrenched by sobs that were muffled on her cousin's flat but comforting breasts. Lynda Warner nodded to him over the girl's bowed head to remain, then led the girl from the room, leaving Jim alone with his cigar.

The clock ticked on solemnly as he went over and over the strange story, the swift turn of events in which he had become involved. He felt impelled to offer his service, keen to undertake any fool's errand in company with such a girl, yet his innate honesty battled against his giving any suggestion of success that his common sense told him was remote. As for the offer of money, he had forgotten that entirely. The matter that had caused the girl's grief was paramount. For twenty-seven months she had fought despair and now, clutching at the straw of hope, revulsion had come, perhaps because in spite of faith she realized the frailty of what she grasped.

The bell tinkled. He heard footsteps descending the stairway, the rustle of a gown. Then men's voices as the outer door was opened, one sharp, deep, and incisive, the other drawling. The Fosters had arrived.

III

Conspiracy

Jim rose as the four entered the room. Kitty Whiting — her cousin had called her Kitty and Jim henceforth thought of her as that — had with feminine magic removed all traces of tears. It was plain that she was not on excessively friendly terms with her uncle by marriage. She treated her cousin, a blood relation, more affably, though Jim formed a dislike to Newton Foster at first sight, an antipathy that he immediately wrestled with. He seemed about the same age as Jim, he was undeniably handsome with his black hair and dark eyes, he was more than merely well dressed in light summer clothes with belt, silk shirt, and buckskin shoes, while he carried himself with an easy grace and assured manner coupled with a politeness that could not be challenged. He wore a somewhat bored expression that heightened as he was introduced to Jim, an introduction that he recognized with an informal nod and a slight raising of the eyebrows.

Stephen Foster was the prosperous, confident man of business, inclined to stoutness. He wore a dark coat and striped flannels and carried a Panama hat. There was some resemblance to his son, but the warfare of commercial life, won by the shrewdness stamped upon his face, had left its marks upon him. His mouth was hard, his lips thin, closing when he delivered himself of any opinion — evidently considered by him the final word — like the slot of a letter box. His eyes were those of a man who has not considered the means to an end, who has matched craft with craft, and learned to keep his own counsel. They were hard as agate, expressionless as the eyes of a dead fish, though there was plenty of life and determination in them. He was clean-shaven, like his son, and the lines of his jaw proclaimed stubbornness. There was something catlike about him, Jim fancied, studying him; an overcare of his hands, a furtive tucking in of his thin lips in a smile that was covert, that hinted at a cruel streak somewhere in his nature. He treated Jim as he might a man applying to him for manual labor, an attitude which helped to color Jim's impressions.

At the outset he showed his attitude toward his niece's views with an attempt at tolerance and sympathy that the girl evidently resented. He refused her offer of cigars.

"Changed my brand for a lighter one, my dear," he said, selecting one from a leather case while his son lit a cigarette. "Now then, tell me everything."

"You know all that I do," she said. "And I realize that you think me foolish in believing dad still alive. But I do. And now I have something definite to work upon. It was good of you to come over. If Mr. Lyman does not mind repeating what he has told Lynda and me, perhaps that will be the simplest way. I will only say that it has determined me to go to the island of which he has the position and where he landed. You are interested in the returns of the expedition," she added with a slight curl of her lip. "I should like to know if you will join me."

"And me," said the spinster quietly. Kitty Whiting slid her hand into her cousin's. "You had no idea I should permit you to go without me?" the latter asked. The elder Foster put up his hand deprecatingly.

"We are going too fast," he said. "I imagined you wished for my advice, for a man's advice in this matter." The girl nodded non-committally. "Now then, my man."

Jim swallowed his gorge and began somewhat grimly. The "my man" attitude nettled him. He was emphatically his own man and intended to remain so. Foster was not the type he would have chosen for employer under any circumstances. And he listened with an increasing incredulity he took scant pains to conceal. As for the son, Jim fancied he saw his assumed boredom enlivened with some interest as the tale advanced. Several times he noticed Newton Foster observing Kitty Whiting closely. When he had finished, Stephen Foster lit a fresh cigar and smoked for a moment or two.

"Those figures, the position of the island," he said, "you have them with you?"

"They are at my room. I can give them to you approximately."

Foster shook his head.

"Figures are tricky things, the foundation of success or failure. And approximate figures are like mortar that has got too much sand in it, a false foundation. Facts, facts, facts," he pounded each word into his palm as if driving home the spikes of argument, "that's what we are after. Then we apply common sense.

"I have no desire to say anything derogatory against this young man's character. I will simply say that we know nothing about it. He comes without references, to tell an interesting story. I am going to be frank, to discuss the matter in a businesslike way, to speak as if he were not present, to set aside all personality, to look at all sides of the question.

"It would be quite possible, for instance, that someone accustomed to seafaring has seen the *Golden Dolphin* and gone aboard of her. Many must have done so, aside from her crew. Such a one, with the trained eyes of a sailor, would have no trouble in registering necessary details for an accurate description.

"He sees — this person, you understand, is quite supposititious — he sees, or hears at second-hand in maritime circles, the account of the *Golden Dolphin* being overdue, coupled with accounts of its building, launching and the story — foolishly spilled to the newspapers against my protest at the time — of her ownership, the romance of her captain returning to the sea upon a quest for treasure.

"This supposititious person later finds himself out of a job at a time when wages are ridiculously high and producers shutting down on production. Ships lie idle, commerce is at a standstill; the shelves and counters of the shops of the world are dusty, awaiting reorganization. He comes, this seafaring man, to Foxfield, spinning an interesting yarn to highly interested parties. Perhaps he looks for a reward; perhaps he smells a soft berth. Pardon me —" Again Foster lifted a deprecating hand. Jim Lyman had half risen from his chair, his hands clenching, his eyes blazing with indignation. Newton Foster looked on like a man at a comedy. Kitty Whiting was on her feet.

"Uncle! Mr. Lyman is my guest, here in my house. You insult him and me." Foster did not lose the urbanity with which he had greased his insinuation.

"Tut, tut, my dear. I am speaking purely impersonally. I cast no aspersions upon Mr. Lyman. That is one side of the question. For the other, assuming that his story is correct in every detail, I can see that he brings no assurance of the success of such a madcap expedition as you propose. We have talked much of this over before, my dear. I can fully appreciate your desire to believe your father alive. I would not for a moment tear down your hopes if I felt they held any basis. As for the pearls — if we could be sure of finding this island and the ship, the chances that the treasure would be still aboard are to me infinitesimal.

The expense would be great, the risk, from a business standpoint, far outweighing any possibility of profit. I am accustomed to looking at such things mathematically. I have made my money upon sound, logical bases of chance. I do not allow my peculiar interests to blind my commercial vision. If a similar situation was laid before me I should, in the light of common sense, proclaim it a wildcat scheme. If your father were alive he would long since have found some means of communication. I have already invested heavily in this enterprise and written it off as one of the few failures with which I have been concerned. I do not care to throw good money after bad. That is my reaction."

His own blood still hot, Jim found it impossible to listen quietly to this cold-blooded argument, though his own opinion had trended in the same general direction. But Stephen Foster's thoughts were evidently centered upon the financial aspect alone. Captain Whiting he callously scored out of the affair. He thought only of his profit and loss columns, of the red ink figures that represented to him his share in the *Golden Dolphin*. He might present the facts in the inexorable light of logic, but it was unnecessary for him to be brutal. The cat had manifested itself. Jim felt the insincerity of the man as a dog scents a taint. The girl spoke coldly, mistress of her emotions, her face pale and set.

"I can readily understand, Uncle, that there being no true relationship, no tie of blood between you and my father, you can the more easily consider his life ended. I can comprehend the hesitation with which you contemplate any suggestion of spending your money without a sure return in sight. I am doing this for love. If I were a man and in your position, I trust I should be a better gambler. I thank you for your advice, but I do not intend to take it. I can sell this business tomorrow by the sending of a wire. I shall do so and spend my last penny in the endeavor to follow up a clew that my heart tells me will lead me at last to my father." Foster looked at her grimly, with tight lips, moving his head slightly from side to side as if to emphasize her folly. His son, gripped by the girl's eloquence, by the restrained fire of her purpose, the beauty of her, was moved as Jim had been and was again. He went swiftly to her side.

"Dad!" he exclaimed, protestingly. Then to his cousin. "Kitty, you and I have some measure of the same blood in us. You are a sport and a wonder. I will go with you."

"Not with my consent. Not with my money," said his father coldly.

The two faced each other. It seemed to Jim that a look of special meaning passed between them. The boy sat down, silenced but not crestfallen.

"If I recover the pearls —" began the girl. Stephen Foster interrupted.

"In the articles of partnership it is provided that a third interest in any profits of the expedition shall be mine in consideration of the money I advanced for building and outfitting. The name of my son, Newton, is mentioned as participant in that third. The duty of bringing back those pearls devolved upon your father, Captain Avery Whiting. It was part of his duty to use all due diligence and precaution in expenditures and the handling of his ship. According to his letters the pearls were secured. One third of them belongs now to me. If, by any miracle, they should be recovered, I should be prepared to stand my proportionate share of any extraordinary outlay — but I will not advance a cent.

"The sale of your business is your own affair, but I can hardly see you, even under the able chaperonage of your cousin, Miss Warner, outfitting and handling an expedition. You have no conception of the difficulties and cost of doing so, the predestined failure. Doubtless this young man will be glad to give you the benefit of his experiences — for a compensation." Jim's furious glance beat against the ice of the older man's expression as inadequately as the wintry sun tries to affect the polar planes. If only Foster had been younger, he thought. He had practically been called a liar, a cheap adventurer looking for a soft berth at the expense of a girl's affection for her father.

"I imagined," Stephen Foster went on, "that you attached some weight to my judgment or you would not have asked me to come over here tonight. You are not conscious of that weight in the very natural flurry of your stirred-up emotions. But I beg of you to sleep over the matter. Tonight you will not sleep; you are too upset. Make no decision until the day after tomorrow. I, too, will give it further consideration. We will take it up again. If you still insist upon what I now believe to be an act of quixotic folly, though praiseworthy from a purely sentimental standpoint, and if I have not changed my mind at that time — say forty-eight hours from now — I will promise to give you every aid possible and wish you God-speed."

Jim discounted the suavity of the speech with his strong sense of

Foster's hypocrisy. He did not think the man had any human feelings. In place of a heart there was a cashbox; his brain was a filing system for commercial logic. He spoke as if he felt he had expressed himself too strongly, had struck more fire from his niece than he had expected, finding flinty indomitableness where he had expected wax. Yet the girl seemed softened.

"I will think it over until then," she replied. "I asked you here as a partner, Uncle. Without doubt you are entitled to your opinions and you have often practically demonstrated their value. But I do not think I shall change my mind. I thank you for your offer to help — for my father's sake as well as my own."

It was said gracefully, but it held a dismissal. Kitty Whiting stood, and the visitors perforce stood with her. She had the poise of a woman twice her age. She commanded the situation with dignity and assurance. Stephen Foster bade her good night with urbanity, Lynda Warner with the suggestion that she was somewhat of an inferior, whereupon the light of humor showed in the spinster's eyes and the twitch of her lip. Lyman he overlooked entirely. Newton pressed the girl's hand.

"Dad will come round," he said. "I'm coming along, anyway."

She gave him a grateful glance. Jim registered the belief that Newton Foster meant to express his ardent admiration of his cousin rather than any conviction in the success of the trip. The two left; there was the whirr of a starting motor, the closing of a door and the girl returned to find Lyman looking for his hat.

"You're not going?" she asked him, a complimentary emphasis on the first word.

"I think I had better," Jim answered, his decision confirmed by a little nod given to him by Lynda Warner over the girl's shoulder. He himself felt some of the strain Kitty Whiting must have been under. It was natural that they should want to be alone. He, too, wanted to think things over. "I'll bring over my diary tomorrow," he said.

"In the afternoon?" suggested Lynda Warner. "Tomorrow is a holiday, you know. The *Golden Dolphin* will be closed and I've an idea its inmates will sleep late." He caught the meaning, illustrated by the tiny brackets of tiredness about the girl's mouth as she smiled, the faint purple shadows ringing her eyes.

"I'll be over about two?"

"Just one question," said Kitty Whiting. "I'll worry about it unless you answer it. If you were in my position and going on such a quest, how would you set about it?"

"I'd take train to California," said Jim promptly. "To San Francisco. And I'd try to charter a power boat. I mean an auxiliary engine aboard a sailing vessel — a schooner or a ketch. Times are hard and they are selling off yachts and launches every day on the Eastern coast. I imagine it's the same way out West. I'd rustle a crew out there. No difficulty about that. And it would save you time and money. But, if I was in your position, Miss Whiting, I am not at all sure I'd go. I don't believe —"

She broke in on him with a pathetic little gesture of her hands.

"You, too?" she said. Lynda Warner suddenly stretched out her hand. "Good night, Mr. Lyman."

"Good night, and thank you," the girl echoed. And Jim found himself out in the street walking toward his hotel. His room there, lacking conveniences, utterly lacking in elegance or true comfort, was a far cry from the place he had just left. It was long years since Lyman had been received as guest in such surroundings, and he carried the contrast to himself, as he turned in, after making sure his diary was in his grip and looking up the position he had copied from the log of the *Whitewing*.

162° 37'w.
37° 19' s.

Cabalistic nine figures and two letters. One hundred and sixty-two degrees and thirty-seven minutes west from Greenwich, the longitude; thirty-seven degrees and nineteen minutes south from the equator, the latitude. Prick the spot on the charts and one would find vacancy — New Zealand a thousand miles to the west, the Cook Islands a thousand to the north, to the east nothing marked save the reefs of Legouve and Maria Theresa in all the long sea leagues to the South American coast opposite the isle of Juan Fernandez; to the south only the Sargasso Sea and the Antarctic drift. Yet those figures in hands no more competent that his could guide a vessel to where the *Golden Dolphin* lay stranded in the jungle with perhaps a million dollars in pearls aboard, with Captain Avery to be found, alive or dead; perhaps with nothing but what he had found and seen. Without the figures certainly nothing at all. Ships might search that ocean wilderness for years and never hit upon that beckoning mountain spur rending the mists, the shadowy highland in the offing.

The whole thing would have seemed like a dream to him had he not the water-stained diary in which he had made entry of the *Whitewing*'s voyage, and memory of the fearful voyage of the open boat north and east, the men dying of exposure and thirst madness, and at last the rescue.

And Stephen Foster had taken him for a sea tramp, with a ready lie coined out of a few printed facts made up to play upon the sentiments of a bereaved girl! His blood surged hot again as he sat on the bed reading over the log. The cold-blooded money grubber, counting his risks! Yet in his heart Lyman was influenced by the decision of the business man, coinciding with his own. It was a wild-goose chase. If he went he had nothing to lose, and he gained a berth and salary, aside from any sharing of the pearls that the probabilities declared were not there. For the girl there would be heart-eating anxiety, hope long deferred, hour after hour of racking suspense, besides the perils of the voyage, and if failure came at last, crushing despair. If it was only the pearls at stake it would be a good gamble for a man, but for a girl, clinging to a faith blindly against all likelihood, it was a different thing. The one would be, at the worst, a glorious adventure; the other carried the hazard of endurance prolonged to the snapping point, the permanent bruising of a brave and sensitive soul.

Lyman suffered a natural despondency born of his treatment by Foster. He began to wonder what the girl really thought of him. He had the diary for proof; he could give her that and slip out of it, dropping all responsibility. To take up her cause would be apt to label him an adventurer in the worst sense of the word, a speculator upon the credulity and sentiment of a woman. Failure would so label him, perhaps leave her penniless. Still —

He tried to thrash the matter out, to come to a decision. It was the remembrance of Newton Foster, handsome and easy-mannered, her own kind, of her own blood, announcing his determination to go if she went, that settled Lyman's somewhat hasty resolution. He would step aside, play the role of messenger as it had been given to him and let the play go on without him.

Love at first sight has been scoffed at by all but the scientists and young lovers themselves. Yet it is sure that certain types are attracted to each other the moment they meet, that such attractions, born of heredity, take no account of rank or fortune save as scruples and pride may creep in to break the attraction. Lyman, though he did not actually formulate the thought, sensed that a voyage with Kitty Whiting would see him tangled in a desire to win her. And what chance had he against Newton Foster, who had rallied to her side, who was versed in the ways of her world and had a hundred ways to appeal to her where Lyman might offend? A young man's first love is often tinctured with humility, with belief in his own unworthiness compared with a girl who has exhibited especial refinement, capable of commanding equality in her mate, trained to scorn any lack of culture, educated to enjoy things of which he was ignorant. He did not know that love levels. He saw himself coarse beside her daintiness, awkward, unfit. Man to man against young Foster — that was a different matter. Put Newton Foster in the same surroundings and he had no fear of contest, but he was nothing but a sea tramp after all, a shipwrecked devil out of a job.

He got to his feet, his mind made up. He would mail the diary and drift on, straightening vanes, working as a rigger, doing odds and ends until things straightened out again and he could go to sea once more. He had thought of the Navy, but enlistments were closed. He thought now of working west, harvesting, reaching the coast, getting across the Pacific — if he had to ship as oiler or stoker — seeking fortune in the Orient where opportunities were more plentiful and white men scarcer. He had marked the street she lived on. No number was necessary for correct address. The *Golden Dolphin* would be sufficient, with the name.

In the hotel office he composed a short note, sincere if it did not contain all the truth:

> My dear Miss Whiting:
>
> Enclosed please find the diary with the position of the island under the date of June 27. I have no further use for the book, which is only the record of a voyage now over with, and I thought you might prefer to see the figures as originally set down. I appreciate the offer you made me, and regret I cannot see my way clear to accepting it, though I wish you all possible luck in whatever you may undertake.
>
> I am expecting to leave Foxfield tomorrow morning so shall not have the pleasure of seeing you in the afternoon at two as I anticipated.

Will you please give my regards to Miss Warner and believe me,
    Sincerely yours,
       James H. Lyman.

The note would do, he decided as he read the final draft. It did not say everything he wanted to but it did not say too much. She would infer, he felt sure, that he believed that the voyage had too great odds against success for him to tacitly, or otherwise, encourage it. She would not suspect that the offer of Newton Foster had anything to do with his refusal. In a week or two, whatever her conclusions, Jim Lyman would be only a shadowy person to whom she would attach a certain measure of thanks for giving her the latitude and longitude of the island.

He signed it with the feeling that he was helping to erect a permanent barrier between himself and the girl, but he believed he was doing the right thing, the best thing, in the long run. He got paper and string from the desk clerk, made a neat shipshape bundle of diary and note, had it weighed and attached the stamps. It was too late for registry but he placed additional postage and marked it *Special Delivery*, more as a way of insurance and means of tracing than to expedite the package. They said they would sleep late. He took it down to the post office and personally mailed it, hoping, after it had passed the lidded slot, that the messenger delivery would not awaken them too early. It thudded down into other mail like something falling into a grave. The burial of young hopes. An illuminated clock over a bank on North Street showed him the time as ten-forty.

Back at the hotel, the clerk hailed him with the news that someone had been trying hard to get him over the telephone and had finally left a number with a request for him to ring up — 2895. He got connection with somewhat of a thrill. No one in all the town would be likely to ring him up but Kitty Whiting — or her cousin. But it was a man's voice speaking, in the tones of Stephen Foster, suave, almost apologetic, in marked contract to that gentleman's manner earlier in the evening.

"Mr. Lyman? This is Stephen Foster speaking. That news of yours swept me off my feet a bit tonight, Lyman. Little out of the usual run of business, you see. I am afraid I may have approached it too abruptly, been a bit brusque with you. If I was, I apologize. It seemed a wild idea to me; I hated to keep open my niece's grief for her father. It is a wound already aggravated by her refusal to consider his death. Out of her love for him, of course, but unwise. Eh? Joy never kills but prolonged sorrow may. Never pays to be over optimistic.

"My son says that he does not agree with me, and we have been talking it over. I am inclined to modify my opposition if there really seems any hope at all. Also the trip may end harrowing uncertainty. If so, there is no time to lose. I wonder whether you could come up here tonight? I have some charts in my library that would help us and you would be of great practical use in discussing ways and means. It's late, I know, but the matter is not ordinary."

Lyman did not reply immediately, a little rushed off his feet by this change of face in Foster, Still he could hardly refuse to talk ways and means. He could stick by his decision not to go. And —

Foster was talking smoothly on. "Anyone can tell you where my place is. Out of town a little, to the south, the first road to the east after you cross the bridge over the river. About a mile, all told. I would send the car but we had some trouble with it going home and my man is tinkering with it. Can drive you back, I expect. May we expect you?"

The new attitude of Foster was flattering; he was putting the thing as a favor, Jim decided.

"I'll start from the hotel right away."

"Fine. And bring the figures with you. Good-by."

He could furnish the figures all right, though not the diary. They were indelibly stamped from now on upon his recollection.

162° 37' w.
37° 19' s.

Foster, as acknowledged partner in the expedition, was entitled to them. It was natural for them to plan ahead; they would probably offer him a berth. He knew the anchorage, just where to find the ship. But he could give them all that. He propped up a resolution that was beginning to waver a bit, railed at himself for indecision, knew it was on account of the girl, knew that he might pass out of her life, but not she from his. She was like a gleam of golden metal in the commonplace strata of life.

He checked directions with the clerk, whose eyes opened with a new respect at knowing that Stephen Foster, millionaire, had called up and invited this none too prosperous guest to his house.

"You'll find it easy enough," said the clerk. "Only house along that road. Stands on its own grounds, back a ways. Can't miss it."

Jim soon decided that Foster's ideas of direction were conservative, as might be expected from a man who invariably motored any distance further than a block. Walking briskly, it took him ten minutes to reach the bridge. The side road opened up like a tunnel, elms and maples shading it thickly. Already he seemed to have reached the open country, so abruptly did the character of the buildings change to the south of town. He had passed only scattered residences of the rich, if not of aristocracy, of Foxfield. Now and then motorcars passed him on the smooth state road, but once in this tunnel of leafage, he seemed to walk in a world remote. He rounded a bend and saw, midway in the curve, the rays of an automobile headlight spraying the trees and hedgerow on the far side. A few strides more and he was in the direct glow. The machine was stationary, well to one side, seemingly out on the road proper if not in the ditch itself.

A voice called to him out of the blackness of the ray, a voice that was eager, hoarse with emotion.

"Give us a hand here, will you? The machine's ditched and my pal's hurt."

Jim ran toward the car. Back of the blinding rays it was hard to distinguish anything but a vague figure. The car seemed to have slewed violently so that the rear end was down in the ditch with one wheel apparently smashed. The man who had called to him was poking about with a dim pocket flash, while the headlights were pouring out a waste of illumination.

"Here," said the man. "At the back. The jack gave way somehow. He's pinned under there. I've got a pole. Maybe one of us can lift it and drag him out. Can you handle that rock? Make a lever out of it?"

His flashlight showed a big stone in the ditch of the type from which stone walls are made.

Jim bent to lift it. Something struck him at the back of his head where the skull meets vertebrae. Golden lights flashed out like an exploding firework and gave way to blackness and oblivion as he pitched forward.

IV

Action

The first conscious sensation Jim recovered was that he was being slowly smothered; the second that he was riding fast, being jolted over rough side roads, presumably in an automobile. He reacted slowly, retarded by a dull headache that seemed to sap the vitality out of him. He was bound ankle and wrist, his arms strapped to his sides and a strap about his knees. They had made a good job of securing him, and not content with rope and leather, they had set him into a canvas sack, a sort of duffle bag into which he had been thrust feet first with the throat of the bad tight about his hips with draw strings. A second bag had been brought down over head and shoulders until it overlapped the first. He could breathe, but the air he got to his lungs was hot and smelly and none too pure. The necessary first aid supply of oxygen was deteriorated; he was like an engine trying to make power on bad gasoline.

It was hard to think consecutively but the searchlight of his objective reasoning played persistently upon the fact — it seemed to be a fact — that he had been deliberately waylaid on the road to Foster's. No one except the clerk at the hotel knew where he was going, outside of Stephen Foster, his son, and perhaps his household. If highway robbery had been their purpose his unknown assailants showed poor judgment in selecting him. They had had excellent chance to gauge him as he advanced in the full beams of the automobile headlights and Lyman was conscious that he looked like anything but a wealth carrier. On the other hand, if they had been deliberately waiting for him to come along, meaning to make sure of their man against any other person who might travel that lonely way at that time of night, the plan adopted was an excellent one. The wrong and curious passerby could have been dismissed with an assurance that the car was all right — as it undoubtedly was. It was more than likely he was now traveling in the same machine. The only slip up, a remote chance, would have been that Jim should arrive on the scene in company with someone else, and doubtless they had provided for that.

What was their purpose? He suspected Stephen Foster. Would

Foster go to the length of having him knocked on the head and kidnapped in order to prevent his niece getting the figures and starting off on the expedition? That Foster was quite capable of such high-handed and unscrupulous procedure, he believed, remembering his impressions of the man, his cold eyes and letterbox mouth. Or was it with reason more sinister? Here Lyman abandoned all attempts at working things out under the circumstances. His head ached intolerably and he was suffering from thirst. But anger accumulated in him, awaiting the chance for action.

Hour after hour, it seemed, they jolted over the roads. There were plenty of good state roads in the region, he knew. They must be purposely choosing unfrequented ways, running like bootleggers to escape observation. Jim prayed that some prowling federal officer or state policeman might halt and search the car. He seemed to be on the floor of the tonneau, otherwise unoccupied.

Torture increased in his cramped limbs as circulation grew sluggish; he lost feeling in them. Still the car sped on through the night.

It stopped at last after climbing a steep hillside; the engine was shut off; the door of the tonneau opened and Jim was lifted, an inert bundle, and deposited on the ground. He could not even draw up his knees. He could see nothing. He was not gagged, but efficiently muffled by the sacking. Through it he could not distinguish what the men who had brought him were saying.

They picked him up again and carried him a little distance. Then the top sack was withdrawn. Jim's eyes, slow to accept the quick change of light, made out ancient and cobwebby rafters high above his head with wisps of hay showing here and there, festoons of old rope, hooks, a pulley. He was on the floor of a barn. There was the reek of old manure. The dawn had broken and the upland air was cold. Twisting his neck, he saw his captors. One wore the leather hood of aviator and motorcyclist; the other had the wide peak of a cap well drawn down. Both wore big goggles with leather nose-pieces. One was unshaven, bristly; the other wore a square beard. A flask passed, Jim caught the smell of whisky. The chill air had cleared his head and he formulated a course of action. Good nature could lose him nothing if he could simulate it and cover the smouldering wrath that possessed him. And a sup of liquor with its quick stimulus might aid him. He was willing to take a chance on its quality.

"You might give me a swig of that," he said. "And loosen up a hole or two. My arms and legs are numb." The man with the hood looked down at him with eyes gleaming sardonically back of the colored lenses. Then he laughed.

"You're a cool customer," he said.

"Too cool in this air, with my blood stopped. You're not aiming to murder me, I figure, or you wouldn't have spent so much gas on me. If you aim to keep me alive, let me have a drink."

"Costs too much and there ain't more'n enough for two," demurred the bearded man.

"He can have my whack," answered the other. "You got him tied up too hard, Bill. No sense in that."

"He's worth money delivered. I'm proposin' to deliver him."

The man with the hood nevertheless loosened the straps a hole, slid off the lower sack, eased up Jim's ankles and supporting him, set the flask to his lips. Jim gulped at the stuff. He needed it. Pain shot through every nerve and artery as his heart, reacting to the kick of the liquor, urged the blood through to proper circulation. He lay back, fighting it as the two moved off, holding a consultation of which he caught snatches. It seemed based upon the question whether one of them should remain with Jim or both go to town. He strained his ears in vain to catch sound of the name of it. The pain in his limbs grew less acute. And while the back of his head was sore, it no longer throbbed.

He was miles from Foxfield. He figured they had averaged at least twenty-five miles an hour through the night for about six hours. And there would be no one to bother about him, save at the hotel where his few belongings were left. The clerk might well think he had left them rather than pay his bill. He had told Kitty Whiting that he was going away.

He was to be delivered somewhere and was considered a valuable package; that was a certain amount of information. Delivered to whom?

"Foster pay you well for this job?" he hazarded as the men came back.

"Shut up," said the one called Bill, now in ill humor. "I never heard of Foster, so quit ravin'. My partner's goin' down to send a wire and get some grub. He'll bring some up to us. You'll eat, but quit your gabbin' because it won't do you a mite of good. Hey, Bud, we can't leave him lyin' on the floor. Where you goin' to stow him?" The prospect of food sounded good to Jim. They might untie his hands. If he were left alone he might clear his bonds himself. He was resolved to wait for the first chance for freedom and then to make a desperate bid for it. He lay quiet while the pair prospected. But he put up a desperate protest when they came back and picked up the sack that had gone over his head.

"No sense in smothering me," he said. The pair did not seem unnecessarily brutal. They had not actually mistreated him since that first smash on the base of his skull. Bill was the harder customer of the two. "I'll not yell if you give me a chance to breathe," said Jim.

"You yell and I'll tap you over the head. It won't be a love tap, either," said Bill. "We'll give you a tryout. Come on, Bud."

They carried him down an alley between two rows of empty cow stanchions. Overhead he could see gaps in the roof shingles. He imagined the place to be the outweathered barn of an abandoned farm. Bill opened a door and he was thrust into a dark place smelling of mouldy grain. It was less than six feet square, too small for him to lie extended. The door closed on a bare glimpse of walls close sealed with tongue and groove, a chute leading upward, and two big bins against the far side. There was a click of latch or staple and he was left alone.

As a rule Jim was even tempered. He had bursts of dynamic fury that he could muster on occasions when rage was needed as lash and spur to urge others to vital effort. Now he had hard work to control his wrath. It steadily mounted until he saw red in the black grain closet, flashes and whirls of red. To get loose, to pin this outrage upon somebody and take it out of their hide was his one wish. That this capture was in some way connected with the *Golden Dolphin* and the proposed trip he did not doubt. Casting about, he wondered whether the maid of Kitty Whiting's, with her insatiable curiosity, had anything to do with it. He remembered the skeleton with the cleft skull, the suggestion from Lynda Warner that she was not surprised at foul play. Though he had not looked at it before from this standpoint, he realized that if there were pearls hidden in a secret place aboard the ship, then his information was indeed valuable.

Foster had told him to bring his figures. Perhaps they had searched him for his diary while he was unconscious. He dismissed the idea. If they were agents of Foster, and Foster wanted to get at the figures, the simplest way would have been the best. As an acknowledged partner Jim could hardly have refused to give Foster the position. Now it was different. Wild horses should not drag the information from him, if that was what they were after. And it was the only valuable, enviable thing he possessed.

But Foster would ultimately get the figures from the girl when they met as agreed the day after tomorrow — tomorrow now. It was a tangle. But Foster did not know that Lyman had already mailed the diary. Did he plan to get hold of the figures beforehand for his own purposes, and then denounce Lyman as the type he had already suggested, a charlatan who had been scared away by the discovery that he had a man of Stephen Foster's caliber to deal with? What would be Foster's purposes with the figures? Merely to dissuade his niece, make her project impossible? Or did he believe that the pearls might be on the wreck and mean to claim the whole for himself by outfitting an expedition in secret while demolishing Kitty Whiting's plans and hopes?

There was the secret place aboard the *Golden Dolphin* that the girl had said only she and her father knew of. But who had devised it? How impossible was it of being discovered? A man of Foster's type would take the wreck apart, crumble it and sift it if necessary, Jim fancied.

One fact seemed to Jim to stand out. He did not reason that he was in no position to argue soundly or logically, that he was biased by his capture and humiliation; but it appeared very clear to him that Kitty Whiting should not give out the precious figures to any one until — if she went — she were well on her way to the island. He had turned one little trick unconsciously in sending her the diary. To warn her further was impossible.

Thus revolving things, like a squirrel in its cage treadmill, Jim got little further than the squirrel progresses. Through some crevice the smell of tobacco came to him. Bill of the beard was outside watching that no one came accidentally to the abandoned farm, ready with an excuse if they did. Bud had supposedly taken the automobile. Jim began to cool down a little, the compression of his thoughts had carried them through heat to cold, to far more effective and energetic anger, once it got an outlet. He was able to shut off the roundabout process of his mind. Appetite for tobacco aided this, another physical need, hunger, assisting. It was with gladness that he dimly heard the arrival of a machine, then the voice of Bud. His door was opened and he was once more packed out like a bale, and deposited, seated, on an empty box. Bud produced a thermos bottle full of hot coffee, some rolls, butter, and crisp doughnuts. They untied the cords at Jim's wrists, giving him his share of the food and a rusty tin cup for his coffee. By pressing his chin into his chest and lifting his restrained hands he could just make connection with his mouth, though Bud had to tilt the cup for him to finish his coffee. Bud did not eat. He smoked. Bill growled.

"Suppose you had 'ham and' in town there?"

"Prunes, cereal, ham and, hot cakes an' maple syrup, coffee, and a cigar," said Bud. "What you kickin' at? You can't drive the car." Bill grunted and Bud gave him a cigar. He stuck a third in Jim's mouth and lit it.

"I'll remember that," said Jim with gratitude. Bud nodded.

"So do, brother, if you figure that'll do you any good. I don't believe you and me is likely to meet again in a hurry, though. Take your time. We've got to tuck you up again soon."

"If I give you fellows the figures now will you turn me loose?"

Both looked as blankly committal as men wearing goggle masks might be expected to.

"I don't know a damn thing about your figures, nor Bill either," said Bud. "We're expressmen in this game. Deliverin' you, brother, as per directions, charges collect, eh, Bill?"

"You talk too much," was Bill's contribution.

The cigars finished, Jim's wrists were once more tied. He begged for a chance to walk about the barn, but they would not grant it. After he was trussed they re-sacked him, despite his protests. He gleaned one scrap of information.

Bud, in response to Bill, answered.

"'Bout thirty miles. Boss expects us round noon. We drive right into the garage, deliver and collect. That lets us out."

Who was the boss?

Jim had hoped to get a look at the license plates on the car but Bud, Bill & Company, illicit expressmen, were too smart for that. This time he was not only deposited on the floor of the tonneau in his sacking, but a rug was flung over all. It was quite a while before they started. Once they stopped and Jim knew they were getting gasoline and oil, for Bill came into the tonneau and sat with his heavy-booted foot close to Lyman's head, mutely promising what would happen if Jim tried to attract attention. The day was warm and he sweated profusely, and an infernal itching started, from which there was no relief. After a time they rolled over smoother roads and finally made a sharp right turn and came to a stop, the engine shut off. They had reached the garage of the boss. One of them went off to report and Jim still sweated in his sacks. Then the upper one was removed and he blinked up into the face of a red-faced man with a squash nose, little blue eyes and a bald head save for a tonsure of reddish hair; a big man with enormous chest and protruding paunch, with hair on his wrists and fingers, spider-wise. He surveyed Jim callously.

"That him?" he asked.

"No," said Bill. "It ain't him. We let *him* go. This is a pal of ours we rigged up this way because that's the way he likes to ride. You got the wire, didn't you? You know he was identified at the other end. What's eatin' you? Come through with that two hundred berries and take your package and we'll call it a day."

The consignee's red face turned crimson, then purple. His pig eyes glittered and he closed his great fists. Then he laughed.

"Comedian, eh? All right. Take him upstairs and put him on the bunk. Make me out a receipt for the money and I'll give you one for the sailor lad."

"Is this the boss?" asked Jim. The trio looked at him as if they had forgotten he was anything but a dumb parcel. The red-faced man nodded.

"I'll talk to you later," he said. Jim had already connected him with the sea. He could not be fooled in several small but significant tricks of manner, aside from the blue anchor tattooed on the back of the right hand — a fouled anchor, one end of the rope continued to form a circle and frame to the design. "Take him up, boys; I'll go and get your dough."

The room above, reached by an open stair, was fitted as a chauffeur's bedroom. The garage was a large one. Through a window Jim caught sight of a big house, elaborately built of stone, many windowed, tiled of roof, with a tower at one corner and wide porches. Like the barn it was set on a hill, though he had not noticed the gradual slopes by which they had reached it. Beyond trees and the tops of other houses he saw a dark blue line, pearly clouds above it, land beyond it; it was the sea, running into a deep bay. They had brought him clear across the state.

The bed was comparatively comfortable, bound as he still was. Bud found pen, ink, and paper on a table and commenced to make out a receipt. Bill strolled to the window. The red-headed man, the boss as they called him, could not be the owner of so fine a place, Jim was certain. Caretaker probably; caretaker of a big summer home not yet opened for the season, perhaps a sort of sailing master for a yacht of the owner later on. He came back by the time Bill had made out his receipt. Bills changed hands and two slips of paper. Bud came over to the bed.

"So long," he said. "Times are hard, pal. It was a chance to get some easy money. No hard feelings?"

"Only on the back of my head," Jim smiled. It was not the underlings he was after.

"You talk too much," snarled Bill. "Come on, if you want to get back tonight." They left the room and backed the car out. Jim heard it spinning over the gravel of the drive. He looked at Redhead, who had drawn up a chair by the side of the bed and seated himself.

"See here, my lad," said Redhead. "Those landlubbers have lashed you over-tight. I'll loosen you up a bit. You and me should get along fine, seein' we've both smelt blue water. Aye, an' sailed it. You slip me your word not to try and get funny and I'll cast you loose entirely. Not that it 'ud do you any good. But I'm an amiable man, when I'm allowed to be, an' a mean cuss when I'm riled." He set his big hands in either pocket of his coat and brought out from the one an automatic pistol and from the other a slingshot — much the same weapon, Jim thought ruefully, that had laid him out at the other end of the trip.

"That goes," he answered. In a moment he was untriced, using his liberty to chafe his arms and legs, then sitting on the bed.

"Nothin' like bein' as comfortable as you kin," said Redhead. "My name is Swenson, my lad. You and me'll get along fine. All I want from you is a little information, and if you're a wise man you'll come through first instead of last, and save us both a heap of trouble. For you've got to come through." The rumbling voice deepened on the last words; the red face coarsened, if that were possible, with an outthrust of the big jaw and a malicious light in the little eyes accompanying the balling up of great fists. "Then we'll have a snack to eat and a taste of grog. The real stuff. They kin make drinkin' unlawful but they can't make it unpopular, an' what the public wants, they most usually gits. How'll that suit you?"

"What do you want?" asked Jim. Swenson winked.

"I want the latitude an' longitude, the true and correct position of a certain island somewhere in the South Pacific. Where's the little log, my lad?" Jim laughed.

"I gave it to a man."

"Name him."

"My Uncle Samuel." For a moment Swenson glowered, then guffawed.

"That's a good un. Fooled me at first. Mailed it, eh? Who to?"

"I'm not telling."

"No?"

"No." Swenson appeared to consider the quality of his refusal.

"That's what I get by treating you so smooth, eh? Well, I'll try the other tack. I'll treat you rough. I hear you've held a ticket. So did I. And they knew me as 'Hellfire' Swenson. Ever hear of Hellfire Swenson?" Jim had heard of the man. A few years before Swenson had been brought to New York on charges forwarded by the American consul at Capetown, accused of violating the seamen's act forbidding corporal punishment, during a voyage from San Francisco to the Cape. Also charged with murder on the high seas. It had been a case discussed on every American ship. There had been handcuffings followed by beatings with knotted towels and a club. The crew had been forced to obey orders at the muzzle of a revolver. A seaman had jumped overboard two months out of San Francisco, to avoid the abuse. Repenting of his act, he had clutched a rope trailing from the stern of the ship, begging to be hauled aboard, and Hellfire Swenson, it was alleged, had forbidden any member of the crew rendering aid. The sailor finally lost his grip and was drowned. Swenson had been backed up by his mates and the charges were, in the main, not proven. But Hellfire Swenson lost his ticket. Jim surveyed him without blanching but he wondered no longer that this blackguard had been named the boss. How he got the position of caretaker, if indeed he held it, was a mystery.

"You're on land now, Hellfire," he said. "Bully driving won't get you anything. But I'll tell you one thing and be damned to you. You can hand it on to Foster with my compliments. The little log is in the hands of the properly interested party." Swenson's fists tightened; he blinked his piggy eyes, but showed no other signs of special interest in what Jim had said.

"That's news. As for Foster, whoever he is, that's news, too. I'm actin' in this for myself, my lad."

Aside from the character of the man, Jim set this down as a lie. If Swenson knew the value of the figures he must know the history connected with them. Whether Foster was hiring him or not, the name would be familiar to him. Swenson went on:

"I reckon you took a good look at them figgers before you mailed 'em. I'm takin' your word about the mailin'. You're a smart lad. Never mind the log. You come through with the position, or it's no grog an' no grub an' worse to follow. I'll leave you to think it over. Lie down, stretch out. Spread-eagle. Turn over on your belly."

Swenson had broken Jim's own parole by his own actions. Liberty was stopped, the prospects of semi-starvation substituted. Hellfire was rising from his chair. He was a big man, but he moved quickly. And Jim was quicker. Pretending to obey, he stretched out his hands, half turned over and then reversed, plumping the pillow he had clutched fair and hard at Swenson. It took the ex-skipper in the face and chest with force enough behind it, combined with the way it shut off his wind, to send Hellfire staggering back a step. That was enough. He tangled with the chair and went over backward while Jim leaped for the door. There was a spring lock on it and the catch had been shot by Swenson when he came in. As Jim tugged at the handle and then sought for the combination Swenson rolled nimbly over, snatched his gun from his pocket and fired from the floor. The bullet slapped into the door panel too close to Jim's head to be either safe or pleasant.

"Stand up to the door there or I'll put a leak in your skull!" The voice of Hellfire roared with stentorian, after-deck purpose. That jig was over. Jim stood against the door Y fashion, arms up and wide. "Turn about, march over to that bed. On your back!" There was the clink of metal as Swenson groped in a drawer with one hand, the other holding his gun trained on his prisoner. Then Jim found himself handcuffed to the bedposts, a pair of cuffs for each wrist. His ankles, spread on request coupled with the muzzle of the gun thrust into the small of his back, were dexterously lashed to the foot posts, and he lay there with some play to hands and arms but secure as a hogtied steer, face upward.

"Now think it over, my bucko." Swenson left the room. Jim heard his tread descending to the garage floor, crunching on the gravel, dying away. Presently a fly began to bother him, a small but persistent tormentor that seemed to appreciate the fact that it was immune from pursuit. Another followed, roaming over his skin, exploring his ears, the cavities of his nose. Jim grinned and bore it. The morning passed; the sunlight shifted on the walls; afternoon came and his enforced position became well-nigh intolerable. He early realized that his ankle cords had sailors' knots in them and that all effort to release them meant only chaffing and cutting of the flesh above his low shoes. He could wriggle his body a little and shift his head on the pillow that Swenson had restored to the bed. He made up his mind to capitulate, but not to do so with too great appearance of eagerness lest Swenson should suspect the truth — that Jim was going to supply false figures. He had no cause to bother about the hurry; Swenson was taking his time. Jim got hungry, then drowsy. Sleep conquered stomach and he found surcease from all inconvenience in slumber. He did not wake up until twilight was approaching, which meant somewhere between eight and nine o'clock in the evening. Now he was ravenous, but he lay there in the growing dusk for quite a while before he heard steps outside coming up the ladder, and the opening of the door. A light was switched on and Swenson stood looking at him as he twisted himself for a survey.

"Had enough, my lad?" asked Hellfire. "I've got some sandwiches here and something on the hip for you if you're goin' to be sensible. I've had lunch and supper myself, piping hot. How about it?"

Jim strove to inject sullenness into his voice.

"I'm not a damned fool," he said. "I'll talk business."

"Nothing to talk about, my lad. You give me them figgers."

"I want to know where I get off. I'm out of a job. I expected to get a berth or money through them, or a stake."

"We'll fix that up. Berth or money. Mebbe both." There was something about Hellfire that dimly reminded Jim of Stephen Foster in the bland, apt way with which he made promises.

"I'll take some of the money now," he said. "Show me a hundred bucks and I'll talk. I'll want four hundred more later."

Jim never expected to see the four hundred. He was willing to accept fifty cash, but that much he needed. If Swenson had been willing to pay out two hundred dollars for the delivery of Jim he ought to be able to advance more for the contents of the package. Jim had no scruples about taking the money. He had had between eleven and twelve dollars in his pocket the night before. If it was there now he did not know, and had had no chance to find out. Bud would not have taken it, but Bill might. He owed seven and a half at the Foxfield Hotel and he did not know how far away he was from there. He was going there by the quickest way he could find and pay for, as soon as he got his release, or made one for himself. He did not trust Hellfire but he sought to allay the latter's alertness by his own acting.

Swenson counted out some bills from a good-sized roll and laid them on the bed, just beyond reach of Jim's hand.

"Five twenties there," he said. "Spiel the figgers and I loosen up; you pouch the money and then you pouch the food. Four hundred more later."

"It's one-thirty-two, fifty-four west, longitude," lied Jim.

"Hold on. Wait till I put it down." Swenson got pen and paper.

Jim repeated.

"One-thirty-two, fifty-four west, longitude. Forty-four, twenty-nine south."

"Got a good mem'ry, have you?"

"Yes. Why?"

"If you should happen to repeat them figgers any time later on and not get 'em the same you're goin' to have a mighty hard time remem-berin' anything from then on. Sure you got 'em right?" Jim repeated them with a laugh. And made a note to mark them down somewhere for handy reference as soon as he got a chance, though he had carefully selected them and felt sure of remembering them. But a threat like this from Swenson was not apt to be vague and he was far from out of the woods yet.

"Pretty far south, ain't it, for jungle?" asked Swenson a little suspi-ciously.

"No farther south than New Zealand. Almost the same latitude as Dunedin. Tropical enough there. And the Antarctic drift is well below fifty in that longitude."

"Some navigator, eh?" Swenson went over to a bureau and took a chart out of a roll, spreading it on the table and poring over it. It was a Great Circle Sailing Chart.

He supplemented that with a colored physical chart of the Pacific Ocean, studying them intently. Jim had picked his false position from memory. He felt certain that it showed absolutely blank on the charts; still — "What did you say them figgers was?" barked Hellfire suddenly.

"Reel 'em off now." Jim repeated once again and Swenson checked. Then he rolled up the charts, unlocked one handcuff, allowing Jim to take the hundred dollars and pocket them, and laid on the counterpane the sandwiches and a pocket flask. Jim bit into the bread and meat with avid content, ignoring the flask.

"Good hooch," said Swenson, almost good-naturedly. "Real, imported American rye, shipped to France and brought back again."

"I'll save it," said Jim. He had no especial taste for whisky and he believed Swenson quite up to the trick of doping him for his own ends — to get back the hundred, for example.

"Suit yourself."

"When do I get the other four hundred?"

"As soon as there's any chance for your using it." Swenson grinned at him without friendliness, a grin of self-appreciation.

"If we'd have got your little book, my lad," he said, "we'd have given you a short trip down the coast — say to Colon. As it is you're goin' along with us all the way, just to make sure you've given us the right figgers. Savvy? Also you're a handy man aboard. You'll know the holding ground and save time in more ways than one. I'll give you second mate's job with full wages, the four hundred an' the one you've got as earnest money. You'll get a share of what we find, same as the rest. But you go all the way. If the island's where you say it is, well an' good. If it ain't — well, *you don't come back.* Splice that into your life-line, my lad. I'll read off them figgers to you. If you ain't *plumb certain* they're right, this is the time to alter 'em. Otherwise, we'll get 'em out of you; if we have to keel-haul you once a day." The emphasis Swenson laid upon his slowly spoken phrases was infinitely malign. Their effect was as bleak as the wind that blows across a polar ice-floe.

"Suits me," said Jim carelessly. "Only I'd like to get my hands on the four hundred. When I've got money coming to me it always seems like it was better off with me. But that's all right. I'm not stuck on your methods, Hellfire Swenson, and, if I'm second mate, I'm not going to carry a belaying pin in my boot and back up every order with a wallop. Otherwise the berth suits me, and the share looks good. I made up my mind this afternoon it was no use bucking you. You're liberal enough and I'd be a fool not to take 'em. Only — I'm no hell-driver. I'll get the work out of my watch by my own methods."

Swenson, watching him keenly, as Jim did the other, carefully calculating the effect of ended resistance, plus a registered kick or two against Hellfire tactics, reached over and patted him on the back with a heavy hand.

"You'll do, matey," he said. "Glad you're sensible. This crew won't have to be tickled with a rope's end. They're all partners, you see. We'll go aboard in an hour, soon's it's dark. We go out tonight. Tide serves at midnight."

"Out of where?"

Swenson winked. "Never you mind. I'll give you your course when you take the desk. Don't you bother about where we start from, sonny. It's where we finish concerns you."

"All right. Turn me loose."

"Not altogether. I'll cast you loose from the bed after I've 'cuffed you up. You'll get liberty when we hit deep water, in case you change your mind about going along. You're a smart lad, Lyman, but I'm a wise old turtle myself." He took away the right handcuff and manacled Jim with the pair still on his left wrist. He cast off the ankle lashings and allowed Jim to get up off the bed and walk around the room, to look out of the window.

The water was no longer visible but there were blinking lights showing through a slight mist. Then the intermittent flash of a lighthouse.

"Hazin' up a little," volunteered Swenson. "Good weather for sayin' a quiet good-by. There's a dozen of us aboard knows the bay in our sleep. Have a cigar?"

Jim took it, accepted the light and sat by the window smoking, elbows resting on the sill. The night gathered and the haze thickened. He wanted to find out the name of the place. Somehow he must make a getaway, and a plan, indefinite as the mist, was vaguely forming. To further it he should know where they were. Looking out did him no good so he turned and started talking to Swenson about the island. He gave him many details that he had not given Kitty Whiting; directions for getting through the reef, for example, bearings, and suggestions for anchorage that Swenson made note of with little nods of his head while he gradually grew more confidential, almost chummy. But if he ever tried to make mooring or work through the lagoon with those same directions, Jim could see his command piled on the coral. If Jim was along — but he did not intend to be. Still Swenson plainly imagined him as having accepted the situation and applauded his common sense — as viewed by Swenson. He insisted upon his sharing his own flask. Jim stuck his tongue in the neck of the bottle, corking it, when it was his turn. Swenson swigged deeply and grew almost jovial, though the stuff had small real effect upon him.

At last a car came up the drive and hooted. Jim saw its lights before it sounded the horn.

"Here's our wagon," he said. "Do I still have to wear these bracelets?"

"Sure do, matey. We're going by the back streets. No one'll see you or know you. Take 'em off when we're aboard an' clear. Give you the run of the ship. You're second mate. Bunk aft. Come on."

They went downstairs out through the garage to where a flivver wheezed and panted. The driver was a stolid individual who barely looked around but sat eating something out of a small bag. Swenson greeted him.

"'Lo, Jakey. Have a little drink?"

"No. Quit it."

"Chewin' candy instead? Suit yourself. Git in, matey." Swenson took seat at the back beside Jim and confidentially slid a hand under his arm. Jim abandoned a hope of getaway from the flivver. They chugged down side streets and roads where lights shone dimly in the foggy night, descending always. The smell of salt water came to them and Jim inhaled it as a desert horse snuffs the oasis. They reached a small creek, ran along its banks and stopped at a little wharf and boathouse, dimly seen, with a dull flare of orange showing in a window.

"Here we are," said Swenson. "Reckon the boys are on deck. All ashore, matey. You first." Jim was directly back of the silent driver who now took the last piece of candy from his bag, screwed up the sack and flipped it from him. It fell on the running board and Jim retrieved it with his fettered hands, opened it swiftly and read the printed legend upon it by the headlights as he passed in front of the flivver. Fowler's General Store, Wareham.

Now he knew where he was and his heart quickened a beat as he dropped the bag and set foot upon it while Swenson followed, unsuspecting. The driver, sucking at his peppermint, noticed nothing.

Wareham is on the Wareham River, head of Wareham County, Mass., emptying into the head of Buzzards Bay! And Jim knew Buzzards Bay! The light he had seen must be Wings Neck Light off Red Brook Harbor. To starboard, as they would run down toward Long Island Sound, there would come Sippican Harbor with Bird Island Light. Mattapoisett Harbor, Ram Island, Nasketucket Bay, West Island, New Bedford Harbor, Dumpling Rock Light opposite Woods Hole, the steamer connection for Nantucket. And, last of all, the Elizabeth Islands with the Cuttyhunk Light at the tip, a fixed white light that Jim knew well from early days. He had been born at New Bedford.

He hid his exultation as, with Swenson's grip on his arm, they advanced to the boathouse, and Swenson knocked on the door. Half a dozen men were playing cards by the light of a lantern. Bottles and glasses were on the rough table. It seemed that wherever Swenson ruled rum was still plentiful. Jim suspected him of pocketing profits on those quarts of rye that were trans-shipped from France — if Swenson had spoken the truth of the course. It was good enough whisky. The men were a sturdy lot, inclined to be secretive, if not surly. Jim knew their type, longshoremen of Nantucket Sound, seafood providers, lobstermen not averse to making a living at anything they might find afloat or upflung, smugglers at heart and by inheritance; good seamen, withal. They gazed at him with wooden faces that might have been carved out of walnut. None of them appeared to notice his handcuffs.

"Mr. Lyman. Goin' to be second mate," announced Swenson briefly. The incongruity of a fettered officer raised no comment. They were used to unusual sights, thought Jim, or else such sights were usual. "How's the tide?"

"Turned ha'f hour ago. Runnin' strong."

"Then we'll git aboard." The flivver driver had turned the car. Jim saw the lights wavering away through the mist and silently thanked the taciturn chauffeur for his candy habit. They made their way down the wharf in a ghostly procession to where a boat swung at a painter, stretching with the tug of the outgoing tide. Jim expected a launch on account of the number of men ashore. Otherwise he had anticipated a dory, but the boat was a double-ended whaleboat into which they jumped with the celerity of saltwater men. Swenson was at the tiller with Jim beside him, and the six men took to the sweeps with a powerful stroke that, aided by the current, sent the boat dancing swiftly down the bay through the fog. They passed Butter's Point unseen, but located by Birds Island Light and swung into the entrance of Sippican Harbor, a long narrow anchorage. Swenson steered as if it had been broad day-light, occasionally hand testing the water alongside for eddies. He brought them up to a trim-looking schooner with masthead light show-ing, and as they pulled forward toward the bows, the reflection of her green sidelight to starboard. Jim looked for a name, but the curve of the bows prevented that. He had seen none on the whaleboat, merely the number 4. A side ladder was rigged, up which Jim preceded Swenson, the men in the boat dropping back to the quarter falls. On deck a man met them whom Swenson called Mr. Peters. There was a crispness to his manner as well as the official handle he set to the man's name that showed that Hellfire had taken up the reins of discipline. He did not introduce Jim but took him to the main cabin, showing him a stateroom.

"Here's where you bunk," he said. "All by yourself. Plenty of room aft. She was a pleasure craft, matey, but we've stripped off the fancy rigging an' made her seaworthy. She's sweetlined as a racing yacht, but she's stiff enough for any breeze. Seventy-two footer, with a fine engine for a kicker. Dynamo, wireless, all the rigamajigs. Take the screw off 'n her an' she'll sail with any fisherman ever went out o' Gloucester."

"Sweet looking schooner," said Jim. "Far as I can see. What's her name?" Swenson looked at him quizzically.

"Didn't you see it on the boat? I don't hold in stickin' a ship's name all over the place, buoys an' boats an' everything. You'll see it in the mornin'. Not much room for cargo, but what we're after won't take up much room, eh, matey? And there's the more space for stores. I'll see you later."

He nodded and went out. A bolt slid outside the door. There was one on the inside also but it wouldn't do him much good, Jim reflected. He climbed on the bunk and gazed through the porthole at the black-ness. Overhead he heard the familiar scuffle of action, short commands, the inhaul of the anchor, the grunts of men as they hauled on the hal-yards, swaying up the sails. There was little wind in the fog, yet they had elected to use canvas rather than the engine Swenson mentioned. It made for silence. But if this craft was going down to the South Seas she must have papers of some sort for clearance, or she would find herself in trouble at foreign ports of call. The truth probably was that Sippican Harbor was not her usual anchorage, and for some reason Swenson pre-ferred to slide out without attracting undue attention. Jim fancied that the schooner had used such tactics more than once. Hellfire Swenson, he imagined, was peddling firewater. But his own affairs concerned him more closely. If he was kept immured in the cabin until the ship gained open water it was likely that he was booked for a trip to the Panama Canal, the first stop Colon.

Carried on the current, more than aided by the light airs, the schooner made good progress. Through the porthole Jim saw Bird Island Light. Now they were heading down Buzzards Bay toward the entrance to Long Island Sound where they would work out to the free Atlantic. The cabin clock chimed eight bells and the ship's bell echoed the strokes of midnight. His bolt was slipped and Swenson came in. He unlocked the handcuffs.

"Fog's breakin'," he said. "Hazy yet, but I wouldn't wonder if 't was clear outside. You'll not take up your duty till tomorrow, Mr. Lyman, but if you want to stretch yourself a bit come on deck. I'm taking the watch. We'll have a little touch of grog first."

He filled glasses in the main cabin and handed one to Jim.

"Here's to a successful voyage," he toasted, and Jim drank to the toast. The whisky sent the blood surging through his veins. They went above together. Swenson kept close by Jim's side, but it was plain that he had partially accepted him as one of his own kidney, or as a tool he could successfully use.

The fog was thinning, shredding away, and there were holes in it here and there through which a star peeped. The beacon lights tore at it, rending paths for their warnings. They stood aft by the wheel. Suddenly the engine started to turn the screw and their speed increased. Jim calculated they were making a good eight knots. They had passed New Bedford Harbor with Clark's Point Light flashing almost abeam. Dumpling Rock Light was the next. Then he would keep his eyes peeled for the fixed white light at Cuttyhunk, westernmost point of the Elizabeth string of islands. There, between Gooseberry Neck and Penikese Island, the inlet was at its narrowest, somewhere about five miles. And the main channel swung toward Penikese.

Jim meant to stay on deck until they caught sight of the light at Cuttyhunk, then to take his chance over the rail. His shoes were unlaced, the ends tucked in, seemingly tied, but ready to kick off the moment he struck water. It was going to be a long swim — how long he could not gauge beforehand — and a hard one. The tide would sweep him down. If he missed Penikese he would have to fight hard to land on Cuttyhunk or be carried out into the ocean proper.

The long odds were preferable to staying aboard the schooner, even if he had not had special reasons urging him. He could not disassociate Foster as the real master mind of Swenson's activities, and he was fired with desire to block all Foster's plans which doubtless were maturing back in Foxfield. He meant to be present at the conference set for the same night — now that midnight had sounded. He had a hundred-odd dollars in his pocket. Let him get away, make a landing, and however roundabout his route, he would get to where autos might be hired, and then travel on the funds of the opposition.

Swenson did not seem to imagine that a man would dream of tackling a getaway by swimming; nevertheless he stayed closer to Jim than Jim relished. And he planned how he could avoid Hellfire's attentions and even matters up with him a bit. So far he had been the underdog; from now on he hoped things would turn out differently.

They chugged on through the dissipating mists which should lend a friendly cloak to Jim's escape. The fixed ray of Cuttyhunk shone like a misplaced star, then was eclipsed by something that must be Penikese Island. He and Swenson were pacing up and down together. Jim had started the topic of rum-running in a manner that suggested that he thought such exploits highly creditable, adventurous, and profitable. Swenson rose to the bait. With a congenial soul inclined to admiration, Hellfire was not averse to boasting.

"Good enough, when there's nothing bigger on hand," he said. "And it's sure good fun to fool the raiders. They sing loud when they happen to light on a buried cargo or board a ship with contraband once in a million times, through some rotten informer telling 'em what they'd never find out for themselves. We keep 'em guessing. It's a fine coast for hide an' seek."

He went on to tell of exploits, not attempting to veil his own personality as a principal. He hinted broadly at the existence of a national ring with ramifications spreading out north to Canada, west to the Orient, east to Europe, south to the Indies, Central and South America. And Jim, with the right word now and then, led him on. Swenson stood at the port rail, elbows on it, leaning back, puffing at his cigar. Jim purposely allowed his to go out. He looked beyond Swenson to where he fancied he could see the loom of Penikese. Fortunately it was thickening up a little. He stood within easy distance of Swenson, judging the space between them.

"Got a match?" he asked. "I'm out."

Swenson took his glowing cigar from between his lips. This Jim had counted on, though it was not vital. He offered it, butt first, in his right hand, the left swinging low. Jim stepped forward as if to take it and brought up his right first smash against the point of Swenson's jaw, with all the impetus lent by the past hours of defeat and ignominy, with all the force of the pivoting weight of his body concentrated in that blow for liberty. Hellfire saw it coming; his cigar fell from his lips, but he was too late to shout, and Jim was well inside his guard. A sudden, fiery pain shot through Jim's knuckles. He had driven them back with the impact against Swenson's adamantine jaw, but they had served their purpose. The big man's head rocked; he half swung around then dropped like a chain. There was no one near but the man at the wheel. He turned his head at the thud. Jim heard the yell as he leaped to the rail, catching at the stays to steady himself for a split-second, then diving clean into the tide, kicking off his shoes and striking out, under water at first, in the direction of Penikese.

V

Reaction

The swift race of the tide gripped him, carrying him along parallel to the course of the schooner before he began to make transverse headway. When he was forced to come to the surface he heard confused shouts aboard and chuckled at the success of the blow that had temporarily paralyzed the brains of the boss. The weight of his clothes handicapped him so that he found he had miscalculated the power of the tide-rip and he settled down to a steady single overhand, swimming on his side, almost submerged, urging progress with powerful scissors clips of his legs, looking backward toward the ship from which he had so unceremoniously departed.

To his dismay a beam shot out from her deck. She was rigged with a searchlight that he in his limited survey had not noticed. The ray swept the waters in his direction, missed him as he promptly ducked, and when he again broke water it was swinging toward the New Bedford shore. But it came back, seeking him out. The churn of the screw had been plain to him across the water; now it stopped. A boat was being lowered. It came in his direction. Evidently they either guessed which way he had gone or they had seen him. Meanwhile the current was carrying down the schooner. As the tremulous finger of the searchlight pointed his way Jim dived for the third time. Swimming under water slowed his progress and there was the danger that when lack of air forced him up again the boat would be on him or the beam spot him. The last risk was realized. He bobbed up in a circle of dull radiance and there was a shout from the boat, a clutter of oars turning to a steady stroke, the flash and report of a gun and the watery spat of a bullet only too well aimed.

On they came, shouting in triumph. He heard the bellow of Swenson. His right hand had swollen with the blow, and now besides paining intolerably, it began to interfere with the diving power of his arm that grew numb.

"Turn on your back. Float, damn ye! Float, or I'll sink ye for keeps!" Swenson was roaring like an infuriated bull. Jim might dodge for a while, might dive a time or two, but they would wear him down, If they got him alive he could imagine what would be in store for him aboard with the humiliated Hellfire; unless —

The gods had taken pity on him at last. A bank of fog, vagrant before the uncertain breeze, bore down on him. For the fourth time he slipped under water and struck out to reach its cover, swimming until he thought his lungs must burst and his body felt like lead from lack of oxygen. Up he came to suck in moist air, to find himself enveloped in woolly vapor. He turned over on his back to float and rest. He could hear the clack of oars, muffled calls. The search ray had long since reached its limit in the mist. Swenson and his rowers were losing their bearings. And the tide was bearing Jim rapidly toward the ocean. He had no hope of making Penikese now. That lonesome rock would have been only a temporary halting place, but a necessary one. Now he must keep on to Cuttyhunk. Out of the fog panic swooped at him. Was he going in the right direction? He knew how easy it was in broad daylight to get turned about while floating. In the fog —

His heart pounded for a few beats, then steadied. He could see a halo in the mist, a rainbow spot of dull, but — to him — glorious tints. The fixed white light of Cuttyhunk, well ahead on his left! Allowing for the tide, as the ferries do trying to make a slip, Jim bucked the rip diagonally, his angle of crossing deflected backward. The light came swiftly toward him and he saw that he must make almost superhuman effort if, when it came abeam, he was to be close enough to shore to make a landing. He strove not to get into a flurry. He turned on his right side now, his left, undamaged arm driving him, while the right gave flotation, depending mostly on his legs for power.

He was almost opposite the light, and it seemed to him that he had made scant progress shorewards for all his exertions. There comes a moment to the stoutest swimmer when the call upon the blood is too much for the over-worked lungs and heart; the limbs grow leaden, buoyancy is deflated and the overcoming of the dead centre of effort between strokes is a Herculean task. To turn upon the back and float and rest is the temptation that assails irresistibly. But to float in such an ebbing tideway, even for a few seconds, meant being carried out to the ocean, or at best down Long Island Sound.

The light grew suddenly clearer. He had battled through the thick belt of mist that had temporarily saved him. He could see surf breaking on the rocks of Cuttyhunk. Past them he went, ledge after spouting ledge where a landing threatened broken ribs if not worse. Now he was past the light, all hope gone. A wave slapped him in the face as if derisively; salt water lapped into his mouth, open and gasping for breath. It was all over. He had failed!

Instinctively he tensed for one last tussle before he quit. As he lifted his head to glance despairingly at the fixed light that shone so inexorably as a mark that he had missed, he saw the ghostly loom of spray that marked a little promontory projecting like a finger to the south of a tiny inlet below the ledges of the lighthouse foundation.

Burying his head, he spent his last atoms of energy in the crawl, flailing the surges with his arms, clipping the water with his legs, plowing through the backwash from the rocks at top speed, then failing —

There was an eddy in the tiny inlet, a small space of slack water, then an opposing current that bore him, still feebly swimming, close to the ledges that were beginning to expose their beards of slippery weed. These he grasped and clung to, twining his fingers like hooks among the pods, his body aswing and horizontal. A great wave came rolling into the inlet, chafing against a hundred obstacles, its force breaking. The tail of it lifted Jim and flung him into a crevice of the rock, scraping his flesh against mussels and barnacles that tore his feet and cut through his thin clothing, taking toll of his blood. It sucked at him as it retreated, spent, part of the general retreat of the tidal waters, but Jim remained, holding with fingers, knees, elbows and his lacerated feet, too spent to move for the moment. A rising tide must inevitably have plucked him from his refuge, borne him off to make a sport of him, half stunned as he was. But now it ebbed steadily. Off shore, the whaleboat was seeking the schooner's searchlight in the fog, Swenson himself bewildered for direction, giving up the chase; cursing and hoping that Jim had sunk; wondering whether he had been given the right position of the island; deciding that he had been tricked, and exhausting his repertory of oaths to meet the occasion. The schooner's engine could not buck the full sweep of the ebb any more than could the rowers. Both craft dropped down below the light, below where Jim crawled to the pitted top of his saving promontory; the boat caught up to the mother vessel, was towed, after the crew got aboard, and the schooner swung out around Martha's Vineyard, past Nantucket, out to the sea until the tide turned.

Jim, with naked feet, stumbled over the dripping rocks, cut and bruised, yet gathering strength in the exultation of having won through. But Nature called a halt, insisting on recuperation, his engines clamoring for fuel. A soaking meant nothing to Jim who had slept curled up on hard planks in a small cockpit many a wet night. He found a patch of sand and dropped to it, shouldering out a shallow bed, scraping a hollow for his hips, dropping asleep in the middle of the work, dreamlessly lost to all the world with the fixed white light of Cuttyhunk streaming overhead.

Gulls woke him, screaming discordantly at this intruder on their sanctuary. The mist had gone, and the morning was sharp and clear with the sun already striking at him over Nashawena Island. He sat up, smarting and aching, a sorry looking sight but refreshed, his hurts lost in his purpose — to get to Foxfield before evening. The prospects were not encouraging, but he clenched his jaws until the muscles bunched, tightened his fists and began to figure out how he could make it. The light was out.

The Elizabeth Islands string out westward from the elbow of the curved arm of Barnstaple — Cuttyhunk, Nashawena, Pasque, Naushon, Nonamesset and Uncatean, the two latter side by side and opposite Woods Hole, railroad terminal and port of call for steamers plying between New Bedford and Nantucket. The straits between the islands, smallest at low tide, are all narrow, that between Nashawena and Pasque the widest. There are a few shacks at Cuttyhunk settlement and at Tarpaulin Cove on Naushon, but they are irregularly occupied. Jim had faint hopes of hiring the use of a boat from one of these and making his way to the train. But it was all of fifteen miles, as an aeroplane might make it, from Cuttyhunk to Woods Hole. Even if he got a boat immediately, there was a long morning's work ahead of him to get to the steamer landing, chancing connections at the railroad. Whether he could hire an auto at Woods Hole to take him to Foxfield he did not know. The owner would charge him both way fare, and his money might be insufficient after all. If he could get to New Bedford —

As he stretched himself he found he had an appetite. Swenson's sandwiches had long since lost their sustaining powers. A man's engines need stoking to be effective. Jim made his way over the rocks toward the shacks at Cuttyhunk. He saw smoke coming out of a stovepipe, promise of breakfast. Better than that, he saw a launch, dirty-white with no glittering brasses — no pleasure craft, but the practical powerboat of a fisherman, engines hooded forward, and a roomy cockpit aft. It was moored to a wharf along which a man walked bearing lobster pots. Another one was in the cockpit fussing with the engines. Jim broke into a run, shouting at the men. The one with the lobster basket-traps turned to gaze at him and the one aboard clambered to the wharf where they stood spellbound, looking at the strange figure that had hailed them, and now came hobbling along on bare feet, hatless, with clothes torn and stained with sea-slime and sand, a right hand swollen into shapelessness, face streaked and caked with blood.

"Wall, I'll be scaled," said the man with the pots. "Where in time did ye come from, stranger? W'ot's the general idee?" Jim had his story ready.

"Got boomed-off last night abeam the light," he said. "Fool amateur on a yacht jibed her, running before the wind. Wish he'd sprung his stick." The fishermen appraised him with professional eyes.

"You bein' hired by him?"

"Yes, Sloop *Gypsy*. Me being sailing master, and my own fault for believing the fool knew enough to steer in a fog. What'll you take for a snack to eat and a trip to New Bedford?" The men looked at each other. Their answer was essentially that of New England bargaining.

"What'll you give? Oughter git that hand of yourn fixed up. Boom hit that?" Jim ignored the thrust. Money would talk.

"Two of you own the launch? Call your profits fifteen a day apiece. That's more than it is on an average. I'll give you thirty dollars."

"We got our customers to consider. Orders to fill."

"Tell 'em it was an off day. You don't always have luck."

"Do it for fifty dollars — cash in advance."

"Deal closed." Jim tried vainly to get his right hand at his money. It would not go into his pocket. But he worked it out and handed over twenty dollars, displaying enough to set the fishermen's minds at rest about their pay. "Thirty more when we hit New Bedford," he told them. "Now for a mug-up."

The launch was sturdy enough, but not designed for speed or grace. It wallowed into New Bedford at eleven o'clock, helped by the tide. They passed half a dozen power schooners, but Jim had not seen enough of Swenson's craft to recognize it, save by the figures instead of name on her boats. Nor would recognition have delayed him. He had evolved a theory that Foster, at back of Swenson — though he admitted even in his biased mood that such a connection between an unprincipled, almost outlawed bully and a prosperous manufacturer seemed incongruous — had planned on securing the figures together with the person of Lyman, and thus get possession of the pearls by making toothpicks of the *Golden Dolphin* if necessary to find the hiding-place of the treasure. He began to suspect Foster of having planted certain of his tools on the *Golden Dolphin* on her original voyage to plot a mutiny — a scheme upset by the tidal casting ashore of the ship.

By this time, he feared, Foster would have learned that Kitty Whiting had the diary in her possession. If Swenson communicated with him, stating that Lyman had got away, there might be an immediate attempt to get the figures from Kitty, to delay her voyage and give Swenson a start. They might even try to kidnap the girl. Men will go to great lengths for the sake of a fortune — even Foster, who, having already made one million, no longer considered it as a definite goal.

If he was correct, Swenson would wire. *And so could he!* At the first store he bought shoes, socks and a cap. Then he found a telegraph office. He had brushed up a little at the store, but the girl looked askance at his desperate looking appearance. He was forced to ask her to write out his messages — one to Kitty Whiting, another to her Cousin Lynda. He believed the latter less likely to trust in Foster, less bound by ideas of partnership. The content of both was the same save for the interchange of names.

> *Arriving this evening. Vital you keep information mailed you absolutely secret. Also my arrival. Trickery active.*
> James Lyman.

He found he could get a train shortly after noon that would take him to South Framingham a few minutes before four. That place was about eight miles from Foxfield. Further connections were bad, but he could hire a machine that should surely land him at the antique shop by eight o'clock.

If Swenson had wired, all his calculations might be upset. Foster would be prepared for his appearance and would, of course, be ready to discredit Swenson. Therefore he would proceed as planned and attend the meeting he had himself arranged.

Lyman could have spared himself a lot of worrying had he known that at that very moment, Swenson, with a broken-down engine that obstinately refused to come to life, was cursing the lack of a breeze twelve miles off-shore.

He filled in his wait with lunch and a visit to a barber's for a shave and a chance to bathe his injured hand. Then to a druggist for bandaging.

"Better show that to a doctor," advised the man. "Looks like misplaced bones, to me. Ought to have an X-ray taken of it. Delay won't help it."

"Then it can't be helped," said Jim. "I've seen worse get well at sea." The druggist shrugged his shoulders.

"Suppose the other chap is in the hospital?" he said as he rang up his money.

"I sure hope so," Jim answered fervently. It was a bad hand, but it would have to get along. If only Swenson's jaw was half-way like it.

At four-thirty he was front-seated beside the driver of a good car, averaging twenty-five miles through incorporated towns and villages with their speed restrictions and wide-awake traffic regulators. At seven o'clock they had a blowout and shifted to the spare. At ten minutes to eight they entered Foxfield by way of a detour for road-mending that brought them over the same bridge that Jim had crossed two nights earlier on his way to Foster's house. The car took him to the hotel. After the chauffeur was paid off Jim had fifteen dollars and sixty cents; Swenson's contribution had paid expenses. The clerk at the desk stared at him unbelievingly as Jim asked for his key.

"That room's rented. Thought you'd skipped. Mr. Foster and his son rang up the other night, wondering why you didn't show up to their house. Then they came down together in their car. Seemed a bit upset about you. Thought you might have misunderstood their directions, but I told 'em you'd spoken to me about it. Thought you might have fallen in the river, maybe. I told 'em we'd take a look at your junk. If it was worth more than what you owed us you might come back. If not, you'd faded for reasons of your own. You ain't the only one that's done it. Mr. Foster figured I was right, but I guess I was wrong. Want another room? What happened."

"I got into an accident," said Jim. "Machine hit me, picked me up and took me along with 'em a ways. I'll take a room, I reckon. And I'd like my things."

The clerk looked at him with an expression that showed he thought Jim was lying, but said nothing. His things were brought to the new room. They had plainly been overhauled. Foster had doubtless been glad of the chance to see if the diary was there or not. And a new thought struck him. Foster might by now be a confirmed believer in his own suggestion that Jim was a fake, and that, seeing his story was to be investigated thoroughly, he had skipped. Though if Foster had seen the little diary, he could tell almost at a glance — any keen-witted person could — that its content was authentic enough with its everyday comments and the stains upon the pages with their more or less legible entries. But — if Foster had suggested the assault and abduction, it was clever of him to have come to the hotel and shown just the right amount of concern. Foster was clever.

Jim changed shirt, collar, and tie, slicked up to the best of his ability, hard put to it to do much to his only suit. At twenty minutes past eight he pressed the bell between the two porches with a side glance at the ship model. He had already noticed light coming from the two windows of the dining-living room.

The gaunt maid opened the door, starting back.

"Land o' Goshen!" she exclaimed. "I —"

Jim pushed past her with an imperative gesture for silence. For a moment the woman seemed dazedly about to try and bar his way. She gasped like a stranded fish, muttering confusedly.

"For the land's sake. I wanter know. Why, I —" Jim grasped her bony wrist with his left hand.

"Shut up," he said. "Are the rest here? Mr. Foster and his son?" She nodded, gathering herself together.

"I'll tell Miss Kitty you're here."

"You needn't bother." Jim went through the hall and abruptly opened the door of the dining room. About the table were seated the four he had expected to find, rising to his entrance. He saw immediately that Kitty and her cousin had received his telegram, though they exhibited well feigned surprise. As for Stephen and Newton Foster, there was no question about their astonishment. The former especially showed some measure of alarm and consternation. They did not seem attempting to mask their emotions. Yet Jim could not construe guilt out of their appearance. Young Newton surveyed him quizzically. The elder Foster swiftly recovered himself. Jim spoke first.

"I've got to apologize for my appearance." he said, "But I've been on the jump every minute that I wasn't tied up since I saw you last."

"Tied up?" The ejaculation was unanimous. Jim could not detect any difference in expressions.

"Hand and foot, with a couple of sacks to boot," he said grimly. "Someone asked me to help them with a busted automobile on my way to your house at *your* invitation to talk things over, Mr. Foster. I stooped and somebody hit me over the head with a blackjack. The rest sounds like a chapter in a dime novel, but I had made up my mind to keep this appointment and here I am."

"But," said Kitty Whiting, "you wrote me that you were going away. And you've been hurt. Oh — your poor hand!"

"I hurt that on someone else, a gentleman by the name of Hellfire Swenson. I met him at Wareham, Buzzards Bay. Maybe you know the place?" He wheeled on Stephen Foster. There was the idea in the back of his head that Swenson might have been caretaker for Foster, the Wareham place the latter's summer residence. But Foster's face was absolutely blank. He was either an accomplished actor or — Jim's theories commenced to suffer from a reaction that immediately grew.

"Never heard it more than mentioned," said Foster. "How about Lyman writing to you, Kitty? You didn't tell me anything about it." Jim looked from one to the other, puzzled. Then Foster didn't know anything about the sending of the log.

"I haven't had a chance," she said. "You and Newton were out of town, to begin with, up to this afternoon. Newton phoned early yesterday morning and told me you were going before the letter came by special delivery. As you were coming tonight it hardly seemed worth while until you told me that Mr. Lyman had missed an appointment with you. That was just before you came in," she explained to Jim. And Jim, who could not suspect the girl of any connivance at his kidnapping, grew more bewildered, less and less sure of his own reasoning.

"I was telling my niece what happened — what I thought happened," said Stephen Foster frankly. "My son, against my own judgment — but I told you that over the phone. I will only say that when you did not appear we telephoned, and then ran down to the hotel in the car as soon as it was adjusted. I had a talk with the clerk, who showed me your baggage. It was, er — not of great value. He considered you had left it in lieu of payment. I must admit that I reverted to my original belief that you had in some way got hold of information concerning the *Golden Dolphin* and had arrived here with spurious information in the hope of a reward of some sort, abandoning the plan on seeing that your proofs would have to be submitted to more than casual investigation. In other words, I thought you got cold feet when I suggested an interview, not with more or less interested and credulous women influenced by sentiment, but with me.

"I apologize. It is evident you have been more or less misjudged by us. Very evident that you have been at — er—some pains to return, after rough treatment that seems to have been extended to both sides of the argument. Now will you tell us what has happened; why you wrote that you were not coming back; why you changed your mind, and, seemingly, fought your way back?"

Despite himself, Jim found his feelings changing toward Stephen Foster. There was a frankness about his regrets, a thawing of his general chilliness, a changing in his eyes, a touch of actual humanity that affected him as the difference between heat and cold. But he did not forego caution, he was unable to cast off all suspicion.

"I went," he said, "because I found myself regarded by you as a faker; because I feared that Miss Whiting was being swayed by sentimentality, and I thought the chances of finding her father on the island remote; because she offered me a share of the pearls in return for the figures which I considered belonged to her.

"Therefore, I mailed her the little diary, intending to leave. I considered you had a right to such information as I might give about landings and anchorages, so I told you I would come to your house. I have changed my mind about the possibilities of the trip. At any rate I am now inclined to think the pearls are there. Others do, also, it appears. In order to get a chance to get away from my host at Wareham I had to furnish him with false figures. It was very plain he intended going to the island. I hope he'll try to go to the position I furnished him. I am afraid he won't. From my short acquaintance with him I should be surprised if he does not make another attempt to get hold of the correct figures — he, or those who may be behind him, who might have been behind the mutiny that Captain Whiting hinted at in his letters to his daughter.

"So, as soon as I could, I wired Miss Whiting, also Miss Warner for security, not to divulge the figures I had given her to anybody under any consideration. And I would advise her to hang on to them until the last necessary moment — that would be after leaving Fiji — if she makes the trip."

Jim said this almost defiantly, striving to detect some clew that father or son, or both, were what he had surmised. Stephen Foster's face showed little but grave attention. Newton Foster displayed close interest. Nothing more.

"I consider that an excellent idea," said Foster. "I commend you, Lyman, for qualities I had not credited you with. Where is this book, Kitty? Have you shown it to anybody?"

"No. It is in my safety deposit box at the Foxfield National." Foster nodded approval, but not surprise. Jim inwardly applauded the girl's business capacities.

"Fine. Go on, Lyman."

Jim told his story, tersely enough. He was a little thrown off his guard by Foster's manner, but he was not entirely disarmed. The connection between Swenson and Foxfield, particularly with regard to his knowledge of his own whereabouts that evening on his way to the Foster house, needed explaining. But Jim felt that it could do no harm to say what had happened in front of the Fosters. If one or both was in league with Swenson they would, sooner or later, know all about it, up to the time of his escape in the fog, if they did not know it already. He was a little inclined to acquit Newton Foster. His jealousy of the son had evaporated somewhat since Kitty Whiting's exclamation of "Oh, your poor hand!" with its genuine sympathy. With both the women, Newton showed no signs of discredence of his yarn, melodramatic as it was. But he fancied that Stephen Foster's pursing mouth disclosed symptoms of doubt. The various expressions that followed his story were typical.

"What a terrible experience!" This from Kitty Whiting. "I think you showed great resourcefulness and bravery, Mr. Lyman. I think a great many men would have given the true figures under such circumstances. If you had not been able to get away, and to jump over — in the fog — with the tide running out — You have increased my indebtedness to you."

"It is just what I should have expected," said Lynda Warner. Her eyes were shining as she nodded at Jim. "I mean Mr. Lyman's share in it."

Newton Foster was ungrudging enough.

"I wish I had been along," he said, "You handled it in bully shape. I hope you broke Hellfire's jaw for him. But how he found out where you were on the road to our house, how he knew you had the figures, how he knew about the pearls, is a mystery to me."

"Quite romantic," was the start of Stephen Foster's contribution. "As to Swenson," he went on, "there has been a good deal of publicity, now and again, concerning the *Golden Dolphin*, when it sailed and when it was reported missing. Swenson may have read it long ago and retained interest. One of your men who was with you in the boat, Lyman, after he was wrecked might have got in touch with him. There are several possibilities. The local end of it is mysterious. The main factor is that Swenson has failed. He may think you drowned; he may think you were hit when he fired. If he has any idea you got clear, he will be likely to lie low. He may well be one of the rum-running community, and he and his schooner will readily disappear for a while. We could stir up the Wareham police, but that again might give notoriety that would be inadvisable. I should advise you to see a doctor about that hand, Lyman, I recommend my own, Dr. Dimmock. I will call him up if you like."

"I thank you," said Jim. "It is not uncomfortable. It seems to me there are more important things right now." Foster was the cold-eyed business man once more, his mouth tight-lipped.

"As you like," he said. "Kitty, I still think that the chances for success are extremely limited. Personally I should vote against it. However, I have already told Newton that if he is determined to join with you I withdraw opposition. My chief worry is for your ultimate disappointment concerning your father. Castles built on hopes that are largely sentimental fall with a crash too often, and you might get hurt in the ruins.

"Newton has money of his own. He has also an equal interest with me in my share of the pearls. . . ."

"I am not going after the pearls, Father. I am going because — because Kitty should not be allowed to go alone. Of course Lynda has offered — but I mean without a male relative."

"Of course. And youth is naturally adventurous. I was about to say that Newton has ample funds to bear the entire expense if he wants to make the gamble."

"I intend to. Let me do that, Kitty. If — if the thing should peter out all round, you wouldn't want to feel that you had nothing to come back to. Unless —" The word and the pause that followed it were eloquent of Newton's personal interest in his cousin, rather than the actual objects of the trip. But he saw that he had been precipitate and hurried on to cover the slip. "It wouldn't do for you to burn all your bridges and sell this business."

"I have already sold it," said the girl. Her uncle made a muffled exclamation.

"The deal has been closed by wire. The transfer will be made tomorrow. The purchaser is coming up from Hartford. It was a good bargain on both sides. I got my price, sufficient, I hope, for expenses. Twenty-seven thousand dollars."

"You don't mean to tell me you got that price for your stock and good will?" exclaimed Stephen Foster incredulously, seemingly annoyed, perhaps at not having been consulted, perhaps — thought Jim — at finding his niece so close to independence.

"I am afraid, uncle, you never did properly value the selling price of antiques as compared with the buying. There is a big demand for them, and I know a good piece when I see it. Most of these were bought for small sums and then restored. At retail the stock would easily bring fifty thousand dollars. It has cost me less than ten. And I had only twenty-five hundred to start with at the very beginning. And there is the good will.

"If Newton wants to come — as he has the right to and as your representative — he can bear half the expense. Mr. Lyman has a master's certificate. I want him to have command of the expedition. It seems to me he has earned it — and the sixteenth share I offered him in the pearls if they are recovered — aside from having given us the position of the *Golden Dolphin*. Please do not protest, Mr. Lyman. It is purely business. I am sure uncle would consider such a bonus only fair. And it can come out of the Whiting share." Stephen Foster got up and walked up and down the room.

"I wash my hands of it," he declared. "I consider it folly, though I shall be more than happy if you find your father, glad also to get my returns from the original investment. Make your own plans. Newton, are you coming with me? I suppose not. You'll be wanting to start tomorrow night, I imagine." He seemed to be trying to be heavily humorous.

"The day after tomorrow," said Kitty. "There are my own things to transfer to storage. Not much to pack to take with us. We are going to San Francisco to charter a ship."

"Why San Francisco? None of my business, of course. But —"

"Mr. Lyman recommends it, uncle. It will save time and expense."

Stephen Foster shrugged.

"Then I'll be going," he said. "Send back the car for you, son?"

"I don't believe Kitty and Lynda ought to be left alone in this house, Father. There's only Ellen Martin, After Lyman's experience —"

"It might make us — me, at all events — seem safer if both of you stayed. You could share the guest room," suggested Lynda to Lyman. "I imagine I am sufficient chaperone. As for Ellen, I know she has been listening at the door. It is a trait that she regards as a privilege. She'll need protection anyway."

"If you would," said Kitty Whiting. The young men looked at each other. Whatever their thoughts, neither could well demur. "But your hand?" she said to Jim.

"I've had a worse one," he answered. "I'll see a doctor in the morning."

"Then I'll send your things over from the hotel," said Foster. "And some duds for you, Newton. See you sometime tomorrow, I suppose. Good night, you pack of adventurers."

With his exit he again achieved a degree of bluff humanity. Again Lyman was in doubt. Foster reappeared, hat in hand.

"About those figures," he said. "I'd recommend you take means to conceal them, Kitty. Even from Newton here, until the time comes. He might talk in his sleep. Lyman, you know them, too. Don't let anybody hypnotize you." His tone was ironical; it might have once more been meant for humor.

"I don't want to know them, Kit," said Newton as the door closed.

"I am going to mail that diary ahead," she said. "I suppose we make certain ports of call, Mr. Lyman, for water and provisions?"

There was a globe in the stockroom under the portrait of Kitty's grandfather. They set this on the table and sat about it. Ellen, discovered suspiciously close to the door between them and the kitchen, was sent packing without excuse for lingering.

"I packed her off for a walk," said Kitty. "She's probably heard more than is good for her. If curiosity was a fatal disease, Ellen would have died long ago. The funny part is that she appears to think herself absolutely entitled to knowledge of everything that happens, and usually offers her opinion freely."

"Taking her along?" asked Newton.

"I'll give her the chance, but I don't believe she'll go. She's got some love affair on. She's close-mouthed enough about that; but I understand he's younger than she is. She has some money saved up —"

"And the bounder is after that. Sure isn't her looks."

Lynda Warner flushed. Jim Lyman realized the sensitiveness that lay behind her plain exterior and wanted to kick Newton for his lack of tact.

Kitty Whiting broke up the awkwardness. "How about the itinerary," she asked.

"We would naturally stop at Hawaii," said Lyman. He had tacitly accepted command. Since the girl was determined to go, and since he was persuaded that there were others determined to thwart her, he had made up his mind to take the trip. The question of the share could rest. It was not an unusual offer, after all. He wanted to pick his own crew, remembering the letters of Captain Whiting.

"Two thousand and ninety-eight miles from San Francisco to Honolulu," he went on. "Call it ten days with power equal to eight knots. We must get a boat with an engine, or we may drift for weeks trying to pass the line. The run to Suva in the Fijis is about twenty-seven hundred. That would be fourteen days more, full speed. But we do not know what capacity we will have for gasoline and we want to sail when the wind favors us. We ought to get a schooner capable of making ten to twelve knots with wind abeam or astern. Fourteen and ten. Call it a month. We should fetch Suva in a month, outside of stopovers or delays from engine trouble. Hardly from storms at this time of the year. There may be headwinds, of course.

"Our real trip begins at Suva. We should take on water and supplies there, and I should like to add to the crew with native boys. They will be wanted to handle the landing boats. They'll be better for many of our purposes than whites such as we are likely to get. We'll ship a working crew at San Francisco."

"How about arms?" asked Newton.

"You said there were no natives, but —"

"It is best to go prepared," said Lyman gravely. "I was only ashore a little while and at one place. That is one reason why I did not want to urge Miss Whiting to go."

"There were women in the war," she said. "I am not afraid of taking the same risks as a man. And I fancy I could shoot on occasion. We can practice on the way down."

Jim had other reasons he could have advanced, but he forbore. The pluck of the girl was wonderful. He had no doubt of her ability to hold her own outside of sheer strength. But the thought of what might happen to her if they fell among the savage tribes locked his jaws tightly and cemented his resolve.

It was midnight when they broke up. The two women got together a little supper. The car arrived with a bag for Newton and Jim's pitiful belongings. He was glad that he possessed a decent suit of pajamas. Such things did not matter, but though much of his first antagonism toward Newton Foster had disappeared, he was human enough not to want to appear at any special disadvantage.

He took a hot bath, somewhat clumsily. Newton shoved his head into their bathroom and asked if he could help.

"Jupiter, but you're banged up!" he said. "I imagine you put up a tidy scrap, Lyman. I envy you your muscles. I'm soft as a rag doll. I'd like to shake hands with you as soon as your fin gets in shape. Over this trip, you know. Mighty glad you're going to be along. It's a pretty serious proposition when you come to think of it. For Kitty — and Lynda — I mean. It's up to you and me to look out for them. And you'll have to make a sailor out of me. So far I'm not a shining light in any profession. But I'm willing to play general utility."

It was impossible to hold much of a grudge after that speech. It began to look as if there was good stuff in Newton Foster after all. With his father Jim still reserved judgment.

"Here's my left hand on it, for the time being," he said. And they turned in together.

There was no alarm in the night. The next morning Jim went to see Dr. Dimmock, the purchaser of the antique store arrived and Ellen Martin gave notice to quit.

VI

Under Way

The trip to San Francisco established a camaraderie between the four. Lyman was the most reserved. He had much to think about and he did not possess Newton Foster's ready knack of conversation. He envied his ready intimacy with Kitty Whiting and devoted himself to squiring with Lynda Warner. His liking for her readily ripened into real friendship. She would have made a wonderful wife for some chap, he thought, but she had been handicapped. Naturally a man preferred a girl with a pretty face and good figure — such as Kitty Whiting — though Jim did not allow his thoughts to wander in that direction, consciously at least. He found in the elderly spinster a quick appreciation of affairs, discussing with her details of the voyage while Newton haled his cousin off to the observation platform. Not that they did not all have serious consultations. Newton was a partner in the enterprise and full of suggestions, but it was plain that to him the expedition was one of romance and adventure intimately connected with his pretty cousin. He was gay, impractical, good-looking and likeable, if he did attempt to monopolize Kitty. Jim acquitted him early of being a snob.

Lynda Warner appeared to weigh Newton lightly, though she made no comments. Jim believed that Lynda understood his own feelings toward the girl and sympathized with him. Naturally, he never discussed it. The gap between them was still open and unbridged, he considered. Only in the matter of his reading was he on equal terms. Her life had held a thousand things he had never come in touch with.

But every now and then Lynda Warner spoke of American democracy. Sometimes she quoted Burns.

"Every man in this country of ours may not be literally equal," she said, "but at least he has an equal start in the race of life. It is up to him to win the race. Some are bound to drop behind, but the real man can gain the prizes. Superficial qualities do not count. They can always be acquired. And the man is lucky who has a chance to show his real manhood in the big things."

All this was pleasant talk to Jim, though he bent his mind to the task in hand, without contemplation of possible rewards. A man's first job was his duty, he believed firmly. And he privately subscribed to Lynda Warner's theories.

"There are only two classes in America," she said. "Some call them the rich and the poor; better perhaps the successful and the unsuccessful. It's grit that tells."

When it came to pedigree — which Lynda declared did not count — Jim knew his forebears to be as good as those of those of the Whitings and the Fosters. He had seen the selvage edge of life, and Kitty and Newton the softer nap, that was all. And Kitty's life had not been without its reverses; had now its present sorrow that she hid under the bright cloak of courage. How she had taken up with business and made a success of it; what a life partner she would make! Too sterling, he could not help but feel, for the airy, ease-loving happy-go-lucky Newton.

It was Jim's idea to try and get the vessel they needed from one of the yacht clubs of San Francisco Bay, rather than attempt to purchase a commercial vessel. Those of the latter type likely to be available would be old hulks moored and half rotting over in Oakland Creek. The war had taken all bottoms that were any good. The Alaska Packing Company's northern fleet consisted of sailing ships; there were scow-bottomed schooners that plied up the Sacramento River and other waterways connected with the bay, but outside these, old hulks and pleasure craft, everything was steam. But he felt sure that on the Pacific, as on the Atlantic Coast, there would be people willing to dispose of their yachts, or charter them. Fortunes had been turned topsy-turvy during the war. Those who had made money were not the kind who understood yachting or looked upon it as a pastime. Those who had lost, on the other hand, were that type of the comparatively leisured class. Moreover, a yacht of the right size and engine power, if they could find out, would be built for comfort aft, and he had the two women to consider.

Newton Foster had brought along letters from his father to business friends. These letters would undoubtedly act as an open sesame to the clubs of the city, and through them to the San Francisco and Corinthian yacht clubs, whose quarters were, as Jim knew, across the bay at Sausalito and Belvedere. But Jim relied upon the advertisements he might read or insert.

Arrived in the city, they went to the Palace Hotel where rooms were already reserved for them. It was late afternoon, too late for Newton to present his letters. He proposed a theatre and they went, but no one enjoyed much of the play. They were on the threshold of adventure and eager to step across. Kitty Whiting's unrest showed in her eyes, in flashes of absent-mindedness. She had not been sleeping since they left Foxfield, Lynda Warner told Jim. Next morning Newton busied himself with his introductions. He was also going, he said, to get hold of all the literature he could concerning the South Seas.

"Not fiction stuff," he announced. "Travel. We'll have to read on the trip to kill time. And I wouldn't wonder if I came back with news of just the boat we want."

There were several advertisements in the papers for the sale of launches and sloops, but none that offered anything suitable. Jim saw disappointment in Kitty Whiting's face, and for a second saw them failing to get anything at all; his suggestions discredited at the outset; himself looking like a fool stripped of all pretense of knowledge.

"I'm going to put ads in the *Chronicle*, *Examiner* and *Bulletin*," he said. She nodded and gave him a look that fired his imagination.

"I know you'll get one," she said. "But the seconds seem like hours and the hours like weeks. Now that we have actually started — it seems to me as if dad was waiting over there eating his heart out for the sight of a sail, waiting, waiting, and growing old. He isn't a young man, my daddy, and I want — I want —"

Her lips quivered; her eyes were moist with tears; she gave a pitifully twisted, brave little smile. Right then Jim would have charged through a regiment of devils for her sake, wished he could. Something of it showed in his look, for she said thank you before he answered her at all.

"I'll get you one, if I have to turn pirate. It might he a good idea if we went across to Sausalito and then over to Belvedere. There is sure to be someone round the clubhouses. The stewards or the boat-tenders would be likely to know of anything that might be available." Kitty's face brightened immediately and she dragged the willing Lynda off to dress. Within the hour they were on the Sausalito ferry, ploughing across toward the strait of the Golden Gate, the loom of Mount Tamalpais ahead of them. The steward of the San Francisco Yacht Club forgot house rules when he saw the ladies and heard Jim's question, recognizing him immediately for a man of the sea and one who knew blue water.

"A power schooner?" he said, a little doubtfully. "I don't know. There's one in the fleet, the *Seamew*, built in the East, Gloucester fisherman type. She can outsail anything round here if there's any sort of weather, and she's got an engine in her. Her owner was a bluewater man. Name of Rickard. Never more than mate, I understand. But he struck oil, or oil was struck for him and he came into a fortune. First thing he wanted a yacht and had this built. Sailed her round himself — plumb round the Horn, just to say it could be done these days. And they say —" the steward sank his voice to a confidential whisper — "they say he bucko'd his crew so they near mutinied. They quit, anyway, and he had to get others. He's always short-handed. He's a visiting member here — we exchange courtesies with a lot of clubs — or I wouldn't be discussing him, you understand. I don't know if he'd sell her outright, or even charter her, but I heard him say he was sick of her. Fact is, he don't get along first rate with all the members. We do most of our racing inside the bay, and he laughs at us for bein' mollycoddles. And he's got a professional crew, you see, whereas we are all amateurs — strictly.

"There's one or two rumors he's going to be married to a widow. He's willing enough, I fancy, and maybe his oil stock looks good to her — begging your pardon, ladies. The point I'm making is that he's always with her and that she hates yachting. Blows her hair about a bit too much, perhaps," said the steward with fine scorn.

"If you could arrange a charter for us," said Jim, "we should be pleased to allow you the usual agent's commission." The steward touched his cap visor.

"Thank you, sir. I'll show you the *Seamew* if you'll come through to the float. I know the caretaker pretty well. I think I could venture to take you off."

"I wouldn't want to do that," said Kitty. "It's like walking into a stranger's house."

"I'm sure Mr. Rickard wouldn't mind, miss. Easy enough to find out. He's got a place over here for the summer. I'll telephone him if you like. He's proud of the boat, you see, and always showing people over it. There she lies. A beauty, all right."

They saw the *Seamew*, black of hull, with a fine gold stripe winking along her run, spoon-bowed, overhung of stern, sweet of line, a typical

Gloucester fisherman model designed for speed and endurance; the type that can come smashing home with every inch of canvas set, and hold deep packed with cod through a gale that makes many a deepwater skipper shorten sail and crawl to windward for open water. All the canvas was stowed aboard the *Seamew*, but it did not take much for Jim to imagine her with topsails full, main and fore, jumbo and jib, fisherman's staysail set between the masts, the sea foaming at her entry, creaming along her run, fanning out in ivory traceries on the green jade of the sea in her wake. Here was no toy, but a ship after his own heart, capable of sailing the seven seas, not needing a large crew to handle her, but comfortable in calm or seaway for all aboard. And she had an engine, almost a necessity in the South Seas, where currents are strong and wind capricious.

Brasswork well polished blinked here and there along her deck. Even at that distance they could tell she was shipshape, controlled by a man who might be a bit of a tyrant with his crew, but knew how to treat a proper vessel.

Jim's face glowed with approval. The steward had gone to his telephone. Kitty watched Lyman's face, unconsciously reflecting its approval. Lynda Warner seemed more doubtful.

"A little small, isn't she," she asked, "for a long voyage?"

"She would be alongside a liner," said Jim, "But she's seaworthy and she's just about ideal for our purpose — if we can get her."

"Mr. Rickard's coming right over," said the steward, coming up. "I said there were two ladies in a party who were admiring his boat and he said he was coming over, anyway. I didn't say anything about a charter over the phone. Best to wait and see what humor he's in." He got them chairs and they watched the shifting panorama of the bay, with San Francisco seated in the midst of her hills; the crossing ferries, lumber steamers and freighters passing through the Gate; scow-schooners high decked with hay from upriver, the helmsman perched high on a scaffold back of the load; the gulls; a destroyer maneuvering to prove up her compasses by the government marks set on the shores. The tide was coming in from the ocean, and all the yachts in the club flotilla dipped and curtsied. The wind came with the tide bringing salty savors. A flush slowly stained the girl's cheeks deeper and deeper until Jim gazed in wonderment at this augmented beauty of one he already thought perfect.

"I love the sea," she said. "It's in my blood, I suppose. And I love the *Seamew*. I hope we get her."

Rickard turned out to be much what they had anticipated, a burly, tanned man who looked awkward in clothes that were too much in the latest mode as to cut and pattern. But he was courteous enough and indubitably pleased to have his boat admired by a party, one of whom, Jim, was an expert, another, Kitty, more than ordinarily wise concerning schooners.

"You ought to own her," he said to Kitty. "You'd sail her in a blow, you would, and not worry about your complexion or your permanent wave. All ladies aren't alike, or all men. If there were more boats like mine here we could have a real race or two — outside, around the Farallones and back, down to San Diego and back, or up to the Sound. But these bay water sailors think an annual cruise down to Santa Cruz is really sailing." Kitty took her cue, and glanced at Jim.

"I wish I did own her," she said. "I couldn't afford to buy her, but I've been wanting for ever so long to take a trip through the South Seas. And this is just the boat."

Her praise was justified, the *Seamew* was more than merely well found. The seamanship of the ex-mate had prevented him from breaking out with his ship as he had done with the unknown quantity — clothes. The fittings were good, even luxurious, but they were convenient and chosen for wear and solid comfort rather than show. There would be a cabin apiece for Kitty and Lynda, one for Newton and one for Jim, as skipper, all opening on the main cabin, besides a small stateroom amidships that would do for the officers. There was even a small bath, a well appointed galley. The engine was powerful, in good condition. There were water tanks and gasoline tanks enough for a long voyage, ample room for stores. The only scant place was the forecastle quarters. Rickard's ideas of a crew's right of comfort were nil.

"She's got everything but wireless." Rickard boasted. "She's a beauty. Eight knots and a half on her engines, and she'll rate up to fifteen when the wind's right. She'll sail right into it and come about for the asking. She's fine lined, but she isn't over tender; you can handle her between spokes. She's a man's boat, but a child could steer her. I might let you have her, if you paid me enough and put up a sufficient bond. I'll want her back, but I don't need her anymore this season. It's hard to get men and keep them in shape when you only have the boat in commission a quarter of the time they have to be paid for. I'd as lief sail round a duck pond as cruise inside the bay. To tell you the truth, Miss Whiting, I'm thinking of getting married — shortly. The future Mrs. Rickard is not over fond of the water, but I hope to win her round later on. I won't sell the *Seamew*, but I might charter her — to the right parties."

Rickard had smiled when he first mentioned price and he smiled again as he finished speaking. Without being offensive, it was plain that he found Kitty attractive, that he was the bluff type, hard enough with men, but wax before the glances of a pretty woman. In his way, and given it, a good enough sort of sea scout.

"What are your ideas on figures?" asked Jim.

"Fifteen hundred dollars for the season, whether you need her for two months or six. A bottomry bond for twenty-five thousand dollars."

"Cash?"

"Or negotiable securities acceptable to my lawyers." Kitty looked at Jim, who nodded. Five hundred a month would be cheap for the *Seamew*; the amount of the bond could not replace her since the war. Arrangement was speedily made to draw contract and make payment. Rickard agreed to meet them the next morning at the hotel.

"I have three good men who might be glad to go along," he said. "I don't know about the steward. You'll need four for crew, outside of a mate. Then there's the engineer and a cook. Steward'll wait on cabin, cook for'ard. That's how I brought her round from the other side. I take it you're sailing her?" he asked Lyman.

"Yes. You don't know of a mate? Rather take one who was recommended."

"I haven't seen one I could recommend to be mate of a brick barge. I'm my own sailing master. I've tried out half a dozen lazy lubbers as mate and I fired the last a week ago. As I say, my trouble is that I pay 'em full time and use 'em less than half. You'll find mates and men scattered all along the waterfront looking for jobs. Some of 'em turned farmers and fruit pickers. Some of 'em in the canneries. Some of 'em fishing for salmon in Puget Sound. But a lot left doin' nothing. Can I take you across to San Francisco in my launch? That doesn't go with the schooner but it's at your service."

But they had an idea that acceptance might conflict with his plans or those of the future Mrs. Rickard and they took the ferry. Now it seemed as if they were really started, with unexpected luck to begin with. The *Seamew* had no cook at present, nor steward, Rickard providing those from his house servants whenever he went cruising. The three sailors of his crew seemed adequate men, two of them Norwegians and the third a Scotch-Irishman. They were deepwater men and they knew the yacht. Jim spoke to them tentatively and they were willing to make the trip, wages to be the same as Rickard paid. He had not used his engine of late, and had no engineer.

"I'll have to hunt a mate, a steward, a cook, an engineer, and a sailor," said Jim. "I don't imagine that'll be much trouble, except about the cook. We don't want to be poisoned. I'd suggest a Chinaman; Jap for second choice. They don't mind the sea. Then there are the supplies, a few charts and — I shall need a sextant," he added after a slight pause. "You see I haven't any tools of my own," he said with a flush. "I imagine Rickard may let us take his chronometers."

"You'll need a complete outfit," said Kitty. "It was stupid of me not to think of that before. Of course you can draw ahead for as much as you need. And you must let me help with the supplies."

"Of course." Jim appreciated the fact with which she had spoken in a manner entirely businesslike of his own lack of clothes and money. He had paid out his last change for the ferry crossings and he could hardly go to sea in command with his one suit of tailor-darned readymades.

"I'll talk the bond over with Newton," she said. "I have no securities, but of course I can put up half in cash, I wish we could buy the *Seamew*."

"What would you do with her after the trip is over?" asked Lynda Warner.

"Keep on sailing. Round the world. I'd love to." She spoke with genuine enthusiasm, in high spirits. Jim wished she might have her heart's desire — and that he might be of the party as sailing master, if not in a more intimate capacity that he merely hinted at to himself.

At the hotel, the two women went straight to the elevators, Jim to the desk for a directory from which to obtain addresses of ship-chandlers. As he passed the telegraph booth he saw Newton Foster handing in a dispatch. He passed on, thoughtful, wondering why and where Newton was sending a cable. There was no mistaking the form of the message. A few minutes later Newton clapped him on the shoulder.

"Wondering where you all were. Girl's back? Good. Let's go to lunch. I'm ravenous. Say, I've got a pile of good books on the South Seas. And I met a fine fellow through one of dad's letters. Invited me up for dinner tonight at the Bohemian Club. He belongs to the San Francisco Yacht Club too. He says we'll be able to get what we want without any trouble. There's a man named Rickard who owns a schooner and who has tried to horn into the club and run things. A bit of a roughneck — used to be a mate one time and now his swollen pockets have affected his head. He thinks he's a gentleman."

"I suppose it's possible."

Newton hesitated, flushed. "I didn't mean to be offensive, Lyman. The point is that this chap doesn't fit with the crowd. And he's stuck on a widow who hates sailing."

"Owns the *Seamew*?"

"Yes. How did you know?"

"We've seen her, agreed to charter her." Newton did not take the news exactly as Jim had expected. He was interested enough, but he whistled softly rather than make the exclamation Jim expected.

"You're quick workers," he said. "That's news. I'll have to wire the old man. He's more worked up over this trip than he lets on. I wired him already that we had arrived safely. When do you figure we can get away?"

"That's hard to tell. We have men to get; supplies; get our clearance; supply a satisfactory bond of cash or securities."

"How much?"

"Twenty-five thousand dollars."

"I've got that in Telephone stock. I imagine he'll take that. Could we get away in a week?"

"With luck."

"And Honolulu'll be our first port of call?"

"Yes." The questions were natural enough and now Newton was all eagerness. But Jim wondered if this supplementary message was also going on a cable form. No one had said anything of Stephen Foster's being away from the United States. It seemed a small matter as he turned it over in his mind, and young Foster had offered to take over the matter of the bond willingly enough, but Jim had not yet shaken off the idea that Newton was on the trip as his father's representative despite Stephen's assertion that he washed his hands of the affair. And he was not at all sure that the elder Foster wanted the trip to be made. Jim mentally shrugged off all complexities. The main fact was that they were going. It was up to him to see that they duly arrived. He had full confidence in himself to accomplish that.

The eighth day saw the *Seamew* passing out of the Golden Gate under her own power, heading south and west for her first leg of twenty-one hundred miles. The call at Honolulu Jim determined upon for several varying reasons. For the first, the diary log with the position of the *Golden Dolphin* island had been mailed there care of the Young Hotel, a precautionary measure that, to Jim, showed the ingenious wit of Kitty. While he had the figures well in his mind, it was vital that they should somewhere be set down in case of accident. They had been posted at Foxfield, and were now waiting in the island capital, carried by the mail steamer that had left the day they arrived in San Francisco.

They would take the opportunity to get fresh meats, ice for a day or two, fruit, water, gasoline, and sundry supplies. The stopover would take about twenty-four hours and there would be scant time for sightseeing if anyone wanted to do so. The important thing was to keep going, to clear up the dual mystery of Captain Whiting and his pearls as soon as possible. Probably the two women would want to do a little shopping; there would be letters to be mailed; perhaps Newton might have another cablegram to send.

The crew of the *Seamew* was made up as follows: James Lyman, captain; Joseph Baker, mate, a capable man of middle age whose chief lack seemed imagination, anxious for the job, with a family ashore, painstaking, reliable, a good navigator and familiar with South Seas work, discharged from a sugar bark from illness and since unable to gain a footing; Jared Sanders, engineer, a sandy-haired Scot who was a queer mixture of caution and desire for adventure, taking the trip purely for the latter reason, careful as to the quality and economic as to the price of his supplies, willing to act in general capacities when the engine was not needed; Emil Wiltz, steward, once assistant on a trans-Pacific liner, ousted from his job by the war, sick of being a waiter in cheaper restaurants, unable to get into the Waiters' Union and secure a better position, a handy, willing man; Olaf Neilson, Henrik Hamsun, Carl Vogt, three Norwegian sailors, stolid men with small initiative but powerful and willing, the first two recruited from Rickard, the third picked up on the water-front with two other sailors, out of work, out of money, out of tobacco, out of luck until Jim happened along, sized them up and offered them the job. These two were a Yankee named Henry Wood and a Britisher named William Walker, both undersized, underfed, inclined to cringe, the type that under a weak skipper and mate prove malingerers, yet seamen understanding their business, with Walker able to relieve Sanders at the engine upon occasion. These five, with the third original member of the *Seamew* crew, a redheaded Sinn Feiner, his name Douglas Moore, made up the six sailors Jim deemed necessary.

The cook proved a more difficult matter. Jim would have been content with ordinary cabin fare, but he wanted something better for the ladies. He interviewed a dozen possibilities and passed them up on the grounds of dirt, incompetence, and lack of sea-service. A seasick cook could not be contemplated. Disappointed at the last moment, he shipped a Greek who had come up from Honolulu as second cook on a steamship and was anxious to return. But he assured Jim there would be no difficulty in getting one at the latter port, and Jim, with the idea of a Chinaman in his head, was inclined to agree with him. Newton Foster, confessedly a novice, was more passenger than anything else, though avowing determination to acquire knowledge and ability.

The trade, that blows north instead of northeast down the California coast, struck them abeam as they laid their southwesterly course across the blue waters that seethed about the bows of the *Seamew*. Lyman was glad of every chance to save gasoline and the schooner justified the praise bestowed upon it by Rickard, reeling off ten knots hour after hour with a run of two hundred and twenty miles logged for the first day.

The weather was more kindly than obstructive. They used the engine less than fourteen hours on the entire trip. For two days only the wind was fitful. The twelfth morning, Jim on deck by sunrise, Baker in charge of the deck, Hamsun at the wheel, picked up the loom of Molokai. By mid-afternoon they had passed inspection and were anchored off Honolulu. While they were still gazing at the town, with its big modern buildings, substantial wharves, naval slips and green-lawned station, its old palace amid the palms with the chocolate colored cone of Punchbowl immediately behind, backed by the blue green splendors of Mount Tantalus, a reporter came alongside in a launch.

He got little from them save their names and the information that they were on a pleasure trip through the South Seas. Such voyages were nothing out of the ordinary these latter days; the reporter was polite but not particularly impressed and they escaped undue publicity. But a smart yawl which followed the reporter with the commodore of the Hawaii Yacht Club in the stern-sheets, his rowers two island yachtsmen, was not so easily dismissed. The commodore was intent upon doing the honors, anxious to save them trouble, eager to make things comfortable for the ladies. Almost by force the courteous Corinthian secured their promise to dinner at the Moana Hotel, promising to call for them in ample time, to take them to Waikiki in motors and to have his wife and other ladies present.

"You are making a trip we all envy you," he said, "You must allow us to give you *bon voyage*. Perhaps we can persuade you to stay over a while."

"When we come back," temporized Kitty. "We have our schedule all laid out to reserve some of the best for the way home." Jim did not go with them. He watched Newton array himself in dinner jacket and white flannels, in silk shirt and hose, in yachting cap and buckskin shoes, and he did not care to display his own rough serge and ducks and coarser shoes — less as a matter of self-pride than from a feeling that he would be a dull patch on a bright party. A dinner at the Moana, with the hints the commodore had thrown out of a Hawaiian orchestra and dancing to follow, was not in his line. Of one-steps and fox-trots Jim knew as little as he did of small talk or playing the ukulele. But he appreciated the look in Kitty's eyes when she heard he was not going. It was distinctly a look of disappointment.

"I wouldn't have accepted if I had known our skipper was not going," she said.

"The skipper has got plenty to do aboard if we are going to get away tomorrow," answered Jim.

Then the commodore arrived, in a launch this time, with ladies aboard who mounted to the deck of the *Seamew*, chatting and laughing with Kitty and Lynda and Newton. Jim was presented — and received as a superior sort of hired man, he told himself with a touch of bitterness for which he was duly ashamed, though the matter had been aggravated by hearing the gay laugh of Kitty coming back from the launch as it sped shorewards.

He went ashore himself, later on. There was really nothing for him to do aboard. He gave general shore leave, Walker volunteering to remain as ship-keeper.

"'Onolulu mykes me sick the w'y it is now," he said. "Hused to be a live plyce. You Hamericans 'ave fair spoiled it. Wot's the good of a bloomin' seaport wivout wine, wimmen an' song? W'ot charnce 'as a pore sailor got to get any of that 'ere? The Japs 'ave chivvied the natives out; the Hamericans 'ave took orl their money aw'y from them. Prohibishun 'as bloody well finished it. I'll stay aboard an' look at old Punchbowl. Bet they'll change the nyme of that to Teacup, afore they get through."

It was not Jim's first visit to the island. He walked to a square where the band was playing, taking a seat in the shadows under the palms. The bandstand alone was illuminated; the square was dusky, save where splotches of brilliant moonlight broke through the plumy foliage and laced the turf that was thickly set with clumps of hibiscus and crotons, here and there touching with silver a gown or the white drill of an escort.

The band played jazz and dreamy waltzes and at last crashed into Hawaii Ponoi. Jim started to stroll off, a lonely mood upon him. As he passed along a path close to the rail of the park, screened off by double hedges, broken now and then by spaces in which were seats facing toward the bandstand, he paused to light his pipe. With the burning match in his cupped hands, poised above the unlit tobacco, he forgot his smoke. Four men occupied a seat perhaps twelve feet away from him. They were talking earnestly in low tones, oblivious of the music and the crowd, intent upon their own purposes. Their backs were toward him. The arm of one lay along the back of the seat as its owner leaned forward emphasizing some point to his comrades. There was something about his bulk that was vaguely familiar to Lyman. A splash of moonlight lay along the cuff of the coat, exposing thick wrist and hand. The two last were hairy, with reddish, spidery furring. On the back of the hand was a tattoo mark of some kind, plain in the brilliant spot of the moonbeam. Jim's keen eyes were aided by sudden memory. The device, in indigo a little faded but visible enough, was a fouled anchor, with the rope continued to make a circle and frame to the design. It was the hand of Hellfire Swenson. Hellfire, whom Jim had last seen firing at him as he swam into the fog off Cuttyhunk, thousands of miles away!

It might have been the striking of his match — it all happened so swiftly — but a man's face turned toward him, the third man on the seat, not Swenson, whose arm remained in the same position. Out of the shadow Jim could see no more than an impression of a face with black moustaches and beard trimmed to a point. The blob of light on Swenson's hand was the only highlight and that vanished as the breeze swayed the long palm fronds above. But Jim, blowing out his match, realized that his own features had been clearly shown. When the dab of moonlight returned the tattooed hand had been removed, and the four men were talking together as if Jim was of no moment. For a pulse beat or two he paused, then walked on, lighting another match. He was quite sure this was Swenson. Who the others were he did not know. It would do him no good to confront him. If Swenson thought Jim had not recognized him it was just as well. It was possible that the black-bearded chap had not known who Jim was.

Jim turned and strolled back. The quartet were gone, vanished in the crowd breaking up after the concert, leaving only romantic couples.

Swenson's presence meant what? That he was still after the pearls? That Jim's dive from the rail had convinced him he had been given the wrong figures? He might have been so advised. Somehow Jim connected his appearance with the cablegram sent from San Francisco. Was Swenson trailing the *Seamew* in his own schooner, foiled through Kitty Whiting's cleverness at having kept the diary in her safe and later mailing it ahead to Honolulu? There was no schooner in Honolulu Harbor that answered to Swenson's vessel.

For Jim to attempt to interfere with Swenson on account of what happened at Buzzards Bay was, as Stephen Foster had pointed out, only provocative of unwanted publicity. The authorities of Hawaii might well excuse themselves from jurisdiction. Probably would. But Hellfire had some schemes on hand that must be blocked. That was certain. He would hardly attempt more kidnapping, or appear openly in any endeavor to obtain the figures. Back on the mainland he appeared to have affiliations and some power, wide reaching and effective, doubtless tied up with his illicit liquor enterprises. On the island of Oahu he could not carry out his plans with such ease. That Hellfire, given the opportunity, would not stop short of piracy in the hope of a fortune, Jim was very sure. Nor would piracy stop him.

At present the pearls were doubly guarded, by the position of the island and by the lack of knowledge of the secret hiding-place aboard the stranded ship. Kitty Whiting alone held that key. Jim doubted whether even Lynda Warner knew where the hiding-place was. Kitty's pretty head held wisdom and caution. So long as she was protected, all was well. After this, Jim resolved to play bodyguard no matter how awkward he might feel in certain situations.

He decided to say nothing about Swenson. He could make inquiry as to whether a power schooner had lately entered the port. He did not know the name, but it was not likely that more than one of her type would have come in within the past three weeks, though it was likely that Swenson, if appearing as her captain, would have changed his name.

As he walked back toward the waterfront Jim began to wonder if he might have been mistaken. He had seen such devices before. The ordinary tattooer at such ports as Honolulu, San Francisco or Shanghai had stock devices from which his customers chose. Duplication was frequent. Jim had not actually seen Swenson's face. Perhaps he was developing nerves — on the girl's account.

The men had orders not to spend the night ashore. Some of them were back when Jim returned to the *Seamew* at five bells. All were aboard by seven bells. Neilson and Wood had the anchor watch; the rest had turned in. Jim, smoking, pacing the deck, waited. Midnight sounded, the sharp strokes of ships' bells in a mingled chime all about the harbor. One bell at last, and then a launch put off from shore. Jim ordered Neilson and Wood to stand by the ladder and effaced himself in the shadow. He saw the figures of the two women come overside and go below after laughing good-nights. There was no sign of Newton. Jim went to the rail and saw him in the light that came from the cabin of the launch. He was in the cockpit aft with another man both smoking cigarettes. His face was flushed and boyishly eager. Jim called down to him.

"I'm not coming aboard, Skipper. Pst!" he answered, standing up while a man in the launch held on to the companion side-ladder of the *Seamew*. "Better come along. There's a native hula on out Diamond Head way. Given for a special blowout. Some old-time chief's birthday. Wouldn't miss it for worlds. Not for ladies, of course, but you don't often see one nowadays. Come along, Skipper. My bid extends to him, eh, chaps?"

One of the local yachtsmen heartily extended the invitation. The ladies of the commodore's party were in the launch's cabin out of hearing. The affair was evidently considered notable. Jim did not feel in the mood for it, but he could understand Newton's eagerness. He'd be no use the next day for anything but sleep, but that would not affect the work aboard. As a sailor, Newton Foster was so far more of a nuisance than an aid. His main asset was spasmodic willingness.

"Don't get lost in the jungle," Jim returned. "I'm obliged, but I've got a lot on hand. Hope to get out of here close to noon. Good night."

The launch backed off, turned and sped for shore. Jim descended to find the main cabin empty, and he turned in. At five he was on deck again. Baker, the conscientious mate, was up and the men were swashing and swabbing deck. Neilson and Wood were in their bunks. The smell of early coffee was in the air. Davos, the Greek, was cooking his last meal aboard. Jim had tried the door of Newton's cabin as he passed. It was unlocked, the bunk empty. He gave an order to preserve quiet on deck. He would let the women sleep until later, though he wanted to get them ashore as early as possible to clear up their errands. He had determined on one thing during the night. To have a talk with Lynda Warner concerning his own suspicions, past and present, of the Fosters, the matter of the cablegram and of Swenson's appearance. He was sure of her commonsense and judgment and her friendly feeling toward him. He would put the question up to her as how much should be told Kitty Whiting. As the head of the enterprise, the one vitally interested, Jim felt that perhaps she should be informed of matters that he doubted whether it would be politic for him to mention.

He went aft to the galley and got a cup of coffee. The tide was flooding, the stern of the *Seamew* had swung toward the land. Jim saw a shore boat approaching, propelled by an ancient Hawaiian, gray-headed, his shoulders covered with flower leis. In the stern were three figures, intertwined, wearing black coats and white trousers, all jovial, friendly to all the wide world, singing a quasi-native song with more spirit than harmony. Here came Newton Foster with two of his companions of the night before! Jim called through the hollow of his hands.

"Tone down a bit there. Ladies asleep!" The trio stared at him half stupidly as the boat came alongside, but they stopped singing. Newton arose, swaying uncertainly while the others supported him none too efficiently.

"'S all ri', Skip. Trifle hilarious as effect of circum-circumventing the Eighteenth 'mendment. Yesh, sir. Native juice of the vine, squeezed from the root of the *ti* plant. Am I ri', fellers? Sounds mixed but the stuff is prime. *Maiti nui*. Thash Hawaiian for heap good, Skip! I learned a lot las' ni'. Wouldn't have missed it for worldsh. No, shir. Wonnerful hos — hos — hoshpitality. Glorioush time. Goo' ni'. I mean goo' mornin'."

He started to sing again at the top of the sideladder, but Jim grabbed him by the arm and he gathered himself together.

"Thash ri'. Mushn't wake the ladiesh. Skip', pu' me to bed an' lemme sleep."

Jim got him below, got his pajamas on him and turned him into his bunk where he promptly composed himself for sleep after insisting that his wreaths be placed about his neck.

"Emblems of love an' frenship, Skip, Everlashtin' tokens of glorioush hoshpitality. Goo' ni'! God bless you, Skip. You ought t' have been along. Goo' ni'." Jim left him snoring stertorously.

At the eight o'clock breakfast he excused Newton, stating the bald truth that he had returned late and needed sleep.

"I heard him come aboard," said Lynda Warner with a twinkle in her eyes, but no further remarks, confirming herself to Jim as a good sport. After the meal, while Kitty wrote a letter she had overlooked, Jim had his talk with Lynda Warner.

"You don't think very highly of Stephen Foster, I believe," he started.

"What makes you think so?"

He told her frankly.

"I think that he is cold-blooded and unscrupulous in business," she said. "In many things he would take great pains to do what he considered the exactly just thing. I do not think him generous. And I have known him not entirely selfish. He thinks the world of Newton. Newton himself does not strike me as a natural conspirator."

"H'm" said Jim. Lynda had not given him a wide opening. "Do you think Stephen Foster considers this trip a business matter?"

She looked at him with shrewd approval. "Absolutely so," she answered.

Then he told her his news while she listened carefully.

"I do not see any good in mentioning this to Kitty," she answered. "Much of it is suspicion, and suspicion against people who are closely connected to her. Newton is her blood relative. It might not help your standing with her. You have nothing really definite. If that was Swenson it means only that we must be doubly careful. You see, Jim —" she laid her hand on his arm as she spoke his personal name for the first time, "you see, Kitty thinks of nothing but her father. Anything else is superficial, as superficial as the affair of that dinner and dance last night. To which you should have come — clothes or no clothes.

"As for the cable, I know that Stephen Foster sometimes goes to Cuba. He has heavy interests there in sugar. So that may clear Newton up. I don't see how anyone is going to get those figures. We sha'n't have a chance to mail them ahead to Fiji, I understand. Swenson may be tricky and desperate in his methods, but he can hardly come aboard and take the diary by force. Just what are you most afraid of?"

"If it was Swenson, he must either hope to get hold of the figures or he will have to trail us. If he could manage to do that I have no doubt but that he would try to capture the pearls, after we had secured them from the *Golden Dolphin*. What we have got to do is to keep him from getting the position, and to shake him off if he attempts to follow. Once we get down there we are first going to try to find Captain Whiting, though I can't help but be doubtful over the outcome of that. If Swenson makes an attack, providing he discovers us, then we must hold him off. Those are risks you should not be subjected to, but I suppose there is no use trying to dissuade Miss Kitty."

"Not in the least. Nor me. We are well armed. So far we haven't practiced with the weapons. Why not do it from now on? Here comes Kitty. I'm glad we had this talk. Are we all going ashore together? I don't mean Newton. As I said, I heard him come aboard."

Next to the shipping commissioner's office on the Honolulu waterfront there is — or was — an agency for the employment of sailing men. Once it was notorious for its connection with the sailors' boarding house of Lewis & Turk, a pair of thugs who made their living by shanghaiing beachcombers and others unfortunate enough to get into their clutches or within reach of their blackjacks and brass knuckles. Prohibition has done more than any law to do away with the crimping game. Liquor was the bait and the drug of waterfront victims. Nowadays the employment agency is conducted on a most respectable basis. There you may obtain names and get in touch with all available mariners; even mates registering. Captain, cook or cabin boy, steward, supercargo, sailor, engineer or boat-steerer, if there are any available Renny & Green, now occupying the abandoned premises of Lewis & Turk, will fill your needs.

When Jim stated his need of a cook, the clerk took him up, asking the length of voyage, number of passengers and crew, list of duties, wages, etc., marking them all down on a form.

"Chinaman?" he asked.

"Preferred."

"One in this morning. Good man. Been a restaurant cook. A bit of a highflier, is Li Cheng. But a good cook and I imagine it's because he has been skinned at fan-tan that he wants a job where he'll have to save up till he's got another stake."

"Seasick?"

"Oh, he's cooked aboard ship before this."

"You know him? Character all right? We've got ladies aboard."

"Know him ever since I've been here. They say Li Cheng was in the opium ring, but that was long ago before the U. S. took over the place and burned up all the pipes and dumped the confiscated opium into the bay."

"I've heard about that," said Jim. "Some say they dumped molasses instead of opium." The clerk grinned.

"I guess Li Cheng's character is good enough. You're not going to tempt him, are you?" Both laughed. "I'll have him in for you inside of half an hour," said the clerk. "You can look him over."

"He'll have to start in right away. We sail this afternoon. Any one else in view in case he doesn't show?"

"He'll show. Needs a job badly, he said. 'Too muchy bloke.' He'll go. And I haven't got any one nearly as good."

Jim did some marketing and saw the stuff carried down to the boat landing by Hamsun and Vogt, brought ashore for that purpose. He needed a little gasoline but took enough to fill up his tank. The water tender was already alongside the *Seamew*.

He returned to interview Li Cheng. The wisest of white men can tell but little about a yellow man until he tests him. Li Cheng was elderly. He was cueless and there were gray hairs among the black, He might have been fifty or seventy, with his comparatively unwrinkled skin and black eyes with their unfolding eyelids that seemed to open like the top of a roller desk.

"Can do," he said. "Me topside cook. Pastly, hot blead, hot biscuit. Good chow. Make up salad, number one salad, fine coffee. Suppose I catch up fifty dolla every month, fifty dolla gold, I go."

"That's pretty high."

"*Maskee*," answered Li Cheng indifferently. "I like go sea becos I no spend. Make um stake. *Maskee*. Suppose you no pay can catch plenty job soon. Topside cook I belong."

"Wages are up," said the clerk, to Jim's inquiring glance.

"I'll sign you," said Jim. "Come in to the commissioner's."

After signing on Li Cheng went uptown again for his kit, promising to be aboard within the hour and to have tiffin ready. Jim had one more errand. At the office of the Collector of the Port. That official's records showed nothing of any vessel's entry that remotely resembled a power schooner. Jim's belief that Swenson had sailed by way of Panama to circumvent and follow them faded, to his relief.

He found the ladies aboard the *Seamew*, their shopping done, anxious to start. Newton still slept off his potations. Li Cheng came off in a shore skiff, bringing his belongings and a pet monkey.

"You no care?" he asked. "Velly fond of pets. No *pilikia* this *kekko*," he said. "Keep him along galley. Make fun for sailor." Kitty Whiting fell in love with the monkey and made friends with it immediately, Li Cheng looking on with a broad smile.

"Plenty *akamai*, that *kekko*," he said. "Heap smart monkey."

They made clearance, yanking the anchor from the stiff mud of the harbor bottom, out through the buoyed channel through the reef, getting a farewell wave from the old keeper of the reef-lighthouse, out past the bell-buoy and then, with the northeast trade blowing fresh and free as the *Seamew* out-swung her booms, they headed straight out into the blue, sparkling sea. There was nothing ahead of them until they reached the equator, save Johnson Island, a barren lift of coral rock and sand that they most likely would not even sight.

The seas ran crisp, the wind blowing off their curling crests like powder. The water was a most intense blue. For all its action it held the apparent hardness of glass, or of a jewel with a myriad facets flinging back the brilliance of the sun. To the north sailed great billows of cloud out of which blew the breeze. In the southeast the other islands of the group swam in a luminous haze, darker blue than the sea, with a hint of green here and there, and on far off Hawaii shore the gleam of snow on Mauna Kea and Mauna Loa, their summits nearly fourteen thousand feet above sea level. Behind Lanari rose the high dome of Maui's extinct crater. Sea gulls and bosun birds had escorted them out to sea. The air seemed charged with vigor; the day one of good omen. Kitty stood in the bows, cuddling Li Cheng's monkey, gazing far ahead, a little anxious frown between her eyes. It seemed to Jim that she was striving to find some hope back of that luminous horizon, as if a little dread was beginning to dilute her confidence that she would find her father.

Baker touched Jim on the arm, pointing south and east to where, on a course parallel with their own, a white fleck showed. Jim took the powerful glass and focused it on that stiffly upstanding speck, watching it for long minutes. It was undoubtedly a schooner, well down to lee-ward, bound on their own course, an unusual one for vessels. It might be a South Sea trader, though not many came to the Hawaiian Group, save on some rare trip to San Francisco. The nearest group ahead was the Phoenix Islands, just below the line, nearly five hundred marine leagues away. Jim handed back the binoculars to the mate with a face he tried to make untroubled.

"Schooner. Going our way, it seems," he said. "We'll make a race of it."

"We've got a good start to wind'ard," remarked Baker. "She'll have come out of Hilo, I'm thinking, through the Alenuihana Channel, likely. Been back of Kahoolawe until just now. Current setting her down. Ah, she's tacking."

"We'll run off a bit and take a closer look at her," said Jim. Baker said nothing. The maneuver would be a waste of time, but if the skipper wanted to get a nearer view of every stray sail, that was none of the mate's business. The sheets came in as Jim gave the order and Hamsun spun the wheel. The *Seamew* came round like a teetotum, heeled to the breeze that sent her reaching, fast closing up the distance to the stranger, sailing now toward them on the same point, though on the opposite tack. Jim did not analyze the impulse that caused him to run out of his way, even for a few miles to leeward. He had set his mind to make all possible speed, yet he felt he could not be satisfied until he had come close enough to see the rig of the fast approaching schooner.

It was still possible that she was merely an inter-island boat making the trip from Hilo to one of the other islands. If she was bound for Kauai, northernmost of the Hawaiian group, she would not, since she had tacked as she did, be much out of her course. Somehow he believed that this was not so. Without anything definite to go on he linked up the schooner with Swenson.

Kitty came toward him, saying nothing, but sailor enough to know they had changed their course. She caught sight of the sail. The two schooners were slashing through the seas toward each other at about their best rate of speed; already on the *Seamew* they could see the lift of the other's white hull as she breasted the seas, making easy work of it. Baker came up again, glass in hand.

"There's a big launch coming like a skipjack," he said. "Either she's after us or out to meet this other chap. Wouldn't be so far off land on her own hook, not a launch."

Jim knew, without further confirmation, that Swenson was in the launch that was tearing along at a furious clip, shattering the seas she charged, half smothered in smoky spray. She was a double-ender, built for island work. As she came on she rolled like a porpoise, showing her bilge heels as she flung herself forward. He got the glass on the advancing schooner once more. She was of the same type as the *Seamew*, a Gloucester fisherman model, unmistakable as she was alien to those waters. There was no need to go closer, but Jim held on. He wanted to read her name, to see the transshipment from the launch. Then, if he was right, if Swenson was trailing the *Seamew*, there would be an even start to the race and he exulted in the belief that the *Seamew* was the better boat of the two, and that he, as its captain, would show Hellfire that there are more ways than one of being lost at sea. Swenson might know, or guess, that they were bound for Fiji. Jim resolved to make Suva first and get away before Swenson showed. The only thing that surprised him was Swenson's willingness to declare himself by leaving at practically the same hour. He must have ordered his schooner to weigh anchor at Hilo early that morning, using the inter-island wireless, and then waited for the *Seamew* to clear before he took the launch to meet his own boat; and he must have reckoned that the chances were all in favor of his being noticed. The maneuvering of the *Seamew* showed unmistakably that the folks aboard her were curious, if not suspicious.

Lynda Warner joined Kitty. Jim wondered what had passed between them about Swenson, if anything. He had said nothing further to Lynda, but it was very plain that the women had a mutual understanding and that they had agreed to ask no questions. It might be feminine intuition; it might be sheer wisdom, but Jim appreciated it. He did not care for Baker or any of the crew to suppose that they were bound on any but a pleasure trip. Later they must know of the search for Captain Avery Whiting; they would be wondering at the stranded hull of the *Golden Dolphin*, but there would be no necessity for letting them know anything about the pearls. If they were in their hiding-place they could be taken out quietly and never referred to. He could understand trouble arising among men who knew they were on a ship that contained a fortune, won by comparative ease, all destined for the lucky one or two, while they got nothing but seamen's wages and seamen's work, hard and exacting. So it must have been with the *Golden Dolphin*, even if the seeds of mutiny had not been sown beforehand.

Now the two schooners were less than half a mile apart, lunging on, almost abeam, a beautiful sight as the wind drove them and the lift of the seas cushioned them on their own buoyancy. Now he could see a name on the bows, letters of metal that glistened in the sun, a short word — *Shark*. A fitting title for a ship run by Swenson.

The launch came on, buffeting the seas. Suddenly the *Shark* shot into the wind, hung there with sails shivering, peaks lowered, rising and falling until from the *Seamew* they could see all the length of her deck with men scattered upon it. Through the glass Jim caught details that the rest could not. The launch came alongside, tossing. Bumpers were flung out. A big man, lithe and active, sprang for the schooner's rail from the lesser freeboard of the launch, caught at the main rigging, jumped down on deck.

He took off his visored cap and wiped his face with the back of his hand as if to clear off spray. Jim caught the shine of a bald dome, a tonsure of red hair. Immediately he handed the glass to Baker and shouted an order. The wheel of the *Seamew* went up; the men sprang to ease out the sheets as she came about. The sails filled and once more she ran before the wind, southwest by five points west, her wake streaming out behind. Smartly too the *Shark* came surging on. The launch turned and went lunging back toward Oahu.

With a glance aft Jim went to the head of the companionway, following Kitty and Lynda down into the main cabin.

"It was Swenson?" asked Kitty.

"Yes. Trailing us. Pretty openly. If he figures he can keep us in sight night and day from here to the island he's going to be mistaken."

"Swenson?" Newton Foster spoke. He had evidently just made his appearance. Behind him stood Cheng, with coffee on a tray. Wiltz was making up the staterooms, not supposed to bother with extra service between meals. "What about Swenson?" Jim did not answer, glancing at Cheng, whose face showed no interest as he set down the tray and left.

"Swenson has just come out in a launch and joined his schooner, the *Shark*," said Jim briefly. "I think the schooner came out from Hilo. That would account for my not finding it entered at Honolulu. I saw Swenson in Honolulu last night. At least I thought it was he. Now I know. He hasn't been able to get hold of our figures so he's taking a try at following. We've got to shake him off. I don't quite understand his tipping his hand so early. He must know we've recognized him. We'll lose him between here and Suva. If we can't out-sail him we'll dodge him some night. And we'll lose him if he doesn't guess we're putting in at Suva. We'll be there a day or two."

"Do we *have* to call there?"

Jim nodded.

"We'll need gasoline, fresh provisions, water. We might get that at Apia. But Samoa's out of our way. I want to get some native boys. We'll need them for several reasons — bush work and landings. We can't get along without natives and Samoa is not easy to recruit from. Why?"

He had sensed a reason back of Newton's remark.

"Just wondering. I've got a horrible head on me." Newton essayed a smile of frank confession, but groaned and held his head with hands as if to prevent it splitting. "They had some native liquor last night. Had me going in no time. That's the worst of prohibition. A chap gets all out of shape for taking a drink when he travels. Good stuff, but regular bottled lightning." He shuddered, pushed away the coffee and tackled a cigarette.

"I'll take a stroll on deck," he said. "Fresh air may help."

As he passed to the companionway he gave Jim a meaning look. Jim followed him. Newton went aft to the taffrail, gazing at the *Shark* throwing up a smother of spray as she came on, down to leeward a little, but holding up as close to the wind as the *Seamew*.

"So that's Swenson and his schooner. Gaining any?"

"I think not," said Jim. "He wouldn't want to pass up. He's doing his best, I fancy. Want to speak to me, Newton?"

"Yes." Young Foster threw his cigarette into the wake, turned and faced Jim Lyman squarely. In that moment Jim liked him better than he had done at any time. Yet he guessed that Foster had a confession to make, and that it was tied up with Swenson.

"I made a damned fool of myself last night," said Newton. "I have hit the hooch once in a while, Lyman — but that native stuff got me. They had plenty of it, and at first it don't seem to affect you. There was a crowd there. Seemed as if everyone in Honolulu was invited. Lots there who didn't know each other or even the host, a fine old chap. Open house, like the old days. Must have cost a mint. Well, there was singing and dancing — poker going on — flowers for everyone, all sorts of weird things to eat. Heaps of regular grub, too. Everything informal. Everybody laughing and talking like old friends. Partly hooch, of course.

"I told 'em, some of 'em — I didn't meet everyone, of course — that we were on a South Sea cruise. That seemed to put me in solid. I didn't say anything about what we were after — at least I don't think I did. But I talked too much; I realized that, and pulled up. I was with a bunch of chaps who seemed interested. The fellows I went with, the yachtsmen, you know, wandered off. They knew a lot of people and they saw I was having a good time. This bunch seemed to know a lot about the islands, told me a lot of yarns. There was one chap who was a bit nosey. Said he'd noticed the *Seamew*. Wanted to know about Kitty and Lynda. Just nosey, I thought. But I didn't enlighten him about them, I think it was that made me shut up. I went off hunting the chaps I'd come with. But I remember telling them we were going to Suva and then on down south to an island we knew about. Some blithering idiot, I know."

"What did the man look like?"

"Oh, it wasn't Swenson. You said he was big and red-headed where he wasn't bald. Swenson wasn't there at all, that I saw. This chap was lanky with a sharp face like a fox. Black eyes. Clipped moustache and a black beard trimmed Vandyke."

The face that he had dimly seen in the dark, turning toward him from the park bench, flashed before Jim's mind.

"Asked you where the island was, did he?"

"Yes, But of course I couldn't tell him that. But he knows we're going to Suva. Do you suppose — ? You said you saw Swenson last night."

"Do I suppose this man was a pal of Swenson's? I do. If I am not very much mistaken I saw them together, long before you first came off. They probably went out to the affair later. Swenson may have stayed away. Meeting you there was a bit of luck for them."

"I'm mighty sorry, Lyman."

"It's all right. No use in saying anything about it. I don't know that there's much harm done. They'll try to trail us from Suva, that's all, and they'll make a race of it from here. They'll try and keep us in sight in case we take a notion to change our course. I'm glad you told me, Newton."

They shook hands, and with the grip Jim's suspicions of Newton Foster disappeared. His confession had been too ingenuous, too unnecessary for any attempt at acting. And no actor could have emulated Newton's expression of regret and self-contempt.

As the day passed it became evident that the two schooners were evenly matched. It was tested out before and on the wind. There was not a cable's length of difference per hour in the speed. They shared the same wind, they might have been built from the same design. Their footage of canvas seemed equal. With the brilliant tropic moonlight nights ahead it wasn't going to be such a simple matter for them to part company as it might seem to a layman. Of course there was always luck at sea. Jim realized that. He had seen wind in the equatorial doldrums fail for weeks at a time; or a squall thrash the sea in one area while a ship a mile away might lie becalmed. But in the present case both had engines. One must be faster than the other. Dark nights would help and they could count on them with the waning moon. Or a storm. But there was no use bothering about such matters until after Suva.

Newton, by his indiscretions, had accomplished one thing. Without doubt the chap with the pointed beard, Swenson's mate possibly, had pumped him dry, and such information would take in the personnel of the *Seamew* and the principal fact that they had plenty of arms aboard. Swenson would weigh the chances of forcible boarding and seizure, Jim was certain. The man was an unprincipled pirate. Without doubt he had already weighed them and decided that it was not worth while. So, for the time being, it resolved itself into a race to Suva.

And they raced every foot of the way, with both crews on the jump to make the constant changes called for, swaying up, hauling in, changing headsails. Jim took only catnaps. Baker was a good man but slow, content to move after he saw that he was being overhauled, lacking initiative, lacking the instinct that Lyman owned for getting the best out of the *Seamew*. For three days and three nights the schooners were never more than a sea mile apart. Both sailed wing-and-wing with booms stayed out. Jim rigged a squaresail on his foremast to offset a big balloner spread by Swenson. For the seventy-two hours they never split tacks. Five times during the night the *Seamew* swung off on a new course, showing no lights, the *Shark*, only a dark shadow flitting over the seas, sometimes to windward, sometimes to leeward, never ahead, hanging on like a hound on scent. Five times the lookout on the *Shark* saw the maneuver and the *Shark* followed suit with gleam of the waning moon turning her sails to glints of mother-of-pearl.

The log of the *Seamew* registered seven hundred and twenty-four miles of sailing. Over a fourth of their distance between Honolulu and Suva. Then the wind grew fitful, the weather, hazy. There were gaps when the breeze seemed to have died altogether, leaving bald spots on the sea. The schooner would come slashing along at ten knots, eleven perhaps, and slide into the becalmed area like a skater suddenly striking soft slush, all speed snatched away instantly. Or a rain squall swept down enveloping her in a downpour that vanished as suddenly as it had come, leaving her with canvas taut, stays and halyards tight as fiddle strings. Meeting with these was purely a question of chance, and luck seemed with the *Seamew*. On the evening of the fourth day she had gained a full sea league on the *Shark* and the sun sank in a mist that veiled the already risen moon.

"If we get wind," said Jim, "we'll dodge her before this clears. If there's no wind we'll start the engine. Sanders has been bothering me to do it all day, but it hasn't seemed worth while. I look for uncertain weather from now on. The closer we get to the line at this time of year, when the southeast trade fights the northeast, the less likelihood there is of any wind to speak of. Ships have knocked about for weeks trying to cross the equatorial belt. We'll plug along at eight knots and trust in the engine. What wind we do strike is likely to come from any quarter. It's a toss-up for both of us."

The sun went down crimson; the moon appeared like a fire-balloon without reflecting power; the *Shark* was swallowed up in the dusk. Sanders, with his engine oiled up and overhauled, turned it over and the screw revoked steadily, the schooner pulsing to the drive of the shaft. Jim changed his course to five points more easting. Sanders' confidence in his "power" proved to be well founded. With Walker spelling him, the pistons never missed a stroke. Dawn came clear with an empty horizon. Jim went to his main spreaders with a glass to make certain, and came down exultant. They might meet the *Shark* at Suva but it had been demonstrated once that they could lose Swenson and it could be done again.

It was almost unbearably hot, with the glassy sea and the sky like a bowl of metal reflecting the heat of the fiery, intolerable sphere of the sun. The *Seamew* reeked of hot oil. The slightest movement brought on a flood of perspiration. Conversation languished; effort died. The sailors had little to do and kept the decks wetted down. This prevented the putty crumbling in the seams and cooled the cabin a trifle. All unnecessary raiment was discarded. Kitty and Lynda kept to their staterooms most of the time. There was a slight general revival at nightfall. Plans for practicing with the weapons faltered, were put off. No fish broke the surface; no far-wandering seabird showed against the fleckless sky. It was a painted ocean that they crossed, but the schooner, thanks to gasoline, was not an idle, painted ship. The engine seemed to pant and labor, but the screw kept turning, every revolution lessening the period of discomfort through which they must pass.

They crossed the line at the hundred-and-seventy-first meridian. Jim Lyman announced the fact without provoking any especial interest or enthusiasm. There was no suggestion of any initiation of crossing the line. All animal spirits were at a low ebb. Even Cheng's monkey was content to hunt the shade. The sea divided at the bows in oily ripples. Some sharks made their appearance, their dorsals streaking the surface and their bodies visible as they sculled themselves along keeping pace with the schooner. Just before sunset a filmy speck showed on the eastern horizon. The *Shark* had picked them up again. But it had vanished by morning.

Still under power, the gasoline getting low in the tank, they passed to the eastward of the Phoenix Group, barely sighting Phoenix and Sydney Islands. The south equatorial current gave them westing and a clear run lay ahead past Samoa down to the Goro Sea and Fiji. Two hundred and fifty miles south of the line they ran into the southeast trades, a steady river of wind flowing just aft the beam and speeding them along mile after mile at top speed. Every one revived. Sanders and Walker turned idlers for a well earned lest. The rifles were got out and the automatic pistols; targets were rigged at the rail or floating alongside as their marksmanship improved. Sanders proved easily the best marksman among them, excepting Cheng, who only shot once but displayed an accuracy with an automatic that was uncanny. Three shots running pierced the bull of a stationary target, four others hit and smashed three floating bottles as they rushed past the swiftly moving boat, bobbing in the run. Kitty Whiting made good progress; Lyman showed himself a fair shot with a rifle, and a better with the pistol. Newton about equaled his performances. Lynda Warner predeclared her inability to fire without closing both eyes at once or to hit anything smaller than a barn door — and lived up to it. Moore shot well but erratically; the others gained familiarity with their weapons, if nothing more. It was not an ideal shooting gallery, a slanting deck on a plunging ship where even the fixed targets pitched unexpectedly and the floaters raced away at a baffling rate. Finally they devised a can painted white and towed.

Li Cheng appeared as a treasure of the first magnitude. Through the intensest heat he suffered least, despite his handicap of working in the galley, and he managed to devise meals that coaxed the most languid of appetites. He was a prime favorite with the men, always jovial, taking their fun in good part, coming back with quaint quips in his pidgin English, winning, not merely their respect, but their confidence. The only two who did not get along with Cheng were Walker and Wiltz. Sanders had little to do with him.

"'E's a Chink," said Walker. "I'm palling with no bloody heathen Chinee." Wiltz's complaint was also largely racial.

"He's a yellow man and he's treacherous. They are a nation of pirates. He's a good cook and that lets him out." There was no open hostility between steward and cook, which was just as well. Cheng smiled on Wiltz as on the rest and showed no offense at the steward's attitude of tolerance. But he undoubtedly was responsible for the attitude of the crew. The three Norsemen had been apt to hang aloof, stolid if efficient. Now all hands went about as if they shared a perpetual joke that never lost its zest and they worked with a will.

"They're too good to be true," said Baker, the mate. "But Cheng is a wonder."

Three days out of Suva, Wiltz sent for Lyman, who found him groaning in his bunk with complaint of dysentery.

"It's that yellow cook," he said, his face shining with sweat on a pallid skin. "He's poisoned me. I know it. Oh, my God!" He writhed with sudden cramps. "I got a cup of coffee out of the pot, as I always do. He knows my custom, sir. The pot's on the galley stove and I help myself to a cup at six bells every morning, regular. At seven bells it took me. I'll be a dead man before night. Skipper, I want to have you write down some things for me. I —" He writhed again. Lyman had seen sick men before. He had a medicine chest aboard and he had prescribed for many sailors. He knew the propensity of a sick sailorman to believe himself fatally ill; he added to that Wiltz's prejudice against Cheng. He took the steward's temperature — not very serious — felt his pulse, consulted his Captain's Handibook. Then he interviewed Cheng.

"Wha' malla that steward?" demanded Cheng, smiling, "All time he come along my galley, take coffee. That all lightee. All same evelly steward I sabe. That coffee topside coffee. I dlink myself light after he go. His trubble he eat too much, all day long he pick-pick this an' that. He too fat that steward. Now he got trubble in his belly."

"He's too sick to wait on the table, Cheng. Or to clean up. Got to stay in his bunk. Why don't you tell him to keep out of your galley. I'll suggest it to him myself as soon as he is better." Jim had noticed the steward's growing tendency toward a rounding port and his habit of eating almost continuously between meals — if he had regular meals at all. He was inclined to accept Cheng's diagnosis of the cause.

"Too gleedy, that man," summed up Cheng. "Suppose he stay sick I wait on table all lightee for day or two. I fixee cabin. Can do."

This he did with speed and neatness while Wiltz groaned in his bunk, refusing to believe himself better. Cheng was almost over-zealous, it appeared. Kitty came to Jim, Lynda beside her.

"Cheng tells me Wiltz is sick and he is to do his work," she said. "You didn't tell me anything about it."

"I really haven't had the chance," said Jim. "Why? Do you object?"

"No. Cheng's splendid. Better than Wiltz. But you see Lynda and I have always taken care of our own cabins. Cheng wouldn't know that. I found him in mine when I came back from Lynda's room. I have been keeping your little log beneath my mattresses since we left Honolulu. Wiltz never has come into our rooms. In fact, I have always kept mine locked whenever I went out of it, even for a minute. But it seems there was a master key and Wiltz had it on his key ring. Cheng got his keys, and I found he had made up my bunk and straightened the room. He had done it in almost no time, and as well as any chambermaid. The log was on the stand beside the bunk. Cheng told me he had turned the mattresses with an air of just pride. 'This I find, missy,' he said. 'Maybe you lose?' Now what do you think? Did Cheng know what the log was? Did he look into it? What can we do about it? Lynda says, 'Nothing'."

"I don't know what can be done," said Lyman. "I have been plastering every incident with suspicion ever since I was knocked on the head. Sometimes I have had cause; sometimes I have been ashamed of myself."

"It would be no use to question Cheng, I suppose."

"It would make him sore if he was merely doing his best, as I am inclined to think. If there was anything underhanded about it you could never get it out of him. Besides, Wiltz, with his master key, has always had the same opportunity of search. We suspect Cheng because you found him there, and he had a perfectly legitimate excuse. Wouldn't he have put the book back? None of the crew know anything about what we are after."

"I am sure Wiltz was never in my room." Baker came below at the moment and the matter ended. Jim thought once or twice of Wiltz's charge against Cheng of poisoning, but the steward was so obviously better that he dismissed it and on the third morning Wiltz was up and about.

At Suva there was no sign of the *Shark*. No such vessel had entered, and Jim hurried to get his native addition to the crew. As he had told Newton, he wanted them for bush work. To find trace of Captain Whiting, to satisfy his daughter, they would have to search the island and one native was worth five white men at making trail. There might be landings to make where the reefs were dangerous, and for that work they were absolutely necessary. Back of all that Jim Lyman had another idea. He believed it possible, without an inordinate amount of effort, to get the *Golden Dolphin* back to deep water, first to the lagoon, then out through the reef. If the channel needed widening he had brought dynamite along, and there again the natives would be wanted for diving and placing the cartridges. He fancied his first observations were correct, now that he knew positively what a short time — comparatively — the vessel had been ashore; and that she was not materially injured by shock or later decay. He had a quick eye for the lay of the land and he thought that the *Golden Dolphin* now lay couched on a jungle bed at no great height above the flood level of the lagoon. If it could be done — and he had his plans for an inexpensive experiment — the salvage would cover all cost of the trip and over and over again. The model had not been included in the sale of the antique shop; it was now ensconced in the cabin of the *Seamew* and Jim had often visualized the original ship back in her element. There was enough spare canvas in the stores for effective jury rigging. He had included special sized hawsers for use in the outhaul, using them meanwhile for duty aboard the schooner.

It took three days of feverish work to stir up the British officials, to get the right natives, take them before the commissioner, secure the necessary permission and put up the requisite securities. But it was done at last, the *Seamew* revictualled, and still there was no sign of the *Shark*. It looked as if they had outwitted Swenson or some good chance for them — evil for him and his schemes — had delayed him. The crew had a run ashore, Cheng lost his monkey the first day and came back late and apologetic for having skipped a meal.

"That damn *kekko* he lun away," he explained. "I have one hell of time find him. I speak him nex' time he go, by golly, I cut off his tail an' make him all same *kanaka*." As almost everyone had lunched ashore, Cheng and his *kekko* were assured of pardon. All hands were glad to see the monkey aboard again with his mischievous but generally harmless capers.

VII

Suva behind them at last, they faced a final run of fourteen hundred miles, a feverish week of hope and uncertainty. Kitty Whiting faced the issue with glowing expectancy and confidence. It was plain that no thought of failure ever entered her head and Jim prayed, against his own convictions, that her faith might not be betrayed. It should not if he could prevent it, he vowed. By now he was self-confessedly in love with her, and however hopeless his cause he knew that there would never be for him any other girl.

That Newton Foster was heels over head in love was also patent. Kitty would stand in the bows hour after hour, looking with yearning glances, with lips half-parted, at the far horizon. And Foster was almost invariably with her. But the girl's heart was in her eyes, searching for the lift of land where she might find her father. Thought of his safety was paramount; it possessed her utterly and not until he was found would she, or could she, think of matters concerning only her own happiness. If he was not found — It would be long before anyone might comfort her, as a man tries to console a woman, and bring about forgetfulness.

Jim saw that Newton made little headway in Kitty's affections though he was quick to say things that fitted her mood, to make suggestions at which she smiled, apt at imagining fortunate happenings for which she was grateful. Yet, as his own love grew for this girl, so plucky, so wise and yet so sweet, so brave and still so feminine, so full of grace and beauty, jealousy sometimes plucked at Jim to the quick. There were perforce many leisure moments when he had nothing to do but think and dream of the future — a future from which he could not imagine Kitty Whiting eliminated, and which often clouded as he considered the vanity of aspiring to familiarity with her.

"They make a fine-looking pair," Jim said to Lynda Warner one night as they came up from below and saw Kitty and Newton at the taff-rail, their figures merging into one in the star-dusk, both gazing down at the wake, Newton's head turned toward hers, his talk provoking a laugh. It seemed to Jim that they were already mating. His prick of jealousy was deepened by his belief that Newton was weak, lacking in purpose and decision, inclined to be lazy, self-indulgent, a laggard in everything but lovemaking and conducting that with a genius that might well involve the girl before she realized it, so cleverly did young Foster submerge his own passion with sympathy.

"Heaven forbid!" said Lynda. "They are both good-looking, if that is what you mean. Being of opposite sex perhaps the one sets off the other when they are together. But Newton is not the only man in the world who would look well by the side of Kitty and she by him. They are not matched any more than opposites can be. When Kitty mates it will be because she falls in love, and when she does that it will be with a man-size lover. I suppose there are possibilities in Newton, but he has much to do to even up his shortcomings. Besides, he is her cousin. He might be willing to ignore the relationship, but I know that Kitty would never marry anyone in whom her own blood ran. The trouble with you, Jim Lyman," she added, in her rich voice that was her one great outward charm, "is that you make two big mistakes."

"What are those?"

Lynda laughed. "I like you enough to tell you. It is doubtful if you would ever find them out for yourself. One is that you don't know how to appraise yourself, not knowing how a woman makes her valuations of a man; the other that you fail altogether to realize that Kitty Whiting is not either angel or fairy, but a very human being. A woman may use her head, Jim, but she has not yet progressed to the place where reason displaces sentiment. Certain types of women need certain types of men. Kitty is ninety percent feminine. She will fall in love with a ninety percent male. A man with a man's force and strength. She would rather have a man who would bully her a little than one who would worship her. I've given you enough to think about. When the right time comes, apply your digested knowledge. Good luck to you and good night." She left him gasping.

The wind began to get capricious the second day out and they had to resort to gasoline, much against Jim's will. He had wanted to save all he could for emergencies, but there was no help for it and Sanders once more took charge of the motive power. They were now where the prevailing wind was southeast, and even if it blew steadily, they, sailing into it on a southeasterly course, could not expect to do better than eight knots, besides falling off in leeway. With the engine, despite the reek of oil, the vibration and the extra heat, all petty annoyances that loom large when the thermometer is over a hundred, they had the satisfaction that every revolution, every turn of the screw sent them ahead, straight to their destination. It seemed to sing a chant of progress:

One foot — two feet — three feet — four!
Five feet — six feet — one fathom more!

Eight hundred and eighty fathoms to a land mile! One thousand and fourteen and a half to a nautical mile! Six thousand and eighty-seven feet divided by six. One nautical mile to a minute, sixty of them to a degree. It was possible to calculate the exact time of arrival, of the moment when they might expect to see the beckoning finger of craggy rock showing through the torn mist.

Newton and Kitty worked out the sums, and checked them off on the chart as they progressed. It was a sort of game calculated to relieve the tension and was not confined to the cabin. Jim gave a talk to the crew. They had cleared from Suva as for "island ports," but he knew that curiosity was rife as to their destination, that the men had speculated on the appearance of the *Shark*, and also on the fact that they had been given firearms practice. He wanted to know how far he could count on them. The Fijian natives were more or less carefree and adventurous. They also had a wholesome fear of the British Government and conceived themselves as lent to the *Seamew*, to be returned in good time and repair, plus satisfactory wage, providing they did their duty and behaved themselves. There were six of them, three of whom had served in the Fijian native police, all good swimmers, brave and faithful, fair shots, handy men, fine sailors; messing, sleeping, and keeping to themselves, unconcerned for the morrow, willing and strong.

Jim held consultation with Kitty and Lynda over his speech. Newton was admitted to the council out of courtesy. Even Baker knew nothing of their purposes. It was decided unwise to mention pearls.

"We've got to arm our landing party," said Jim. "We can't count on my experience as to there being no natives. If on visiting the ship we should uncover a million dollars in pearls, it might turn the heads of our crew.

"I don't want to discriminate against any of them. I think Baker's all right. I am sure of Sanders and Wood, and Douglas Moore would fight like a fiend for whichever side his temperament happened to attach itself to. He could argue himself right under any conditions and spill his blood as freely as the other chap's to prove it. Walker's game and square. I don't know that any of them are not, but I am sure the best way would be to ally them with us by taking them into our confidence to a certain extent. I'll call 'em aft at the end of the dog-watch."

"We are going down to an island where I was once wrecked," he told the listening men, all hands assembled down to Li Cheng and the monkey, the *kanakas* grinning in a rear circle of their own. "When I was there I discovered a fine ship stranded in the jungle where some big wave had flung it. That ship, men, was called the *Golden Dolphin*. Its model is below in the main cabin. It was built by the father of Miss Whiting, who has chartered this schooner to search for him, believing him to be alive.

"It is to the interest of certain people, for business reasons, to get in touch with Captain Whiting before we do, to prevent our finding him until they have secured what they want from him. We believe those men to have been following us from Honolulu, in fact from the States. We hope we have thrown them off the trail. If we have not we are not afraid of them. We look to you to stand by us."

There had been a shuffling of feet and a rolling of eyes when Jim mentioned the pursuit. Nods passed between the men.

"There may be hostile natives," Jim went on. "I am authorized to state that there will be extra pay — a substantial bonus — for all those who volunteer, but it is distinctly understood that you do volunteer, for shore duty. Nothing will be held against you if you prefer to stay aboard. But — the main factor of this trip of ours is the rescue of Miss Whiting's father, to crown with success a venture that has brought her nearly ten thousand miles by sea and land. She takes the chances that I ask you to share, not for the matter of wages or bonus, but as men for the sake of a brave woman."

It was the longest speech that Jim had ever made. He was conscious that he had injected into it much of his own feeling for Kitty Whiting's venture. It self-inspired him with fresh belief in their ultimate success as he conjured it up in words of crisp, stirring appeal. He saw her flushed face and shining eyes as he finished. The men were cheering. Strangely enough, they were led by Li Cheng, who stepped out in front in his cook's white drill apron and cap, his Oriental face a mask of approval and enthusiasm.

"Thlee chee' fo' Lilly Miss," he cried. "Hoolay!"

Jim dismissed the men, feeling that he might count upon all of them. Baker spoke to him.

"That was a good talk you made, Skipper. Good idea to make it. You know how things leak out aboard ship, and how little things roll up. The men savvied there was more than just a chance meeting with that *Shark* schooner, and there's been a heap of talk about this being a trip for buried treasure. A word of talk starts in the cabin, and by the time it drifts forward, it's a whole book. Now they know what they're after, and if there's a spice of danger to it, why it'll tie 'em up."

"How did they ever come to talk about buried treasure?"

"It's the most natural thing, I reckon, to tie up with a trip like this where it ain't given out at the start just where you're goin', an' then there's the pistol an' rifle practice. You don't look like a tradin' outfit. I've done some wonderin' myself, but my motto is to get orders, an' outside of that to be deef, dumb an' blind. You can count on me, Skipper. I hope the young lady finds her father. Looks like a long shot to me, though. I understand you've been to the island an' didn't sight him?"

"I was only ashore for a little while."

"It's derned funny he didn't show if he was there. I've bin wrecked myself, an' I spent night an' day on the highest point I c'ud find. Leastwise, I was there often enough to make sure nothin' went by me."

"He might have been ill; broken a leg?"

"He c'ud have made a smoke. Not that I'd aim to discourage Miss Whiting, Skipper."

"Of course not." But Baker's common-sense had taken a lot of the elation out of Jim. He almost dreaded the moment when they would land.

In the early afternoon of the eighth day, after the noon reckoning had shown them close to landfall, they sighted the distant peak. Off the starboard bow was a cone of deep blue, a thimble-shaped stain against a clear sky; to port, a crooked crag rising from a wide-spreading base.

"Clearer than when I was here," said Jim after the first tumult of discovery had died down. "No storm brewing. Fair weather ahead. A good omen, Miss Whiting."

"Do you think so, Jim?" In the moment of excitement formality dropped.

Perhaps the girl spoke as she had secretly thought of him. A wild hope leaped in him, and he thrilled to the touch of her eager hand on his arm, confiding, more than merely friendly. He saw the quick frown gather on Newton's handsome features, the glance of understanding and endorsement from Lynda.

By sunset they were close up, the men gathered at the rail, discussing the landing. The hump of highland to starboard had changed color, faded, diminished, dissolved as they headed for the island of the crag. About the latter evening mists had gathered, and the one talon-like peak, high above the forest of emerald where the shadows lay in deepest blue and violet, showed more than ever like a finder, blood red in the sunset. Along the line of the barrier reef the surf pounded and was tossed high, gold powdered, shot with rainbow glints, thundering ceaselessly in its perpetual cannonade. Jim himself mounted to the main spreaders to seek for the opening, masked by the spray. He gazed across the coral barrier to the quiet lagoon, recognizing at last the creek where the mate of the ill-fated *Whitewing* had gone for water, the spot where he and his own boat crew had landed, and the mass of jungle where the *Golden Dolphin* lay with a fortune hidden in her hold.

He searched low level, beach and bush and grassy uplands, from deep forest where the plumes of cocoa palms thrust through the mass of tangled foliage and broomed in the gentle wind, up to bare slopes, down to the beach again — looking for some thread of smoke, some flutter of signal, some sign of habitation, and found none. So far as humanity was concerned it might have been an island of the dead. Here and there birds rose and wheeled, settling for the night; the pungent scent of tropic flowers and fragrant herb and bush came to him at the masthead; he could see fish rising in the lagoon, a school flushed from the water by dolphins, a turtle floating, a giant ray hurling itself from the surface — but no sign of man, no eager figure hauling up a makeshift flag or bursting through to the beach to stretch out his arms toward the rescuing schooner. Solitude was all that met his eye.

He stayed aloft as they cruised along toward the opening under power, calling out directions from his perch to Baker at the wheel, as they threaded their way through the jags of the channel while the rapid dusk settled fast about them. The sun was down, the colors of the island had faded, the tip of the finger-like crag tipped with pink, for a fleeting instant. Then it was night, purple night, water and air and sky and the bulk of the island against the stars. The chain went rattling down to fifteen fathoms, the links stirring up a streak of phosphorescence as they shot down; the schooner swung gently to the last of the flood, a light shining in Cheng's galley, another in the cabin. The native sailors were chanting in the bows, there was a chatter among the men. The clock in the cabin chimed eight bells and the mate gave instructions to "make it so" on the schooner's bell. The coupled chimes rang out and Kitty Whiting came on deck to Jim.

"You have brought us here," she said. "But, Jim, somehow I am afraid. It all looks so lonely. Surely he would have seen us by this time, I am still sure he is alive. I feel it here" — she pressed a hand over her heart. It looked like a tired bird, Jim thought, and he battled with an impulse to take it in his own for comfort and assurance. "But — I don't know. That island broods with mystery. It frightens me — a little." She took her hand away from her bosom and put it out in a little appealing gesture Jim could not resist. He grasped it and laid it on his arm, his palm over it.

"It'll look far more cheerful by daylight," he said. "As for your fear, that's just natural reaction at having arrived. We'll search every square yard of it, and there's the other island we sighted."

"Yes, I know. I had nerved myself not to meet him, but — somehow — I pictured him waiting on the beach."

Jim ached all over with the restraint he put upon himself not to take her in his arms and comfort her. She seemed so small, so helpless, so appealing to his manhood. He was almost grateful when Newton came up with Lynda and Kitty drew away.

There were no sleepers an hour before daylight aboard the *Seamew*. The smell of coffee came from the galley where Cheng stood in his doorway gazing at the shore at intervals between cooking. His monkey perched on his shoulder. They were to start ashore immediately after breakfast. Cheng, Wiltz and Hamsun were to remain aboard, the rest of the outfit to go with the landing party in two boats, one covering the other, all armed. For all its silence Jim knew that the bush might hide scores of naked savages, might at any moment vomit a bloodthirsty, cannibalistic, howling horde of them. He was taking no chances. He had trade goods with which to secure peace or truce if there was any chance of it, bullets if there was not.

The night held its secrets. In the east the sky grayed, appeared to shake like a curtain, and with the shaking, the spangled stars suddenly lost luster. High up a cloud caught fire, flamed like a burning rag. Another took form and color lower down. Radiance showed beyond the rim of the sea. The fingertip of peak glowed golden, orange, and rosy coral. Light and color swept down the crags, the forest, the grassy uplands and the bush, like the passage of a magic brush restoring life.

Parrots screamed to welcome the sun, doves cooed; a little wind blew off the land, ruffling the lagoon where fish flashed; gulls started out to sea, wheeling uncertain, to gaze at the thing that had appeared within the reef overnight, proclaiming their displeasure with raucous cries. Day had come with a leap, bringing warmth and cheer, the renewal of vitality and hope.

"Bleakfast all leady!" piped out Cheng from the galley.

Wiltz served them a rapid meal. They took their rifles, the women armed with holstered automatics. Both had donned knickers and shirts of light flannel. Jim discovered to his surprise that Lynda Warner had another treasure beside her voice; her figure was almost as youthful, almost as gracious in the revelation of the boyish costume, as Kitty's. The men had had their meal; guns and cartridges were served out, instructions given. Baker was to take charge of the covering boat, Jim steered the first. With him went Kitty and Lynda; he assigned Newton to Baker's outfit, much to the latter's protest, overruled by the statement that two passengers were enough.

Kitty, Lynda, Jim, Moore, Sanders, Neilson, Walker and two *kanakas*.

Baker, Newton Foster, Vogt and the four remaining Fijians.

On board Cheng, Wiltz, Hamsun and Wood.

The boat-keels struck the water; the falls were released, oars put out. Cheng stuck his yellow face over the rail, the monkey squatting on his head like the familiar spirit of an Oriental wizard.

"Goo'-by an' goo' luck," he called. Wiltz and Wood stood at the forestay, glum but waving farewell. Hamsun was invisible.

They rowed softly along the quiet lagoon where the ripples were like opals in the dawn. Cautiously the leading boat edged in toward the white beach of powdered coral and shells where sea pinks patterned the sand. The sunrise wind had died. There was not a sound but the splash and drip of the oars. Baker kept distance, two men rowing, the rest ready with their guns. But not a leaf of the thick wall of bush back of the beach waved. No canoe shot out from the mangroves guarding the freshwater creek.

"Why are there no islanders here?" asked Kitty. "It is a beautiful place and fertile."

"They may have all been killed off in an epidemic," Jim answered. "The place may be *tabu* after some such disaster. There are islands like this that seem never to have been inhabited for many centuries. Out of the currents, you see. The big migration never reached them."

"An Eden of the Seas," suggested Lynda.

"Minus snakes," said Jim. "Mighty few snakes in the South Seas proper."

The keel grated on the bottom; the *kanakas* sprang out and ran her up the slight slope with strong arms. Jim trusted to their sizing up of the situation more than to his own.

"No *kanaka* walk along this island," one of them pronounced. "Too much already they raise plenty hell an' bobbery suppose they here this time."

They landed, and the covering boat came up.

"Everything to ourselves," said Newton. "Now then, Lyman, where's the *Golden Dolphin*?"

Jim took his bearings and led the way into the bush. It was much thicker than when he had last penetrated it. The almost level sunrays stabbed its green mantle with long lances. They climbed through, over and about dense masses of creepers and palmetto, saw-leaved pandanus, with tree trunks grown close together as the stakes of a palisade. Here the Fijians first proved themselves, hacking a way through the tangle. Soon there were no longer any shafts of sunlight, they walked in a green twilight, as they might at the bottom of a sea with weird water-growths twining all about them. The sight of the ship vaguely showing amid a mass of verdure heightened the resemblance. It was hard to see at first even when the grinning *kanakas* pointed it out, but then their eyes traced it and they hurried forward as fast as they could, with their hearts pounding with excitement. To Kitty Whiting it was the visible confirmation of her hopes, the sight of it reinforced her belief that, having found her father's ship, she would find her father. Lynda Warner naturally shared her cousin's feelings. To Newton the ship represented a fortune of which he had been somewhat skeptical, though not so much so as he was at heart concerning the fate of Captain Avery Whiting. Jim was not unthrilled by the thought of the pearls hidden in the hulk. He found some triumph in showing what he had promised, in proving up. He wished Stephen Foster were there beside his son. Kitty Whiting's joy was his.

There was an open space above the ship where its weight had crushed the growth and prohibited any revival. So thick was the jungle that the *Golden Dolphin* seemed to lie at the bottom of a green shaft. Away up the topmost branches of the trees had caught the rising sun but it was not high enough yet to send full light to the bottom of the well. It would not be long before it did so, Jim noticed. Looking at his watch he saw that they had been four hours struggling through the bush from the beach, four hours to make half a mile of progress. It had originally taken him a quarter of the time. Another year and this ship would be utterly lost, swallowed by the jungle.

The native boys attacked the barricade with fresh vigor, their bodies, naked save for loincloths, glistening with sweat that ran off them in streams. Now they could make out the mast that lay over the side, festooned with green vines. Vines had climbed the mast-stumps and the tangle of ropes, smothering the vessel with a cloak that seemed to hide it from the shame of its disaster.

Suddenly the sun peeped over the edge of the rift in the trees. A ray came down and touched the half-hidden figurehead. Kitty gasped. Jim saw her eyes fill with tears that she winked away.

"The *Golden Dolphin*." She flashed one look at Jim, a reward that amply satisfied him. Then her eyes closed for a moment and her lips moved. She was praying.

They clambered aboard breathlessly, leaving the native boys below. They peered down through the broken skylight through the tarnished bars into the dim interior where more green things writhed. The sun, as if directed for their search, sent one beam, almost vertical, probing through the gloom, disclosing a mast, outlines of a table, chairs, a cushioned transom, a stateroom door.

"I got down through there," said Jim. "The companion doors were jammed. Maybe we can move them."

They were closed, but united effort shifted them more easily than they expected. The companion ladder was in place and unbroken.

"I'll test it," said Jim. It was sound and he called up the news. The sun, almost directly overhead now, beginning to flood the shaft with golden light, illuminated the main cabin with beams in which golden motes danced, and rendered the darkness still blacker by contrast. They had brought along electric torches and Jim turned his on the stairs as Kitty descended. She held out her hand to him naturally for assistance though she did not need any, he knew. Lynda followed, then Newton. Baker tactfully kept the rest back, telling them this was "the lady's party."

The quartet did not notice that they were not followed. Kitty stood in a ray of sunlight, her hand over her heart, leaning forward, looking, listening; listening, it seemed to Jim, as if her love was conjuring from this stranded ocean habitation of her father's some clew to his where-abouts. She spoke in a whisper that fitted the occasion. There seemed something uncanny about the place. Jim fancied he heard movements back of the passage that led from the cabin forward. He sent an exploring pencil of light down its dark tunnel, showing stateroom doors on either side, half open, a door closed at the far end.

"There may be some message," said Kitty. "We must look." They moved forward through the vines that caught at them like seaweed or like detaining hands.

Jim thought of the skeleton alongside, well covered now with ver-dure. Their searchlights flicked through the dense patches of shadow.

"Spooky," muttered Newton, close behind him. "She'll find no message, Lyman. Wonder where the pearls are?"

Jim, sympathetically possessed by the girl's real quest, had tempo-rarily forgotten the pearls. He half turned on Newton to bid him hush.

Suddenly there was a rush and a scuffle on the deck, a stifled cry, a shout half strangled, in Moore's voice:

"Look out, belo-o-w!"

A shot sounded, distant, as if from the lagoon. Another and another. As they grasped their weapons, turning for the companionway, at the top of which they saw to their amazement, Walker, fighting viciously with Vogt and Neilson, a deep voice came from the passage leading for-ward.

"Up with your hands, all of you! Chuck your guns over to the port transom. Hurry, or I'll bore the lot of you. Up!"

The ray from Newton's torch as he jerked his arms aloft lit up the great figure of a man that almost filled the entrance, fell on his sardonic face, squash nose, piggy eyes and bald head with a tonsure of red hair. Over Hellfire Swenson's shoulder leered the features of a man with a close-clipped beard and moustache, mouth open, the tip of a tongue showing between white teeth, for all the world like a wolf gloating at the survey of a victim. This in a flash; they vanished as the torch dropped from Newton's nerveless hand.

Some one called through the skylight bars. It was Sanders.

"They've got us, Skipper. They've got you covered." Then there was a thud on the deck. Other faces looked down. The sun caught the glint of rifle barrels trained on them. Swenson spoke out of the dark.

"No nonsense, now. I've come too far to monkey. Short work from now on. Lyman, throw that gun away or I'll start with you. I don't need you any longer." The bleak purpose of his voice was appalling in its menace. Sullenly Jim tossed his automatic to the port transom. A man swung down through the skylight and secured the weapons.

"You poor fool," said Swenson. "There are other harbors in the Fijis besides Suva. I got there first and put in at Levuka on Ovalau. My good friend, Cheng, whom you were good enough to hire at Honolulu, sent me the position from Suva by wireless. I've been here forty hours waiting for you to show up. The *Shark*'s on the other side of the island, snug. Your schooner is in my hands. Cheng is a good persuader; I've got five of your men in with me. The rest are damaged and your *kanakas* have chucked the job. Now then, young woman, where are those pearls?"

He switched on a torch that sought out Kitty's face and held it, pale in the circle of light but with chin up, lips compressed and eyes that shone defiantly. Jim, his useless fists clenched, furious at the trickery he had not detected, the mutiny of the five, which were, he supposed, the three Norsemen, Wiltz and Cheng, saw the girl's finely cut nostrils dilate.

"I'll not tell you," she answered and there was a ring to her voice that told of true metal. "Not if you kill me."

"Mebbe you wouldn't," said Swenson, and there was a grudging acknowledgment in his voice, "but I don't aim to kill you. You're the goose that lays the golden eggs, you see. Get back into that sunshine, all four of you where I can get a good look at you. I don't aim to kill you, miss, but there's some things almost as bad, some worse. So you'll please get back while I'm giving you the option of doin' your own moving. Got those guns, Pete? Then you can get to hell out of here. This is a private conference.

"This is my partner, Ned Stevens, sometimes known as Slick Stevens. He was too slick for young Foster. Pumped him dry. Not that he held much. Now you're introduced, let's talk.

"There's young Foster here, miss. A good-looking lad. Mebbe you've taken a fancy to him. Or mebbe it's the skipper there. Personally I'd recommend Lyman to you. He's somewhat of a bearcat. I owe him one or two scores, though. But I'll call it all off if you come through with the pearls. If you don't, I understand you think your father's on this island or mebbe the other one. You see I happen to know all about your affairs. Everything. Sometime, if we come to terms, I'll tell you all about how I got my information. It'll open your eyes. But I ain't got time now. What I am after is a quick getaway. I want to turn those pearls into cash. Now, Miss Whiting, if you want to see your father again, and not be ashamed to meet him, you come through. That's one threat, and I mean what I say.

"First thing I'll do, if you don't, is to cut short the career of one of these two beaus of yours. I understand from Cheng, and he's a good judge of human nature, that they're both stuck on you. I think I'll take Lyman first, seeing I'm not quite even with him. I'll give you while I count ten. One — two—"

Swenson was standing himself in full light now and Jim saw his pistol go up steadily, remorselessly.

"You can put down your hands, Lyman, if you want to," he said.

"Three — four — five —"

"Stop." Swenson did not lower his gun. "Do you mean that you would kill him in cold blood?"

"It's you doin' the killing, miss, not me. As for bumping a man off, I don't make any account of that. Not when there's a fortune in sight. When a man's dead he's dead. He won't worry me any. Now, if you think he's worth the price of the pearls to you? No? Six — seven!"

"Stop. I'll tell you."

"No. Let him shoot — if he dares."

"Oh, I dare, Lyman. You first and Foster afterward if I have to. But she'll tell. You ought to thank me. You're the one she wants, it seems. Now, where are they?"

"In my father's stateroom, aft."

"We'll go there, all of us. Get on."

The captain's room was a large one, to starboard of the companionway, connected with a similar room to port by a passage back of the ladder. It was well lighted ordinarily by two large ports, but after the jammed door had been forced back by Stevens, Swenson meanwhile keeping his gun trained on the four prisoners, the electric torches were necessary to break the gloom. The *Golden Dolphin* had been well fitted. There was a brass bedstead in place of a bunk; there were lounging chairs, a table and desk and a washstand with running-water plumbing, both hot and cold, to judge by the labels on the faucets. The place smelled musty as a grave but it was free from the encroaching vines. The bed was unmade, the sheets, spotted with discoloring, flung back above the blankets. But, though Jim had half feared it, there was no moldering body here. Kitty's eyes roved to the desk, still hoping to find some written message. Lynda stood close to the door. Stevens, eyeing her slenderly rounded figure, suddenly put a grossly familiar arm about her. She struggled, tore his hand loose, and as he clawed viciously at her, struck him. With an oath Stevens struck her in the face. Jim sprang across the floor. Stevens lifted his gun, but Jim struck it aside and smashed Stevens in the jaw before the latter, reeling, closed with him. He got a hand on Stevens' throat, throttling hard and swift in the darkness. A ray of light shot out and showed Stevens' face, distorted, his eyes protruding, his tongue forced out of his mouth. There came a crash on Jim's head and he collapsed, half-conscious, while he heard, as if far off, the bellow of Swenson.

"Damn you, Stevens, keep your hands off! I'll have no fooling with the women; I've told you that."

"It's her own fault. Hell, she ought to think it a compliment with a face like that."

Jim got to his feet again, blood streaming down the back of his neck. The blow had been a glancing one, and the flow of blood relieved the pressure. Stevens had his gun trained on him, finger on trigger, a look of deviltry on his face that showed that firing would be a delight. Lynda spoke close to Jim's ear.

"Don't, please. We need you. It was nothing."

"You heard me, Stevens," roared Swenson. "You obey orders or, by God, you won't be able to hear 'em! Now, about these pearls?"

"They are back of the washstand," said Kitty. "The panel moves. The hot-water pipes are not practical. One of them . . ."

Swenson rapped on the mahogany panel while Stevens, subdued, held a gun in one hand, a torch in the other. Jim contemplated a rush, a grab for the gun, but he was weak with the blow Swenson had given him. If he failed it might be the finish for all of them, for there were Swenson's men on deck, with his own traitors. Mist gathered in front of him from faintness that he fought off valiantly.

Swenson impatiently smashed in the panel after his test had shown a hollow space back of it. The plumbing was disclosed, two pipes leading to the faucets, the one to the left connected with the impractical hot-water system.

"Those joints screw up and down, then a section of the pipe comes loose," said Kitty in a hard little voice. "The pipe is plugged. If father did not take the pearls with him they will be there."

Swenson manipulated the joints. As he shifted the lower one a section of the pipe came out in his hands, an ideal hiding place. Even in systematically wrecking the vessel it would never be suspected but torn away with the other fittings. The top of the pipe was closed by a tightly fitting cork. Swenson dug this out with his knife. Cotton packing followed. Precaution had been planned to prevent a rattle of any kind. The end of the section was closed by metal. Swenson tilted the pipe, shook it, examined it by the light of the torch and flung it down with a volley of imprecations.

"Tricked, by God!" he wound up, glaring at Kitty.

"I have not tricked you," she said calmly and Jim could see conviction register on Hellfire's inflamed face as he stared at her. "That is the hiding-place. I am sure father would never have disclosed it. I am sure he would have kept it secret. If the pearls are gone it is because he himself removed them." And her voice proclaimed the joy she felt at this evidence of her belief that her father had mastered his situation and escaped from it with the gems.

"If he's on this island," said Swenson, gritting his teeth, "I'll find him, dead or alive, and I'll get those pearls if I have to go to hell after them. One thing you can be sure of," he went on, "none of you'll leave this ship until I've combed this island and the other one. If I get the pearls I may leave you a boat. Your schooner's at the bottom of the lagoon by now. Or I may not. You can stay here and play you're married. Don't try to leave this ship until I come back. I'm leaving guards. And I'll see that you get some grub. Come on, Stevens."

"She may have lied to you about the hiding-place."

"You're nothing short of a damned idiot, Stevens, at this sort of thing. You boast you know women, an' don't know that she told the truth. You haven't trailed with her kind. Would a man have two hide-outs like that? You told me the truth — on your honor?"

"On my honor," said Kitty.

"That's something you may not understand, never havin' had any of your own," sneered Swenson at Stevens. "But it's good enough for me. Whiting got clear somehow. You saw that skeleton alongside. I'm saying he got clear and we'll find what's left of him somewhere about. In a cave, likely. Where he is, the pearls are. Come on."

"I'm not going on such a fool's errand."

"Then stay behind and be damned to you! Glad you brought some *kanakas* with you from Suva, Lyman. They are goin' to come in mighty handy for me, choppin' bush. You four have got the run below of this hulk. Hatches will be guarded and so will the skylight. If you try any funny stuff it'll be boarded over."

"What about my men?" demanded Jim. "You said they were not all traitors."

"One of 'em's got a busted head. Another one, a wild Irishman, had to be choked before he quit. Your mate's thrown in with us. Your engineer was put out of business with a broken arm. The steward and the squareheads have been my men for two weeks or more. As to the other man you left aboard, Cheng was going to give him a chance, but I heard a shot or two fired; mebbe you did. I don't much imagine you'll see him again. I'll send the cripples below for you to take care of."

He stamped out of the stateroom into the main cabin with Stevens, and up the companionway to the deck. Stevens lingered to give a look malicious and evil before he disappeared.

"You're hurt badly." Kitty had come to Jim's side. There was a break in her voice that acted upon him as an elixir.

"I'm all right," he managed to say, but the girl had touched his head and found blood. She went back into the stateroom and ripped at the sheets but they shredded under her hands. With a shrug of petulance she closed the door behind her and came out in a moment with some strips of sheer linen. This she bound about Jim's head despite his protest.

"The others will need it more than I do," he said.

"I don't agree with you," Kitty answered almost sharply. "We'll attend to them as soon as they let us have them."

"Here they come now," said Newton. The companionway opened and their wounded men were delivered to them, roughly and gruffly, Neilson and Vogt acting as two of the bearers. Sanders had a broken arm from manhandling. Walker was insensible, with a skull that seemed as if it might be fractured. Moore, too, was unconscious. He had put up a notable fight, it seemed. His clothes were torn to rags, his face a mass of contusions; his neck showed black bruises and his naked torso was smeared with blood. Jim was hard put to it to keep his hands off Neilson and Vogt, whose sullen pose was not proof against the steady look of disdain the two women bestowed upon them. Stevens lolled in the entrance, gun in hand.

"You'll get fed tonight," he said. "Sorry you've lost your cook. Treat me right and I'll reciprocate. The skipper's by way of being a woman-hater. I'm not. You may see me later. He won't have any women aboard ship. That's where I differ from him, if they're reasonably attractive. It would be a shame to leave you ladies on the island and tha's what the skipper intends to do for his own protection. Think it over."

His eyes bulged and he pressed trigger as Jim leaped for him, stumbling backward up the ladder as he saw his shot had missed. Jim caught him by the ankle, but two of Swenson's men had flung themselves upon him, for his own safety, since Stevens dared not fire again for fear of hitting them. Instead, Stevens scuttled up the companionway through the hatch and the two flung Jim to the floor where he lay panting. The rest left, and the companion hatch was closed. The evil face of Stevens looked down through the skylight. They heard him give orders to shoot on suspicion.

"You make a move that looks phony," he shouted down, "and we'll finish you. Meantime, starve and be damned to you!"

The shifting sunlight showed that soon they would be again in comparative darkness. The ports were undoubtedly crusted tight; leaves masked them. The only light would be what filtered down through the natural shaft and the skylight. Their schooner — if they could believe Swenson and the shots they had heard — was sunk. Wood was killed. Three, aside from Jim, were badly injured. Sanders and Walker needed medical treatment. Their chief jailer was a cruel beast; the main villain, Swenson, meant to leave them stranded on the island. He had gone to seek Kitty Whiting's father. If he found him alive, Swenson and his men would indubitably possess the pearls. They were helpless, almost hopeless, prisoners. Jim went about with clenched teeth and a jutting jaw trying to do something for the injured men. It was stifling in the cabin and they had no water. To beg it from Stevens would only provoke mockery. Sanders' arm had to be set. The Scot sat with his face chalky in the gloom, hanging on to himself.

"They jumped us, you see," he said huskily. "That dirty dog of a Neilson and Vogt. Cracked Walker with a blackjack or something and there were three on my back at once. I think Moore tackled half a dozen. They grabbed our arms so we couldn't shoot. They were hiding back of the deckhouses. Tried to warn — you — but . . ." He closed his eyes and set his teeth into his lips.

"Lie down," ordered Jim, himself with a blinding headache. "We'll fix you up. Newton, I want you."

They went exploring and found a cabin where the two bunks had decent mattresses that were not too badly molded. They took their undershirts and made them into bandages, then, with the aid of the broken pieces of the panel that Swenson had smashed, Jim managed a splint, feeling fairly sure that he had the ends of the broken upper arm in place. They put Sanders in the top bunk, carried Walker to the lower.

Kitty and Lynda had vanished into the room that connected with Captain Avery's. They came back to the main cabin triumphant.

"It was stupid of me not to think of it before," said Kitty. "The ship's medicine chest! I knew where dad kept it, with the extra drugs. We broke the lock. There are bandages but they are pretty rotten. Some of the medicines, like iodine, have dried up but there is permanganate, and —" she hesitated — "some other things. We must cleanse that head-wound of Walker's and do the best we can for poor Moore."

"Without water?"

"I think I can get some water."

"Not from those brutes."

"I'll trade it. For liquor. I'm not demented. There was always a supply in the lazarette locker back of the starboard cabin where I got the medicine."

"See here, Kitty, if you tell them there is any of that stuff aboard," broke in Newton, "they'll take it all. You know what that means with beasts like Stevens. We haven't any weapons."

"I have," said Kitty. "A woman's weapons, and I am going to use them for the sake of our wounded men. I may find a way out for all of us. I want you and Jim to force the hasp on the locker. Lynda and I are not strong enough for that. But we have our wits about us."

"Lyman, you're not going to let her get that stuff?"

"I have more confidence in her weapons than you have, Newton," said Jim. "We're in a tight place and Miss Kitty realizes that as well as we do. Come along."

Newton went reluctantly with Lynda. Kitty, hanging behind, thanked Jim for his backing. "There is no necessity for the 'Miss'," she whispered. "I am calling you Jim. You'll trust me in this? Not ask me how I intend to do it? Lynda knows and approves."

"Of course." But Jim wondered. There was an almost tragic note to her talk. They broke the hasp and brought out a dozen bottles — one of brandy, three of whisky, the rest port and sherry.

"If you are figuring on making them drunk — ?" started Newton.

"I am not," the girl answered. "Leave me a torch please, and go into the main cabin with Jim. Lynda will stay here with me. We've got to open these. I don't want to break them."

"Those chaps up there have got a nose for booze a mile off," said Newton. "I could do with a slug myself." Jim took his own knife and Newton's and eased out the corks before they left. Soon the two women come out with some of the bottles.

"I am to do the talking," Kitty whispered, then called up through the skylight, "Mr. Stevens."

Immediately the leering face appeared.

"Well. Seeing the light, little lady?"

"Will you let us have some water — for the wounded men?" Stevens laughed.

"I might. What will you trade for a pint of it — say in kisses."

Kitty put out a hand to grip Jim's arm without looking at him. Instinctively she seemed to know that he was quivering with blind rage.

"I'll need more than that," she said, her voice unfaltering. "Give me a gallon of water and I'll give you a quart of brandy."

"Brandy?"

"I knew where my father kept a bottle for emergencies. I just found it."

"Pass it up." Stevens' voice was hoarse from eagerness.

"No. Send down the water first, or I'll smash the bottle."

"Don't do that. I'll bring the water."

"Let it down. Then you may come."

"If he comes into this cabin to start drinking," said Jim in a tense whisper, "I'll not answer for myself. I —"

"Sh!" He felt her fingertips on his lips. "It will not matter. Trust me."

The water came down in a demijohn, lukewarm, cloudy stuff, but water. Jim unfastened it from the cord and took it to the cabin where Sanders and Walker lay. Moore, on the transom, was slowly beginning to come back to consciousness. The companion hatch slid back, letting in more light, and Stevens came running down.

"No tricks now," he said. "I trusted you. Where —? Ah, you're a sport! This is the real stuff."

He tilted the bottle at his mouth and drank greedily.

"Just the one bottle?" he asked between gulps.

"There is some wine. I thought the men . . ." Kitty had purposely spoken loudly. Heads appeared above. "One of you can come down and get it," she said. "Only one. You'll have about a bottle apiece. Hurry."

An unshaven villain came clattering down and stacked up the wine in his arms, returning shouting to his comrades.

"You're a cunning little devil," said Stevens, and his voice sounded drowsy. "Thought you said only one? Here's to your bright eyes — to your red lips — to —"

He pitched forward to the floor. On deck the men were shouting ribald toasts to each other. They heard nothing, suspected nothing.

"Drugged?" whispered Jim.

"Chloral in the brandy," she answered. "I don't know how much. I hope I've killed him," she said with a fierceness Jim had never credited her with. "The wine has morphine in it. I crushed the pellets. Quick, get his gun. Newton, here's the whisky. It is all right. Give some to the boys. Get it down Walker's throat." Newton went off with the bottle. Jim knelt to get the automatic and the belt with its holster and cartridges, buckling it about him.

"You are wonderful," he said to Kitty.

"I think you have been too," she said. And he knew that in the stress of danger and trouble all suggestions of caste and difference had been removed. Kitty and Lynda mixed water with permanganate crystals and bathed Walker's head and Moore's cuts and abrasions. The whisky had brought them back.

"Where the divvle am I? Who's singin'?" said Moore.

The men were roaring snatches of songs. The morphine had lost virtue or was slow to act. Walker, revived, was still confused.

"They busted in my nut," he said. "Oh, Gawd, it's split in 'arf."

"Buck up," said Newton. "Have another swig of this."

Jim checked him.

"Not too much," he cautioned.

"Then I will." Already Newton's breath smoked with the stuff and his speech was thick.

"Take it away from him," said Kitty. "You need some yourself."

"Not in this weather."

"Lynda and I are going to have a little, to make the water drinkable. Give me the bottle, Newton."

"Where's the other? Hang it, Kitty, that stuff puts new life in you."

"You've had enough," said Jim sternly. "We don't want to pack you." His disgust showed plainly. Newton muttered and subsided. The diluted drink that Kitty mixed ran through their veins with swift reaction that cheered them. Above the singing had died down.

"I'm going on deck," said Jim, "To get their weapons. We'll tie them up."

"If they're alive. Do you suppose I've really killed them? It is murder. I was desperate. Stevens, the beast, was different. I'm not sorry for him if he is dead. But —"

"I'll see," said Jim. "I don't think you need reproach yourself." He saw she was shaking with revulsion. Lynda took her in her arms. "You haven't killed Stevens, anyway," Jim added. "Chloral is the same as knockout drops. He's breathing all right. He'll come out of it after a few hours. I'll get him out of here, if the rest are drugged. Newton, I'll want your help. Step quietly." Newton staggered a little, but braced himself and followed Jim up the companion ladder. On deck, in the queer twilight of the jungle they saw five men sprawled on the planks amid the wreckage and the vines, arms flung wide. One or two twitched in their stupor as they cautiously approached. They secured two pistols from the nearest with another cartridge belt. Jim had reached for a rifle leaning against the skylight when Newton gave a cry of warning, and a shot shattered the silence and a bullet sang by Jim's head. A volley followed out of the bush through which men were crashing at top speed, aiming as they ran. Jim flung himself on deck with Newton to dodge the fusillade. Men were swarming up the bows of the ship, hidden by the screen of greenery and cordage, firing fast. The bullets whistled about them as they fled before the superior force. Swenson's bellow sounded as he forced his way aft with at least ten men back of him.

Jim and Newton heard him cursing as he surveyed his prostrate men while they slammed the hatch and returned to the alarmed women. Moore was on his feet, demanding a gun, Walker feebly struggling to get out of his bunk, Swenson's thunderous oaths continued as he swore at his fallen men. He seemed to be kicking them and the emptied bottles. The others pounded at the hatch that had jammed again. Jim shouted up.

"The first man that shows a head will be shot. We've got their guns and plenty of shells, Swenson."

There was silence then Swenson suddenly guffawed.

"Tricked again!" he shouted and seemed to take delight in the fact. "Drugged! I bet the girl thought of that, Lyman. Have you got Stevens down there?"

"What there is of him."

"The blighted fool. Damn me, but it was smartly done. Look here, I want to have a talk with you. I've a proposition to make. You've got guns. I'll come down without any, I'll trust you for a truce. What do you say? We'll make a deal."

"Shall we?" asked Kitty in an undertone.

"He can't hurt any. Come on, Swenson. You shall have a drink of whisky. We've got plenty of stuff that isn't drugged. Canned goods, too, for grub."

Kitty gave a start.

"There may be, at that," she whispered. "I know where they are stored. Right under our feet, above the bilge."

"Prepared for a siege, are you? How about water? But I'll go you, providing you sample the liquor. Pete, you take charge here. Souse those drugged fools. Walk 'em up and down. Kick sense into 'em."

"Only you," warned Jim.

"All right, my fox. Lyman, you're a wise one and you've a wiser head with you in that girl of yours. I'm coming."

They could barely see each other in the cabin as Swenson, with a great show of heartiness and good humor, took his drink without asking for a test.

"Wouldn't pay you to drug me, more ways than one," he said. "Now, then, I've come back from that wild-goose chase. It 'ud take a month to search this island. I'm going to leave that to you. Your *kanakas* gave us the slip in the bush somewhere. They may come back after we're gone.

"We're going, I reckon. I've struck a better idea than trying for the pearls. That's too big a gamble and this is a certainty." He chuckled and took a pull at the bottle. "Don't know why I didn't think of it before. I'm going to leave you all, maybe. It depends. I want to ask a question and I want the little lady here, Miss Whiting, to answer it. On her honor, again. If my information is correct, and I haven't missed much of what has happened, you gave out the figures of this island's position to no one. Lyman here advised you not to. You kept this book in a safety deposit, then mailed it to Honolulu? I haven't got much use for women, Miss Whiting, but I take my hat off to you for pluck and cleverness. What I want to know is, does any one, outside of those aboard your *Seamew*, know those figures? Does Stephen Foster, father of this young sprig here, know? Has he, to your knowledge, any means of learning them since you sailed?"

Jim started. Swenson and Foster were not in collusion. His suspicions of the millionaire were unfounded.

"Wait a minute, Kitty," he said. "Before you answer that, let him tell you how he got his information."

"I don't mind that, young cock of the walk," returned Swenson, setting down the bottle that he had finished, half empty as it was. "Open up another from your cellar, and I'll tell you. Damn my eyes if you haven't earned that much." The whisky had mellowed him, that and his propensity to brag. "It's simple as A. B. C. I won't see any of you again. After I've collected my half million, I shall disappear to a freer country than the U.S.A., hidebound by prohibition and blue law cranks. I'll leave no trail. I'll be far afield by the time you are home again.

"I'm a sworn enemy to restrictions of liberty, my friends. When they tried to cut off my liquor and that of other good men they trod on my personal rights. There were a lot of others felt the same way. We got together after a while and we became friends of liberty. Rum-running, not to put too fine a name to it. Bound together in an organization that will keep the sleuths jumping like fleas on a kerosened dog. Coast to coast. Top of Maine to bottom of Florida, Cape Cod to the Golden Gate! Over seas! And under 'em.

"I wasn't one of the smallest links in that chain. I had my own territory, savvy? All Massachusetts was mine as head of that ring. And I could call on the other bosses. I handled as good stuff as this, at a profit and at some risk, I grant you that. That's why I'm going to get out of it.

"That place you found me at, Lyman, belongs to a gent who is a good friend of mine. His only fault is that he must have his liquor regularly and often. He's got the same trouble as young Newton here. I've sold young Newton many a quart, only he don't know it. He got it through his father's chauffeur, one of our sub-agents in Foxfield, one of the lower-downs, same as I am one of the higher-ups.

"Now the plots thickens, eh? Gets close to home, I'm going to get closer. You next, Miss Whiting.

"You've got a maid, had one, who is a love-sick fool. She's got some money saved and that chauffeur of Foster's has been kidding her to get the handling of it. Let her talk marriage and a little home and borrowed a hundred every now and then. Savvy? She worships the ground he walks on, when he does walk. He's a good-looking devil, younger than she is, a fast worker with the girls, a persuader. She told him everything she knew. That time she went for a walk, when you thought she might have heard something, she phones him as soon as he has taken Old Man Foster home. And he, being a wise young feller, knowin' I was by way of bein' a seafaring man, phones me long-distance. It listens fine to me. I'd heard and read about the *Golden Dolphin*, you see. Later that night he phones me again that Lyman here is coming to talk things over with Foster's old man and bring the figures.

"So I tell him to get some of his pals with a car that we've used for shifting the booze. That's as far as I have to go. I got Lyman. Lyman took a long chance and went overboard. You know all that. I got the rest of your talks via the same route before I started for Panama and Honolulu. I was pretty sure then you'd call at Suva, but I wanted to make sure. I thought by that time young Newton here might have got on to the figures and Stevens pumped him. It's dry work talking. You can figure out the rest of it. Simple enough. I knew when Lyman slipped off he'd given me the wrong position. Guessed he had from the first when I meant to take him along. There you are, miss; there's my end of it. How about my answer? I don't know what you may have wired or written back."

"On my honor and to the best of my belief," said Kitty, "Mr. Foster knows nothing of the figures."

"Good. Then here's my proposition. They say a bird in the hand is worth two in the bush, but I've got one bird here in the bush that is worth a whole lot more to me than a chance scramble after pearls. Young Foster's father made a small mint out of blankets and such like with his mills during the war. Now's his chance to help equalize things again. I don't know how high he values Newton here. I'm setting half a million on him as a minimum. Personally I wouldn't give a plugged nickel for him. I've got him sized up as a lightweight, but his daddy may consider him the apple of his eye and fruit's expensive in my market. He's all the old man's got and folks are foolish about their kids. Seem to figure because they are theirs they must be wonderful. I'm goin' to give Stephen Foster a chance to prove up on his love and affection. If folks was as wise as the dog-breeders they'd kill off all the runts soon as they were born. Old Man Foster has made a show dog out of his boy here. Not bad looking on points, I grant you, but a wise judge would give him the gate. Same as you have, miss.

"So — I go away and leave you on the island. Cheng scuttled your schooner an' she's at the bottom of the lagoon. I'm goin' to take your landing boats with me. Three of my men and Cheng have gone across the island to get the *Shark* an' bring her round here. Tomorrow morning we'll be off. Month or more from now, I get in communication with Stephen Foster and offer to sell him the position of this island so he can send out a relief expedition to take you all off. That won't cost him much more than a cable to Suva and your passage home. Just so he won't think I'm pulling his leg, I'll take him a note from you, young Foster, telling him how you feel about bein' cooped up here for the rest of your natural."

Newton, sharing drinks with Swenson, growing more surly at the depreciation of his merits by the rum-running blackguard, sat sullen and silent.

"Better get busy, young feller," said Swenson. "You can use the fly leaf of one of those books, that'll be convincing evidence. If I'd thought of all this I'd have brought a camera along and taken a flashlight of the crowd of you. But the book'll help. I'll loan you a pencil."

"What if I don't?"

"Ah!" The exclamation wiped out all the good-natured banter from Swenson's face. It grew evil, repulsive. "If you don't? For one thing you'll stay here, anyway. Maybe to rot. Maybe not. This old hulk would make a rare bonfire. Keep your hand off your gun, Lyman. I've come unarmed. Shoot me and you can imagine what would happen to you — and to the ladies. You're inside this hulk and my men are out. You haven't got any water to speak of, don't forget that. Now it's up to young Foster, and I want it settled. His father bunked the government out of the money he rolled up on war contracts. Half a million don't mean any more to him than a hundred would to most men. It'll hurt him a little, like taking off a patch of skin might. But the graft'll save his son from a life down here. Lucky it ain't you, Lyman; you'd be apt to be contented with the lady here. Regular Paradise for two. But not for the rest of you. What d'you say, Foster?"

"Give me your pencil."

Swenson chuckled and took another drink as Newton got a book from the shelves that had the name of Captain Avery and his ship on the fly leaf and began to write. Swenson finally read it aloud.

My Dear Father:

Swenson will tell you his story. I write this in the cabin of the *Golden Dolphin* to corroborate this much of his story. The *Seamew* is sunk; we have no boats and the trip has fizzled out. The pearls are not on board. So far there is no trace of Captain Whiting. If you do not meet Swenson's blackmail I see nothing for it but for us to stay on this damned place until we die.

One man of ours has been killed; three more are badly hurt; Lyman is injured. Otherwise, we are all well, so far. To check Swenson's figures I give them to you. For God's sake, pay the blackmail and get us out of here.

Affectionately,
Newton R. Foster.

"You write a cheerful letter, but you use better sense than I thought you had," said Swenson. "That touch about the figures is a shrewd one but you haven't put them down. Otherwise it's a grand little note."

"What are the figures, Lyman?"

Lyman gave them and Newton wrote them in long hand. Jim sat with head between his hands. His head throbbed abominably and he was weighed down by sense of failure. If the *Seamew* had not been sunk he was confident he could have got off the *Golden Dolphin*. Now . . . If only he had not been taken in by Cheng. Wood had been murdered in cold blood with Cheng, Wiltz, and Hamsun against him. And, by the irony of fate, it had been Wiltz who had warned Jim against Cheng before the wily Oriental won him over by a golden bait.

"Thanks," said Swenson dryly as he pocketed the book. "That ought to make it worth three-quarters of a million, at least. The pearls would not have brought that at a forced sale, and my men will want their shares. Also the hounds that came over from you, Lyman. Any of the rest of you like to add anything to the note? No? Nothing I can do for you?

"Eh, Lyman? You seem downhearted. Fortune of war. It's checkmate this time. No message I can deliver for you? To the widowed mother? Shall I have your engagement announced in the *Foxfield Gazette* society column?"

"Damn you," said Lyman. "I may beat you home yet!" Swenson laughed. "There are two things you could do for me. One is to get out of here before I give you another clip like the one I did off Cuttyhunk. The other is to give me two minutes with Cheng — barehanded."

"I'm going. As for Cheng, he had some idea of that sort, I think. Anyway, he elected to go with the others to fetch the *Shark*. We'll be here the rest of today and tonight, so don't try to interfere by coming on deck. You might get shot. I wish you good meals and pleasant dreams. Thanking you for the whisky."

He put the second bottle in another pocket, lifted the limp body of Stevens with infinite ease, though with utter disregard for the man's comfort, and went up on deck where they heard him fling down the drugged body and roar out reproof and orders to his men.

The day dragged. Walker grew delirious and Jim gave him a hypodermic of morphine. He did not think the skull was fractured but he could not be sure. Moore was swathed in makeshift bandages and adhesive plaster but full of fight. But the assurance that they would have to expose themselves to the fire of Swenson and his men bit into all of them. Newton helped to forage and they found cans of meat and even fruit, unspoiled. They roamed the hull and made many useful discoveries, including oil sufficient to fill one container, and an unbroken chimney.

Toward dark, following a glare of afterglow high above them, a mass of heavy timbers was thrown across the skylight bars, suddenly shrouding them in blackness, Swenson's voice called down through a crack.

"You might start some monkey business, after dark, Lyman. I don't quite trust you. The hatches are battened. After we're gone tomorrow you can break your way through this. Meantime, pleasant dreams."

All through the smothering night they stayed awake, save for the sick men, who dozed off — Walker still under the merciful drug. And Lyman discussed plans.

"If the *kanakas* come back to us — and they may —" he said, "I can get them to dive to the *Seamew*; the depth is nothing for them. The hatches will be blown off. They can carry down a line and haul out the thick hawser. We'll get this old hulk to sea. We can't raise the schooner. That's beyond us."

"But you can float this?" Newton's contribution was an open sneer.

"We can try."

"How?" asked Kitty.

"Tide and sun. The lagoon's on a lower level. We'll clear away the bush — burn it if we have to. We'll secure the end of the hawser on the reef and take up the slack with the windlass aboard. At high tide most of it will be covered. We'll soak the rest by hand. As it takes in water it'll shrink. Hydraulic power that will test the breaking point of the rope. We may have to dig out, but it can be done. It'll move the *Golden Dolphin*, by inch and foot and fathom. At low tide the sun will make the hawser slacken. Then we take up the slack again. If only the hull is sound! And I believe it is."

"Oh!" said Kitty, a world of admiration in her voice. "I've seen the halyards tighten in a squall so that we had to let them up and take them up again when the sun and wind dried them. Taut as fiddle strings. Will the hawser stand the strain?"

"I think so. There was a bark dragged two miles across the sands up in Hecate Strait, British Columbia. It wasn't my idea. While we're working, and waiting on the tide, the others can search the island for your father."

"Yes. You know I'm still certain that he is alive. Sure of it. Sure."

The morning found them without water. The sufferers had used it all. Their watches gave them the time by the light of the lamp. Newton Foster had been steadily drinking.

"You ought to be ashamed of yourself," said Kitty. "When we need all your manhood."

"'F you get off this dump it'll be because my father comes through with a fortune," he answered sulkily. "Not from any schemes of Lyman's. Fine mess he's made of things, so far."

On deck a bustle began. A voice hailed from the bush and Swenson answered. Then he pounded on the skylight covering.

"*Shark*'s arrived. Good-by. If you hustle you may get out in time to wave to us."

Scuff of feet and then silence. They had found the rusted carpenter's kit and two axes. Jim swung at the skylight barrier with crashing blows, standing on the cabin table. Newton, fuddled and surly, slumped on the transom. Moore tried to assist, but had no strength. Kitty seized the other axe and helped to strike and pry, Lynda relieving her. Jim wormed through the exit they achieved and Kitty handed him up the axe. With it he freed the companionway hatch, blocked by baulks of wood angled against it and across it. The two women came up.

Above the jungle shaft the sky was gray, the treetops bending in a strong wind. All the bush shivered before the myriad tiny draughts of air that were forced through its mass from the sea.

"It looks like a storm," said Lynda.

"Probably a downpour of rain," said Jim. "They've gone. The wind's onshore. They'll be aboard by this time, but they'll not have got far off the land yet, sailing close-hauled. Let's get to the beach." Newton came on deck.

"Moore says he can look after Sanders and Walker," he said. "Going down to the beach?" Nobody answered him.

"I should have stayed off that liquor," he said. "But the stuff gets me whenever it's round. There's a tug inside of me pulling for it. I've got to apologize all round, I suppose. I'm trying to do it. Swenson wasn't far out. I'm not worth more than a plugged nickel. All I can do is to be sorry." The women did not answer. Jim did.

"I guess that's enough, Newton," he said. "We've all been strung up. Let's forget it."

"That scheme of yours about the *Golden Dolphin*? Will it work?"

"I think so, but it will take weeks."

"How about masts and sails? How about a compass?"

"There are trees that would do at a pinch. We couldn't build a seaworthy ship from them green, but they'll serve for sticks. We can weave matting for sails. I know the stars well enough to get us back to Suva before a stern wind, as it would be."

"You've got the stiffening I lack, Lyman," said Newton. "I — There they go, damn them."

They had broken through the edge of the bush to the beach and saw the *Shark*, close-hauled, beyond the tumbling breakers of the reef, clawing her way out to sea. Her canvas showed white against the slate-hued sky, where lightning was beginning to flicker. The sea was a tawny yellow. To the north a great black cloud lifted and grew, out of which javelined streaks of electric flame. The wind was strong. The sun struggled through masses of rolling vapor.

"I wish a hurricane would fling them ashore," said Newton.

"It's going to be a bad rain, nothing worse. *Look out there, coming round the point.* See them! *War canoes.* Get back out of sight. There are hundreds of them!"

They found a hillock up which they struggled through the vines and trees, peering from their point of vantage that gave them clear view across the tumultuous reef. The sun shone on first one, then another and another — five all told — great curving sails, double peaked, lifting above catamaran craft of lashed canoes with outriggers, each carrying a platform and a small deckhouse of thatched grass. They came sliding over the ocean at incredible speed to cut off the *Shark*. Lower canoes and decks were close packed with savages, some paddling furiously in the wash of the canoes, though they could not have aided progress. Others brandished weapons that glinted in the pale sunshine at spearhead and arrow tip. The canoes were high-prowed and pooped, carved and inlaid with shell that occasionally winked in the light. The bows were decked with streamers. The wind bore a faint sound of savage yells.

"Fifty men, at least, to each canoe," said Jim. "Three more coming. Must be a whole tribe. The *Shark's* doomed."

Flashes of guns showed from the rail of the schooner as the canoes raced up, and the big sails came down while the paddlers dug in their blades. Flights of arrows answered the firing. Then came detonations. A canoe seemed to break in half in a sheet of flame. Swenson was tossing dynamite. They could see his men at the rail, flinging the explosive, firing pistols, then driven back by the horde that poured in upon them, twenty or thirty to one. Cries and shouts blended. With the helmsman clubbed, the *Shark* swung off and wallowed in the trough, the wind slanting her until it seemed she would capsize. Then the canvas flapped loose, the sheets cut, and the mainsail came down with a run. Over its folds men moved, fighting like frantic ants. The yells changed to cries of unmistakable triumph. The canoes formed on the lee of the stricken schooner, refilling with men. Bodies in white clothing were handed down. The canoes forged off; smoke rolled out of the hatch of the *Shark*, smoke shot with flame that licked at the sails and rigging, enveloping the ill-fated ship.

The watchers had not noticed the increasing darkness in the horror of the massacre. They saw the canoes disappearing around the headland, stroked hard, the great sails still furled. The wind had suddenly ceased, and out of the swollen black cloud came down a deluge that blotted out everything and drenched them to the skin in a moment. They struggled back to the stranded hulk as if to an ark of refuge. The barricade over the skylight was some protection and over the apertures they hung scraps of old canvas and tarpaulin before they went below, listening to the torrent battering on the deck, seeing and hearing again the sudden horrors of the massacre.

It was hard to hear speech. The lamp was a comfort.

"They may come ashore?" asked Kitty. Jim shook his head.

"I think not. Not unless they are wrecked. They came from the other island. They must have watched the schooners arrive and come over in the night."

"Then they would know there were two ships."

"They may have only noticed ours.

"They may have seen the *Seamew* sunk, and thought no one but the survivors of a white man's feud left. I believe there's a *tabu* of some sort on this island. Or there would be natives living here. And I'm almost certain none are."

He spoke bravely. He did think that the island must be *tabued*, but the dread of a visitation from the cannibal canoes would be ever with them. With Walker raving, the lamp failing, the rain pelting down like lead, the intolerable heat and the memory of the flaming ship, their souls were blanched with despair.

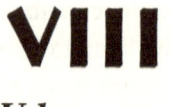

VIII

Udanwaga

It was long before the memory of the massacre dimmed sufficiently for them to go about without the dread of a landing overshadowing them. The cry of a parrot would seem the yell of a savage sighting them, the rustle of a wild pig in the bush the rush of a spear-flinging warrior. But time seemed to bear out Jim Lyman's theory and they came to accept the idea that the island might be *tabu*.

The five Fijians came back to the stranded hull the day after the rain with many protestations of fealty and proclamations that they "had been make walk-along but mighty soon make getaway and come back." Through them Jim recovered the hawser from the *Seamew*. With their aid as expert surfmen he recovered a lot of tackle from the half burned remnant of the *Shark*, impaled on the reef. They got her foremast, also, and some provisions. But her boats were burned or smashed. So the long task of clearing the way for the launching of the *Golden Dolphin* commenced and slowly progressed. The bush was burned and cleared with infinite labor after an examination had shown the planking sound. A trench was dug beneath her keel and the accumulated soil removed. At last the hawser was attached, and the trial made. With much groaning of protest the pull of the hawser, half drenched by the rising tide, half soaked by a hand-chain of buckets, tautened; the hull creaked, moved a stubborn prow, stopped, moved on again, almost imperceptibly, but nevertheless moving, a full two feet to one tide.

Jim delegated two *kanakas* to accompany Kitty, and Lynda in the untiring search over the island for some trace of habitation; some clue that her father might have lived there, and be in hiding, perhaps for fear of savages. Burnt as brown as a native, with limbs scratched and bruised from struggle through the bush, the girl preserved, and one day came back with tidings, though not of her father. She refused to think of him in the grim connection she had uncovered.

There was a stone causeway half hidden in the bush, an ancient road with some of its mighty flags upheaved but still passable. It led straight up, with steps here and there to the summit of a flat hill where there stood a pyramid of faced stone, and on its top an altar of three stones, like those of Stonehenge. It seemed placed so as to receive the first rays of the rising sun and allow them to pass through an opening in the pillars. Beneath the flat top was a block of lava that in turn held a stone chalice. Whatever was placed in this cup must bathe in the sunbeams. The bottom of the pyramid was a charnel house of bones: ribs, pelvises, skulls, and leg- and arm-bones, flung pell-mell. The stone cup was black with sinister stain that had splashed and dripped all about.

Some of the bones, most of them, were bleached and disarticulate. Others bore unmistakable signs of comparative recent dumping. They were unbleached, hair clinging to the scalps, grisly details of a not too thorough cleansing of tendon and sinew. That the flesh had been stripped by man and not decay, was hinted by the ground at the back of the pyramid showing plainly the signs of fires, of fire pits where sacrificial meats were wrapped in leaves, and steamed on hot stones, after the sacred portions had been offered to the gods.

Yet nowhere could they find actual signs of very recent visitation. The land was fair, the sea full of fish, the bush of fruit and wild pigs. Here and there the girl came across crumbling stone platforms built on ledges, the foundations of grass houses long vanished; vanished long before some of those skeletons had been flung down by the priests, in Jim's opinion. A pestilence, a hurricane, a tidal wave greater than that which flung the *Golden Dolphin* ashore might well have made the place *tabu*. There might be an occasional pilgrimage from the other island to placate the gods.

He tried to turn the discovery into a certain sign of immunity, but it was hard to be convincing. From that day on someone stood watch on a high point that commanded the channel between their island and the next. They stored provisions in a cave where fresh water dripped, and where they might make a valiant stand, and prayed that they might get away before any canoes appeared in sight. There were days when the tortured cable threatened to break, when a sunken rock rose up beneath the keel and had to be dug away laboriously. But, foot by foot, and fathom by fathom, as Jim had predicted, the hull crept closer to the lagoon.

They made numerous repairs. They worked with increasing vigor as the sick men mended. Sanders and Walker, his cracked pate sound again with the exception of violent, but decreasing, spells of headache, sewed on jury sails made from scraps of the *Shark*'s tattered canvas, or spliced ropes. The foremast was made ready for sloop rig, shears prepared to hoist it into place, the broken rudder repaired, with Jim Lyman hardest worker and foreman of them all, unceasing in vigor and determination to overcome all obstacles. He was the idol of the Fijian boys, who called him in their own language The-Quick-Thinking-Strong-Armed-White-One, a title that Kitty made him translate and kept secret for her own edification.

The year rolled slowly round. December came and found the *Golden Dolphin* thirty yards from high tide. Jim began to talk of a launching by Christmas. Then one day Moore, whose turn it was at the lookout, came racing down with evil news. A flotilla of canoes was in the channel, winging toward the island. He had counted ten craft and figured they would arrive by noon. With one impulse they rushed to the lookout and saw the dread confirmation of all their fears, after long weeks of labor, with victory almost in sight.

To fight off the landing of so many scores of warriors would be impossible. They had already seen how little they cared for gunfire. To retreat to the cave, to trust that the *Golden Dolphin* might be overlooked, was their only hope — and a slight one. The ship stood out on the beach, visible from the reef entrance. The sight of it surely meant a swift search all over the island, with destruction of the precious ship as the least of calamities. The best they might do was not to be taken alive.

They stayed until the canoes, profusely decorated, streaming over the quiet sea, were lost to sight behind the headland of the landing bay, then hurried with their weapons to the cave. From it they could view, through a gap in the jungle, a section of the stone causeway. In the entrance they waited with grim fortitude, resolved to give stern account of themselves, to die as white men and white women should. Kitty, of her own accord, stood close by Jim. He smiled at her and she smiled back wanly.

"At the last, Jim, you won't leave me alone?" He shook his head, not trusting himself to speak.

Suddenly they heard shouts. The canoes had landed. Then, to their surprise, a mighty chanting mingled with the beat of drums, the shrilling of flutes and the belching roar of conch shells. Whatever the reason for the visit, it was stronger than the curiosity that the inevitable sight of the ship set out upon the beach must have excited. The sounds came nearer, mounting. There was a procession coming up the causeway to the hill of sacrifice. Their discovery was delayed. Some vital ceremonial was forward.

They waited breathlessly. They had brought binoculars with them on their first landing and Jim trained the glass on the strip of causeway. They could have picked off some of the savages with rifles but to commence a fight was to invite annihilation. The music, if such barbaric rhythm might be so termed, grew steadily louder. The leaders of the procession came into view, weird, leaping fantastic figures of naked men who wore high headdresses of feathers fluttering on frames that extended five feet above their bushy hair, itself tied with strips of gaily colored fiber. They were striped and patched in red and white and yellow, their faces hideously daubed. Some had picked out in white their ribs and the bones of their arms and legs. On their necks and all their limbs were strings of shells and teeth. Each held a drum shaped like an enormous wooden stein on which they beat as they sprang and shouted.

Then came file after file of warriors, armed with spears and clubs, with bows and arrows, painted like the rest, leaping along in unison to the throbbing, screaming drum and whine and roar of the unseen orchestra.

He handed the glass to Kitty at her request.

"I wouldn't look at it, if I were you," he said.

"I'm not afraid of them," she said.

She slightly changed the focus of the glass. A litter came by, a platform borne by six enormous cannibals, so braced that it could easily be carried horizontally along the ramp. On it, beneath a canopy supported by poles, reclined a figure of commanding pose. His upper body seemed to be covered with light pigment; the lower was kilted with patterned cloth of native pounding from inner bark.

Jim heard an indrawn sigh from Kitty. The binoculars fell from her hands to the dust of the cave, and her face glowed with some strange ecstasy. Instinctively he put out his hand to restrain her but she swerved and leaped from the cave mouth to the tiny trail they had contrived. She flew down it with arms extended, sounding a glad, impossible cry of, *"Father! Father!"*

For a heart-beat Jim thought she was demented; then he raced to overtake her, gun in hand. The others followed. The procession had halted. The man in the litter was looking toward the direction of the voice that had reached him above the clamor. The music stopped at a lift of his hand. He spoke to the savages in a high, imperious voice. Kitty fled on the wings of love. For all his efforts Jim could not reach her before, light as a fawn, she broke through the mask of green that ended the trail and was out by the side of the litter, reaching up her arms, sobbing and laughing — *"Father! Father!"* And to Jim's amazement, the man stretched out his arms, and in a broken voice called back to her.

He ordered the litter carried aside and waved the astounded procession on and upward. They obeyed, casting half fearful glances at him, looks of chained hatred at the little group of whites, Lynda among them, that gathered round the litter as the bearers set it down. Kitty was in her father's arms and they drew to one side as the files passed — rank upon rank of warriors, priests carrying a strange representation of a fish in wickerwork frame, painted red and black; then the musicians with conches and panpipes and larger drums slung between four carriers, two men beating. As they passed their white leader — for such he plainly was, if not their god — they started once more to play their savage instruments. The chant recommenced and they went on up the hill. Last of all came men bearing baskets in which was flesh, the carcasses of pigs. Others carried giant yams. There was also another great wicker fish, red and black, toiling blindly along with two men inside of it, their spotted legs, red on black, showing strangely beneath the fetish.

Jim turned to Captain Avery and saw on his breast the same emblem, a fish tattooed in red and black.

"I saw my ship on the beach," said Captain Avery, "and I marveled. I thought it might have been the work of the men who were killed some months ago by the tribe — without my knowledge — though I wondered why they should have salvaged it. After the ceremonial I should have investigated, of course. But nothing is allowed to interfere with this sacrificial visit.

"This is the island of Lukuba. We came today from the island of Tudava where I am half chief, half god, the impersonation of Lono.

"The *Golden Dolphin* was flung up on Lukuba by a tidal wave from a marine earthquake. The islands are both volcanic. At intervals there are shocks; on Tudava an occasional eruption and overflow from a crater.

"I wrote you, Kitty, from Suva, that I feared trouble among my crew. It was ripe when the wave caught us up. After we were crashed down and found ourselves alive, they were still resolved to get the pearls that I had secreted in my cabin. I would not tell them where they were and they prepared to torture me after they had killed one man who tried to warn me of their coming.

"This island of Lukuba is slowly sinking into the sea. One time it sank twelve feet, with frightful landslides. Then the tribe deserted it. But, by the order of their priests, they visit it once a year to make sacrifice on their ancient altar to avert more disaster, for each shock affects both islands.

"The pilgrimage had landed just before the wave that carried us ashore. Terrified, they had seen nothing of our landing, flung through the jungle on the crest of a wild wave as we were. But returning, they heard the noise of our struggle, for my men were drunk and reckless. And they found me stripped, about to be tortured by fire. Had I not been naked they would not have seen the fish of Udanwaga, the totem of their tribe, tattooed upon my chest.

"This was the totem of Mafulu, my blood-brother, part of the fraternity ceremonial. The tribes of the Pacific are far-flung. They break up and migrate, but their customs and their sanctities hold. They gazed at me almost in awe, and when I spoke to them in their own tongue, they fell down and worshipped me. The others they killed. I could not prevent that. And they sacrificed them to their gods — in their own way.

"Me they took back to Tudava, and as we crossed the channel the crater was spouting smoke and flame and a flow of lava smoked down toward their main village, firing the forests. Their priests made incantations, and at last they called upon me. It may have been coincidence or the holier manifestation of God, but when we reached the landing the flow stopped, the eruption ceased. It was attributed to my *mana*, the godlike power within me, the manifestation of Lono who wore the sacred badge of Udanwaga, the fish from whom they were all descended. Had it not been prophesied that I should come?

"So I have lived with them and made laws for them and striven to make them wiser. Twice we have visited this island and I abolished the sacrifice of human flesh. I was ill with a fever when the flotilla left to take the strange craft they had sighted, or I would have forbidden it. For while they have given me all power, they are loath to loose me. I have had no chance to escape.

"When they came back that time with the corpses of white men in canoes almost swamped after two days and nights of paddling, bewildered by the rain and carried offshore by the great waves following, I told them it was the anger of the gods against their act. And to think that ever since you must have been here!

"I have always told them I should leave them some day. They will not dispute me after this miracle of your presence. For I will threaten to bring back the volcanic fires that have not flowed since I came with them. You see my godship has been precarious. But — it ends well. And now, tell me your story."

"Jim," said Captain Avery Whiting, as the *Golden Dolphin*, under a jury rig, bore sluggishly, but surely, on her way for Suva, while the peak of Lukuba — no longer beckoning — dimmed and diminished, "Lynda Warner tells me that you are in love with my daughter. She tells me also that Kitty is in love with you. I have told you what I think of your behavior. I have no son. I have often wanted one."

Jim stood silent, the two at the taffrail alone.

"Well?"

"Kitty is an heiress, sir. I —"

"You have a share in the pearls."

"If I must take that, it is to be divided with the others who stood by."

"Tut! You talk like a very young man sometimes, Jim. What are pearls? Would you deny Kitty for pearls? If that is what lies between you and her happiness I will fling them all overboard, and regret that I ever heard of them or brought them from the stranded *Golden Dolphin*. I am getting to be an old man, Jim. I had hoped to retire. Let me keep my pearls, or what they bring, for my old age. I may live long enough to see grandchildren. If so, I promise to let them be the inheritors. You see we are both talking foolishly and you are eaten up with a very false pride."

"Perhaps," said Jim, "I am willing to be convinced."

"Then go and talk to Kitty. She has bragged all along of your courage. Of late she must be beginning to doubt it. Wait — stay here and I will send her up to you."

THE MAROONER

I

El Cay de los Quatros Hombres

Like herrings cured in sun and wind
The four lie side by side.
Dry as a husk of coco-rind
Above the creaming tide.
Buccaneer Ballades.

"Turtler Tom" was the man who discovered them and gave name to the islet. He had beached his sloop in the leeward lagoon the better to calk a leaking seam and found them lying on the sand just above tide reach, the desiccated rinds of what had once been human beings, mummified, distorted husks of shriveled skin and flesh and bone, their bleaching skulls wisped with hair, a few discolored rags flapping about the pitiful remnants.

What tortures had forerun the giving up of their ghosts on this arid shoal that thrust itself above the blue Bermudan waters, Tom could well imagine. There was no water on the cay, no shade, no growth but scanty herbage and brown palmetto scrub that survived between the rains by some miracle. He looked for identification traces in the shreds of personal belongings and found none.

"Dead of hunger and of thirst," Tom said to his Carib sailor. "What brought them here? There is no wreckage."

Then his foot kicked up an object buried in the sand and wind-drift. He stooped and picked it up.

It was a boarding-pistol of unusual design.

Forged of the same strip to which the trigger-guard was attached and deep-set in the wooden frame of the barrel was a heavy blade, machete-shaped, sickle-curving, a formidable weapon for close quarters after the discharge of the pan-primed powder and bullet, a thing designed by the genius of deviltry.

Turtler Tom had seen this pattern before though it was rare those days, the recent invention of a buccaneer scourge of the Caribbean. His moody eyes gleamed as he hefted the cunningly balanced weapon by its carved grip.

"Marooned, poor devils! Marooned by 'Long Tom' Pugh!" he exclaimed. "One of his bullies dropped it from his belt, likely, and it got shuffled under the sand. Come, Tampi, we'll bury what's left of 'em."

Turtler Tom bore the news of his grisly find with him back to Providence and to Port Royal and all along his devious water wanderings but the score of Long Tom Pugh was a long one and *los quatros hombres* lay beneath the weather-fluted sands on the cay that bore their name as only epitaph, unrecognized though doubtless not unmourned.

▌▌

The Mercy of Long Tom Pugh

The chase had been a long one and Long Tom Pugh raged like a thwarted devil. From dawn until a scant half-hour of sunset Pugh's schooner had trailed the other, both vessels tacking on long reaches with canvas set until their tall masts bent like whips and their lee rails were gutters of foam.

Foot by foot Pugh's *Scourge* had overhauled the fugitive until the weapon from which Pugh got his name, the "Long Tom" couched in the bows, had found first its range and then its target, so that now the trader lay wallowing in the choppy seas off the tiny cay, hull riddled, foremast gone, its decks a clutter of rope and canvas that served as shrouds to five of its crew that the last charge of partridge had dismembered and disemboweled. Three men stood near the stern, weary, bloodstained, helpless, yet defiant, watching Pugh's longboat crowded with his bullies dance over the water to take them off.

"A murrain on the luck!" said Pugh. "A stinking shell-peddler! And I thought it a gold-carrier from the Plate! And we short of powder. But they'll pay for it, the dogs!"

He cupped his hands and bellowed across the crisp waves.

"Bring 'em away and let her sink, blast her. The wind's ashift."

The hair upon Pugh's broad and naked chest was black save where a streak of white marked where a cutlass slash had sliced his brisket, but the hair of his head and of his long beard was dyed a rusty purple as if it were stained with dried blood. His fierce face, deep-tanned, deep-scored, was split by a great, bony nose like the beak of a macaw with nostrils that were narrow slitted and twitched as he watched the progress of his boat. One black eye had Pugh and one of hazel and from both of them the devil looked out as it leaned on elbows across the sill of his brain, never free from the fume of liquor and never seemingly affected by it.

He was bare to his belt that was studded with pistols tucked into a gaudy over-sash and to which swung a hanger in a leather scabbard. Wide pantaloons were thrust into wider sea-boots of leather and he stood with his legs wide apart and his furry hands upon his hips. Almost alone of all his crew of forty ruffians who overcrowded the capacity of the *Scourge*, Pugh wore no earrings. The lobe of one brown ear lopped in twain where some desperate foe had torn away the ornament. His teeth were naturally divided and Pugh had filed them in the manner of the Madagascar savages, the better to characterize his evil countenance.

The sun dropped rapidly and the sinking schooner swashed about in water that was incarnadined with the sunset. Nine of Pugh's bullies were in the longboat, now returning with the three prisoners, forty-odd watched at the rail or made ready for the tack to come, for the fickle day's-end wind was setting them down to the shoals that outribbed from the cay.

The three men were set aboard, their arms pinioned behind their backs and shoved aft to where Pugh stood agrin. They were of varying age and stature and one was bald save for a fringe of hair. But there seemed some link of related features common to all of them and they looked Pugh fairly in the face though the blood was running into the eyes of one of them from a scalp wound.

"So," said Pugh. "Ye thought to outsail the *Scourge* in that coffin-box of yours?"

The bald man answered.

"We could not fight. We had no weapons to match yours."

"Then ye would have fought, priest-face? Eh? Ye would have fought with Pugh?"

"I'll fight with ye now, an ye let one arm free," answered the other composedly.

Pugh's face grew purple with a rush of choleric blood. He whipped a pistol from his belt and leveled it, the hammer slowly cocking to the pull of his finger. Then he lowered the weapon.

"Sink ye for a bragging fool," he said. "But I will not kill in cold blood. I must remember my vow. I am a merciful man. Yet ye crow well. What is your name?"

"We be three Graemes."

Pugh glanced to where the yellow lettering on the pitching stern of the wallowing vessel showed the name *Three Brothers* and nodded.

"Of Nassau? Turtlers?"

"Aye. Our port is Nassau but we are Carolinans."

"So? What know ye of the schooner *Belle Isle* bound from the River

Plate. She should be hereabouts. Speak up."

"Naught. Nor would I tell ye an' I did."

"Say ye so? Look ye, Graeme, I am a merciful man. And ye are a fool to be stubborn standing on the edge of trouble. It is in my mind that ye are lying. So, I give ye another chance. Tell me what ye know of the *Belle Isle* and join my crew. We can find room for all of ye and a full share apiece if ye come willingly?"

Silence hung for a few seconds.

"No? Still stubborn? Then we but waste time, brethren three. Into the boat with them!" Pugh ordered as a stronger gust set the *Scourge* to shivering where she swung in the eye of the wind, uneasy and restive, her keen bows pawing the waves, "Give them the usual provender and set them on the cay."

For the first time something like anxiety showed in the faces of the trio.

"Ye would not maroon us on yon cay?" said the eldest Graeme, "'Tis waterless. Man, 'twill be worse than murder. It means —"

"A fig for what it means," said Pugh. "Ye will shortly find that out. And I am a merciful man, Graeme. I am sending meat and drink."

The brothers exchanged glances. It was as if they nodded acquiescence with their eyes. The bald-headed one spoke.

"Then may God curse ye for a murderer and a coward, Long Tom Pugh!" he said. "May ye come at your end to linger till your tongue grows to the roof of your mouth and your belly shrivels. May your soul shred out into the darkness and whine in the winds for mercy."

He suddenly shot out neck and head and spat full in the buccaneer's face.

Pugh turned livid and his eyes became points of fire. He snatched the scarlet bandanna from the head of one of his crew and wiped his face and beard, then flung the gaudy silk overboard where the wind snatched at it and whirled it far astern.

"Ye are a cunning knave, Graeme," he said and his voice held hate and breathed it as an iron holds heat. "I would that I had time to handle ye aright. Yet, before ye die, ye will wish a hundred times that I had shot ye as ye would have me do. Over with them! Ye will find company ashore, Graeme. Ask the four I left there a while ago to play hosts to ye."

"And speed back," he called to the quartermaster in the stern of the longboat. "These are tricky waters. Ah, look at that!"

The foundering schooner had taken her last sudden plunge and disappeared, but her maintop spar protruded from the water, warning of a shoal toward which wind and sea were slowly backing the *Scourge*.

"We'll pick ye up outside!" roared Pugh. "Let her come up! Pay off there! Starboard tack!"

He leaped to the wheel, active as a tiger for all his bulk, and laid a guiding-hand to the spokes to aid the helmsman. The lithe schooner gathered way and hurled herself ahead as she caught the wind in the shallow hollows of her sails, close-hauled, fighting free from the threatening reefs and bars. The longboat sped to the shore, tumbling out the three Graemes, hurling after them two kegs, one of which fell short and swashed about in the tide fringe till two of them retrieved it.

The boat went racing back after the *Scourge* as, clear of shoals, it once more hung in the wind. The bullies clambered aboard and left the longboat, riding to a line, to lunge after the schooner like a leaping dog after its master. Then the sun fell below the horizon and darkness jumped up from its ambush beyond the rim of the sea.

Presently a spark of light appeared on the leeward side of the cay and grew to a crackling radiance as the crisp palmetto fans flared up. About the fire squatted the three brothers, their faces grim in the ruddy glow as they took counsel.

"I would not care so much, save for Margaret," said Will Graeme, the youngest of the three. "The babe was to come this week. I had thought to be at home." And a spasm contracted his features.

"Take heart, lad," said John Graeme, the bald-headed. "We will win through. Aye, and settle accounts with Long Tom Pugh. The rains are not so far off. A month at most. We can eke out. We will. Fret not, Will, the child will be born ere she begins to worry over ye. But we must go carefully. Just keep the life in us till the rains come or we sight some ship. Mayhap we'll get enough from the wreck to build some sort of craft."

"The current swings about the cay," said Alec Graeme. "There was no driftwood on the beach. And we were chased by the *Scourge* far off the travel lanes. Ye heard what Pugh said about company? How he left four here? This is Quatros Hombres Cay where Turtler Tom buried them that Pugh marooned."

"Yet we will win through," said John Graeme. "I'll handle the rations. Alec, see if the water-keg is full. We can do without tonight."

"'Tis but a double anker," grumbled Alec Graeme as he rolled the keg closer to the fire and John Graeme did the same with the barrel of meat. "Now may the flesh rot on his bones while he lives in anguish!" cried Alec passionately. "This is no water anker! 'Tis brandy! And the other bully beef! The lying, grinning devil with his talk of mercy! Brandy and salted meat and the rains a month away!"

III

The Inn at Porto Bello

Oh, sing me a song of a rover,
A tale of the Spanish Main
Of a buccaneer living in clover,
And drink to the jolly refrain.

Ho, yo ho, as black as a crow
Is the flag the bullies sail under;
To Long Tom Pugh and his rollicking crew
And the roar of his carronades' thunder.

Ho, yo ho, for the swing of the surge,
Show me a schooner as swift as the Scourge.
Gallant and free are the men of the sea
Who sail under Long Tom, the Wonder!

They beat out the time of the tune with their rummers and mugs on the scarred tables while their crimson faces loomed through the blue haze of the tobacco-smoky, low-ceilinged room like sundogs through a mist. The song ended and Pugh tossed a couple of gold pieces to the singer who spun them with a flick of thumb and finger and roared for more liquor.

There were twenty rowdy, blousy wenches, *mustees* most of them, bred of full whites and quadroons, olive-skinned and flushed with their portions of the tankards thrust upon them by the pirates who shared them, each woman with either arm about a buccaneer, ogling, cajoling for a dividend of the freely spent, lightly gained gold. Presently the wail of violins joined in a pulse-quickening hornpipe. There was a scuffle for partners, half-jovial, half-ugly, and a score of couples thrust back chairs and tables and swung and lurched upon the sand-gritted floor.

Long Tom Pugh and his bullies were in Porto Bello. There were no hovering king's ships to annoy and the town was theirs, as long as their gold lasted. Pugh did not dance. He sat apart with the quartermaster of the *Scourge* and his mate and chief gunner, his evil face seamed in a smile that split his henna-stained whiskers.

"I'm done," said the quartermaster, glowering at the dice he had just cast. "I'm clean as a whistle, curse the bones. There's the devil's own luck in them!"

"There should be," answered Pugh as he scooped in the stake. "They are shaped from the thigh-bone of the man 'Roaring' Raines left to guard his treasure-chest when he buried it on Ransom Cay. Raines buried it and I found it with the skeleton of the poor devil he took ashore to do the digging sprawled atop of the chest. Raines didn't figure on the shifting dunes.

"We got hold of a member of his crew and persuaded him to tell which cay Raines chose to leave the loot on. He told us what he knew and luck did the rest. The wind had blown the sand and there was the hand of Raines' gravedigger sticking up like a sign-post, beckoning us to come and get even with Roaring Dick. And my bo'sun shaped me the dice. Try your own, man. Come, you've a ring there I fancy. I'll stake a gold doubloon against it."

The quartermaster hesitated, then drew the ring from his finger. It was of crude workmanship, fashioned to form a snake of gold with a flawed emerald set in the flat of the head and two diamond chips for the eyes.

"I'll set it against five and no less," he said.

"Three and no more," answered Pugh and piled the stake. A minute later and he stuck it on his own hairy digit.

The quartermaster smothered his resentful oath in his tankard.

"Where did ye loot the ring?" asked Pugh, twisting it about. "I do not recollect seeing it in the sharing."

"I got it from a wench," lied the quartermaster.

He had taken it from the finger of Will Graeme when he had bound his arms behind him. And in this, he, the chosen representative of the crew in the division of spoils, had cheated. But the lie passed.

"She gave it ye for your handsome face, I suppose," said Pugh and the others at the table laughed, for the quartermaster's face was pox-pitted so that his features seemed to have crumbled.

"A winner's jests come easy," he growled and the look he gave Pugh was murderous.

The scrape of the fiddles and the shuffling of feet ended and once more the sweating servers scurried about replenishing the empty mugs. A fight over a girl broke out in a corner and the *mustee* ran squealing from the grappling men.

"Bring 'em out in the open," bawled Pugh.

With all the blood lust in them flaming from the liquor they had swigged, a dozen men hustled out the combatants to the open space between the tables.

"Take away their knives," ordered Pugh. "I'll lose no good men for the sake of a worthless wench. A doubloon to the winner!"

Left to themselves the two pirates, roaring like bulls, rushed at each other swinging arms like flails, locked, swayed and fell together to the floor. One got astride of the other and gripped his throat while the under man's knees played a tattoo against his back and he squirmed like a seal. The topmost lost his balance and they rolled over and apart to scramble to their feet amid the yells of their comrades.

There was no science to it and much comedy, for one was squat and bow-legged and the other lanky and gangling. But the latter bashed the short one in the face with a straight left so that his nose seemed to split like a rotten pear and the blood spurted. The squat man bellowed, grabbed his long opponent about the buttocks and sent him hurtling over his shoulder to smash against the table-leg with his head.

The unsound support splintered at the impact and the table pitched forward with all its contents while the room echoed with ribald laughter. The lanky man lay stunned and was hauled out by his feet to have a tankard of ale dashed in his face as the victor advanced to Pugh for his doubloon.

A door had opened in the rear and a girl came in whose appearance drew the swift attention of those nearest to her, halting their jesting and buffoonery to a silence that rapidly spread so that she advanced in a strained quietude to the center of the sanded space where she stood for a moment before she gave a nod to the fiddlers and began to dance.

She danced like a reed in the wind, swaying with infinite grace of posture, her feet scarce leaving a circle less than that of an ordinary platter. She was tall and lissome, though full-busted and she looked like a half-opened flower, fresh, unsmirched with paint and holding an air of aloofness that was eerie.

Her dark gray eyes, almost violet at times in the uncertain lights, seemed to gaze far beyond the tavern walls, she danced as one might dance at will on the sea-sands, as a nymph might dance, strangely incongruous in that assembly of gross-passioned men, unconscious of her surroundings. Her golden hair was coiffed in classic simplicity and her sable draperies were at odd variance with the tawdry gauds of the *mustees* who viewed her with palpable disfavor yet shared the silent concentration of the buccaneers.

The air the fiddlers played was soft and low, a crooning rhythm that sounded like the murmur of surf after a storm or a breeze playing amid young birches. And, as she danced, to the masterful, masterless men about her, came visions of Spring woods where hyacinths and primrose clustered, of brooks winding amid lush sedges, all set in the far-off days of their own innocence.

The rhythm changed and she floated 'round the room, light as thistle-down or a foam-bell, her eyes passing over the rough, seamed faces with no hint that she regarded them as indices of humanity, hypnotizing them by the sheer beauty of her dance. Then she snapped her fingers to the players and they swung their bows to a wild *tarantelle*. The violet eyes became black, sudden roses flashed out on her cheeks, her posturing became of the flesh rather than the spirit, provocative, yet so infinitely graceful that it still held the audience in thrall though their heads swayed to the increasing lilt and their pulses pounded.

She was no longer a foam bell, but a curling wave that leaped, upcurving, cresting to the very feet and then swept back in furious eddies that bewildered with their whirl.

A fiddle-string snapped. She stopped, ivory arms flung back, audacious, challenging, as a shower of coins fell upon the floor and one of the pirates, snatching a tambourine from his quondam consort, gathered up the gold and humbly offered it to her as she curtsied low before Long Tom Pugh, whose eyes were ablaze and whose beaked nose showed its ridge of bone as the nostrils twitched and dilated and the great chest lifted and fell.

He rose, sweeping the table aside and, in one great stride, reached and raised her, crushing her to him while his bearded lips sought hers. Then he drew back with an oath as she twisted free and stood, less at bay than ready for attack, a dagger she had drawn from between her breasts flashing in her hand, her eyes holding Pugh's while one of his great paws fumbled at his beard where blood was oozing its way through the mat of hair just beneath the line of his chin.

All breaths were held, sensing the verge of tragedy. But Pugh, still fumbling at his beard, slowly retreated until his other hand, back-stretched, felt the edge of the table he had pushed aside. His eyes, no longer blazing, but ablink, were fixed on those of the dancer and, as he leaned against the support, he shivered.

"She is a witch," he muttered. "Look at her eyes. They are not human! By God, she missed my jugular by an inch! She would have let the life out of me!"

And still the room hung on the scene, marveling to see Pugh so strangely tamed yet conscious of the weird power of the woman. Pugh's hand fetched up against a rummer and tightened about it. He lifted it and drained the raw *caña* it contained. As he set it down the dancer's gaze suddenly fastened on the ring he had won from the quartermaster.

She seemed to stiffen in a sinuous pose, while the arm that held the dagger glided like a white-skinned snake, back in an almost imperceptible movement that presaged a lightning thrust. It came, but only to sheath the knife between her breasts once more, and she laughed.

"Know ye not ye must not touch me?" she asked, and her voice, clear as a bell, seemed to come from afar off like the sound of a distant chime. "Ye must not touch me, for I am Death," she said. "I am the White Death and this dress is the shroud of Love." Her eyes, absolutely fearless, burned in their absolute belief of what she spoke to Pugh's brain and to all in that still silent room. The light in them was uncanny, as if the soul no longer reigned behind them in its seat, they were lambent with the high glaze of madness. And they held Pugh as a snake charms a bird.

"You are Death?" he muttered. She nodded.

"But you need not fear me yet," she said. "I have not harmed you. Only warned you. Did I not dance for you? And you sought to take me. Know ye not that it is Death who comes for you?"

She advanced her hand and the great bulk of Pugh cowered. He crossed himself and many of his men did likewise.

"Where got ye that coiling ring about your finger?" she asked.

He took it off and offered it to her.

"Take it," he said. "Take it and go."

"There is blood on it," she answered. Pugh looked shudderingly at the circlet and laid it on the table, not realizing it was his own gore from the fingers that had pressed his neck that stained it.

"It is yours," he said shortly. "Take it."

"Nay, I have not yet earned it. Nor have ye told me its history.

Surely it has a history? Mayhap it was a love-pledge once upon a time? Tell me. Then I will sing for ye and so I shall have earned it."

"I know naught of it," said Pugh. "I won it but now from him."

He nodded at the quartermaster and the woman's eyes scrutinized the pitted face for an instant.

"Ye shall tell me presently," she said, and smiled.

And with her smile the dread that had stiffened the face of the quartermaster passed and he grinned at her with yellow teeth. The witch had turned siren and his vicious blood responded.

"I'll spin the yarn," he said. "I am not so timid as others." And he glanced sneeringly at Pugh who had sat down and was shading his eyes with his hand.

"No?" she asked. "Then why do ye make the holy symbol?" For the pirate's bundled fingers still touched his tunic above his heart. "He who woos Death does not always win. Yet Death is kind."

She stepped back and commenced to sing:

> Where lies he now?
>   Lost love of mine;
> His marble brow
>   Is creased with brine,
> His lips caressed
>   Are chill and gray;
> How warm they pressed
>   The other day.
> His body swings
>   To shifting tide,
> No twilight brings
>   Him to his bride.
> Yet do I know
>   Our tender vow
> Shall ever bind,
>   As then, so now.
> When fails my breath,
>   When life grows dim,
> I'll thank grim Death
>   For finding him.

It was a dirge that changed into a paean of joy. While she sang there was not a soul-calloused sea-rover, not a hardened drab but sighed to the memory or the lost hope of love, tender, gallant and enduring, not one but thrilled to the credence of the last triumphant lines. In a spell they sat as she took the ring and glided from the room, the tambourine with its golden offerings untouched.

Then Pugh shook off the mood that compassed him.

"Go, bring her back," he ordered. "Fiend take me, but I'll teach the jade. I'll take her, aye, and break her till she sighs for death. Rot me, up and after her, I say."

No one moved till the quartermaster, with a contemptuous look at Pugh, got up.

"I'll find her," he said. "But I'll not promise to bring her back."

Pugh started up, coughed and set a swift hand to his mouth. The stab had pierced through to his throat and his mouth had filled with blood as his anger quickened its flow. And the quartermaster, catching up the tambourine as he went, vanished into the night outside.

The tavern-keeper came hurrying with a bowl of water and a pannikin of rough salt. Pugh swallowed his own blood and waved him aside.

"'Tis no hemorrhage, fool!" he said, "Only a scratch. Unless," he added, half to himself, and his ruddy face paled, "the witch poisoned it."

"Best let me fetch a leech," said the tavern-keeper. "Indeed I know little of the wench, save she is a bit mad. She comes from Nassau, some say. She has an infant. She lost her man at sea and it crazed her. But this is hearsay. She has danced here and elsewhere and sings among the sailors, seeking news of her man. Yet she seems not to know her own name. And she was ever harmless until now."

"I have a leech of my own," said Pugh. "If the fool is sober? So, Folsom, here ye are. Take a look at this slit the she-devil put in me. Where is the quartermaster?"

"Gone after the witch," said the discredited medico, who had joined the outlaws of the *Scourge*.

"May she slash his weasand agape," said Pugh. "We would be well rid of both of them, What think ye of the wound?"

"I think 'tis clean. Some ointment and a stitch, maybe — "

"Then come off to the schooner. Lads, we sail on the flood close after dawn. I have news of a gold-ship. And," he added as he left the tavern with the leech, "if she bewitches the quartermaster we'll sail without him, He is too solid with the men now, for my liking."

As they went down the beach the chorus broke out again behind them, muffled by the closing door:

> *Ho, yo ho, as black as a crow,*
> *Is the flag we bullies sail under,*
> *To Long Tom Pugh and his rollicking crew*
> *And the roar of our carronades' thunder.*

IV

Margaret Graeme

It is hard to say if Margaret Graeme was mad. Perhaps it was merely the passing fever of a brain lit by the exaltation of one great concentration of purpose, bred of a mating love and hope — the finding of her man. Will Graeme had promised to be back for the birth of their son; no ordinary circumstance would have held him.

Now he was two months overdue and for six weeks she had been seeking news of him, bending her will to the best ways and means of cajoling sailormen, the use of her beauty, of her voice and of her grace, so used as to keep herself inviolate for Will. So had grown in her a wondrous cunning coupled to her gifts of dance and song that had bubbled up within the sweet fountain of her body in the happy days of love and mating.

She had thought of the *boucaniers*. There were other perils of the deep, but it was not yet the season of hurricanes, and the *Three Brothers* was a stanch and speedy craft, while Alec and John and Will formed a trio of mariners who were innate masters of the sea rather than doomed to be its playthings. In her six weeks of flitting from port to port she had heard more than once of Quatros Hombres Cay and the way of Long Tom Pugh and others of his calling.

Earlier pirates had been different, men big in a crude way, moved by fits of cruelty or generosity as the mood swayed them. Sometimes they would kill, kill for the sheer joy of blood-letting, drunk with the fight, the reek of powder and the drive of blade or point through elastic flesh and stubborn bone. And again they would give some gallant foe his ship after they had glutted their fancies from the cargo, or send the survivors adrift in an open boat to take their chance of landing after having sworn them not to inform.

But Pugh and his ilk took no chances. They were marooners, leaving their victims on desert cays to perish, destroying all witnesses, yet styling themselves merciful.

And Margaret's grief-shocked brain had determined that buccaneers had taken her Will and his brothers. True, the *Three Brothers* hull held nothing worth the rifling but she had the heels of the trading fleet and the pirates were apt at changing to a faster or sounder vessel than their own. On these lines Margaret had hidden her identity, asking rather than leading up to information, listening, piecing together, charming her crews and selecting by her woman's wits the natural chiefs among them.

Even the child came second. With her on her wanderings went a coal-black West Indian negress, a giantess in size and strength, a child in loyalty and admiration of her golden-haired mistress, who played nurse to the infant and guardian to the mother.

Margaret knew, when she left the tavern, that the pox-pitted quartermaster would follow her. It was the compelling urge of her sex, grown to its utmost power in the hothouse of her love, that called to such rough spirits yet held their coarseness in check by the purity of her own spirit's flame. She was a Circe and she bent men's passions and wills as one might weave osiers to a basket.

As the quartermaster, the hot blood flooding his brain to one mad desire that was only tempered by a certain dread, emerged, tambourine in hand, its golden coins jingling slightly on the taut parchment, out from the heated tavern into the quiet night, he saw, between the interlacing shadows of the palms upon the shell road, silver where the moon lustered it, the figure of the dancer, vague, uncertain, almost ghostly in the checkered light that shifted with the play of the land wind in the plumes of coco-palms. She had a *mantilla* about her head, but he caught the gleam of her eyes as she glanced his way, and marked the play of her beckoning hand.

Involuntarily he crossed himself, then swore at his own weakness with a crude sea-oath and followed her in his lurching deck-gait. Followed, for she glided ahead without ever looking back, on beyond the clustering houses of the port, on to where a path led through the seabush. She went fast, and the quartermaster, his heart pounding a devil's jig against the cage of his ribs, lunged after, striving in vain to gain without breaking into a run, from which the same latent, tugging fear at the back of his inflamed brain prevented him.

They came into a scanty clearing where a mud cabin stood and a little stream flowed from the hills and spent itself in the sand. An owl hooted and the quartermaster checked his pace at the omen. It might be the witch's familiar. But he was a slow-witted man, save in the practice of his calling, and the strength of his body and the triumph of a hundred personal skirmishes had endowed him with a sturdy belief in his own prowess that built up a dogged courage born of the flesh rather than the mind. His purpose once set, he would hold to it. And he followed.

Lights glowed suddenly in the two visible windows of the little cabin and he saw the door open as the woman reached the threshold and, turning for the first time, drew aside her *mantilla*, showed him the witching oval of her face with its gleaming eyes and, with the tiniest beckon of her head, passed in.

There was but one room in the low-roofed place. By the light of two brass lamps burning whale oil, he saw that it was empty, saw too, that the only other door, at the back, was barred on the inside. There was little furniture. A low bed stood behind a screen and, near the pillows he saw what seemed a small bundle underneath the coverlet.

Who then had opened the door or lit the lamps? He felt the hair rising at the nape of his neck and the incipient goose-quills lifting down his spine. His hands tapped the pistol butts in his belt and the handles of his dirks and the swift wish came to him that he had a silver witch-bullet in the muzzle of one of the former.

But the woman had turned and, radiantly alluring, pointed to a rough chair in which he sat, even while he felt little cold beads break out upon his brow beneath his headkerchief. A slight draft caused him to slightly turn his head and roll his eyeballs toward the door through which he had just entered. It was slowly closing of its own volition. The dancer was holding out a pewter mug toward him.

"It is *caña*," she said. "I will pledge you first."

She sipped a little and swallowed it. He could see the moisture of the liquor on her crimson lips and he took the mug and drained it. The ardent stuff fired him, his eyes became bloodshot and he leaned toward her, swaying a trifle like an amorous bear. God, but she was beautiful! White — and tender and sweet! But some tingling touch of restraint still thralled him.

"What if I should take you, mistress?" he uttered in a deep guttural.

She surveyed him unafraid with her shining eyes. They held a hint of amusement.

"You would be dead long before the dawn," she said, and the utter conviction of her voice hammered home to him the feeling that she spoke sooth.

"Did I not tell you I was Death?" she almost crooned. "I could kill you in a hundred ways, so very easily. They say I am a witch. You think so as you sit there. Wouldst see my familiar? Look at the window."

Swiftly she lowered the wicks of the two lamps till they barely showed. The moonlight came in at one window and made a wedge-path to where the quartermaster sat. The path began some two feet from the window where the shadow of the wall below the sill ended. It was very white and luminous, squared off by the woodwork of the panes.

Slowly a blotch began to eclipse its brightness. A drumming noise commenced and quickened as the blotch enlarged and the pulse of the mariner beat faster until it seemed as if the sound were that of the blood flowing through his own veins. Then, suddenly, a face leered in at the window.

The face of a demon, livid, emitting a pale lambency that set off a great, grinning mouth set with pointed tusks between which lolled the tip of a lusting tongue, staring eyeballs floating in white circles, wide nostrils eagerly agape and crisp hair that seemed alive with mysterious lights. The skin was black, like that of a devil from the pit, and it appeared fungused with the phosphorescence of decay. It blotted out the moonlight and shone by its own radiance.

Santa Maria! This dancer was no woman! She was a ghoul, a succubus! The quartermaster snatched a pistol from his belt and pulled trigger. By some mischance the powder had fallen from the pan and it missed fire. But his brain gave no such ordinary explanation. The face was still there. And, by the living God! A snake was twining through the tresses! He flung himself at the door that opened outward. It was of solid hardwood and it resisted his heavy thrust as if it had been of iron.

Behind him the dancer laughed. He turned, sweat clammy on him, at bay, fumbling for a knife. The lamps were turned up again, the face had gone.

"Sit down," she said. "Since ye can not go, sit down. I mean ye no harm."

"No harm? Then why —"

"So ye should not harm yourself by trying to harm me. Take more *caña.*"

She handed him a fresh measure and took a pipe from a stand, filled it and handed it to him with a paper spill that she had lighted above the flame of her lamp. Half-mechanically he drank the liquor and accepted the pipe, sitting down once more. "Are ye human or what?" he asked, gaining false courage from the *caña* and the homely elements of her hospitality. "Or have ye tricked me? By the wounds of God's Son, that head cast a shadow on the floor. 'Twas no spirit!"

He half rose.

"Wouldst try another pistol at it?" she asked smiling. "Or will ye go outside and seek it. The door is open now. Or closed, as I will. But I am flesh and blood. See."

She took his rough hand in her smooth one and set it on the warm satin of her forearm. The beast in him leaped to the front. He sprang up, coarse mouth open, eyes crimsoning, his clutching hands apart.

"Sit down," she said, and her voice rang like the crack of a trainer's whip. "If ye would win me ye must woo me. Sit down!"

His half-befuddled brain obeyed the dominance of her will and he crouched rather than sat, as an unwilling brute going through a disliked performance.

She had said "if." Would she come willingly to him? Would she play an obedient, eager beauty to his beast? If only she would take her eyes off his. She might be human, but those eyes were not. They made him blink as they had made Pugh blink. Yet she had preferred him to Pugh. Why not? He was the better man for all his ravaged face. Some day. . . .

"Ye are a brave man," she was saying. "Ye have done brave things and ye will do braver, with my aid. Come, ye were going to tell me about this ring."

There may have been some subtle herb steeped in the *caña*. The negress, voodoo-worshiper, who had so ably backed her mistress by her startling apparition, her sooty face smeared with match-phosphorus, fireflies in her wool, a harmless snake looped in the kinks, knew many secrets.

It was not the first time she had raised a devil to her mistress' conjuring, using such simple but not necessarily transparent means as in the present case when she had lit the lamps and swung the door at sight of Margaret's approach backed by a sailor-gaited man. Then, descending through the cellar-trap, kept covered by a grass rug, she had emerged by the outer hatch to play her demoniac role and set a prop against the entrance door as she and her mistress had planned for such emergency.

And it was small wonder that, with the setting, the suggestion and eerie atmosphere that environed Margaret, the quartermaster, knowing nothing of the existence of her sooty slave, had deemed the apparition supernatural.

Perhaps Margaret Graeme's stress of will gave her hypnotic power. The quartermaster gazed upon the dull emerald and the twinkling eyes of the golden snake and felt his own will melting into a desire to serve. If she was Circe, he was Caliban.

He had meant to lie about the ring, to spin some yarn redounding to his own prowess, but his words came aside from his own volition and he spoke the truth.

"There were three of them left, all brothers," he said. "We chased them all day, thinking them a gold-ship from the Plate, for there was one due in that neighborhood. The schooner was fast. We overhauled it at sunset and we sank it. We killed all the crew, for'ard and amidships, with a round of partridge. *The Three Brothers* it was called. Their name was Graeme.

"We brought them aboard in the longboat. I bound the youngest of them and I took this ring from his finger as I made it fast. One was bald and he mocked Pugh, who sent us ashore with them. We left them with a keg of salt-horse and an anker of brandy. 'Pugh's provender,' we call it. They are dead now and you have the ring."

"Where did ye land them. Where?"

"Nay, I know not. I told ye we chased them all day. We took no sun that noon. Nor did I check our bearings in the log for Pugh and I were at outs and I bunked for'ard for a week before. And since. Somewhere to the southeast of the Wind'ard Isles."

He had told all he knew. In the longboat he had not heard Pugh mention the four men set ashore at a time when he himself had been ashore at Skull Cay, their own headquarters, recovering from fever and a bad shot-wound. Nor did Pugh himself know that Turtler Tom had found the shriveled men and styled the islet Quatros Hombres. Margaret repressed a sigh. She was balked of the pith of what she sought even while she heard what caused her heart to leap. For Will was still alive — she was strangely confident of that. He had been on a barren cay for eight weeks, nearly nine, for the quartermaster had said Sunday, and the babe was born on Thursday night. Nine weeks with the food that was an aggravation rather than sustaining, the rains had not yet come though they were overdue, but she was sure that her Will, her gallant, strong, loving Will, would win through. As her love had made her do wonders so his would help him to a miraculous preservation. Then there were John, the canny, and Alec, the capable. Oh, it was impossible to think of them perishing!

So now she bent her wits to locating the cay. "Somewhere southeast of the Windward Islands" was like saying "somewhere in the haystack lies the needle." There were hundreds of cays — no man yet knew how many cays, since the charts were acknowledged vague — humping themselves above the waves, just awash, arid isles of the ocean desert.

But Pugh knew. And Pugh must tell. Pugh would be more difficult. He was not as plastic as his quartermaster, quicker-witted, more — due to his imagination — of a beast when aroused. Margaret swiftly made up her mind to ply the quartermaster of all he knew of Pugh, his rendezvous, his habits, his next intentions. This she would take to the king's ship — there was one expected soon at Providence, and she would make her bargain. News of how to capture Pugh in exchange for information to be dragged from the pirate as to the whereabouts of the cay on which he had set the Graemes. She might go farther and ask for passage on the king's ship.

Yet this course — and she reasoned so swiftly that the quartermaster knew naught of her mental process — was uncertain. Pugh might be kiled in the fight. And the *Scourge* had outsailed many a king's ship. She must have two strings to her bow. The quartermaster was her surest method. Later would come the ultimate revenge if aught really happened to her Will.

While the shuttle of her mind shot nimbly through the warp and woof of her brain, weaving in bright strands of hope, the land-wind swept down from the hills in a sudden rush, bringing with it the swift patter of rain. Her heart leaped. It was a sign — a sign that before many hours the season's fall would be mercifully drenching that scorched cay where Will fought off death. She turned to the quartermaster.

"It is a pretty ring," she said. "I am sorry it has no stranger history or that we do not know it. Thank you."

"Thank me not. Thank Pugh, or, rather, thank no one. You paid for it with your dancing. God, it was like the swaying of the seaweed in the lagoon pools when the tide shifts and all the colored fish swim in and out. And that last. It was a flame! See, I forgot the gold they gave ye."

He took up the tambourine with its jingling coins from the table.

"I need it not," she said. "Take it. Ye can use it."

Open-mouthed, he goggled at her insistence, then pouched the gold.

"Ye care not for money?" he said incredulously.

"Not for coins. They pass through a thousand hands a hundred times a year. They are counters in the game. I like jewels. I love jewels!"

She sighed, and looked at him with deliberate languishment.

"I have seen rare ones, aye, and owned them," he boasted. "I will get ye jewels that have adorned princesses, jewels from sacred shrines, jewels from the hilts of chieftain's swords. I will outweigh thee with jewels. Why, look ye, once —"

"Go on," she said. "Tell me of yourself, brave man."

There is no flattery so subtle as that of Desdemona's gift. All the world loves a ready listener, and the quartermaster talked until his own experience, his own limited invention, and what he remembered of the yarns of others were combined in his Ulyssean tale. Ever and anon the wind would rise to a gale with spit and slap of rain that passed unnoticed by the teller. At last he paused and emptied the mug she had kept replenished.

"I knew you for an adventurous man and a brave one, Simon Hart," she said, for he had told her his name. "You have told me your past. Give me your hand. I will read ye the future."

Then from his horny palm she conjured a vision of success, tinged with suggestions to her own end that so accorded with Simon Hart's self-estimation that it knit his will to achieve these things. She read and leavened his jealousy of Pugh, of any master, she cajoled him and held out hints of reward until he swore by all the gods of sea and land that she was a marvel and that he would prove her so.

"The men are with me," he boasted. "Pugh is puffed up with pride and has forgot his fellowship. They are tired of seeing him with the lion's share and, with their smaller measure, only harsh words. He would forbid them the freedom of the cabin, he would curb their shore liberty, he calls no conferences, he gives only half an ear to what I set before him.

"The wind blows my way now. And when we have given him the black spot, when he is deposed and I rule and reap a harvest of the Caribbean, wilt come with me to Skull Cay and queen it? I will build you a house and bring you *mustee* slaves, white slaves and black, and I will be the chiefest of them. I will make Pugh your servant. I will humble him as I will elevate thee. Wilt come?"

"Come back to me soon and tell me ye have done these things. We will reap the harvest later. Prove to me you are a better man than Pugh, Bring him to me or me to him —"

"What want ye of Pugh?" he asked with sudden suspicion.

"I hate him. He tried to kiss my lips. He would have taken me by force. I could have killed him but I would rather see you break him and then give him to me. See, the lamps are wan. The day breaks."

Simon Hart leaped to his feet and looked through the rain-streaked window at the graying east.

"We sail on the flood," he said. "Pugh would go without me. Farewell!"

He would have embraced her roughly, but she eluded him, and a hint of struggling rose stained the sky above the hills and flushed the room.

"Farewell," he cried again and left the cabin, running heavily across the clearing. Margaret watched him with eyes from which the glaze of fever had lifted to show exaltation struggling with weariness and saw him plunge into the bush path with a hasty wave to her. Then she turned back into the cabin and leaned above the small bundle on the bed behind the screen.

"Babe, babe," she breathed softly. "Your father, whom ye have never seen and who has never seen your little straight limbs and his own image in your eyes and shape, is coming home again."

And the pattering, saving rains told the beads of her prayers.

When the great negress came softly in she found Margaret Graeme asleep on her knees beside the bed, continuing her grateful petitions in her dreams.

Fox And Hounds

For the third time the *Scourge*, with mutiny mounting in the hearts of her crew, headed up for Skull Cay, Pugh's rendezvous in the delta of the River Plate. For the third time the chagrined lookout in the top saw through his glass the king's ship in the offing, visible to him by her higher spars and canvas. Behind them, outdistanced for the time, more by luck than speed, for the Scourge's bottom was fast gathering a drag of weed, Pugh knew the *Thetis*, sloop-of-war, was following relentlessly.

Somewhere below the sea rim her consort was cruising. And they were all after the *Scourge*. The hunt for Pugh was on, and these three indomitable, untiring gaze-hounds of the sea had viewed him and never had one of them, or two, failed to loom on the horizon at nightfall and again at dawn.

Once, after a gale that blotted sea and sky, a frigate had shown so close to them in the swift clearance that the bullies of the *Scourge* could see from their deck the yellow hull with its blue top-works and the scarlet gun-ports that opened eagerly to belch a broadside that came skipping and scattering across the waves. Pugh had run for it, outmetaled by this frigate of the fourth class but not outsailed. Then the sloop-of-war had appeared, heading them off, and Pugh and his bullies fought a smashing encounter.

The sloop had them inshore and the frigate was plowing along far astern, so that there was nothing for Pugh to do but run the gantlet of the sloop's broadside until he could forge ahead on his superior speed. This the *Scourge* had finally accomplished, but not until showering round-shot had taken toll of the crew and damaged the gear so that Pugh had to fish his fore-topmast. Five bullies went overboard to the ground sharks, seven still tossed and groaned in the stuffy cockpit, their jagged wounds attended by the leech with the rough surgery of those times.

Their best suit of sails had been sadly rent by the iron hail and they had been given no time to patch, only to change foresail and two of the jibs for extra canvas, well worn and none too sound. Altogether they were in evil case. Their bottom was fouling rapidly so that already they could note the difference of speed and answer to the helm. Their water was low and beginning to smell musty. Worst of all, the powder was running short.

They had made but a brief stay at Porto Bello on account of the tip given Pugh by the tavern-keeper concerning the gold-ship and they had been unable to buy munitions there. They had missed the gold-ship, or the tip had been false, the men were tired and lacked sleep, the grog was none too plentiful and Simon Hart assiduously encouraged the idea that it was all the fault of Pugh, that the captain's luck had gone, that he had had his day and that the passing of the "black spot" was in order. Such whisperings went about without any knowing who started them.

Pugh sensed the trouble, sensed too that the quartermaster was the brewer and cursed the day that he had taken among his crew a man who knew navigation. So far the common peril kept the snake of rebellion coiled and only sleepily resentful. Once out of it, Pugh determined that Simon Hart must die, in such fashion that the crew should not suspect Pugh of the deed. And Hart read the wish and the will in Pugh's demeanor so that the two went warily, watching each the other.

It was the continuous presence of one or other of the king's ships in the Plata Gulf that gave Pugh greatest uneasiness. True, he might, at nightfall, slip into one of the many mouths of the Plate and work his way through the labyrinth of creeks, but it was vital to refit and careen and to reach the stores and powder in the magazines at Skull Cay, but it seemed evident that the enemy knew of the existence and location of that rendezvous.

Someone had blabbed, Pugh knew not who. There were moments when Simon Hart wondered if the dancing witch had played him false, but he could see no reason for such vindictiveness toward himself, and her hate of Pugh he set down to a woman's whimsy, a flare-up that would die as swiftly as it had flamed. Nor did it curb his ultimate ambition to displace Pugh and see himself as a master buccaneer, a swaggering, colorful figure to be sung of ashore and at sea.

Meanwhile they were in jeopardy. They were closer to the land and to their haven than the frigate, but the *Scourge* lay in a belt of alternate calm and sudden, forceless catspaws that sent the schooner surging forward for a little footage, then died away to leave her with slapping canvas and jerking rigging as she pitched on the ground-swell. But the frigate was coming in on a full breeze. All her courses were set and studdingsails had been spread in her captain's eagerness to head off the chase.

On she came, lifting higher and higher until they could see the gleam of her wet side, its airy roll as it lifted, and the creaming rush at her bows. And still the sharp line of the wind, dark against the sluggish shore waters, showed sharp and clear and steady, two miles seaward of the Scourge. Presently the frigate ran out of the breeze, her studding-sails hung idle, course after course wrinkled from their bellied fullness and the crew began to take in some of the useless kites. Under her own impetus she glided into the calm belt that girdled the schooner and lay there heaving to the swell.

Pugh looked at the distant land and at the haze that hid the crests of the range. He looked at the sky that was a blue flame and he looked at the sea about him, a sea of greenish brass. He looked at his crew and at Simon Hart and gritted his teeth as he walked his quarterdeck.

"May their souls crisp in hell!" he muttered, and the oath included king's men and his own.

He was trapped. He had less than thirty able men and presently boats would drop over from the king's ship, filled with fighting men, two at least to his one, and they would come swinging over the swell with the bosun's pipe of "boarders away" still ringing in their ears. His men, if they could be called his, would fight hard and well, but there would be no spirit in them, only the sullen, desperate courage of the cornered pirate while the king's men would swarm over and through the nettings with cheers.

He leveled his glass. Already tiny figures were swarming at the davits of the frigate. Pugh snapped the telescope shut.

"Lay aft here, all hands," he roared. "Men, we're in a tight box. See to it they don't nail the lid down on us. The devil's own luck is in the weather, and, hear me all, I'll serve a mass to Satan an he'll but send us enough wind to slide by that frigate! We've got to beat off their boarding-party. So up double-nettings and fight like the devil's own. Gunner, I'll lay Long Tom myself. Double-shot your carronades. Use partridge and canister. Lively, all of ye, or ye'll be squirming on hell's griddles in an hour."

Pugh went forward and saw to the loading of his long bow-chaser, one hand fondly on the sleek metal skin of his barking serpent while he hung over the breech, watching the foremost boat from the frigate as it came up on the long surges of the ground-swells and hung on the crests for a moment, the oars of the men dipping in rhythmic man-of-war sweep, making the four craft that had been dispatched against them look like water beetles, straddling on top of, rather than in, the water.

Little specks of white light broke out from the weapons of the fighters, soon the pirates could see the gay colors of the uniforms, the figures of the officers in the stern sheets, urging their rowers on in the gallant race for the honor of being first aboard the chase. They could see the spurts of foam from the quick, even catch of the ash blades, working with toy-like precision. The little flotilla split apart, they were going to attack on both sides.

The pirates worked like fiends, raising a double-net above the rail, piling up their ammunition, setting handy pike and double-ax and pistol and musket. Many were armed with Pugh's special boarding pistols, he himself carried a variety of small arms in his belt and slung from a sash that ran across his bare and matted chest.

Every man was nude to the waist, belts were taut and kerchiefs wrapped tight about their brows and each man's face was grim for the encounter. Swabs stood beside the inhauls of the carronades and buckets of water ready to cool the heated metal, By the foremast they were taking turns at a grindstone, edging their cutlasses afresh and the sparks shone orange in the sun before they died.

And still Pugh waited, calculating the range and the lift of the water before he fired. He was the master-gunner of them all, and their only hope lay in smashing at least one boat, no easy mark as it raced on. The leading cutter poised on the rounded summit of a swell and Pugh, squinting through the sight, dipped the glowing linstock to the powdered touch-hole. The Long-Tom roared and white smoke cauliflowered up from the muzzle in the still air. Pugh, peering through the screen, saw the shot souse into the sea beside the boat, shearing off the blades of the port oars and throwing the crew into temporary confusion.

"Jump to it, damn ye, jump!" he yelled, lending his strength to the inhaul of the gun, seizing the swab himself and plying it dexterously.

The charge was set and rammed home with almost incredible swiftness and Pugh's hawk eyes fiercely sighted the mark. The missile plumped fairly into the cutter, fragments flew and the sea was dotted with the black forms of struggling men, survivors of the deadly aim.

The second boat swung in to the rescue and Pugh laughed.

"A taste of our metal they didn't relish," he crowed. "We'll try 'em again."

But his next shot ricocheted harmlessly past the target and a puff of white smoke from the bows of the frigate, followed by a hollow boom, sounded the recall.

"Done! They're done, the sniveling hounds!" cried Pugh.

"No, by God, the wind is coming!" He had seen the flattened royals and skysails on the distant frigate puff and fall to puff again while a line of foam showed faint at her bows. The boats had turned with the men they had rescued from the wreck of the cutter and were speeding back. Twice more the Long-Tom roared without a hit.

Seaward the sky had suddenly darkened, wind pouring out of gathering clouds as from a bellows, the swift riffle of it all about the frigate now and reaching toward the *Scourge*. The king's men had to get aboard, which equalized to some extent the fact that the schooner was last to get the breeze, A fine haze had veiled the sky and tarnished the sun, a moan came out of the source of the wind, a hurricane was forward. It was not a Plate *pampero*, but a true sea-gale.

"A black mass to thee, Satan!" shouted Pugh, "We'll beat 'em yet!"

The sudden unleashed gale grew in intensity. Aboard the frigate they were shortening sail as she rushed on toward the *Scourge*. But now the schooner had caught the breeze and was fleeing northward, the wind abeam, the sweet lines of her entry slicing the long rollers that had replaced the heave of the swell. The heavier frigate heeled, her bows deep to the catheads, her masts abend. A faint sound, like a pistol shot, came to the *Scourge* and an unfurled royal flew from the frigate like a bird. Yet her superior canvas, while it held, smashed her through the seas faster than the *Scourge*, which trailed a beard of weed along her keel, and she held the windward gage.

The frigate did not fire. The distance was still extreme for her range and the pitch and toss of chaser and chased made targetry a waste of powder. But her canvas held in the bolt-ropes, the lighter sails having been furled before the full fury of the gale broke, and she gained, little by little. A drenching area of rain from an overswollen cloud passed between the two ships, hurrying to gain the shore with the remnants of its load and for a minute or so blotted out all view.

Following it came a gusty squall and the wounded topmast of the

Scourge smashed at the crosstrees. Still the frigate gained and now a long headland loomed up, barring the way. The schooner could not clear it, but Pugh held on to his tack until the last moment before he ordered —

"'Bout ship!'"

The pirates hauled madly on the sheets as the *Scourge* spun on her keel and clawed a frantic way seaward into the face of the gale with the king's ship, plunging like a bull, coming fast up. As the schooner crossed her bows the frigate yawed and fire spurted from her dripping sides. Round shot screeched through the rigging above the voice of the storm, round shot gouged the *Scourge*'s planks and tore away her rail, round shot slugged into her side-planks as she rose to the roll of the sea. Peak and throat halyards of the mainsail were torn away as the blocks came smashing down, the canvas drooped like the broken wing of a bird and the schooner fell off in the trough.

Two men swarmed aloft with repair tackle, but as she rose to the pitch of the great waves another volley came and men dropped groaning while Pugh cursed at their impotence.

"Satan take me, but send rain," he bawled as he stood at the wheel astride the headless helmsman who had fallen at his feet in the last discharge.

Above them an ebon cloud was rived with lightning, and from the gash a blinding torrent fell, hiding sea and sky, battering the deck and hissing in the scuppers, striving to flatten the rearing waves that ran and leaped uncontrolled as the hurricane reached its height.

The mainsail, reefed close, rose again, and the stricken schooner gained headway. Pugh could not see the frigate for the storm and darkness, but he knew she too must have tacked to avoid the cape and was now using every effort to combat the gale. Out to sea they fought, foot by foot, under the inky pall of the sky, while the thunder pealed and the rain thudded down. Once only as a blue javelin split the clouds from the zenith did Pugh catch a glimpse of the laboring frigate.

Hour after hour they beat out until they had struggled through to the skirts of the tempest, and at sunset sailed a troubled but subsiding sea without sail in sight or fall of land.

VI

Reprisal

At midnight Pugh sat alone in his cabin. Neither his lieutenant, Folsom, the leech, nor Simon Hart, who slept in tiny cubbyholes that opened from the main cabin, had come aft since they had run out of the storm. All three were forward with the men, and though Pugh had closed transom and door against the sound, he was conscious of snatches of song and drunken shouting in the bows.

For the first time he had lost control of his men. They had refused to clean ship after they had run out of the gale, and Pugh, swallowing his black wrath, had let the matter go under Simon Hart's smiling excuse that the hands were dog-tired.

It presaged trouble; Pugh realized that very plainly. He was not the man to brook tamely the taking away of his authority and a place forward among the hands with his share the same as the least among them. He could hardly believe that he had dropped the whip and lost the power over his bullies. They were all brainless — save Simon Hart. Left to themselves they knew naught but to drink, sing or listen to bragging, evil yarns. They never thought. A story-spinner could hold them, any one with initiative could get an audience, the last thought placed in their heads was the prime one, and Simon Hart, the crafty devil, had worked upon them as a modeler would handle clay until they were all of his pattern. With Hart out of the way, he, Pugh, could bring them 'round again.

And he walked the cabin pondering the best way of disposing of Simon Hart. He might challenge him or start a quarrel?

The medico came down the companionway and sank down unbidden on a chair at the table beneath the gimbaled lamp. His face was drawn and his tired eyes were set in black caverns.

"'Ranting Dick' has gone," he said. "Bates and Willett will go out with the dawn. I may pull Ames through, but he'll lack a leg. And Bartlet is in evil case."

Pugh scowled. Of all the crew Bates and Ranting Dick might have been depended upon to stand with him against the rest.

"Stop your croaking," he said angrily, then changed his note. "Nay

Folsom, I meant it not. Ye need somewhat to bring back your own blood. Art white as a corpse. Mix yourself a rummer of grog. Mix one for me."

The leech looked craftily at Pugh as he mixed gin, water and the juice of limes with sugar into a cold toddy. There was malice in his eyes.

"There's trouble for'ard," he essayed tentatively, and as Pugh did not forbid him, went on.

"The men say that Pugh's luck has broken, that ye have given your soul to Satan and that ye are accursed. They have held a council and they have voted to slip ye the spot."

He squealed suddenly like a rabbit when it feels the fetters bite, and his glass fell from his palsied hands as Pugh clutched him about the throat and shook him clear of the floor.

"So, they will slip me the spot, will they? And they have sent ye sneaking aft to deliver it. You dog, you drug-pounding, treacherous dog. Ye dare to come to me and tell me I am to be deposed!"

He flung the doctor from him with a crash and the leech landed in a huddle upon his hands and knees.

"Nay, I bring nothing. I — I voted against it. I came to warn ye. They will slip ye the spot in the morning. I tell ye some wanted to see ye walk the plank but I would none of it."

"Aye, ye persuaded Simon Hart to mercy, I doubt not," said Pugh grimly. "Get up, man, and finish your grog. Mix more. Now listen. Where are your drugs? In Hart's cabin?"

"Yes."

"Have ye enough to mix a sleeping draft for the quartermaster, have ye enough to mix one so deep for Hart that he will wake up in hell? Listen, Folsom, do this for me and we will win through yet. We'll slip through this cordon, we'll repair ship and sneak back to Porto Bello or some other port and refit. We'll get more bullies to replace our dead and you, Folsom, shall be my right-hand man. A double share for ye in all. We'll set up another rendezvous and ye shall have a house there of your own, a house for your loot and your women. What say ye?

"It must be a cunning drug or that devil Hart will note it in his liquor. And one that acts swiftly. With him down I will drive the rest of them until they beg for me to forgive them. Have ye such a drug, Folsom? Look ye," he clapped the leech upon the back. "I have gold and jewels here aboard the *Scourge*. I'll share the gold with ye and give ye the pick of the jewels. Gems to win a woman's favor with, Folsom, gold to buy it."

"Where is it?" asked Folsom, still with the malice cold in his eyes, though now it was tinged with greed.

"There is a false bottom to the locker in my room cabin below floor-level. Slip for'ard and take the drug, put it in Hart's drink and then come back to me. Art game for it?"

The leech nodded and pushed Pugh's second toddy toward him.

"Ye'll pledge me your word?" he asked.

Pugh picked up the rummer and gulped down its contents.

"I'll play fair with ye," he said.

Suddenly his face contracted, his mouth drew back in a snarl, and he set an uncertain hand to his head, looking at Folsom through a thickening haze. His voice came in a husky growl that choked in his dry throat as his staring eyes began to glaze.

"Double-dealing knave, I'll —"

He lurched heavily against the table and groaned as Folsom watched him with fascinated gaze. Then Pugh squared himself with a mighty effort and stood erect, a dirk in his hand.

"Drug me, would ye? I'll slit thy weasand!"

Folsom made a sudden dive for the companionway, but Pugh towered between him and escape. With the dose that the leech had mixed in the second toddy it seemed incredible that the pirate chief could keep his senses. He dodged behind the table and Pugh came toward him with a certain grim dexterity, wedging him in a corner of the main cabin behind the table and reaching for him, his head nodding as if with the palsy, dry lips apart, eyes protruding with the effort of the will back of them.

Pugh's fingers closed, twisting the medico's cravat, and dragged him across the table, turning him on his back, wind and speech cut off, weak and limp from semi-suffocation, gaze goggling at the blade that descended in inexorable jerks that marked the failing co-ordinations of Pugh's mind and body, descended until its sharp edge broke the skin and gashed flesh and windpipe while the air from Folsom's lungs rushed whistling out with his escaping soul, his half-severed head fell back across the table's edge, and Pugh, groping toward the sealed companionway, bolted and barred it before he slumped and lay inert.

Pugh came back to consciousness with a frightful, pounding pain in his head, a searing almost unendurable torment. His mouth was foul and dry, when, with an effort, he opened his gummy eyes. The vertical rays of the sun glared into them and added torture to the pulsating agony of his brain.

He was lying in the bottom of a small boat, his bulk wedged and crumpled between the thwarts. The boat floated on even keel in a dead calm. There were little sucking noises at the bow that sounded to him like drum-strokes. Along the thwarts lay a mast with its sail wrapped about it, together with two oars. In the stern were two kegs and a baling pannikin.

Pugh managed to get one arm across his face to shade the furnace of the sun. Slowly recollection came back to him in disjointed fragments as it had registered. He remembered the drugging and the killing of Folsom — that was a deed well deserved and well done — then the breaking of the skylight, the battering down of a door, with himself rising and fighting like a man in his sleep. He remembered the taunting face of Simon Hart, then he had fired at it and missed, but had hit some one, for a face back of Hart had changed from a triumphant grin to a mask of pain. Some one had struck him on the head from behind — and that had been the end.

And they had not killed him. Why? He lifted his head and exquisite agony spread from a spot above his right ear until it surged like a white flame through his consciousness. The blow must have laid bare his brain. He feared to touch the place. It seemed to him he would feel the pulsing matter oozing at the contact. As an egg when the shell is broken but the membrane holds intact and dimly shows the yolk. That was how his head must be, and the sun was frying his brains! Yet he could use them. He was still alive! It was the remnant of the cursed drug that bound him. Presently he would get up, make an effort, plan the future.

He lapsed again. When he revived he lay in shadow. The sky was a bowl of jade above him and the boat was moving, tossing to one side and another unevenly as if in the jobble of a tide-rip. The pain in his brain was less, the vitality seemed to have come back to him somewhat, though he was terribly cramped and terribly weak, so that the best he could do was to crawl and twist himself to a huddle in the stern close to the two kegs.

There was no wind, no tide-rip, no motion on the placid sea of peacock-blue.

Blunt muzzles reared above the surface, gray forms rubbed against the planks like great cats that arch and scrape their backs while waiting to be fed. The boat swayed and swerved as the sharks forged under the keel and lifted it. There were two score of them or more, silently, persistently striving to upset the thing that kept from them the food they sensed and craved.

It was cooler. It had rained yesterday, tomorrow it would likely rain again, since the rains were fairly started. But meantime, with his partial revival, there came a craving for food and water, principally for water. Pugh knew what was in the kegs beside him before he made certain of it. They had given him "Pugh's Provender," the same brandy and salt-meat he had devised for those he had marooned. If he could only strike land somewhere and find puddles and pools of yesterday's downpour. He seemed partly paralyzed from the drug, and he hitched himself up with elbows and hands to a higher position.

Far to the south he thought he glimpsed the blue phantom of a sail. That would be the *Scourge*. There must have been a breeze when they had put him overboard. Pugh prayed that one of the king's ships might come up and demolish the schooner and hang Simon Hart to the yardarm, kicking and jerking like an impaled crab.

The sun dropped and evening swiftly fled before night. Pugh could no longer quite control his mind. He was still afraid to touch the wound he had received. It must have been from belaying pin or marlinspike, he thought, and he held the belief that only a thin integument lay between his brain and the air. Once let that be pierced and he would die.

All night gray sharks trailed with the boat, muzzling, nudging each other in a ghastly cortège. Sooner or later what was in the boat would come to them. Sooner — or later. Once Pugh thought he heard the boom of guns across the watery sounding board, but he could not be sure.

Soon after that he began to see shapes, seated on thwart and gunwales, some with their dried arms folded and their desiccated bodies in the water. There were others who grinned at him from the bows. Folsom, the leech, with his severed throat, and Simon Hart! Good — if that was Simon's ghost Simon was dead and he, Pugh, was still alive, very weak, but alive! And therefore still the better man.

The shapes were those of men and women. Vaguely he remembered some of them. He had marooned them. There was one phantom of a girl with great black eyes. She had died by her own hand — after. . . And there were the four men he had left on the cay. He had left three there just recently. Where were they? Ah, there — there on the next thwart! One was bald-headed. Priest-face he had called him.

The boat began to slide along in the grip of some mysterious current, for there was no breeze, no veil in the sky to herald rain. Water! There it was, a hidden stream running underneath the keel. And he too weak to dig for it. Once he had seen a man with divining rods. . . .

Dawn rushed up and the phantoms disappeared. The boat rocked. The gray shapes were breaking water now. Pugh essayed to pick up an oar and batted feebly at the snouts that showed. The boat swerved. They were trying to capsize it. The boat moved on, grounded and now the blood-beat in his brain grew louder. It was surf breaking on low land. Pugh craned his head painfully. He was being carried fast by flood and current to a sandy beach dotted with gray shrubs.

Land! And somewhere in some rock crevice there must be water. The boat bumped, dragged, lifted and bumped on again. A swell tilted the stern and swept the boat on to strand it on the shore. The gray shapes were cheated, left behind in deeper water. He was ashore.

Somehow he got out and collapsed on the wet sand. Then some vital spark brightened and he began to crawl mechanically up the slope. There were no rocks about that his bleary eyes could see, but there were marks that showed that turtles had been there. How fresh the trail he could not tell. He could no longer reason, his moves were instinctive. Some low mounds loomed ahead. They should be where the turtles had covered their eggs. He clawed with painful effort and unearthed a grinning skull.

He tried to scramble from the place and bones grasped at him from the loosened sand. With a prodigious effort he got to his knees and so to tottering feet. Out of the palmetto scrub three grisly figures came toward him, ragged, thin — one of them had a bald head. The others. . . .

Pugh turned and lurched down the slope. He was blind and dizzy, his brain afire. He could not see his boat, and staggered on with outspread arms, pursued by the phantoms. He heard the lap of water. It was the old swimming pool! He would dive and escape. There was a gap behind an old root. Waist-deep he splashed into the lagoon, scooping up the salt sea and thinking it nectar. Then he struck the verge of a tide-swept gulf and plunged forward.

A gray shape, followed swiftly by another and yet another, rose, swirled and lunged. There was a commotion under the surface that sent long ripples diverging on the top, ripples stained with crimson that rapidly dissolved to streamers of pink.

"'Twas Pugh himself!" cried Alec Graeme. "The sharks have got him!"

"He has left his boat," said Will Graeme hoarsely. "He has left his boat! See, there are mast and sail. Come Alec, come John. We've won through. Margaret!"

He fell to his knees on the sand in thankfulness, and his brothers dragged up the boat.

"We'll broach the kegs and clean them," said Alec. "It is clouding for rain. With these and the two others filled with water we can essay the trip."

Will Graeme came up.

"We start now," he said fiercely.

Alec set an arm about his shoulders.

"Tonight, lad," he said. "'Tis an uncertain trip. Pray God there be stars to set our course."

VII

The End of the Chase

In the gray of the dawn Captain Thorne of His Majesty's sloop-of-war *Thetis* chuckled as he picked up the pirate schooner that he had fought at long range as they drifted through the starlit, almost breeze-less night. Now the wind strengthened with the dawn, the canvas filled and they bore down upon the *Scourge*.

It was the end of the long chase. The schooner sailed but sluggishly compared with the sloop, and while her stern-chaser fired intermit-tently, the aim was bad and the shot fell short.

"They are saving on the charges. Powder's low," he said to his lieu-tenant, "We've got them now, Blair."

The woman standing by the rail moved over to him. Her sleepless eyes were brilliant. Captain Thorne nodded to her.

"We'll have them inside of an hour, Mrs. Graeme," he said kindly. "Thanks, in great measure to you."

"Pugh must know the island where he left them. You'll get it from him, Captain."

"Aye, we'll persuade him to tell all he knows." As she moved back to the rail where she had watched ever since the first shot had been fired, Thorne added in an undertone to his junior. "If we get him alive. We'll keep bargain with her and seek the island, but they can hardly be alive for all her faith. Look — look at their flag! They are surrendering."

The black flag of the pirate was fluttering down its halyards. Then it stopped and through his glass Captain Thorne noted a commotion on her decks. A figure broke from a mob of men and fled down a hatchway. But the flag came on down to the deck. "Cease firing!" ordered Thorne. Suddenly the schooner seemed to split apart as a gush of black smoke rushed up from her amidships. A dull roar came over the water and the smoke spread above a flash of red while fragments of spars fell slowly. There was a momentary vision of the stern and bow of the schooner plunging beneath the waves and then, as the smoke drifted off before the wind, a few blackened scraps of floating timber, a struggling speck or two that vanished, and the career of the *Scourge* was ended. Simon

Hart, cheating the gallows, had broken through his spirit-crushed men and fired the remnants of the magazine.

Margaret Graeme, pale-faced, gazed horror-struck at the spot where the *Scourge* had vanished. Now the last hope of finding Will was surely gone. Slowly, with hanging head, she went below to the cabin Thorne had assigned her, where the negress sat with the babe.

She was still there, sick, despairing, when a cry came from the masthead.

Hardly discernible, a black dot showed against the salmon of the sunset sky. The *Thetis* shifted course and soon the dot became a boat making steady headway to the northwest under a lugsail. Closer and closer the sloop came toward the tiny craft until all aboard could see three men in the stern and then a waving cloth.

"Mrs. Graeme, a miracle has happened," said Captain Thorne. "Your husband and his brothers are alongside."

Margaret rose with shining eyes.

"An answer to prayer is not a miracle, Captain Thorne," she said. And, with her babe in her arms, she went on deck.

"There must have been a hurricane somewhere," said Alec Graeme, "the kind that comes before the rains arrive. Probably it destroyed the growth on some isle, and it's to be hoped there were none living on it, but the drift brought the uprooted palms to us and scattered five of them along the beach. Two more we got by wading off the point. Seven in all, close to two hundred nuts, with nigh to half a pint of life-saving liquor in each of them. That saved us. Sheer luck, I call it."

"Plus sheer pluck," said Captain Thorne.

But Margaret Graeme, safe in her husband's wasted arms, knew otherwise.

FORCED LUCK

The flame of the fire leaped high, rocketing sparks into the air, fighting against the cold white moonlight. It checkered the brushwood in black and scarlet and painted the lower trunks of the palms that soared up from the heavy-scented bush. The moonlight frosted their plumy crowns and, beyond the fluctuating ring of firelight, changed the highlands of Tortuga del Mar into a mystery of ebony and silver. The narrow strait between Tortuga and Hispaniola and the broader scope of the Windward Channel showed like spilled mercury. On a rocky headland gleamed the orange lights of the fort where the governor, M. le Vasseur, held the island against the Spanish.

Over a second fire of charcoal, kept fierce by palm-leaf fans, the figures of the cooks attending to the broiling of two pigs that lay on wooden frames over the vermilion coals, were splashed by the same vivid hue as they passed to and fro. The gutted bellies of the pigs were kept open by sticks, the cavities stuffed with partridges, packed about with crushed pimientos and citrons, seasoned with salt and pepper. The savor of it broke down the fragrance of the bush, making the nostrils of the men who lounged away from the direct heat twitch with anticipation and their mouths water.

Half a hundred dogs, pendulous-eared and long-headed, part mastiff, part bloodhound, descendants of those imported by Columbus to hunt Indians, lay with their red tongues sliding eagerly back and forth over their white teeth, too well-trained to offer at a morsel uninvited, even though they had made the kill themselves.

The men were in three groups. The hunters, the actual *boucaniers*, kept apart from the *engagés* — their duly indentured apprentices — by right of caste and authority. The Indian guides stayed in the deep shadow between the *boucans*, the smokehouses where the sun-dried meat was curing on wicker frames over fires of charcoal augmented by the fat, bones and skins of the cattle. Sphinx-faced, imperturbable, puffing at their pipes, they preferred to be alone.

The central fire was burning for light rather than heat. The tropic night was warm, and the buccaneers were almost as thinly clad as the Indians. They were all to leeward of the smudge that discouraged the attacks of mosquitoes. Some smoked, some drank as the bottles passed.

"The moon's overhead and no sign of him. If he's stayed to eat at the tavern, hang me if I don't carve it out of him. My belly's wedded to my ribs." The voice was half-surly, half-jocular.

"The pork'll give you an easy divorce. I'd be careful how I tackled 'Lucky' Bart. He's a rare hand with knife and cutlass. As for pistols, he can split the lead on a knife blade at ten paces. He'll be here, and in good time, never fear. He sent the same word to all of us. He was *boucanier* before he became *filibustier*.

"What of it?"

"So he knows by instinct when the pigs will be done and he still likes *pore boucané* better than any other meat. He'll be coming upwind, mind you, and he'll march in on us just as the crackling is ripe. He's a knack of arriving at the right minute, has Lucky Bart."

"Aye, he's been lucky enough, so far."

"He's not the only one. Did you hear what King Louis did to Pierre le Grand when he reached France with the galleon he took off Cape Beata? The word came last week by the captain of the *Celestine*."

"Took the gold away from him, like enough. It would serve him right for not spending it on Tortuga. We were not good enough for him to drink with, it seems."

"*Peste!* You are jealous as well as surly, Pierre. The king made a knight of him. Aye, and they rang the bells for him at Notre Dame de Bon Secours in Dieppe and held a high mass in honor of his victory over the Spaniards. Pierre is no outlaw. When he won from Spain he fought for France and the winnings were his. Bars of gold to the tune of a hundred thousand pistoles, to say naught of the value of the ship. But twenty-nine to divide it.

"There was a bold stroke for you, to sink his own boat and climb aboard the vice-admiral's ship! Better than sweating in the bush and sweltering in the *boucans* for a few pieces of eight. So Lucky Bart comes in from sea with his pockets so full of gold it rolls out on the floor when he sits down. The women will not look at a *boucanier* while Bart and his men are in port. They say he chases men while we hunt cattle."

"There are getting mighty few cattle left to hunt of late. And it takes three years for a calf to grow to meat."

A sudden clamor rose as every hound gave tongue, baying in bell notes, racing forward toward an opening in the bush and standing reluctant as their masters shouted at them.

A band of men came swaggering into the clearing. They were gaudily dressed with silken sashes beneath their broad leather belts, with silken kerchiefs binding their heads beneath the wide-brimmed, feather-decked hats. Each wore high boots of Spanish leather with the bucket-tops turned down to show hairy legs or silk hose beneath the wide, short breeches of striped patterns.

All carried pistols in belts and slings, all had cutlasses, naked or in sheaths, according to the fancy of the owner. Earrings gleamed golden. Rings twinkled and a gem or two flashed in the firelight. They ignored the dogs which slunk back again, recognizing folk who understood them, if not actual friends.

"Am I late, bullies all? I trust, at least, the pigs are not overdone. I like to see my stomach well-filled, as well as my purse."

A shout of laughing greeting went up from the buccaneers who crowded round the newcomers.

"There are two hampers of wine close behind us," said Lucky Bart. "As an aid to digestion. Tell me, are the pigs cooked? They smell like a breath of heaven."

"Done to a turn."

The cook came up.

"A dozen partridges to each porker. The gravy has oozed through the skin and the crackling is crisp and sweet as a palm-cabbage."

"Good! Here comes the wine. Let's fall to before we talk."

He was easily the dominant figure among his followers and the beef-smokers. Not over-tall but big without being clumsy. His gay raiment somehow became the man, though the others of his party looked like masquerading swashbucklers. Every gesture, every word, the flash of his black eyes and the gleam of his white teeth in his black beard, showed confidence, vitality, leadership. From nail-joints upward to where the stoutly supple wrists disappeared under lace ruffles, black hair curled crisply.

His beard ran heavy down the strong throat to join the mat that showed on his chest where the wide-collared shirt lay open.

His skin was Indian red with exposure and the whites of his roving eyes gave emphasis to his glances as he called the buccaneers by name while they seated themselves ready for the feast. He had the nose of a hawk and his chin showed prominently for all its bushing. On one finger a great diamond shot iridescent rays. A golden neck-chain caught the light. Instead of cutlass he wore a rapier at the end of an elaborate belt hanger. There were pistols with carven butts ornamented with silver in his belt between silken scarf and leather, pistols in the silken sling across one shoulder.

There was little said for a time as the pig was carved at will by the ready knives while good wine went gurgling down brawny throats from bottle-necks. Every little while Lucky Bart would roar a pledge across the fire to some one of the buccaneers, his jewel spraying fire as he raised his hand. Between the huts the Indians devoured their portion of the feast.

At last the dogs were fed, the last of the wine was drained and long crude cheroots of Trinidad tobacco lighted. In complaisant humor the men sat about the fire.

"A song!" cried Bart jovially. "Who'll tip us a stave? What, no volunteers? Then here's one for you. 'Tis good, for I made it myself."

He roared it out in a lusty bass and the men who had come with him joined in the refrain with a will, timing the lilt, beating out the rhythm with closed fists on their thighs or imitating the inhaul of ropes as they sat, like performers in a South Sea *hula*.

> *"The galleon's hold was filled with gold:*
> > *Oh-ho, let the wind blow!*
> *As she put out to sea,*
> *The breeze did stream athwart her beam,*
> *Jamaica on her lee.*
> > *Yo-ho!*
> *Jamaica on her lee.*
>
> *"Yo-ho, let the wind blow!*
> > *Let it blow high, let it blow low,*
> *But blow right steadily.*
> *North or south, or east or west,*
> *Any breeze that blows is best*
> *For our good Company!*
> > *Yo-ho!*
> *For our good Company!*
>
> *"Her captain's gay in silk array;*
> > *Oh-ho, let the wind blow!*
> *A sparkling jewel he wears.*
> *But, oh, his face is turning gray*
> *As up the wind he stares.*
> > *Yo-ho!*

As up the wind he stares.

"Yo-ho, aloft and below!
     Haul on the sheets, let the ship go.
And man the battery.
Prime your pistols, whet your steel;
Fast we glide on tilted keel.
Yo-ho the Company!
     Yo-ho!
For our good Company!

"The scuppers' wash is red with blood;
     Oh-ho, let the wind blow!
The air is filled with groans.
We fling the corpses in the flood
And hoist the skull and bones.
     Yo-ho!
And hoist the skull and bones!

"Yo-ho, let the wind blow!
The galleon's captain's gone below
To sup with Davy Jones.
Gold galore to spend ashore,
Then to sea to gain some more
Beneath the skull and bones;
     Yo-ho!
Beneath the skull and bones!"

Roars of approval greeted the song. Bart's followers chanted over the last stanza and Bart, unfolding a bundle he had carried under his arm, displayed a sable flag on which was stitched the death emblem.

Some one brought a bamboo pole. In a trice the banner was fastened to the staff and the filibuster stood waving it. The moon silvered the device, the glow of the fire tinged it with sinister crimson. The final note found the whole company grouped about him, shouting in enthusiasm born of the feast, the wine, the song and the infection of Lucky Bart's enthusiasm.

"That's the flag to fight under," he cried, "Death to our enemies! Death to all Spaniards unless they hand over the loot they have robbed from the Indians. We'll let 'em off then, if they're humble enough, but we'd rather cross blades. Eh, lads?

"There are three things to warm the blood — wine, women and a good fight! There are three things that smell sweet to a real man, the scent of a woman's hair, the perfume of wine and the reek of burned powder! Three things that are good to hear, the laugh of a girl, the clink of gold and the clash of steel!

"Join in with Lucky Bart, my hearties, and we'll give you all of them. Why, look you, a year since and I was toiling through the brush on Hispaniola with a collar of raw beef around my neck, lucky if I earned enough to stay overnight in a tavern once a month. Now —" he made the big diamond flash — "a don, a hidalgo of Spain made me a present of this ring. He had no further use for it."

He grinned and the crowd guffawed.

"Another gave me this Toledo blade."

He whipped out the supple blade of bright steel from its sheath, making a hissing circle before he took the point and curved the rapier until end touched end within the jeweled guard. As it swung back to true, quivering, sending off rays of dazzle reflected from moon and fire, it seemed like a sentient thing, live as an adder's tongue.

"Booty, my lads! Spoils of war! Taxes on Spain! Yours for the collecting. Who'll join? I've a stout ship though it's small. I've four cannon. We've done well with them, but we must do better. We must fly at bigger game. We need men. We'll be crowded for a few days until we find a ship big enough to hold us with comfort. We'll take that as we've taken all the rest.

"Follow Barthelemy's Luck, my men. Every cast wins. Luck's a handsome jade, but she'll pout and she'll flout you if you do not read aright the look in her eyes. Run after her and she'll leave you bogged, like a will-o'-the-wisp. But when she walks within your grasp, look you, seize her, woo her, flatter her and she'll give you all she has, being a woman, to be wooed and won."

"Aye, and the jade will fling you aside as she'd toss away a frayed ribbon, when she's put you through all your tricks."

There was a laugh at this and Bart twisted to see the owner of the voice, pushed forward by his comrades in jest.

"So, old growler, Luck jilted you, did she? In faith 'tis no wonder, with those swivel eyes."

Lucky Bart swiftly traced the sign of the cross in the air, shrinking a little, for all his boldness and the knowledge that every one was observing him.

"Swivel-eyes or no," retorted the other, a gray-bearded, bald-

headed veteran in whose shrunken flesh the muscles still stood out efficiently; "they can sight cannon perier and culverin as well as any ordinary pair. Nay, they are rightly set for that same trick of sending a shot
true to the mark. Every man squints when he sights along a barrel. I do it
without effort.

"I fought against the Spaniards in '24 when the French chased them
out o' the Val Telline. I fought 'em in the Netherlands in '21. I'm not too
old to fight 'em yet, give me the chance. I've no son of my own, let me
adopt one of those four cannon of yours and I'll warrant it'll speak for
me!"

The old man, half-drunken with the unaccustomed amount of wine
he had drunk at Bart's expense, was working himself up into a fury.
Barthelemy, quick to recognize his quality as a recruiting agent, let him
talk.

"They got me once, in Madrid. I was there to — never mind that,"
he muttered, "but the friars caught me for a Frenchman and a heretic.
They tried to save my soul by squeezing my body. Look at those twisted
arms."

He tore off his tunic, exposing misshapen arms, distorted shoulders
and scarred ribs.

"They gave me the rack and the boot; they took the nails from my
fingers and toes in their sweet zeal. They made me walk in procession
with yellow and red flames on my robe — pointing upwards, mark you.
I was handed over to the seculars; I was to be burned to ashes.

"But I escaped their deviltry. There was a girl in the city. My eyes
were straight then. Never mind that. Now the Bishop of Cuba is Inquis-
itor General with full power of fine and fetter, dungeon, torture and the
stake. The Inquisition of the Galleys covers the friars aboard all Spanish
ships of war. Give me a chance to aim your cannon against Spaniards,
Lucky Bart, and I'll call it the biggest luck that has come to me in
twenty years."

Bart clapped him on the back.

"I'll give you your chance," he said. "If there is ill fortune in your
crossed sight, fire it at the Spaniards with your priming."

The talk had been all in French, the common language of the buccaneers, though the crowd was a mixture of French and English, Scotch,
Irish, Welsh and Dutch with Barthelemy himself a Portuguese and
sworn enemy to Philip of Spain. A short, rotund man who had joined

lustily in the singing, put the question to the newly appointed gunner:

"You've not said what crossed your eyes, Simon? Was it making love to two wenches at once?"

"No. It was trying to make a Welshman look me straight in the face."

In the roar that went up the Welsh quizzer backed out of the front rank of the circle surrounding Bart. Simon reverted to the leader's first sentence.

"'Tis true Luck jilted me at the end," he growled out, emboldened by his acceptance as gunner. "So she will all. And when she's tiring of you and seeking a new favorite, see that you force her not, Lucky Bart. That's my word to you, and a wise one."

"I've a charm to keep her favor, Simon. But for that, good gunner as you are, I'd not have risked the evil eye aboard my ship. I took this myself from the beard of an oyster that I brought up in fourteen fathoms. It has been with me ever since.

"There's Bart's luck for ye, come out of the sea as a sign from Neptune himself. Whiles that's above my heart I have no fear of forcing my luck, nor need those who sail with me."

He hauled up the gold chain about his neck and displayed its pendant in his broad, horny palm as they crowded in. The pendant was a baroque pearl that had been tipped by some clever artificer with goldwork. The same clever craftsman may have used his tiny chisels to emphasize the natural design. That was hard to determine, for the nacreous luster was perfect.

Baroques are freakish things, and this bit of pearl, thrown off by a sick shellfish, about the size of a man's thumb-nail, showed plainly the modeling of a face with hooked nose above a grinning and wide mouth, with cavernous eyes suggested beneath beetling brows; the semblance of a satyr exquisitely wrought in miniature. Strangest touch of all were the horns that sprang from the temples. These may not have been matched, for they had been tipped with gold, accentuated perhaps until projected forward, curving slightly inwards above the sardonic face.

As they looked at it in superstitious awe, Bart, with the fore and little fingers of his left hand, made the sign to ward off evil that the Italian fishermen call *gettatura*, the gesture common to all the Mediterranean coast. Tiny branches of coral that suggest such horns are treasured and worn as charms. Many in that crowd had seen them, some possessed them, but never had they seen a charm like this, a veritable *diabolus*.

Swayed as they were by their common hatred against Spain, by the growing scarcity of cattle that had backed Bart's arguments for freebooting, by the prospects of following the notable example of Pierre le Grand, nothing could have cemented them like this. It was incontrovertible, miraculous. They watched in strained silence as Bart put the baroque back into his hairy chest and nodded at them triumphantly.

So tense was the momentary hush that even Bart started when every hound gave deep-throated warning in a sudden clamor that heralded a small party of men, advancing authoritatively into the clearing; belted, booted and armed with pistols and hangers, dressed with a certain uniformity. Bart wheeled to face them.

"Now what the deuce is this?" he demanded as the newcomers halted, standing close as if uncertain of their welcome, yet determined to maintain their mission. One of them stepped forward.

"We come by virtue of the warrant of the governor," he said. "We seek certain buccaneers whose names are set forth in these warrants against the sums long overdue the French West Indian Company for goods and other provisions and supplies. Moreover we act under special authority from his Majesty Louis the Thirteenth, who graciously granted the charter to the said trading company, and by whose order we have come overseas to protect the traders in their lawful enterprise which hath been imperiled by the refusal of these buccaneers to take up payment of these accounts." He stopped for breath and to gather his resources, somewhat scattered by the attitude of these debtors of the French West Indian Company, by the presence of Bart and his men, whom he had not expected to find on this collecting expedition to the chief rendezvous of the beef-smokers. Bart stood with folded arms, but a hand grasped a pistol to right and left and the filibuster was grinning contemptuously.

"I will read the warrants — and the names," said the officer. "In the name of the king —"

"Spare your breath, you may want it when you go down the mountain," said Bart. "We'll take it that most of us here are on the books where we are charged such prices as would bring a millionaire to beggary. I'll venture mine is there. Mayhap you have heard of it? Lucky Bart, they call me, or Barthelemy Portuguese, of the *Swan*, sometime buccaneer, now turned freebooter. There is not one of us but has paid the company twice what their goods are worth at a high profit. How do you propose to collect your money, my man?"

The officer drew himself to his meager height. His voice shook with sudden rage as he answered the titter that echoed Bart's speech while his men held off the suspicious hounds that snuffed at their calves.

"I have heard of you," he said. "And for you and your pirate crew there is especial mention in the warrants. Unless these bills are met, not one of you nor any man whose name is written, shall leave the island under penalty of imprisonment in the fortress. So says the governor. The guns of the forts will back his words. None shall put to sea nor cross the channel. Attempt it without showing a receipt and the *Swan*, or any other craft, will be blown out of the water."

"You hold a strong hand," said Bart, and his tone had mellowed. "The company seems to have a friend at court as well as one at the fort. Yet how shall we pay unless we ply our trade? What we make we spend. We do not hoard our gold. It is gone. How shall we pay?"

"That is your concern."

"Are you empowered to give such receipts? Will your signature satisfy the governor?"

"Without doubt. The company but wants its lawful rights."

"Good. Prepare the receipts."

"You said just now your gold was gone." The uneasiness of the collector increased. It seemed to him he saw meaning looks passing between Bart and his crew.

"By the seven winds, do you think because my gold is spent I am a beggar? Can I not borrow from my friends? I have no desire to have the *Swan* blown out of the water. And Le Vasseur is a man of his word. My four three-pounders are popguns against his cannon. What I ask you, my friend, is this: Have you the authority to sign for these moneys? Have you the forms for receipt?"

Bart's grin had lost its mockery, his voice had softened still deeper. The collector stiffened. After all, he had counted on the weight of the governor's pronouncement. And there were fees attached to each bill.

"I have the forms and the authority to receipt and to collect," he said. "It is all set down in the warrants."

"Then read them to us," said Bart. "My own memory is short. I may have forgotten certain items. It will suffice if you read off the totals against each man's name. I warrant few of us are forgotten."

"Then call off your dogs. Trompette, read the warrants."

A few harsh commands sufficed to send the hounds back. The buccaneers farmed a circle about the officer and his guard, listening attentively to Trompette reading his warrants and then the list of names with the debts set down against them.

Soon after Tortuga was won from the Spaniards by the buccaneers, a governor was sent over from St. Kitts, a fort built and some order established; the rumor flew overseas to certain canny French merchants, Gascons, many of them, that on this West Indian islet named after the sea turtle, Tortuga del Mar, the buccaneers thought no more of a doubloon than a seashell. Colonists were pouring in, men of doubtful character, women of whose character there could be no doubt at all. Tortuga was a place where there was a golden harvest for the shrewd storekeeper.

The buccaneers bought only the best, without asking the price. Boucan beef was in high demand with all ships. The cattle were wild and cost nothing for breed or feed. The buccaneers found money easy come and easy go. They had too much of it. More than was good for them. They had gold fever. A little judicious gold-letting would be as efficacious in diseases of this sort as blood-letting in fevers of the sanguine fluid. *Peste!* It would be a charity not to let this money flow too freely into the hands of keepers of brandy-shops and brothels.

So the French West Indian Company was formed under royal charter. Storehouses were built, trade shipped. Good wine, groceries, firearms and clothes — above all fine raiment — were provided. The prices were high, but seldom mentioned. The buccaneers stayed in the bush weeks at a time. They came out with physical and mental appetites stimulated to the nth degree by enforced abstinence. They reveled until those appetites were sated. When this happened they found themselves head over heels in debt to the company, little better than bound-men.

And for the credit they paid five prices. They were careless, but they were not entirely fools. They coined a name for the officials of the French West Indian Company — *Les Sangsues* — which may be translated either as leeches or bloodsuckers. The characteristic of man and animal was the same — once attached, they never let go until they had more than they could hold.

The buccaneers, lacking law and lawyers, hating both, proceeded to even matters according to their own judgment. They had paid five times too much for what they had already secured — therefore they would get four times as much on credit and for this they would refuse to pay, in gold, in hides or in boucaned beef.

Now the mercantile agency was in trouble. That was to be expected. The interference of their own governor, whose arrival from St. Kitts they had celebrated as proof that Tortuga was on the map — that was another thing. It complicated matters — matters that had come to a head.

Even Lucky Bart saw that; he was willing to knuckle down. Yet it was sure he had spent gold freely — unless he had a hoard stowed away. It must be close by or he would not have called for receipts. Perhaps he designed to pay the debts of all the buccaneers and so win them to his service. Still —

The officer pondered the pros and cons as the reading went on.

Bart was passing quietly round the circle, whispering in this man's ear and that one, sliding an arm about another's shoulders. The crowd gave out a distinctly jovial atmosphere as the long list of names was called. They cracked little jokes with each other. None murmured at the amounts, none disputed them.

"You have missed none of us," said Bart as Trompette folded up his crackling warrants. "Eh, but they have good bookkeepers, have *Messieurs les Sangsues!*"

It was the first time the collector had heard the local epithet. He did not quite like it. Besides, there was no move toward the production of money.

"Now for the receipts," said Bart. "Doubtless you have brought ink and pens. Sit you down and sign them. Bring him a log for table and another for chair, a torch to see by. Some sand, perhaps, to dry your writing?"

Bart's tone had changed again. It was charged with derision. The collector looked about the circle. Every one of the buccaneers had somehow secured his musket and the officer had heard many tales of the marksmanship of the bull-hunters. These weapons, loaded and primed, had been brought to them through the shadows by their apprentices while Trompette read the roll. Barthelemy and his filibusters were palpably quick hands at fighting.

The collector felt sweat break out upon his brow underneath his hat as he fought against the emotion, calling up his own sense of importance, the protection of the governor, the royal sanction to the warrant. His will turned fear to bravery.

"I have yet to see the gold," he said, facing Bart.

"Will no other metal suit you? There are three precious metals on Tortuga — gold, silver and lead. There are times when an ounce of lead, properly cast and carefully distributed, is worth a ton of gold. It seems to me this is one of them. Sign the receipts."

The last sentence was a command. The mask was off. Bart's knuckles had whitened to the grip on his weapons.

With an exclamation that was half-oath, half-prayer the collector snatched a pistol from his belt and fired at the freebooter. A feather fluttered from Barthelemy's hat as the bullet clipped the clasp that held up the brim and secured the plume, and passed through the crown. Weapons were raised, the moon and fire shone on lifted barrels and blades; the circle became a threatening ring of death.

Bart's great voice roared out with the full blast of his lungs, yelling an order not to fire, not to attack. He leaped to grasp the officer who drew his second pistol and snapped hammer on a spoiled priming, jumping back to draw his sword. Out came Bart's rapier, licking swiftly about the other's steel, wrenching it from his hand to send it into the fire, scattering red flakes.

"Yield!" shouted the freebooter. "Surrender, you fool; we're three to one. Throw down your weapons if you want to keep your lives."

It needed no order from the officer. The deputy collectors flung their pistols and hangers to the ground. Freebooters and buccaneers pressed in and quickly bound them, laying them on the ground in a long row like so many foot-roped calves.

Barthelemy himself secured the officer and held him until he could turn him over to two of his men who grasped each an arm and bore him back sputtering maledictions.

"Put them on the platforms in the *boucans*," ordered Bart, pointing to a row of the curing huts.

"We surrendered," protested the officer, his face white under the moon. "What manner of brutes are ye? Would you roast us alive? We but attempted our duty. I was the one who fired. If you must torture, ply your devilish trade on me and let the rest go."

"There are no fires in those *boucans* — yet," said Barthelemy. "Nor will there be if you sign those receipts. It is not convenient for us to make payments at present nor can we ever do so unless we put to sea. So, you see, we are between the deep and the devil, and we prefer the deep.

"If luck is with us we may pay those claims or such charges as may be adjudged legal. There are two sides to every question. Since you give us no choice with those wondrous warrants of yours we must ask for receipts rather than argue with the guns of the fort.

"Sign. You will find it very unpleasant in the *boucans* after the charcoal gets properly started and the ammonia comes from the burning bones and hides."

The collector strove to read the freebooter's mind but could only decide that, whatever course it was set to, it was inflexible. His men, carried to the *boucans*; fully believing they were to be smoked to death, a credence strengthened by the coarse jests of the buccaneers, their cries drowned in laughter, appealed to him by name.

"If my second pistol had not missed fire," he said desperately, "I would have settled your account in full — with a bullet."

"Not you. Bart's luck is not to be broken by a bill-collector."

The freebooter touched his neck-chain lightly to feel the charm move against his flesh.

"I like you none the less for crowing with the knife at your throat. You are a gamecock. I take it you will sign?"

For full three minutes the doughty little officer cursed Bart with a tongue that never tripped, a facility of imagination that depicted the pirate's ultimate end with precision and full detail, his temper lashed to eloquence by Barthelemy's smile of open admiration. Then, his men within the huts, the buccaneers making a show of arranging the fire beneath the platforms on which they had been flung bound and helpless, he gave in and subscribed his name and titles to quittances against the trading company.

Bart called up the men and presented each with his receipt.

"'Twill serve as passport," he told them. "Sooner or later our friends here will be missed. This will be one of the first places they look for them. Tortuga may not be healthy for any of us until we can return with plenty of golden salve to heal all offenses. The *Swan* will sail at sunrise. Who sails in her with me?"

The recruiting was absolute. Only the Indians had melted quietly into the bush, willfully blind to all that had happened, stoic to the white man's affairs, resolved to have naught to do with them.

"We will give you a *boucan* to yourself," Bart said to the collector. "I do not think you will stay here long. We'll leave the hounds on guard for a bit, so do not be too anxious to get free. For the receipts, we thank you. We go to sea. I should suggest you return to France. You will not find your calling popular on Tortuga. Yet you are too good a man to be smoked. To a more fortunate hour!"

The sun was lifting behind the Caicos Islands and Turk's Island Passage was a flood of golden splendor when the little *Swan* weighed anchor and stood out into the Windward Channel. The sunrise gun had been fired from the fort that loomed dark on its shadowed crags against the dawn. The waterfront patrol challenged Barthelemy on the wharves, but the sight of the receipts removed all suspicions from its sergeant if he had any, the half-dozen doubloons pressed into his palm by the jovial Barthelemy — his last coins — dissipated them into thin air. It was not for him to think of forgeries in connection with so generous a freebooter. He had no special instructions, merely an addition to general orders that none should leave Tortuga without a clean bill of credit from the French West Indian Company.

There were thirty men all told besides Barthelemy aboard the *Swan*, and they overcrowded her space both above and below decks. The craft that Barthelemy proudly called his "ship" had been originally brought across from France and legitimately purchased by Bart when he decided to invest his small capital in freebootery under the black flag.

It was a *bilandre* type, of less than thirty tons, square-sail rigged on the mainmast with foresail and two topsails, with staysail, jib and flying-jib. Aft, there was a lateen-sparred, triangular mizzen acting both as spanker and driver. A mizzen-topmast stay allowed for a staysail when the breeze permitted. She was clinker-built, an alongshore craft capable of work in deep or shoal, sailing fast with the wind a trifle aft the beam, able to point high. Barthelemy could handle her as if she were a racing yacht. Her three-pounders peered through rail ports, two to an insignificant broadside.

"She is small, is the *Swan*," cried Bart, "but that is her only fault. She has served me well enough. You shall not be cramped for long. We'll trade her for the first Spanish vessel big enough to suit us. There is a rare breeze coming with the sun; we'll use the mizzen staysail and shoot through to the Caribbean in rare style. Bells of Doom, there's the fort!"

A second flash had spurted from the dark walls, followed by the boom of the discharge. It was no salute powder-burning, there was grim earnest in the charge, as the solid shot skipping through the water perilously close to the *Swan* attested.

"Someone bungled a job of tying," shouted Bart, his face purpling with rage. "Those plaguey collectors have got to the governor! Le Vasseur would pistol the devil if he roused him from sleep before mid-morning. He'll try to sink us. Lively, lads, strain on those topsail-halyards. Curse that gunner, he's too wide awake this morning."

A second shot came ricocheting, breaking water within a biscuit toss of the *Swan*'s taffrail. Bart's own trained sailors jumped to their work, the buccaneers tailing on and lending main strength to the haul as they were directed by the mate and bosun. The wind blew strong and the *bilandre* heeled to the push and drive of it as the canvas went up and the sheets were belayed to Bart's liking. He roared his orders from the tiller. His black rage had passed into more exultant mood as the *Swan* gathered way and went seething out of the harbor. The governor controlled no craft but a sailing-galley that could not hope to catch the *Swan*, even if its crew could be persuaded to cope with the pirate fighters.

"Bart's luck!" he howled. "Good shooting for them, but better sailing for us. We'll win clear."

Flash after flash now came from the fort, alternating with the dull thunder of the guns. The sea geysered all about them. Once more the men jumped to his order and the *Swan* shot up into the wind and about on another tack as a cannonball split the waves where the handy vessel would have been targeted had it kept its course.

A short leg and he tacked again, zigzagging out across the channel while the range grew too great for the fort's artillery. Then he brought her up, heading on a long reach down the channel, careening to the light gale, dancing over the crisp blue waves that were creaming as they raced with the ship.

"Up with the skull!" shouted Bart, and the bosun bent the flag to a whip and hoisted it, flaring on the wind, the grim device plain on its sable ground.

"I would we had those cannon aboard, Old Swivel-Eyes," he said to the new-recruited gunner. "We'd send 'em back an answer. We'd give 'em a receipt, eh, Simon? Couldst do as well as they did? They aimed well enough, but we outguessed them. What do you think of Bart's luck now?"

"'Tis well enough if you do not force it. But I fancy there'll be trouble if ever you put into Tortuga again."

"Trouble?" laughed Bart, his strong hands on the bar of the tiller, lending his weight to keep his course, his eyes on the taut canvas, watching the flag for his wind. "There was never trouble that could not be cured by gold-grease. Le Vasseur is not in Tortuga for his health. He has an itching palm. We'll treat with him easily enough. If not, there's Jamaica with rarer fun than ever was shown on Tortuga for men with money to chink. Who knows? If the luck holds we'll sail back to Europe. Philip of Spain reigns over Portugal now, but we'll see the Duke of Braganza on the throne before long. There's insurrection brewing in Lisbon now. We could join Braganza's crowd. There'll be honor and loot to be won. A bold man can go far these times."

He stopped talking and gazed ahead, withdrawn into himself, brooding over his ambitions, seeing himself at the head of a resolute band, with money to aid the cause, allying himself with the duke's fiery wife, Donna Luiza. Knighted perhaps, a power in the field, lording it in Lisbon.

Tortuga diminished, faded and was lost behind the headland of Saint Nicholas as they sailed due southwest. The breeze held through that day and all the night. Dawn found them pointed west, Jamaica looming up to port. At sunset of the second day the course was changed again to northwest, clawing into the wind, making for the channel between Cape Cruz on Cuba and the Cayman group. Noon of the fourth day found them cruising along the islands called the Gardens of the Queen — *Jardines de la Reina* — the wind yet with them, far enough out for sea-room, all eyes searching for a sail that might turn out worth capturing.

Nothing hove in sight but fishing-craft and Indian pirogues and they held on, heading up into the Cazones Gulf, out again to sea between Cayos Largo and Rosario, rounding the Isle of Pines.

On the seventh day, with nigh to eight hundred miles of sailing back of them, Cape Corrientes looming ahead, they saw a great galleon sailing south and east, a whale to their sardine, a sea castle that would carry twenty guns at the least and probably have close to a hundred men aboard.

Bart held to pirates' rules. His men had a say in any venture and they gathered round the mast in consultation, discussing the stranger as she came on, her sails like a mass of pearly cloud, her hull crushing the waves, high-pooped and ponderous. They had not yet chosen their representative who would be given the run of the cabin and a right to speak with the captain at any time.

The fact that Barthelemy actually owned the *Swan* put matters on a footing somewhat different from the regular routine and scale of sharing of the Brethren of the Coast as the filibustering buccaneers were beginning to style themselves. His share of booty would be a quarter of the total taken, the remainder would be divided equally, a share to a man, with an extra share to the crew's representative, with certain specified rewards for the man who first sighted a prize, the one who hauled down the enemy's ensign, who uphauled the skull and bones on the captured vessel during the fight, the first boarder to cross the enemy's rail; and fixed recompenses for wounds.

Simon the swivel-eyed, by virtue of his record as a fighting man, and his ready tongue was, it was plain, likely to be made spokesman for the crew. It was he who came finally aft to the tiller, his black eyes apparently gazing at the tip of his long, blue-veined nose as he essayed to look Bart in the face. Simon was grinning; he trod the deck resolutely and showed that he had sea legs and a sound stomach.

"Yon ship, they tell me — not being very sea-wise myself," he said, "is not a warship of the fleet, but a merchantman. She is the more likely to be well lined, yet she is well provided for fighting. Twenty culverin show from her ports, ten to a broadside. There will be soldiers as well as mariners aboard, passengers as well as officers. One well directed broadside would make splinters of us while we were trying to dent her sides — trying, I say, for she would sink us long before we could get into range.

"But we have sailed a week without other prospect. It began to look as if Bart's luck had failed at last. Now that this galleon shows and we can smell the gold in her hold we would be willing to risk a fight save for the great odds of her guns. It stands this way. Unless you press the matter we will not attack."

"It was you who gave the advice about the guns, I take it?" answered Bart. "Think you that all prizes are won by cannon fire? This will be a fight where you will have little to do as gunner, Simon. Down in Brazil, Simon, there are certain small fishes called *piranhas*, little longer than your hand. But they have jaws like bulldogs, their teeth are so sharp that the Indians use them for chisels to point their arrows. Once they taste blood they are merciless. They will tear to pieces man or beast within a few minutes. So — we are *piranhas*, the galleon yonder is a lumbering bull trying to cross the water. Call the men aft."

They came with their eyes gleaming, shifting occasionally to the galleon, standing on, her big bulk and press of sail holding her to the water as if she was cargo-logged — so little did she lift or roll — compared with the quick motion of the *Swan*.

"Two thirds of you know naught as yet of filibuster ways," said Bart. "You will know more before the sun sets, I'll warrant. There was nothing ever won at any time, in any part of the world, without risk. Our, cannon are small use, we will take her with hot lead and cold steel. We'll grapple with her and board her and then, 'tis up to you to fight like devils from the pit.

"We must risk their first broadside. These merchantmen are not overly practiced in gunnery. It is big odds they will miss us entirely. Once draw their fire and we'll board. Bart's luck will bring you through. That's all. Stand by to wear ship. Then to your weapons. And, remember this, you buccaneers, a sharp edge cuts quickest and deepest!"

They went about before the wind and hauled off for the galleon. The black flag flaunted impudently at the masthead, the *Swan*, like a tiny, impertinent terrier dancing up to a mastiff that could make one bite and swallow of it. The galleon kept serenely on as if disdainful of them. Bart could see many men moving on her poop with now and then the flash of a steel morion, in the sun.

His mind was busier for the moment with the probable tactics of the Spanish commander than with his own. His seeming foolhardiness was calculated. He figured that the arrogant don would deem this a good opportunity to teach all pirates a lesson and would wait until he was within close range and then deliver a broadside. In Bart's experience the Spaniards were good fighters but poor gunners; he thought the risk well offset by his luck. One or two of his men might be killed; the *Swan* might be sadly damaged; but even her sinking under them might work for the test. He remembered the glorious example of Pierre le Grand, who deliberately scuttled his boat to cut off his possible retreat.

Giving over the tiller to his mate, Bart took a hand-stone and whetted his rapier delicately to razor edge, plucking a hair from his beard to test it. So with his knives.

He fired the charges from his pistols and replaced them, carefully adjusting the priming in the pans.

Then he proceeded to make his fighting toilet. He took off his boots, he stripped himself to the waist, discarded his silk scarf of ornament and tightened his belt.

He bound a kerchief tightly over his curly poll with the ends hanging down like lop ears. He took the chain and its charm and tucked them into a flap pocket of the belt, carefully securing it. The scabbard of his rapier he tossed down the companionway into his cabin. His only actual article of clothing was a pair of short drawers, though, so dense was his hairiness, he seemed far less naked yet more terrible than any of his crew.

Simon, ordered away from the guns, sulked and predicted failure, but nevertheless ground smooth the edges of a double-headed ax, and there was a glint of war-light in his twisted glance. The men sat on the deck for the most part, stripped for action as was Barthelemy; the new recruits followed the example of the crew, all hands preparing weapons, cutlasses, knives, axes, pikes and pistols. The pin-rails bristled with them, the sun glanced from the new-ground blades with flecks of light that flitted over planks and canvas.

The *Swan* swam steadily on, Bart back at the helm with four pistols in his belt and two at the end of the sling over his shoulder — good for six lives, as he used them. They were weapons of his own design, and several of his crew had their duplicates.

Once fired, in the turmoil of a boarding or repelling rush, a pistol was little good, save as a possible missile to be flung into the face of a foeman. To use the butt meant shift of grip, and a knife or sword was better. A pistol was only an encumbrance. One had no time to reholster in a fire-and-slash affair with the press all about you. Pistols were deck gleanings for the victor.

But Barthelemy had a saw-blade attached to the support of the barrel, welded in one piece, an extension demi-bayonet that could hack through the mesh of a boarding-net, sever a cable or serve as a dagger. To balance the pistol he weighted the butt with lead. It was a touch of genius born of Bart's concentrated joy in his profession.

The galleon held to her chosen course, a little south of east. The *Swan*, twice as swift, five times as agile, closed in on an intercepting angle that would bring the two together well out from land. Bart wanted sea room for his maneuvers.

Slowly the details of the Spaniard's richly carved and ornamented hull revealed themselves: curving, gilded scrolls, elaborate iron work in the railing of the poop-ladders and the stern and sprit lanterns. Her buff bows lifted now and then with a dazzling flash as she felt the ground swell of the Caribbean. For the most part she seemed to ride on an even keel, her canvas unfluttering, her ensign stiff in the wind, the culverin muzzles unwinking in their regard of the swaggering *Swan* coming on pot-valiantly into the jaws of death.

Poop and lower decks of the galleon were packed with crew and passengers, waiting for the spectacle that would show when the curtain of the broadside smoke had rolled up; the show of a pirate craft sinking, of pirates striking out feebly while their blood drained and stained the water with trails of paling crimson, A rare show — talk for the voyage — gossip to relate at the other end — a plume in the commander's cap.

To the Spanish all Europeans in the West Indies other than themselves were foes and outlaws. The buccaneers were not all the riffraff of the Old World, despite their occupation of butchering cattle. Many were men of good family and education, cadets of fortune. There were British university men among them and Dutch spendthrifts, adventurers from Germany, Scotch exiles, Irish rovers and many emigrant officers from France, disgusted with the iron rule of Louis. Nor was Barthelemy the only revolutionary Portuguese.

Such men made good fighters and, now that they were beginning to graduate into filibustering and piracy, the Spanish deemed it a righteous and a necessary act to sweep from the seas these Brethren of the Coast. Here was a chance to use the broom. Aside from the sailors, the galleon carried a detail of marines, for she was a treasure ship and had right to government protection.

The commander, Don Montalvo, was of noble blood; there were some wealthy, important merchants aboard, returning to Spain with their profits; there were friars; there were musicians. It was a varied and a gallant company in their contrasting robes and suits and uniforms. The gunners stood by their culverin, the slow matches handy but unlighted, the crews ready to haul and sponge and ram.

The passengers of higher degree joined the officers of the ship on the poop, the marines stood idly to arms, their light helmets flashing, their superiors smoking, listening to the music of fife and tambour, jesting at the audacity of the little square-rigger standing up to cross their bows.

The *Swan*'s speed served Barthelemy well. She had the weather gage of the galleon and she came up on a slant that kept her out of anything but the extreme range of the heavy culverin. These were not swiveled, they projected only a set distance beyond the ports, they were practically a fixed arm with their direction changed only when the galleon shifted. Bow-guns they did not have.

The *Swan* headed its course, stuck its nose into the wind and hung there, sliding slowly down as the galleon lumbered up. Bart held on as long as he dared; then, when collision was imminent, he bellowed orders for the jibs to be backed as he flung his weight against the tiller-arm. The *Swan* spun on its keel and caught the wind as the crew inhauled the sheets, shooting with a burst of speed toward the starboard side of the galleon under a rattle of small arms that made no damage beyond boring the sails. It was a bold maneuver, cleverly conceived and smartly carried out.

The astounded Spaniards looked over rail to see the *Swan*, blanketed out of wind by the bulk of the larger vessel, but with way still on, making for the side of the galleon, a score and a half of men, armed to the teeth, where they carried their spare knives, standing by the rail, ready to spring, while the thirty-first, black-bearded, hairy, of naked torso, gripped the tiller and howled defiance and encouragement. The top-hamper glided by with the streaming skull and bones flaunted in their very faces.

The broadside roared out with flame and billowing smoke; the ten balls went whistling through the reek of black-powder gases; the breeze piled back the vapors to fog the galleon's middle deck. There was a splintering crash of the *Swan*'s topmast. The black flag toppled, disappeared. Then came the bump of the smaller ship, and out of the smoke shot grappling hooks that caught in the galleon's rigging and tied the craft together.

Bart left the tiller with a prodigious leap, his men already scrambling up by the easy path of the galleon's strakes, the carved port sills, the hot muzzles of the guns; silent, because of the steel they lipped, eager to slay, pouring over the rail, jumping down to tackle the swiftly formed resistance of the marines with their musketry, the baffled gunners with their rammers and the Spanish officers, springing into the fray with flashing swords. Bart retrieved his flag and severed it from the whip, binding it about his left arm, roaring as he scrambled upward. There was the crack of pistols and the bark of muskets, lunge of pike and grating of cutlass against sword in the sharp rally, muffled shouts and cries of desperate men fighting in the drift of smoke. Bart's bosun fell from the rail, shot through the throat, toppling against Bart, who caught at a shroud to steady himself. Three of his men were a-sprawl on the deck. The rest had barely got their footing and were fighting with their backs to the high bulwarks, one against two.

Swiftly he discharged his pistols and saw his targets fall or go staggering back. His rapier gleamed as he poised himself for the jump to the deck, his last pistol still in his left hand. He saw a marine on one knee, aiming a musket at him pointblank, and he flung his weapon. The saw-edged knife caught the man fair in the throat and the blood spurted from the severed jugular as Bart joined his men, yelling the war-cry of the filibustering buccaneers —

"From the seas!"

The odds were too great, fight as they would. The musketry fire was too galling. Eight of the thirty were down in the first five minutes. The Spanish commander had established a firing squad on the poop, aiming over the heads of their own men at the bunched pirates. Furious, reluctant, yet prudent, Bart's great voice boomed out ordering the retreat.

Overside they dropped, sheering off, Bart at the tiller again, the panting, bloodied crew cursing as they hauled. The *Swan* caught the wind, clawed off, got way and came about before the starboard battery could be reloaded and order reestablished in the galleon.

Now Bart gave; full vent to his wrath, his face convulsed, his lower lip bitten through, froth on his beard. More than a fourth of his little company lay on Spanish planks, dead or wounded. Repulse to him was like the sting of a *banderilla* to an Andalusia bull. His pounding, furious blood stimulated his brain to new tactics.

"Muskets, buccaneers!" he cried. "Now show those Spanish dogs how you can shoot. Pick off the gunners!"

The *Swan* remained within short range, a tempting target. Bart's original crew handled her, and she frustrated every effort of the galleon's crew to work their clumsy vessel for effectual shots. There was wind enough, and the *Swan*'s sailing qualities, with Bart's seamanship, did the rest.

Wherever a Spaniard showed in porthole or rigging, or exposed on the poop, there sped a bullet from men expert in their arms, with skill gained in hunting the cattle or defending themselves against Spanish raids on the mainland. They crouched behind the rail and yelled whenever a shot found its mark. It was thrasher against whale.

The wallowing galleon, out-maneuvered, floundered in the seas while, like wasps, the stinging missiles sought out the harassed sailors. Again and again the broadsides roared harmlessly, and the pirates yelled in derision. Hour after hour the long-distance fight went on while Bart kept rough tally of the Spaniards put out of the fight.

He marked with satisfaction every time a sniper hit a man who exposed himself on the poop-deck. The passengers and all those not actually concerned with the working or fighting of the ship had gone to shelter. A man down on the poop meant an officer, an increasing demoralization of the galleon's company. Two he had himself accounted for. Both wore corselets besides the morion helms, but this insufficient armor served as guide rather than hindrance to Bart's sighting. One he shot in the face, the bullet ranging upward, the other in the armpit.

He served out food to his men, and, at intervals, measures of rum. Their blood was kept at battle fever by the concentration of their shots, the excitement of hit or miss. Sweating, begrimed, gory, many with minor superficial injuries, they egged each other on, realizing the wisdom of Barthelemy's stratagem, waiting for the time when they could once more attack.

Bart gave the order in the middle of the afternoon. Pannikins of Jamaica rum were handed round and then the *Swan*, maneuvering at will, sailed up wind, paralleling the course of the galleon, forged ahead and drifted down again, repeating her first tactics. Out and up went the grappling-irons; again they swarmed the bulging sides, the skull and bones once more flying to the stump of the topmast.

A man fights at his best on the tide of victory or with defeat cornering him. This time the Spaniards were no longer triumphant but desperate and lacking leaders. There was not a buccaneer of Barthelemy's crew who had not had to fight his own battles in the bush, often back to back with his apprentice, holding off a troop of Spanish horse who feared the accurate fire of their muskets.

They were accustomed to handle themselves as units. Boarding, after the first overside rush, was always an affair of every one for himself, and in this the freebooters were supreme.

Bart pistoled three men before he reached the deck, stabbed another and ran through the second in command. The Spaniards had massed and the pistols, fired from the rail, did fearful execution. The howling pirates, swinging their cutlasses, herded the dons, broke them up and struck down man after man. They were not without their own losses, but their hardihood was the greater.

Over thirty Spaniards were dead or dying. Wounded crawled into the scuppers where the blood collected to the swing of the ship or trickled back on the opposite roll, making the planks slippery with the crimson fluid, clotting in the sun. Dead men lay with arms outflung and legs drawn up, blind eyes looking to the sky. Couples were locked together from the final struggle. Not a fighter on either side but bore some wound.

The buccaneers, more than half-naked, smeared with blood of both sides, appeared devils rather than men. Their ferocity was not to be withstood. The Spaniards retreated pell-mell to the poop, flinging down their arms and calling for quarter.

Bart headed off his own men and stood before them with outspread arms, forcing his hoarsened voice to dominance of the uproar.

"Back," he shouted. "The ship is ours. Back, I say!"

He faced them with his face a-snarl, his teeth showing white in his beard, red rapier in hand, threatening them as a hunter cracks whip over the heated pack, leaping for the kill. As they subsided unwillingly he picked out two and bade them stand guard over the huddled dons on the poop, ruefully surveying the bloody waist of the galleon where nearly fifty men lay helpless, gouting blood. Two more he told off to go through the lower decks, disarming all they met and at the same time relieving them of personal wealth. For this he picked his own men, choosing the cooler heads. The new recruits were the hardest to control. Simon stepped forward, panting hard, his right shoulder sliced, his calf torn with a pike, squinting horribly, like a Japanese devil-mask.

"Twenty of us joined," he cried. "Twenty, I say. Twelve of us are gone, and you would give quarter. Down with them! Let them walk the plank. Where are the friars? Let them go first."

He was mad with blood-lust and his own especial obsession against the priesthood. His cutlass had been shivered, and he held the jagged remnant of it in one hand, a stained knife in the other, crouching, ready to leap, like a savage beast that only half fears its trainer.

"I am no murderer," replied Bart. "Drop those weapons, Simon, or I shall tickle your ribs with my point. Drop them, I say. Who is captain here? I give the orders, sirrah."

He conjured up a fury that licked up that of Simon as a greater fire consumes the less.

"Blood enough has been spilled," he challenged. "Now we look for gold!"

"*Gold!*"

The word held them. The light in their eyes changed. In the rage of conflict they had lost sight of the prize. Bart saw the turn.

"Gold!" he repeated. "Gold and jewels and wine! Silks and satins! Loot! Spread through the ship, you landlubbers, while we sailors handle it. The man who conceals a trinket gets the lash and shall be driven from the crew. All booty is to be brought to foot of the mainmast and distributed by lot. He who injures a Spaniard I will deal with myself. Send them aft to me."

Simon dropped his weapons, and, turning, followed the rest of the lately joined buccaneers, who ran whooping through the vessel, decking themselves extravagantly with snatched raiment, breadths of cloth and sashes, staining them, regardless of the drying gore on their flesh, breaking the necks of such bottles as came their way, cutting their lips in their haste, swallowing blood and wine together.

Bart's sailors came back, herding trembling prisoners. Then they went to work methodically clearing the deck of bodies, flinging overboard the Spanish, laying aside their own for later banal, covering them with a sail. They knew that Bart would take care of the loot, that there would be wine enough for all, that there were things that must be done before the feast was commenced.

From the poop the affrighted survivors of the galleon watched the splash of the corpses, the feeble striking out of some who quickened when they struck the water. From the depths sharks, vultures of the ocean, came swarming, ravening, tearing at their meal.

Don Montalvo, one arm rudely bandaged and slung, his head bound up, stood at the break of the poop. When Barthelemy fronted him he did not lift his head, but gazed up at his conqueror from under his brows.

"Gather your wounded and all that is left of your company," said Bart, "and go aboard my ship. I make you a present of it, or an exchange, as you will. She sails well, and I am loath to leave her. But we were somewhat overcrowded. I' faith," he went on a bit ruefully, "I take it that we shall be lost aboard this galleon, seeing I have lost half my company."

"And I more than half mine, sir. But I thank you for your courtesy and your mercy."

Bart grinned as he turned away and left Montalvo to salvage the forty left of all the complement. The pirate flag had been brought aboard and nailed to the truck by a freebooter, displacing the Spanish pennant. Now he gave orders to dismantle the rudder of the *Swan*.

"I would not have them make shore too easily," he said to his bosun. "They'd have half the fleet after us before we get off the horizon. By the time they have fixed a jury rig we'll be well away. We're for Jamaica. If the gold is sufficient we'll send enough of it to Le Vasseur to square those receipts and get a general discharge from him. Enough of it will stick to his palm to set him in good humor, I'll warrant."

The disabled *Swan* drifted off; the galleon headed east, the loot piled up at the foot of the main with Barthelemy superintending the division, the men casting dice for choice of lots as he apportioned them.

There were seventy-five thousand crowns in money and a cargo of cacao worth five thousand more, besides the trinkets, watches and personal cash taken from the dons. It was a goodly fortune. Twenty thousand crowns to Barthelemy, four thousand crowns apiece to each of the fifteen survivors of his crew.

They were drunk with their good fortune long before the wine they found affected them. Under a favoring wind they drifted on, carousing, shouting chanties, praising the luck of Barthelemy and toasting him again and again. The dead were forgotten; the wounds of the living, patched up in rude fashion, discounted in a golden dream. The galleon itself was worth a big sum, and Bart purposed to sell it to the best bidder and get himself a craft less cumbersome and with the speed his trade demanded.

He almost regretted the *Swan*; but he knew that the fame of this his latest exploit would bring him recruits by the score. He had his fortune, but his ambitions had swelled. His luck was with him; there would be other strokes like this, easier victories with an increased crew of picked rovers.

Simon was the only growler. The more liquor he consumed the greater became his grouch. The setting free of the friars was his main grievance.

"'Tis forcing the luck," he declared. "No good will come of it. Had we lost they'd have racked us, taken us to Cuba, burned us. Now they have set a curse on us."

"A murrain on their curses," answered Bart. "Old Cross Eyes, next time you shall have a real battery to handle. My luck has but begun."

He had dressed himself in clothes belonging to Montalvo, in waistcoat and breeches of rich crimson, a red feather in his hat, a diamond cross pinned to a lace cravat, a ruffled shirt, bucket-topped boots with silver buckles, making a figure more barbaric than gallant, but a striking one, not without dignity. Now he felt to find his pendant charm in place and touched it with his fingers beneath the ruffles.

"Time will show," persisted Simon, gazing gloomily at his emptied bottle, reaching drunkenly for another.

He had thrown the dice with ill fortune and been forced to take the refusal of the mixed loot, his share of which was tucked between his legs as he sat on the deck — not yet cleansed of battle stain — his back against the rail. Some of the others cast black looks at him and began to mutter about Jonah.

"Let him alone," said Bart good-naturedly. "His disposition but mates his eyes."

Before the laugh ended he started up a song and soon the chorus lifted to the stars as they surged slowly Jamaica-ward.

The next day brought work of cleansing and restored discipline. Compared to the *Swan* the galleon sailed like a barge, and the winds that had served them hitherto so well, failed them. What breezes came to break the long calms headed them inevitably. Try as they would they could not make easting past the Isle of Pines. Every league of slow tacking into the wind, with the ship behaving like a tub when the yards were close-hauled, was more than lost by drifting in the offshore current that slowly bore them westward.

While the wine lasted few cared but Bart. Their unleashed appetites finished this at last, and with fevered heads they took to water. The galleon's butts were half-filled, carelessness spilled more and they were down to the last gallons.

Bart made a forced landing on Cuba's extreme western point, at Cape Santo Antonio, anchoring in a little bay. There were wounds that needed close attention, fevers running high in blood inflamed by drink; and he decided reluctantly on a rest ashore. Often he walked apart from the rest, fingering his charm, fighting against a disposition to lose faith in his luck, now and then eying Simon doubtfully.

That croaker was in sorry case with the hole in his calf that would not heal. Bart could not quarrel with a man who was near death, as he fancied. He brought himself around to his normal confidence. The men were better for the laying up, eager to start back for Jamaica. One night the winds began to marshal and, as Bart paced the surf-edge, he resolved to sail the next morning.

They worked out of the deep indent north of the hook of the Cape and headed for the Caribbean and Jamaica. They had barely cleared the point when it seemed that every able man was at the rail, staring and pointing to where, coming fast down upon them, converging on three tacks, with towering canvas, three galleons came on.

For the first time Bart cursed his luck.

With only fifteen men, half of them weak and unable, he could not hope to work the ship with any speed or precision. To fight against such odds was worse than foolishness.

A hail came from the leading ship; flag signals were exchanged with the rest. Bart chewed his lips and gave the order to lie-to while a boat's crew boarded him, an officer in the stern-sheets.

To lie was ridiculous. The great cabin showed plainly all the signs of nightly debauches. There was not a man among them who could speak Spanish without an accent. To a nautical, observing eye, traces of the fight were everywhere, aside from the bandages yet worn by the freebooters. More boats' crews came aboard, and a muster was made from the three ships to man the recaptured galleon. Bart and his despondent men were taken aboard one of the ships, stripped of all they possessed except their drawers, flung into the lowest hold, foul with stinking bilge; slavery, torture, perhaps execution ahead of them. Stale crusts were flung down to them, a jar of impure water lowered and the hatch clamped down.

They sat in silence, pitching to the heave of the ship. A croak came out of the dark.

"Said I not so? You forced your luck when you set free the friars. Now —"

Simon squeaked as Bart gripped him by the windpipe.

"I'll choke the voodoo out of you," he said savagely. "That, or you keep silence. We're not dead men yet."

He fumbled with the band of his drawers. In the deep hem he had run his chain and charm when he knew capture certain. In the blackness he felt the outlines of the tiny face with its horns that held off evil, and felt comforted. While that remained his luck was with him. As to forcing it — *peste*, one must be the master of one's fate!

The galleons, merchantmen all, it seemed by a chance word caught before they were thrown into the hold, were bound for San Francisco Campeachy. That lay to the north. In the hold they had no sense of direction, and on the second day a storm struck the flotilla. Bart and his men were tossed until they lay bruised and exhausted, caring for nothing. By some strange perversion Simon's wound had ceased to suppurate and commenced a healing process that all the roughage did not check.

When, not so much from sympathy but in the desire to preserve his prisoners alive for judgment, the captain had them taken on deck after the storm subsided, Simon disguised his convalescence easily enough. None of them appeared to have much more than a spark of life left in him. They lay on the planks in the waist, gasping the fresh air like outhauled fishes, filthy, cramped, pounded to apathy.

The captain picked out Bart to be revived with wine. Quick to snatch at any straw, Bart bestirred himself, showing bravado enough and telling his tale with such a devil-may-care good humor that the captain gave him back his crimson clothes and took him into the cabin.

Montalvo, it turned out, was no favorite of his. The daring of Bart and his little band roused in him a certain admiration.

"What they will do with you at Campeachy, I know not," he said. "My consorts have separated in the storm. If we arrive first, beshrew me if I do not claim you for myself."

"I know not how to behave well as a slave," said Bart.

"There are degrees of slavery. Any, I should think, are better than the rope or block. If you are ordered to Havana or Santiago, look you, there may be the Inquisition. You are a subject of Spain. That might or might not mend matters."

"I spared all lives after the ship was captured," said Bart, dodging the issue of citizenship.

"True. I wonder where Montalvo landed. There will be jests at his expense. He will pay us salvage on his gold and goods. Come, if I can compass it to keep you aboard, will you join my crew? I could use you and some of your men. Maybe all."

Things looked a little brighter to Bart. Not much. He had not given his name, but he might well be recognized at Campeachy. Barthelemy the Portuguese was known, and not favorably, to many merchants. If he acquiesced there might be a chance to escape.

"We'll wait till we reach Campeachy," he said. "Let us find out if we have eggs before we plan an omelet."

The captain nodded and then chilled hope.

"I will provide you better quarters," he said. "But I must keep you under heavy guard. Take another glass of wine. I would give a butt of Xeres to have seen Montalvo's face."

Bart went out with his escort to the deck. Land was in sight. The next morning would see them off Campeachy. His pendant was still in the hem of his drawers, for he did not know when he would lose his fine clothes again. His men were on their feet, being driven forward. A figure lay prone in the scuppers, face downward.

"It is the cross-eyed one," an under-officer said to the captain. "He is near death. Shall we throw him overboard?"

"See if he comes to later. If not, tie a round shot to his feet and launch him."

The captain spoke carelessly, passing on, sealing the fate of Simon, but in a fashion he had not intended.

An hour after nightfall, when the watches were being changed,

Simon the cross-eyed slipped over the rail. He could swim like a seal. The shore was less than a league away. Fear of the friars made fins of his legs and arms. One watch thought the other had thrown his corpse overside. He was not worth mentioning. Once Bart thought of him as he gnawed his nails in the fore-room underneath the butt of the sprit.

"That's what he gets for croaking," he told himself. "He's no great loss, even to himself, I wonder if he crossed my luck, after all. We'll find out at Campeachy."

They made a peep-show of the captured pirates at San Francisco Campeachy. A cage of wild men from Borneo could not have attracted more attention, or a band of tattooed cannibals. Bart was placed with the rest under the forecastle head where the townsfolk peered timidly through the windows at the pirates and asked questions of the sentries.

There was one gleam of hope; the convoying galleons had not arrived. The galleon would sail in two days without waiting for them. They were not taking on cargo, but delivering.

At noon the ship was cleared of sightseers and Bart breathed easier. To make a part of the galleon's crew was not so bad a fate. With luck they might mutiny and take the vessel. In the mean time they would be subservient.

A barge came alongside. The captain went to the gangway to receive a guest. Bart's heart sank as he shrank back from the window. He knew this angry man. It was Montalvo.

Soon two men came for him, bound his arms behind him and took him aft into the great cabin where they stood him by the butt of the mizzen, remaining on guard. Barthelemy faced the angry don, mustering all his fortitude.

"I have pleaded with Montalvo," said the captain of the galleon, "but so far with small use. In that he recovers his ship, his cargo; in that you are no Frenchman but a subject of King Philip and therefore an outlaw perhaps, but no foe; in that you gave him quarter, I thought he might be disposed to strike a bargain with me. I have even offered him a fair sum for your services."

"The man is a renegade," said Montalvo.

His arm was still slung; the scar of his head wound showed raw.

And he manifested only a cold politeness toward his fellow captain.

"A revolting Portuguese. He has so declared himself. Mine was not the first ship he has plundered — nor the tenth. His wickedness is known through the West Indies; there is no more bloody and desperate pirate in the world. He is a scourge to our commence, a villain who deserves only to be hung, and that speedily."

"Yet you thanked me for my courtesy and mercy, if my memory serves," said Bart quietly. "I should be glad to return that compliment. I held off my own men from hanging you at your own yardarm or walking the plank, Don Montalvo. I furnished you a ship —"

"After you had killed half my crew, you butcher and traitor. I made no treaty with you."

Bart shrugged his shoulders.

"I doubt whether you would have kept it in any event," he said.

The swarthy Spaniard turned the color of a ripe olive, the scar on his brow swelled until it seemed it must reopen. He turned his back on Bart, addressing the captain.

"Either give him up to me or I go to the governor," he cried. "As for the vermin he commanded, keep them for galley-slaves an you will. This man deserves neither shrift nor trial. I hold you responsible."

The captain threw out his hands in a gesture of inutility. He had done his best.

"Take him away," he ordered.

Bart was led back to the forecastle. He still had spirit enough left to laugh at his men's commiseration.

"When the rope is brought there is yet the noose to tie," he said. "And the noose must tighten before one chokes."

He tapped at his charm.

"I have seen a man lose all he had and all that he could borrow. I have known that man to go out into the street and pick up a battered piece of silver and so return and win every main. One thing is certain, luck never stays with a coward."

Montalvo did not return, but a guard came off from the governor, soldiers who hustled Bart into a barge and rowed him off to a great galleon that lay at anchor. They loaded him with irons so that he could barely walk. They thrust him down a ladder into a sort of lazaret and left him there. His crew they left on the merchant galleon. Before they clapped on the hatch the sergeant of his guard told him of his fate.

"There will be no trial for you, pirate and traitor!" said the man. "Cuba has had enough of pirates. They will make a glorious example out of you, renegade Portuguese that you are. All Vuelta Abajo will be here in the morning. They are putting up the gallows in the public square. It is to be a holiday. You will tread air until sundown when they will take you down, dip you in tar and sling you in hoops of iron on the end of the mole."

The sergeant held a lanthorn so that the light from the sputtery candle within sprayed through the holes punched in the tin and freckled the captive pirate's face, hoping to read some sign of quailing. Bart looked at him composedly.

"The meanest cur barks loudest at the caged wolf," he said.

"Cur, am I?"

The sergeant hung up the lanthorn on a hook driven into a deck-beam.

"Look you. There will be many to apply for the privilege of playing hangman to you, Bart the Unlucky. But I have seniority and a special claim. I shall put the noose about your neck. There is a good fat fee in it, besides much praise and satisfaction for a worthy act.

"Long after your throat tightens up, never again to suck in air or swallow wine, I shall be slaking my thirst with good liquor bought for me by those who are anxious to clink glass with the man who hanged Barthelemy. I shall make good money selling the rope, besides. A crown an inch."

"You have a jovial way with you," said Bart. "You go deep into details. You should have been a lawyer, my friend. Yet it is no news to me. I could have told that you were the executioner by your hang-dog look."

The sergeant scowled.

"It remains with me whether you die swiftly or dance long, whether your neck is broken or you slowly choke to death," he went on. "The people would rather see you dance with the ends of your toes just touching the planks as you swing. I have chosen a well-stretched halter for you. Your clothes are mine and all your valuables."

"The most valuable thing I have about me is my life. And I lose that I care not for the rest. But I was not born to meet death at such hands as yours, my friend. Make no mistake of that. You filthy scum, a brave man to bait a bull through the bars! A wine-swiller and a swaggerer! I suppose you will boast in the wine-shops how you made me wince at your words. Liar!"

He wondered at the ferocity of the sergeant. While crowds would assemble to see a pirate swing, Bart knew that a subtle sympathy for the victim, a sneaking admiration of his defiance of the laws and his free life with its chances for riches or death, was predominant.

This man was not merely callous, he was a deliberate torturer. It was no fault of his if his taunts failed to affect Bart as he desired. Inwardly Bart was burning with anger, but he was helpless as a toad filled with lead shot. They had enough irons on him to hold an elephant.

"My brother was on Montalvo's ship," said the sergeant. "He was a corporal of the marines. You flung a knife at him and pierced his throat. That is why I applied for the hangman's job tomorrow."

"Then let it keep for tomorrow and do not kill me tonight. Your words are far more annoying than any noose. I am weak with hunger and thirst, and since I do not suppose you will relieve those conditions it might be well to leave me to gain some rest or I may give a sorry exhibition in the morning.

"As for your brother, he had his finger triggered to shoot me down. It was the fortune of war. Even you — an you had the courage to stand — may have killed in your time, though you prefer the rope to the musket, it seems. There is less risk.

"Your brother and I were enemies. Because Philip lords it over Spain that does not make me a Spaniard. Because Portugal is subjugated it does not follow that all Portuguese are slaves. Now leave me. You weary me. I would sleep."

The sergeant drew off and looked at Bart, baffled. He could not understand this sort of man. His taunts were as useless as throwing mud against a stone wall to level it. More so, for the mud did not seem to stick.

Since he could find no epithets that would rankle he ascended the rough ladder and before he closed the hatchway spat down at Bart, who dodged philosophically. He sat in his clanking fetters and racked his brains. He felt confident of being able to get out of his irons. They were clumsy as well as cumbersome. Some were locked and some riveted. The first he could pick, the others open by main force.

His eyes, adjusting themselves to the dim light, made out a ring stoutly bolted to the floor. He could set foot on the ring and pull against the bolt-head on a fetter link. The lanthorn hook seemed secure. He could use that for leverage. He fancied he had talked the sergeant into forgetting the lanthorn. But he might come back.

The galleon was larger than Montalvo's ship. Bart's glance had told him she was laden, almost ready for sea, waiting perhaps for a full crew, a lengthy process of late with labor growing scarce. That was why the captain had been so anxious to retain Bart and his men. It was probable that only the guard was aboard, and an anchor watch.

The rub was that Bart could not swim a stroke. He held the old viewpoint of mariners that to be able to swim was only to prolong agony. That was for accidents at sea. This was different. He was only half a mile from shore. And he could see himself free as far as the rail. Then —

Bart clucked softly to himself. Among odds and ends of storage in this little room where they had stowed him he made out two large earthenware wine-jars in which liquor was exported from Spain. About each was a coarse net of cordage for convenience in handling. Bart knew such jars well, knew their buoyancy. If he had the luck to find some tarpaulin —

He felt the blood running more freely through his cramped limbs. Strength, reduced by the starvation of the trip up the coast, returned with new hope. Bart's luck was still working. Now for the irons.

There came a gush of cooler air, and he glanced up to see the stars through the spars and rigging. Stars glittering in a sky of sapphire. Out there was freedom. He took a deep draft of the salty air, tonic to his resolve.

A soldier — not the sergeant — bore in a leather demi-bottle and a dish.

"Oh-ho! Bart's luck was working well."

The sergeant hangman had taken his hint that the star performer at the hanging might be but an indifferent actor without meat and drink. Or it might be orders. Bart did not care. His eager nose caught the savor of wine and cooked flesh.

"Eat hearty," said the soldier. "'Twill be thy last meal. They are working tonight on the gallows. You can hear the strokes of ax and hammer across the water."

"Thanks, friend. I am more interested in my supper."

The hatch clamped down again and Bart fell to. The wine was fair;

there was goat's flesh, beans and corn pancakes. It was a feast. It was his freedom. With the steam drawn from this timely fuel he went at the irons. Some he twisted, some he forced apart, the locks he picked with a bent nail torn from a bulkhead. He had to work quietly, muffling the metal with his coat as soon as he could get that off. He heard the ship's bell striking through the night. At two in the morning he was clear. There was toll of skin and blood on the metal; he was soaked in sweat and infinitely tired, but he was clear.

For the space of another bell he forced himself to rest, and when the five strokes sounded he started work on his jars. They were empty and they were sound, uncracked. He found the remnants of a hatch-cover and with the cords by which the jars were slung he drum-headed them, joined them together, making twin buoys. He finished the last of his stoup of wine and then adjusted himself to the hardest task of all — to wait, dependent on the actions of another, not knowing whether such actions would favor him.

He counted on the revengeful disposition of the sergeant. When the man thought his prisoner had slept sufficiently he would be almost sure to visit him alone and try to harrow him.

Eight bells struck at last. Then one. Half after four. It was close to dawn. He heard a shuffle of feet, felt the fresh wind come down the open hatch. He lay groaning at the ladder's foot, his irons gathered about him. The sergeant came half down the steps and sat on the tread.

"Dost repent, pirate? Would'st confess thy sins? I am the only priest will visit you. You are beyond the Church. Half way to Hell already."

"It is not my soul, fool," Bart gasped laboriously. "It is my stomach. I have been poisoned. The wine, or the food. I am dying!"

He rolled over, careful not to displace his chains too much, breathing hoarsely, simulating a death-rattle. The sergeant, deceived, wondering if the prisoner had not poisoned himself to cheat the gallows, came down and stooped over him.

Bart promptly kicked him in the belly, driving him against the side and knocking all the wind out of him. Rising like a jaguar, straight into a spring, Bart leaped and brought down one of his fetters full upon the sergeant's pate. The bone of the skull cracked dully and the man dropped.

With his jars Bart fled up the ladder. He had stripped himself down to shirt and drawers once more, shedding again the crimson suit that fate denied him. On deck he paused, glancing up and down. He heard voices forward, caught sight of the light of a lanthorn slung to a yard and half a dozen men beneath it, gossiping, their weapons set aside.

There was no time to lose. Light was gathering behind the hills, the stars were fading, or so his nervous vision fancied. Like a shadow he made the rail, climbed upon it and with a jar under either armpit, the connecting rope across his chest, leaped into the sea.

There was a resounding splash as he sank beneath the surface. The guards came running to the rail. Bart spat the water out of his mouth as he bobbed into the air once more. They were firing from the galleon; but now he was sure he was away, not to be captured. Not a bullet came near the jars. The other ships were not aroused.

The flood tide caught him and sped him landward, while he struck out with his legs for better speed. The east was gray when he crawled out upon the beach, patted the friendly jars farewell, felt for the charm in his waistband and plunged into the thick jungle.

They would be after him — hotfoot. Spaniards and Indian trailers and the famous bloodhounds kept and trained to follow escaped slaves. If they once struck his trail that was the end of it. He plunged on through the woods, thanking his stars for the meal that, gave him the energy.

Striking a morass in the midst of the forest he waded through the water and at last roosted in a tree, draped with curtains of moss, satisfied he had baffled the pursuit for the time at least.

Before noon he heard the baying of hounds on the edge of the swamps, the shouts of the trainers. He caught a glimpse of Indians gliding along the margins and lay quietly hidden in his tree.

To escape along the coast to Golfo Triste, more than half-way to Havana, some forty leagues of mangrove swamp, forest and jungle, through streams infested with caymans and crocodiles, through a wilderness where he must live on roots and shellfish, unarmed against jaguars and the giant boa — that was his objective.

Golfo Triste was a pirate rendezvous. Sooner or later he would find kindred spirits there. Sooner or later he would get the revenge already forming in his brain — nothing less than the capture of the very ship from which he had just escaped. Give him time — a week, ten days — and he would do this before it made up its complement and sailed. He was certain it was a rich prize, richer even than Montalvo's ship.

And it would be a rare revenge — to come back under their noses and take the galleon. It could be done — with luck. He was forcing that luck now, with a will that must stretch it to the limit. He realized that; but Fortune favored the brave, and the brave had to use means according to the occasion.

All day he heard the baying of the hounds. At night, perched in his tree-fork, hammocked with thick folds of moss, he saw torches flickering in the search.

So for three days and three nights. Bart was weak in the knees when he made his way out of the morass at daylight. Such water-roots as he could scrabble in constant fear of being sighted had proved scanty provender. They had been bitter and had given him dysentery. Insects had stung him and he was in a fever. Out of the trees he mounted a hill and looked back over the deserted crescent of the beach toward the sleeping town. The ships lay at anchor, mirrored in the calm water. No figures moved on the waterfront. In the public square, deserted, he saw the gallows that had been set up for him.

Bart shook his fist at it — good-humoredly enough, if ironical.

"If you wait for me as your fruit," he said, "you'll be a long time ripening. *Adios!*"

He had brought out from the morass a half-rotting gourd that he had found there, relic of some former fugitive. This he used for water-canteen, knowing well that he would often have to carry his supply. It was a wretched substitute. He had to balance its precious content as he fought through stiff jungle where he had to worm his way between twisted trunks, thorny undergrowth and lianas. Food, as he could obtain it, was scarce. There were doves and rabbits, but they mocked his efforts.

Stones had to be picked up and carried. In the muggy heat of the bush they were more than a nuisance. It is a hard thing to hit bird or beast with even a bullet in a primeval tangle.

Parrots, macaws and the yet more brilliant trogons flew through the glades, screaming at him. Humming-birds gleamed like jewels flung at random through the forest. At night the great fireflies with their greenish lamps seemed elfin spirits.

His main food was shellfish; but often the mangroves, with their hooped roots curving out of deep mire, blocked his progress along the coast. Sometimes he found oysters clinging to the mangroves, but only at the edge of the sea and so infrequently as to make the tedious, tiring trip out of his direct path unprofitable.

The mangroves were his greatest trial, growing thick from the ooze that stank under the sun and offering no footing, save at low tide. Through their thick groves he had to swing from bough to bough ape-fashion, his calabash tucked into his rag of shirt. Here the mosquitoes attacked in clouds that forced him to brush them away almost continually to prevent blindness. Every step was a drain on his strength. He never found food nourishing enough to replace the loss.

He grew gaunt, his eyes sunken, ribs protruding, arms and legs mere bones set with muscles held there by sinews. His belly was a pit between ribs and hips. The fever never left him. He went on in semi-delirium, automatically. It was as if he had lashed the tiller of his will as the last selective act of consciousness, the course set for Golfo Triste — forty — thirty — twenty and — at last — ten leagues away.

He looked like a dead man staggering through the thickets, a dead man dug up and driven on by an uneasy soul. His hair and beard were matted, his eyes bloodshot, all his skin ripped with thorns or spotted with swollen stings. Scorpions bit him and made sloughing wounds, and he did not notice them. Jiggers got into his feet for all their horny soles, and he kept on.

Every mile or so he would come to a stream, dreading always to find one too deep to ford. At his approach caymans would slide into the water, lurking in their favorite nooks. The heavy air reeked of musk. Up and down stream Bart wearily plodded, seeking infrequent stones. He flung them into the water with rasping cries and then risked passage in the hope that he had scared the brutes away.

On the seventh day he came to a little headland and surveyed the coast ahead. As far as he could see, league upon league, stretched nothing but mangroves, running far inland. Bart groaned aloud, but never faltered. They had to be crossed. He had made some sort of meal with mussels and a fish caught in a rock-pool. Some sapodillas, a paw-paw and an overripe alligator pear — last of a lucky gathering — made his dessert.

The phrase of Simon the Swivel-Eyed had grafted securely in some convolution of his brain and with his fever it began to bear strange blossoms. This was forced luck, indeed — this defiance of all danger, of hunger, thirst, fever, wild beasts, this rape of the jungle.

He began to see his luck as a vision of a woman flitting on before him in a mirage that held by day and turned to dream by night, or whenever he essayed to rest. A luring woman who looked at him seductively with eyes and lips that beckoned but never promised.

She formed out of the swamp mists, stirred in the jungle depths, laughed up at him out of the water. A wayward minx who had given him much and now tested him to the uttermost. As he withstood, so would be the reward. She was a woman — therefore she loved a strong man. And he would show her he was strong. He would bend her, force her to his will. Simon — dead and drowned Simon — was a fool. Fortune favored the brave.

He declaimed such resolutions aloud in a cracked voice, then plunged on, croaking a chantey, a specter fighting on the borderland of life and death and winning back.

For four leagues through the mangrove swamp he barely set foot to ground. It was clutch and swing and clutch again. Now and then he drew himself up to a stout bough and rested before he made his weary way along. The palms of his hands were raw, deeply cracked, swollen, festering. But he kept going — famished, with a temperature at which a doctor would have thrown up the game of life — clutch and swing and clutch again — a human pendulum.

It took him two days to cross. The second sunset, flaring through the thinning trees, revealed the fearsome sight of a whitish body, half-covered with matted hair, with bent knees, aswing at the end of bony arms that had hooks instead of hands, jerking from one elastic branch to another — the travesty of a man, the caricature of an ape; jerking on with set face and staring eyes under the rustling canopy of glossy leaves until at last it swung itself out upon the grassy margin of a river and lay there insensible.

The current ran deeply to the sea. And the sea itself was far away. To keep direction in that swinging flight had been impossible. Bart slumbered heavily through night and forenoon before he stirred and looked at the river cutting through the jungle. It was a full quarter-mile across, a turbid flood that would surely swarm with caymans, that showed without testing that it was too deep for fording. A soggy tree came lunging down the center of it, swirling, sucked down now and again by undertows.

His sunken, somber eyes held no light now, only a dull gleam that showed there was still fire left. It almost died out at sight of the watery barrier. He gazed round dully at the trees he could not chop down, whose lesser limbs, green and elastic, he lacked strength to tear away. They would not have helped him. He was at an end.

He dug his thumbs into his waistband at the hips, felt the charm and took it out. For a moment reason was dethroned, and Bart gazed at the little fetish with the face of a maniac. He raised his arm and flung the thing from him, watching with glazed eyes to see it spurt the water.

The golden chain looped about his wrist in the clumsy aim of his shapeless hand; the amulet fell, to strike against his knee and hang suspended. Bart looked at it stupidly; but reaction was coming. He had swung off-course, but the lashed tiller of his will brought him slowly back again. His broken lips parted; his eyes widened between their swollen lids.

To him it seemed as if a miracle had happened, though the thing must have been there from the first — an old board, a plank two inches thick, some four feet long, floated from some region far up-river. In it bristled some heavy spikes and nails, rusty — but of iron, malleable; tools!

He lugged at the prize with sudden strength, and even as he dragged it up the bank made another discovery. This was a clump of a species of croton, its broken leaves and juice capable of stupefying fish. That this rolling river held many was sure. He had but to find a pool. Inside of an hour he had five big fish chosen from the shadows of his pool, carried there in the eddy and stupefied — three *guayacon*, two *viajocos*.

A nail struck, sparks from a stone to moss-tinder. He had his fire, his belly full of cooked meat once more. It seemed as if the wheel of fortune, turning so long away from him, was coming his way again; as if the luck lady had relented. The river held no terrors now. He pounded at his nails with stones for hammer and anvil. He heated them and tempered them and made chisels out of the spikes, cutting-blades of the smaller nails.

He manufactured two efficient spears with hardwood shafts, spending the rest of the day in prodigious, inspired effort. To the plank he added branches that he hacked down and bound with withes, crossing on his raft triumphantly, poling, paddling himself over, his legs tucked under him for chance of caymans. That same night he speared a chameleon, then its mate, and feasted on their tender flesh with soursops for vegetable. He was coming through.

Vigor came back to him with better food and fortune — as a dried sponge sucks up water. He fought off the fever. The day — the four-teenth day — that he struck the open sea and saw the Golfo Triste gleaming in the sun, he cast off the subjective lashings and resumed full control of his mental tiller. There were no more mangroves, only grassy headlands for a while, with pleasant growths of timber that the sea-winds kept fairly cleared of brush on the scant soil.

Sucking in great breaths that filled his capacious chest, Bart strode on to the cliffs' margin and looked down on the rendezvous, the mouth of the Rio Triste. Its name belied itself in that moment. Here was no river of sadness, for a ship was careening, there were canvas shelters and palm arbors on the sand, figures with bright cloths about their heads moving here and there — Brethren of the Coast!

Bart let out a yell and began to run before he checked himself. He did not want to appear before his fellows like a frightened child running home out of the woods. He was still a leader. He wanted to impress some of these men into his service. He made a shrewd guess as to the ship that was laid up and, with it, the name of its buccaneer captain. They knew each other, had gamed together and drunk together; they respected each other's prowess, though Bart, younger at the business, was the more famed.

He reached the higher reaches of the river — no need to cross it — and took stock of himself. There was little that he could mend; but he managed to comb out beard and hair, painfully enough, to suspend his chain and amulet about his neck, to wash away blood and dirt and to make the most of what rags were left. So with his chisels and his two spears he strolled toward the camp as carelessly as if he had merely left it for a walk in the forest.

The first who saw him was the buccaneer chief, superintending the scraping and calking of his ship from the beach. He hardly knew the distorted figure, at once shrunken and swollen. The altered voice held some link of recognition. Bart's smile was wry, his bold eyes hidden by puffed lips and lids; but the amulet made the connection. It was Lucky Bart!

"They told me you were to be hanged at San Francisco Campeachy two weeks ago," cried the other.

"I was never born to be hanged," said Bart, "nor to be drowned either, methinks, though I can not swim. In the name of fellowship give me some wine and meat. I stink like a fish and I am sick of chameleons."

"You came by the coast — afoot?"

"By the coast, and, since I can neither fly nor swim, afoot; yet for a while I traveled through the air."

Bart enjoyed their mystification as he swigged down the wine they brought him, cup after cup of it. He was his own man again. His prestige had returned. The freebooters quit work and crowded round him.

"How did you know I was to be hanged?" he asked. "You seem to have been here for two weeks at least."

"We have one of your men here with us. He came in an Indian canoe, escaping from the galleon that took you off Cape Antonio."

"A man of mine? He must have jumped overboard."

"He did. Wounded though he was. An old veteran with eyes that seem to look only at the tip of his nose. Though he misses little."

"Simon? My gunner? Swivel-Eyed Simon?"

"That is his name. A canoe picked him up. They knew of our being here. He came easier than you did."

Bart's jaw dropped. Simon, whom he thought dead and drowned, the more certainly since his own luck, so close to breaking utterly, had begun to mend. Then he laughed. His charm had been potent against Simon's crossfire optics.

"Where is he?" he asked.

Simon came to answer the question, creeping out of a palm shelter, yawning, half-curious, half-annoyed at the general commotion.

"Ha, croaker!" called Bart, gobbling beef without regard to starvation precautions. "Hast some luck of your own, 'twould seem. And here I am, for all your voodoo talk. Luck is still with me. I have my grip on her wrist. She's like any other woman — force her first and she'll love you afterward."

Simon looked at his leader as if half-dazed, shaking his head doubtfully.

"Who told you I was hanged," demanded Bart, "since you rolled off deck before we reached Campeachy?"

"The Indians — they know everything that goes on. How, I know not. But they told me you were taken, that the gallows was building and that you were to be swung in iron hoops at the harbor-mouth."

"Oh-ho! Racine, now you have fed me, will you go further? Will you put me in the way of recouping my own fortunes?"

"Surely. What I can do. Weapons, half the contents of my pocket, though that is not heavy-laden at present. First, some clothes."

"Anything will do. For the present. There is a certain crimson suit that I fancy. It fits me fairly and it is my favorite color. I left it behind me at Campeachy in the cabin of the galleon where I escaped. It is in my mind to go back for that one."

They looked at him in amazement, yet with admiration and a growing belief in the prowess of this man who had safely made a trip that none of them would have attempted and now sat in the sun, forgetful of sting and bruise, his fever overmastered by the joy of achievement, packing his paunch with solids and drinking heady wine like water.

"To go back and put your head into the mouth of the lion? Eh, that would be a simple trick," said Racine.

"Simple enough. Are all these men of your own crew? They seem over many for her size. As I remember."

"The *Falcon* lies on the reef off Purgatory Point. She was my consort, and a cursed galleon swept her with a starboard broadside, killing Jean Vaurin, her captain, and eight others. The rest ran her ashore. We did not take the galleon; but we made her sheer off, for all her metal. I picked up what was left of Vaurin's crew and came here to careen. I was dragging a fathom of weed on my keel."

"Which are Vaurin's men?"

Racine gave an order, and seventeen stepped out to one side. Bart surveyed them complacently. They were an average lot, but they would serve. Added to Racine's complement all was well in time of plentiful provisions and no loot to divide; but if food were scarce or if a prize were captured the regular crew would with cause grumble at their lessened shares. Racine would be glad enough to get rid of them; they would sense their own position.

"What say you?" asked Bart. "Racine here will give us a long-boat, I make no doubt. 'Tis some fifty leagues by sea to Campeachy. You have your arms. We'll lay off, send some one ashore to con the chances, and at the end of the night, 'tween gray and red, we'll take the galleon and be outside and bowling for Jamaica before the lubbers are awake. They sleep like stuffed dogs at Campeachy. Listen, and I'll tell you how readily I befooled them."

If they had any hesitation they were lost the moment they began to listen. Bart was a born storyteller, and he had a great first-handed yarn to spin. With him they broke irons, struck down the taunting sergeant-hangman, floated ashore on the jars, lay in the swamp and struggled through cayman-haunted streams and mangrove thickets until at last they rafted across the final river. Bart was no boaster; neither did he hide his light under a bushel.

"That's the kind of a man I am," he ended. "That's the way I hang on when luck seems indifferent. And when she smiles, her smiles are golden. Eighty thousand crowns and more was the value of Montalvo's galleon. This one will be richer picking. We'll put her to sea and go find Montalvo. I have a grudge against him that still aches. Are you with me, bullies?"

They gave him three cheers, and even Racine's men seemed envious of the chances.

"How about the longboat?" Bart asked. "I'll pay you back her worth some day."

"Choose for yourself and never mind the payment," said Racine. "I may be asking you for return favors before the year is out. Our trade has its ups and downs."

"So! Seventeen of you and myself. Pity 'tis not an even score."

His eye lighted upon Simon. With a perversion carried by this swelling wave of fortune on which he was launched, he laughed at any suggestion that Simon's awry glance could menace success. Half-jestingly he took the baroque pendant and held the tiny horns tipped toward Simon.

"Come on, Sour-Face! I'll put you back of a battery yet. Here's nineteen of us. Luck in odd numbers. It's enough."

Arms were always plentiful. The survivors of the *Falcon* had not left their wreck without them. The longboat that Racine promised so readily had also come from the stranded ship. Racine contributed only some powder and ball, sidearms and muskets for Bart and Simon, wine and provisions. Without doubt he was glad to see them go.

He had his own reservations as to the probability of Bart's venture. Bart had nothing to lose beyond his life, everything to gain. If he won he would hold generous feelings toward Racine. If he perished there was a strong rival out of the road.

Bart rested until evening, not that he felt the need of leisurely recuperation. He overhauled the longboat, saw to its equipment. He was keyed up to tune. The emotions of revenge ruled his body, quickened it with vitality. A fair wind promised; the longboat had a square-sail lug. He would make best speed with canvas or oar, timing the trip to make Campeachy after nightfall.

About midnight, he calculated, was the best time to loaf along, to send two men ashore to some wine-shop to find out about the threatened galleon — how soon she was to put to sea, the numbers of her complement, how many were ashore. What was her cargo? The possibility of her having put to sea never entered his mind. He was convinced that he had forced his luck to loving obedience and sympathy for all his plans, from now on.

His absolute faith communicated itself to his crew with the exception of Simon, who had little to say in the matter. Simon's private belief in the vagaries of luck were somewhat shattered. The matter of the friars still stuck in his mind. To have let them off scot-free, perhaps to practice inquisition rites upon unfortunate prisoners, seemed to him like deliberately throwing pebbles in the face of Fate. Fate might have been blinded temporarily, but when it regained sight the smart of the flung grit would not be forgotten.

He allied himself to Bart in this new enterprise because he had small choice in the matter. The men at the rendezvous had made small secret of the opinion in which they held a cross-eyed man, wizard though he might be as a gunner. They spat across the back of their hands and crossed themselves whenever they fancied him looking at them — wrongly nine times out of ten. They openly referred to him as a *mascot du diable*, a left-handed blessing. In the longboat they still looked askance at him as he sat in the stern with Bart, his calf-wound, though nicely healing, releasing him from the oars. He was glad of Bart's protection, on the whole.

When they sighted Campeachy at last, it was after dark, the lights twinkling as they rowed softly on the tide and landed their two spies an hour before midnight with a gold piece to spend. They came back within two hours, smelling of strong liquors, rolling in their gait a little more than usual but coherent and full of prime news.

The galleon was to sail the next afternoon.

"I knew it. Bart's luck!" exclaimed the leader.

The recruiting of the crew was practically completed. It had been hard to get men. The two spies had been made an offer. The marines, being government troops, were an easier matter. They had been aboard for several days. The sailors were enjoying shore-leave up to the last moment. They had spoken with several of them, drunk with them. Some of them had never been off to the vessel, and the marines — the sentries — were therefore unacquainted with them by sight. The cargo was reputed the richest kind of merchandise.

Bart slapped his thigh as they floated in the blackness. All was falling out perfectly.

"What did you hear about me?" he asked.

There were a dozen stories. That he had been drowned trying to swim ashore — for they had discovered and recognized the jars — that he had starved in the swamp — that the devil had flown away with him. The governor had taken three of his men away from the friendly captain and hanged them to ease the Spaniards' disappointment at losing the big offender. Bart exploded in great oaths at the news. That the sergeant he had felled with the irons had died did not console him.

At almost precisely the hour when Bart had jumped overboard from the galleon with his jars, a longboat arrived alongside that vessel, gliding gently in with oars tossed inboard. The rowers had made little noise, but there was no especial attempt at concealment. A sentry, holding out a lanthorn, peering down at the dim faces looking upward, challenged them.

"Hist!" Bart said softly. "There is no need to wake the ship, comrade. This is not a feast for officers. We have things in the boat that have paid no duty."

"You belong to the crew?"

"Do you suppose we are making a present of ourselves and what we bring to a strange ship? Let us aboard, friend, we are late enough as it is, and we'll sneak our stuff with us into quarters."

The sentry had a fellow sympathy with smugglers. He had no suspicions, only a desire to graft.

"You will not forget me?" he asked as Bart swung up the rope ladder that was accommodation for shore-going sailors.

"I have been thinking of you all the time," Bart answered.

He caught the astounded sentry by the throat with one hand and fetched him a tremendous buffet with the other. The man suddenly went slack and pitched to the deck.

Up came the seventeen, with Simon tailing, because of his lamed leg. The deck-guard was smothered, three to one. With pistols clapped to their heads they were hustled under hatches for the time. Bart sped through the vessel from poop-cabins to forecastle, disarming, threatening, subduing. It was practically a bloodless victory. No shots were fired.

With all Spaniards temporarily secured, Bart swiftly set to sea, sailing out between the ships at anchor, rousing no suspicions, if any sleepy guard bothered about them. They were two leagues from land when the sun lifted over Cuba. Bart assembled the galleon's crew and made them set full sail. He had found his crimson suit tucked away in the chest of an officer and had donned it, the golden chain and charm about his neck beneath a ruff, certain rings and trinkets that had taken his fancy adorning him, the captain's rapier at his side.

The galleon's officers stood shivering in the early morning in their underclothes, as they had been hurried out from sleep. The seamen were better clad, having turned in all standing. Sixty in all, counting marines. Inspection of the galleon's papers had put Bart in high humor. Here, under foot, was not less than a hundred thousand crowns.

"Thirty to a boat," he said. "Give them one of their own and the longboat we came in. About two hours' row, gentlemen, as the tide sets. 'Twill give you an appetite for breakfast. Give the compliments of Barthelemy Portuguese to the governor and tell him the next time I come to San Francisco Campeachy it will be with my own fleet. It is a sweet city and should pay a fine ransom. Tell him also to sleep in a halter nights to accustom himself to the feel of it. For when I come back I shall set up my own gallows. Over with you."

His words were not all vainglorious. Bart was not through with his grudge against Campeachy. First Montalvo, then the governor. To sack the city would be a profitable achievement. Then at last back home to Portugal to muster his bullies under Braganza's banner.

With folded arms he stood at the side and watched the chilled dignitaries get into the stern-sheets of the two boats while the crew and marines crowded on the rowing-thwarts. He had no especial grudge against them. He could be complacent in victory. The sergeant had deserved his fate. Montalvo and the governor were a different matter.

He turned to Simon.

"There is a battery for you, gunner," he said. "Twenty-four guns. We are short-handed for this vessel, but it is as well to be prepared to bite. We may be pursued. See to it, Simon. Is there a sail-maker among ye?"

A man stepped out.

"Hunt the stores and make us a proper flag," ordered Bart. "Black — with the skull and bones."

The flag was in place before sunset, with the galleon heading south toward Cape San Antonio, bound for Jamaica to recruit, bowling along at eight knots, undermanned but with all things in her favor. In the poop-cabin, masquerading in silk and velvet like so many peacocks, gaming, screaming out snatches of song, spilling wine as they swilled it, Bart's buccaneers went wild.

Bart himself drank measure after measure without effect. He sang his share of songs, he stayed until, one by one, the rest succumbed, sprawling on transoms or the heavy rugs, sodden and fumed with liquor.

Bart went on deck to find the helmsman dead drunk. Shifting the helpless body with his feet, he took the tiller himself, elated but not intoxicated, master of a prize, master of a crew, master, he told himself, of his fate.

The wind hummed through the rigging, coming up behind, bellying out the sails that the defeated crew had set, a moon silvered the sea that broke into bright splinters under the galleon's bows. Barthelemy Portuguese was his own man again. Luck was surely perched on his bowsprit.

He was not quite so certain that Fortune was his figurehead after a day had passed. In some ways all went well. No sail appeared astern. If they had been followed, as seemed inevitable, they had shaken off their pursuers. Probably because they were carrying greater stress of canvas than was entirely wise, even for a man fleeing from the gallows.

But these seventeen men of the wrecked *Falcon* were not as his own crew of the *Swan* had been. In action Bart might have handled their forward inclinations; in comparative idleness they were hard to manage. Their late captain must have been somewhat slack in most things. Given time, Bart could have whipped them into line; but reaction had set in upon him. Strong as he was, his reserves had been burned up in the fearful trip to Golfo Triste. Excitement had offset the wine the first night, the liquor had given a fuel to his laboring engine that had produced a spurt of energy and, passing, left little but ashes.

A tremendous lassitude of body and mind took possession of him. The slightest movement, even to think, without action, was a strenuous matter. Nature, too far stretched, was inevitably relaxing. The supreme essence of the man, his spirit, had dwindled, the steam was low, the water low, the draft bad. He forced himself to eat a meal or so, and when that nauseated him took to wine.

All the crew were drunk — aggressively, humorously, sulkily drunk, according to their natures. Simon went round naming his twenty-four culverins, cuddling them, talking to them, polishing, swabbing, trying to make up guns' crews, cursed out and buffeted by those he addressed, but persistent, half-crazed with liquor. As the men grew maudlin they lost control of their muscles. They could neither understand an order nor execute one.

Long observation and habit feebly asserted itself from time to time in Bart. The wine slowed him down, dulled his eye, broke up coordination, but he was conscious of increasing pressure, of lowering temperature, mounting winds and clouds piling, piling up to windward until they seemed like the toppling walls of a mountain; of blue seas that turned gray and lost their buoyancy, chopping at the ship rather than lifting it.

To shorten sail with his eighteen, less than half of whom could be really termed sailors, would have been a slow but entirely possible process. Now they were tipsy beyond redemption, wallowing on deck or in the cabin, laughing inanely at him when he sought to enforce an order, or dead to the world in the scuppers.

Bart cursed the fancy he had conceived of making the Spaniards set full sail off Campeachy, though it had been the saving of them at that time, distancing pursuit. He had not spared them from sprits to mizzen. All told there were thirty sails with all their infinite detail of bowline and brace, clewlines, buntlines, tacks and sheets, as complicated to the sodden brains of the drunken men as cat's cradle to a newborn babe.

Harder and harder blew the wind and heavier the seas as they rounded San Antonio and drove for the Isle of Pines. To go inside, to thread the archipelago between that and the mainland, while it might give them some lee, was impossible. Bart could not tack and navigate with drunken sailors, far too few at any time properly to handle the big galleon. He could only drive.

Before the wind they sped, with the canvas straining at clew and tack and sheet, blowing up to a hurricane. There was no one to take the helm but Bart, and he stayed on deck with the bottles and broken meats he brought up gradually littering the deck about him.

At times he slipped the tiller into a becket and dozed off. One by one the crew gave way to stupor, overcome by alcoholic fumes. They would sleep it off after a while and would begin to come slowly back with their poisoned blood making them feel as if they had been clubbed, nauseated, weak.

In the mean time hour after hour the breeze strengthened on to gale, the gale heightened to hurricane. The sea lost all aeration. The galleon labored in it as if struggling through slush. There was no color to the water, only an expanse of yeasty white, furiously whipped, the spindrift flying in level sheets. The sky, like teased gray wool, seemed close to the tops, scudding along.

They were on the line of twenty-one south latitude, thirty miles south of Cape Pepe on the Isle of Pines. The wind was due west, and they held before it. Two hundred miles of open water lay ahead of them before they should reach the Gardens of the Queen. There they must man the braces for a shift of yards, making a southerly course to clear Cape Cruz, lowest point of Cuba. And they would need leeway for the galleon, with wind abeam, battering the towering stern, sagged off like a molted duck's feather in a pond.

All this, with his will fighting a losing battle against the all-encompassing weariness, Bart realized but could not help. He stood swaying at the helm, half-dead on his feet, the sleep-demons tugging to close his eyelids, his fine crimson raiment soaked through with flying spray, the galleon driving at ten knots toward the jagged reefs of *Los Jardines de la Reina*, Gardens of the Queen in all their beauty when the weather was fine, but veritable jaws of the devil when it was foul.

There was nothing he could do if he left the wheel. He might cut certain ropes and let the canvas tear loose to lighten ship; but the wind was doing that for him with reports like mighty guns as the sails disappeared in the smother or flapped to ribbons. The deck buckled as the masts bent and tugged at their restraining shrouds. Each shroud was fixed with a movable toggle-pin. Bart might have struck these out; but to risk having a mast go by the board and, still held by the lee rigging, drag and pound against the sides, was worse than to trust to the storm destroying the excess sails.

More than once he strove to bring his men back to some realization of their position, to some capability. Many of them were violently sick, retching until they brought blood. Two, in their tipsy helplessness, had struck their heads against some projection, and one of these had fractured his skull. One had been knifed in a quarrel, by whom none knew, not even the murderer. The corpse rolled about the waist of the ship, swashing in the lee scuppers, hurled against a living comrade who had no more senses than feebly to thrust off the body.

Night came, not with sunset, but early in the afternoon, the dusk piling up with the fury of the storm. Rain lashed at them; lightning seared the dark pall and showed the ghastly waves, lunging and leaping, roaring as they whipped on the galleon to its doom.

Toward five o'clock the blackness slowly diminished to gray. It narrowly revealed a raging sea that swirled under a lowering sky. Between waves and clouds the wind shrieked as if blown through a great chimney, flinging the galleon, stripped of sail, with cordage slackened or thrashing at loose ends, straight toward where masses of spouting, thundering foam announced the reefs of the Queen's Gardens.

Wind and rain and spray had somewhat revived the crew. They groped for lines and dragged themselves to the rail, some crawling up the poop-ladder to where Bart stood, gray with salt, his eyes like those of a dead man, his skin wrinkled, rime on his beard, clutching the tiller with hands that had hooked about it.

They yelled their fears at him and he stood stolid, a contemptuous giant among pigmies. It was every man for himself. Simon was on the poop, his cross-eyes seeming to shrink from the sight of the leaping death all about them.

The sea shouldered and heaved beneath them. It appeared to be putting itself to one supreme effort as a man moves to toss down the heavy burden he has carried to the dump.

For a moment the ship seemed to be tossed free of the water, slung through the air. Then it crashed down, creaking, breaking, dissolving in the ravening pack of breakers.

Below the surface, swept irresistibly along, yet striking out by blind instinct, rolled by whirling currents, Bart fought for dear life. He had filled his great lungs before he leaped far out from the poop-rail. He had used every atom of that air, and a raging fire was burning inside his chest that seemed constricted with red-hot hoops of iron.

His flailing strokes brought his head above water in the hollow between two waves, a hollow filled with a scud of bubbles, aerated fragments of the crests. He gulped both air and water, shaking his head like a bull, scenting hope of salvation in his sniff of the gale.

Then a living bulk washed upon him. Frantic arms twined about his waist, fighting upward, legs twisting around his. He sank down, struggling to release that drowning grip, bludgeoning, trying to break loose the fingers that sank into his flesh like steel. One hand dug into his shoulder; another was at his throat; the legs were about waist and crotch.

Down they went, down, with streaks of light breaking before Bart's starting eyeballs. Over and over they whirled and the light enveloped him in spiral flares. He was gone — done — shrouded in light — Mother of God!

Bart discovered himself digging fingers and toes, elbows and knees, deep into sliding shingle, trying to stem the backrush of a wave that plucked at him as if he were a stalk of uprooted seaweed. It grasped him, dragged him back, and a second billow tossed him again onward.

It was no effort of his own that won him to safety. He was flung there as if, the wanton sport over, Neptune had contemptuously thrown him aside.

The tide receded and left him lying on the sand that was formed of broken shells and coral grit, face down amid masses of uptorn weed. The hurricane went on its way, dragging its ragged mantle of clouds, revealing the blue field of the sky.

Out came the warming sun, mounted to zenith, slanted westward. With the ebb there came in fragments of the galleon, gilded sections of the carved poop, an empty wine-keg and five dead men, stranded at intervals down the placid beach on which the emerald water rippled. None of these looked less alive than Barthelemy.

Five others of his men had won ashore, sobered, battered and lamed. Two of these had gone exploring for food, for water and for signs of natives. They had stranded in a little cove apart from Bart's landing-place and the three less vigorous lay on the sands in the sunshine like basking seals. The man killed in the quarrel and the one whose skull had been fractured were missing with the remainder of the company.

Bart roused an hour before sunset and groaned as he raised himself on his elbows. He felt as if he had been beaten to a pulp. Blood was thick on his hair where he had struck a rock; seashells had deeply scored his body and torn to rags the faded glories of the crimson suit. His ruff was gone, the doublet open at the throat, his shirt torn away. His neck still ached from the clutch of the drowning man, and the hurt brought back full recollection of that struggle, up to the point where he lost consciousness.

His fingers, gingerly feeling his gullet, missed something familiar. The golden chain that had borne the pearl amulet was gone — the charm vanished. Frowning, Bart stripped himself and searched his clothing — the baroque had disappeared.

In vain he traced the beach to the sea and back again. On his once gay coat was still pinned a diamond brooch; there were some valuable rings deep sunk in his sodden fingers; there were a few crowns in his pockets; but what he prized more than anything on earth was lost. His luck had deserted him. The man who had clutched with him in the undertow must have wrenched the links of the chain, the sea washed out the amulet.

Moodily Bart got into his clothes again, He cast a casual glance at the bodies on the fringe of the tide, then turned to the hail of one of his men from a low cliff. The buccaneer came toward him, followed by his comrade, giving him news of the three survivors.

"We have found an Indian encampment," said the man. "They have goat's flesh, fresh water and fruit. And they have a large canoe which they will trade for a gold piece or two."

A gleam of interest came into Barthelemy's eyes.

"We can get from this accursed place then," he said. "We can make Jamaica. Put me once ashore at Spanish Town and I'll never leave it."

The two stared at him.

"I'm through with the sea," he said, "It gives with one hand and takes away with the other."

"Yet if one has luck?"

Barthelemy turned upon the speaker with a visage so murderous that the other leaped back and half-drew his knife.

"Luck? Prate not to me of luck!"

Bart uttered a volley of blasphemy.

"Luck! A false-faced, treacherous jade! Woo her and she flouts you. Force her and she comes along beguiling — to leave you ditched. Luck was conceived and born in Hell, bred in the ways of purgatory.

"Simon was wiser than I, after all. Old Swivel-Eyes could see more ways than one. Forced luck is luck departed. I —"

Walking toward the little cove where their companions rested, they had come upon the first of the five corpses thrown up by the sea. The two buccaneers turned the man over on his back, then hastily crossed themselves. The eyes, fixed and wide open, stared inward. It was the face of Simon the gunner, Simon the Cross-Eyed!

Something glittering caught the eye of Barthelemy. He stooped and forced open the contracted fingers. Looped about them, twisted across his horny, seamy palm, was a length of the chain that had held the baroque. It was Simon who had snatched loose the charm in his death-struggle. Somewhere, on the shifting sands of the lagoon or in the belly of some fish, attracted by the gleaming thing with its gold-tipped horns, lost irretrievably was the amulet, and with it the luck of Barthelemy Portuguese.

How can luck profit a man when he believes it gone forever?

www.ingramcontent.com/pod-product-compliance
Lightning Source LLC
Chambersburg PA
CBHW031226020726
47499CB00002B/653